EDWD. KELLEY A MAGICIAN

In the act of invoking the spirit of deceased person

The Book of Black Magic and Ceremonial Magic

INCLUDING THE RITES AND MYSTERIES OF GOETIC THEURGY, SORCERY, AND INFERNAL NECROMANCY, ALSO THE RITUALS OF BLACK MAGIC

BY

ARTHUR EDWARD WAITE

AUTHOR OF "DEVIL WORSHIP IN FRANCE," ETC., ETC.

TWO HUNDRED ILLUSTRATIONS

This Edition Prepared for Publication Under the Editorship of

L. W. de LAURENCE

Author of "The Great Book of Magical Art, Hindu Magic and East Indian Occultism," "The Sacred Book of Death, Hindu Spiritism, Soul Transition and Soul Reincarnation," "The Mystic Text Book of the Hindu Occult Chambers," "The Magic and Occultism of India, The Wonders of the Magic Mirror, Hindu and Egyptian Crystal Gazing, Astral Auras and Colors," "The Immanence of God, Know Thyself," "God, the Bible, Truth and Christian Theology." Owning and controlling the publishing rights of the only standard and exclusive line of Occult Works by The Old Masters and Adepts extant today

KALPAZ

ISBN: 978-93-5128-378-2(PB)

First Published in 1910
Indian Reprint in 2017

Published by

Kalpaz Publications
C-30, Satyawati Nagar,
Delhi – 110052
E-mail: kalpaz@hotmail.com
Website: kalpazpublications.com
Ph.: +91-9212142040

Cataloging in Publication Data—DK
Courtesy: D.K. Agencies (P) Ltd. <docinfo@dkagencies.com>

Waite, Arthur Edward, 1857-1942, **author.**
The book of black : magic and ceremonial magic : including the rites and mysteries of goetic theurgy, sorcery, and infernal necromancy, also the rituals of black magic / by Arthur Edward Waite ; this edition prepared for publication under the editorship of L.W. de Laurence.
pages cm
"First published in 1910"
"Two hundred illustrations."
ISBN 9789351283782 (PB)

1. Magic. 2. Occultism. I. De Laurence, L. W. (Lauron William), 1868- editor. II. Title.

BF1611.W35 2017 DDC 133.43 23

PREFACE

IN the year 1889 a learned expositor of Kabbalistic doctrines edited in English a work on Ceremonial Magic, entitled *Clavicula Salomonis,* or, the "Key of Solomon the King." In an introduction prefixed to the work he stated that he saw no reason to doubt, and therefore presumably accepted, the tradition of its authorship.[1] Mr. Mathers, it should be added, undertook his translation more especially for the use of occult students, that is to say, for those persons who believe in the efficacy of magical rites, and may desire to put them in practice. With this exception, the large body of literature which treats of "Theurgic Ceremonial" in its various branches has remained inaccessible to the generality of readers, in rare printed books and rarer manuscripts, in both cases mostly in foreign languages.[2] There is probably a considerable class outside occult students to whom a systematic account of magical practices would be not unwelcome, perhaps mainly as a curiosity of old-world credulity, but also as a contribution of some value to certain side issues of historical research; these, however, an edition for occult students would deter rather than attract. In the present work both interests have been as far as possible considered. The subject is

[1] The work as it now stands quotes Ezekiel, Daniel, the fourth Gospel, and mentions SS. Peter and Paul. Most of these anachronisms are to be found in the pentacles accompanying the text.

[2] A judicious and excellent paper was contributed some time ago to the *Transactions of the Bibliographical Society* under the title of "Some Books on Magic," by J. H. Slater. It does not, of course, pretend to be exhaustive, and, though informing, is not entirely accurate.

approached from the bibliographical and critical standpoints, and all the sources of information which many years of inquiry have made known to the writer have been consulted to render it complete. At the same time, the requirements of the professed occultist have been studied in two important respects, which will not, it is believed, be a source of offence to merely historical readers. They have been studied, firstly, by the observance of strict technical exactitude; the ceremonial produced in this book is absolutely faithful to the originals, and removes all necessity of having recourse to the originals before determining any doubtful point of magical procedure in the past. For convenience of reference it is indeed superior to the originals, because it has been put systematically, whereas they often exceed understanding owing to the errors of transcribers, the misreadings of printers, the loose methods of early translators, and seemingly, it must be added, the confused minds of the first compilers, "Solomon" himself not excepted. The innumerable offices of vain observance which constitute Ceremonial Magic, as it is presented in books, will therefore be found substantially intact by those who concern themselves with such observance.

The second respect in which the interests of the occult student have been considered is, however, of much more importance. Robert Turner, the English translator of the "Magical Elements," written, or supposed to be written, by the unfortunate Peter of Abano, describes that treatise as an introduction to "magical vanity," a term which was probably used in a transcendental manner, to intimate that all things which concern the phenomenal world are indifferently futile. The occult purpose of the present investigation is to place within reach of those persons who are transcendentally inclined the fullest evidence of the vanity of

Preface

Ceremonial Magic as it is found in books, and the fantastic nature of the distinction between White and Black Magic—so far also as the literature of either is concerned. It would be unbecoming in a professed transcendentalist to deny that there is a Magic which is behind Magic, or that the occult sanctuaries possess their secrets and mysteries; of these the written ceremonial is either a debased and scandalous travesty or a trival and misconstrued application. Let a transcendentalist assure the "occult student" that he is dealing therein simply with curious researches. The statement just made will explain why it is permissable to bring forth from the obscurity of centuries a variety of processes which would be abominable if it could be supposed that they were to be seriously understood. It will explain also why this work is entitled "The Book of Black Magic," when it deals, as a fact, in a fairly exhaustive manner, with most extant Rituals. These are all tainted with Black Magic in the same way that every idle word is tainted with the nature of sin. The distinction between White and Black Magic is the distinction between the idle and the evil word.

It would, however, be unsafe to affirm that all persons making use of the ceremonies in the Rituals would fail to obtain results. Perhaps in the majority of cases most of such experiments made in the past were attended with results of a kind. To enter the path of hallucination is likely to insure hallucination, and in the presence of hypnotic and clairvoyant facts it would be absurd to suppose that the seering processes of Ancient Magic—which are many— did not produce seership, or that the auto-hypnotic state which much magical ritual would obviously tend to occasion in predisposed persons did not frequently induce it, and not always only in the predisposed. To this extent some of the processes are practical, and to this extent they are dangerous.

Preface

For convenience of treatment the present work is divided into two parts. The first contains an analytical and critical account of the chief magical rituals known to the writer; the second forms a complete Grimoire of Black Magic. It must be remembered that these are the operations which gave arms to the Inquisitors of the past, and justified Civil Tribunals in the opinion of their century for the sanguinary edicts pronounced against witch, warlock, and magician. It is, in truth, a very curious and not reassuring page in the history of human aberration, nor has it been wholly a pleasing exercise which has thus sought to make it plain, once and for all.

CONTENTS

PART I

The Literature of Ceremonial Magic

CHAPTER I

THE ANTIQUITY OF MAGICAL RITUALS

CHAPTER II

THE RITUALS OF TRANSCENDENTAL MAGIC

CHAPTER III

COMPOSITE RITUALS

Contents

CHAPTER IV

THE RITUALS OF BLACK MAGIC

PART II

The Complete Grimoire

CHAPTER I

THE PREPARATION OF THE OPERATOR

CHAPTER II

THE INITIAL RITES AND CEREMONIES

Contents

Contents

CHAPTER VII

CHAPTER VIII

CHAPTER IX

EXPLANATION OF FULL-PAGE PLATES

PLATE I

FRONTISPIECE.—Edward Kelley, the Alchemist and alleged Magician, in the act of invoking the Spirit of a Deceased Person.

The plate is reproduced from the second edition of Ebenezer Sibley's "Illustration of the Occult Sciences." The companion of Kelley within the circle is presumably Paul Waring, who, according to Weaver ("Funeral Monuments," 1631, pp. 45, 46), was associated with him in all his conjurations. The scene is intended to represent the churchyard of Walton Ledale, "in the county of Lancaster." The information of Sibley is derived from Weaver, whose authority is said to have been Waring. On this point and the general question of Kelley's necromantic pursuits, see "The Alchemical Writings of Edward Kelley," Biographical Preface, pp. xxvii-xxx.

PLATE II

The Angels of the Seven Planets, their Sigils, the Signs and Houses of the Planets, the names of the Seven Heavens, according to the "Magical Elements" of Peter de Abano, with the names of the Olympic Spirits of the Planets according to "Arbatel of Magic," and the Infernal Sigils of the Evil Planetary Spirits according to the "Red Dragon."

The name of Michael, the Angel of the Lord's Day, appears over his Sigil, together with the Astrological Symbol of Sol, the Zodiacal Sign of Leo, which is the House of the Sun, and the name of the Fourth Heaven, Machen. The name of Gabriel, the Angel of Monday, appears over his Sigil, together with the Astrological Symbol of Luna, the Zodiacal Sign of Cancer, which is the House of the Moon, and the name of the First Heaven, Shamain. The name of Samael, the Angel of Tuesday, appears over his Sigil, together with the Astrological Symbol of Mars, the Zodiacal Signs of Aries, and Scorpio, which are the Houses of the Planet, and the name of the Fifth Heaven, Machon. The name of Raphael, the Angel of Wednesday, appears over his Sigil, together with the Astrological Symbol of Mercury, the Zodiacal Signs of Gemini and Virgo, which are the Houses of the Planet, and the name of the Second Heaven, Raquie. The name of Sachiel, the Angel of Thursday, appears over his Sigil, together with the Astrological Symbol of Jupiter, the Zodiacal Signs of Sagittarius and Pisces, which are the Houses of the Planet, and the name of the Sixth Heaven, Zebul. The name of Anael, the Angel of Friday, appears over his Sigil, together with the Astrological Symbol of Venus, the Zodiacal Signs of Taurus and Libra, which are the Houses of the Planet, and the name of the Third Heaven, Sagun. The name of Cassiel, the Angel of Saturday, appears over his Sigil, together with the Astrological Symbol of Saturn, and the Zodiacal Signs of Capricornus and Aquarius, which are the Houses of the Planet.

PLATE III

'Mystic Figures of the Enchiridion.

Figure I., the mystic symbol of the Tau, converted into a monogram which has been supposed to signify the word Taro or Tora. Figure II., the triple Tau. Figure III., an arbitrary figure supposed to represent the fortieth part of the stature of Jesus Christ. Figure IV., the Labarum of Constantine, with the usual inscription, "In this sign thou shalt conquer," and the emblems of the Passion of Christ. Figure V., a double door, connected by a bar, and inscribed with the first seven letters of the Latin alphabet. Figure VI., a composite symbol of unknown meaning. The second circle contains twenty-two letters, which recall the Keys of the Taro. Figure VII. represents the dimensions of the wound produced by the lance of the Centurion in the side of Jesus Christ. Figure VIII., a two-edged sword, for which various simple meanings may be conjectured. Its inscription has been adopted by alchemists.

PLATE IV

Mystic Figures of the Enchiridion.

Figure I., the reversed form of a well-known occult symbol. The Hebrew words signify Jehovah, Elohim, Agla, Elohim Tsabaoth. Figure II., the Labarum of Constantine, another form. Figure III., the inscription on this talisman is unintelligible. Figure IV., the occult symbol of the pentagram, reversed, and therefore the sign of the Demon, according to Eliphas Lévi. Possibly misplaced by the ignorance of the printer, but it occurs in this manner in many books which do not apparently connect with Black Magic. Figure V., a talisman with the monogram of Michael. Figure VI., undescribed, but belonging to a prayer of St. Augustine addressed to the Holy Spirit to receive a revelation. Figure VII., the characters of this talisman would seem to be Hebrew, but are so corrupt that they are unintelligible. Figure VIII., a talisman with the monogram of Gabriel. Figure IX., the talisman and monogram of Michael.

PLATE V

The characters of Evil Spirits, from the so-called "Fourth Book" of Cornelius Agrippa, and described as follows in the original.

1. A right line; 2. a crooked line; 3. a reflexed line; 4. a simple figure; 5. penetrate; 6. broken; 7. a right letter; 8. a retrograde letter; 9. an in-

verted letter; 10. flame; 11. wind; 12. water; 13. a mass; 14. rain; 15. clay; 16. a flying creature; 17. a creeping thing; 18. a serpent; 19. an eye; 20. a hand; 21. a foot; 22. a crown; 23. a crest; 24. horns; 25. a sceptre; 26. a sword; 27. a scourge.

PLATE VI

The Sabbatic Goat, from the "Ritual of Transcendental Magic," by Eliphas Lévi, who identifies it with the Baphoment of Mendes, and does not regard it as connected with Black Magic, but as "a pantheistic and magical figure of the absolute."

PLATE VII

The instruments of Black Magic, from the Grimoire entitled "True Black Magic."

Figure I., the knife with the white handle. Figure II., the knife with the black handle. Figure III., the arctrave, or hook. Figure IV., the boline or sickle. Figure V., the stylet. Figure VI., the needle. Figure VII., the wand. Figure VIII., the lancet. Figure IX., the staff. Figure X., the sword of the master. Figures XI., XII., XIII., the swords of the assistants.

PLATE VIII

The Magical Circle used in Goëtic Theurgy, according to the "Lesser Key of Solomon the King," showing the position of the operator, the divine names and symbols to be inscribed within and about the double circle, and the situation of the lights.

The figure and place of the triangle into which the spirit is commanded will be found in the text, pp. 190-192. The Divine Names differ in some of the manuscripts.

PLATE IX

The Goëtic Circle of Black Evocations and Pacts according to Eliphas Lévi.

The circle is formed from the skin of the victim, fastened to the ground by four nails taken from the coffin of an executed criminal. The skull is that of a parricide; the horns those of a goat; the male bat opposite the skull must have been drowned in blood; and the black cat, whose head forms the fourth object on the circumference of the circle, must have been fed on human flesh. There is no authority for any of these stipulations. The small circles within the triangle show the place of the operator and his assistants.

PLATE X

The Apparatus of Ceremonial Crystallomancy according to White Magic, showing the crystal in a frame, which should be of polished ebony, ivory, or boxwood, the torch, and the engraven candlesticks of brass.

The process of Ceremonial Crystallomancy is analogous to that of the Mirror of Solomon.

PART I

THE LITERATURE OF CEREMONIAL MAGIC

CHAPTER II

The Antiquity of Magical Rituals

§ 1. *The Importance of Ceremonial Magic.*

THE ordinary fields of psychological inquiry, largely in possession of the pathologist, are fringed by a borderland of transcendental experiment into which pathologists may occasionally venture, but it is left for the most part to unchartered explorers. Beyond these fields and this borderland there lies the legendary wonder-world of Mysticism, Magic, and Sorcery, a world of fascination or terror, as the mind which regards it is tempered, but in either case the antithesis of admitted possibility. There all paradoxes seem to obtain actually, contradictions logically coexist, the effect is greater than the cause, and the shadow more than the substance. Therein the visible melts into the unseen, the invisible is manifested openly, motion from place to place is accomplished without traversing the intervening distance, matter passes through matter. There two straight lines may enclose a space; space has a fourth dimension, and further possiblities beyond it; without metaphor and without evasion, the circle is mathematically squared. There life is prolonged, youth renewed, physical immortality secured. There earth becomes gold, and gold earth. There words and wishes possess creative power, thoughts are things, desire realizes its object. There, also, the dead live, and the hierarchies of extra-mundane intelligence are within easy communication, and become ministers or tormentors, guides, or destroyers, of man. There the Law of Continuity is suspended by the interference of the higher Law of Fantasia.

But, unhappily, this domain of enchantment is in all respects comparable to the gold of Faerie, which is presumably its medium of exchange. It cannot withstand daylight, the test of the human eye, or the scale of reason. When these are applied, its paradox becomes an anticlimax, its antithesis ludicrous; its contradictions are without genius; its mathematical marvels end in a verbal quibble; its elixirs fail even as purges; its transmutations do not need exposure at the assayer's hands; its marvel-working words prove barbarous mutilations of dead languages, and are impotent from the moment that they are understood; departed friends, and even planetary intelligences, must not be seized by the skirts, for they are apt to desert their draperies, and these are not like the mantle of Elijah.

The little contrast here instituted will serve to exhibit that there are at least two points of view regarding Magic and its mysteries—the simple and homogeneous view, prevailing within that charmed circle among the few survivals whom reason has not hindered from entering, and that of the world without, which is more complex, more composite, but sometimes more reasonable only by imputation. There is also a third view, in which legend is checked by legend and wonder substituted for wonder. Here it is not the Law of Continuity persisting in its formulæ despite the Law of Fantasia; it is Croquemetaine explained by Diabolus, the runes of Elf-land read with the interpretation of Infernus; it is the Law of Bell and Candle, the Law of Exorcism, and its final expression is in the terms of the *auto-da-fe*. For this view the wonder-world exists without any question, except that of the Holy Tribunal; it is not what it seems, but is adjustable to the eye of faith in the light from the Lamp of the Sanctuaries; in a word, its angels are demous, its Melusines stryges, its phantoms vampires, its spells and mysteries the Black Science. Here Magic itself rises up and responds that there is a Black and a White art, an art of Hermes and an art of Canidia, a Science of the Height and a Science of the Abyss, of Metatron and Belial. In this manner a fourth point of view emerges; they are all, however, illusive; there is the positive illusion of the legend, affirmed by the remaining adherents of its literal sense, and the negative illusion which denies the legend crassly without considering that there is a possibility behind it: there is the illusion which accounts for the legend by an opposite hypothesis, and the illusion of the legend which reaffirms itself with a distinction. When these have been disposed of, there remain two really important questions—the question of the Mystics and the question of history and literature. To a very large extent the first is closed to discussion, but, so far as may be possible, it will be dealt with a little later on. As regards the second, it is the sole concern and purpose of this inquiry, and the limits of its importance may therefore be shortly stated.

There can be no extensive literatures without motives proportionate to account for them. If we take the magical literature of Western Europe from the Middle Ages and onward, we shall find that it is exceedingly large. Now, the acting principles in the creation of that literature will prove to rule also in its history; what is abscure in the one may be understood by help of the other; each reacted upon each; as the literature grew, it helped to make the history, and the new history was so much additional material for further literature. There were, of course, many motive principles at work, for the literature and history of Magic are alike exceedingly intricate, and there are many interpretations of principles which are apt to be confused with the principles, as, for example, the influence of what is loosely called superstition upon ignorance; these and any interpretations must be ruled out of an inquiry like the present. The main principles are summed in the conception of a number of mysterious forces in the universe which could be put in operation by man, or at least followed in their secret processes. In the ultimate, however, they could all be rendered secondary, if not passive, to the will of man; for even in astrology, which was the discernment of forces regarded as peculiarly fatal, there was an art of ruling, and *sapiens dominabitur astris* became an axiom of the science. This conception culminated or centered in the doctrine of unseen, intelligent powers, with whom it was possible for prepared persons to communicate; the method by which this communication was attempted are the most important processes of Magic, and the books which embody these methods, called Ceremonial Magic, are the most important part of the literature. Here, that is to say, is the only branch of the subject which it is necessary to understand in order to understand the history. Had Magic been focussed in the reading of the stars, it would have possessed no history to speak of, for astrology involved intellectual equipments which were possible only to the few. Had Magic centered in the transmutation of metals, it would never have moved multitudes, but would have remained what that still is, the quixotic hope of chemistry. We may take the remaining occult sciences collectively, but there is nothing in them of themselves which would make history. In virtue of the synthetic doctrine which has been already formulated, they were all magically possible, but they were all subsidiary to that which was head and crown of all—the art of dealing with spirits. The presumed possession of the secret of this art made Magic formidable, and made therefore its history. There was a time indeed when Ceremonial Magic threatened to absorb the whole circle of the occult sciences; it was the superior method, the royal road; it effected immediately what the others accomplished laboriously, after a long time.[1] It had, moreover, the palmary recommendation that it was a conventional art, working by definite formulæ, a process in words.

It was the fascination of this process which brought men and women—all sorts and conditions of both—to the Black Sabbath and to the White Sabbath,[2] and blinded them to the danger of the stake. It was the full and clear acceptation of this process as effectual by Church and State which kindled the faggots for the magician in every Christian land. As-

[1] Thus, the abstruse processes of astrology might, on the hypothesis, be dispensed with altogether in favour of the evocation of one of those numerous spirits whose office it was to give instruction in astrology and on instantaneous knowledge thereof. It is otherwise obvious that the least occult of the esoteric sciences was exploded by an art which provided familiar spirits who could discern the past, present, and future. In like manner, Alchemy was superfluous for a magician who could cause treasures to be transported from the depths of the sea or the bowels of the earth, and even from the royal exchequer, in the more convenient shape of current coin.

[2] There is much the same ground for this distinction as for that made between the Black and White Magic of the Rituals. They were abominable or fantastic according to the disposition of those who frequented them. As a whole, they have probably been much exaggerated. Jules Garinet, in his *Histoire de la Magie en France, depuis le commencement de la Monarchie jusqu' à nos jours* (1818), speculates that the monks, who abused public credulity for the sake of diversion amidst their idleness, may have assumed ridiculous disguises, and may themselves have committed the extravagances which they attributed to devils. The same author affirms, as certain and incontestable, that in all the criminal trials of sorcerers and sorceresses the scene of the Sabbath was invariably in the neighbourhood of a monastery. "Since the destruction of the monastic orders," he concludes triumphantly, "no more is heard of such assemblies, even in places where the fear of the devil still exists." Add to this that seventy-five years later, Papus, the French occultist, would persuade his readers that all the Grimoires of Black Magic were the work of priests, and the case is almost as complete as French reasoning can make it. It is cited here to show that, outside the demonologists, the Sabbath is viewed rather as a moonlight mummery, where the presiding genius was not the fallen star Wormwood, but Venus, and, even on the monkish hypothesis, the mysteries were those of Priapus rather than Pluto. The records of trials for sorcery rest under the gravest suspicion, firstly, because there is no guarantee that they have not been garbled, and, secondly, because information extracted by torture is, in the ultimate, always of the nature which it was intended to extract; but they are also mainly records of sexual mania.

trology was scarcely discouraged, and if the alchemist were occasionally tortured, it was only to extract his secret. There was no danger in these things, and hence there was no judgment against them, except by imputation from their company; but Magic, but dealing with spirits, was that which made even the peasant tremble, and when the peasant shakes at his hearth, the king is not secure in his palace, nor the Pope at St. Peter's, unless both can protect their own. Moreover, in the very claim of Ceremonial Magic there was an implied competition with the essential claim of the Church.[1]

The importance of Ceremonial Magic, and of the literature which embodies it, to the history of the occult sciences being admitted, there is no need to argue that this history is a legitimate and reasonable study; in such a case, knowledge is its own end, and there can be certainly no question as to the distinguished influence which has been exercised by the belief in Magic throughout the ages. In order, however, to understand the literature of Magic, it is necessary to obtain first of all a clear principle of regarding it. It will be superfluous to say that we must surrender the legends, as such, to those who work in legends and dispute about their essential value. We need not debate whether Magic, for example, can really square the circle, as magicians testify, or whether such an operation is impossible even to Magic, as commonly would be objected by those who deny the art. We need not seriously discuss the proposition

[1] That is to say, the Church communicates the supernatural world by a sacramental system, and the direct communication which Magic pretends to establish must, if established, supersede the Church. It is not surprising that a sacerdotalism so acute, especially along the lines of its own interests, as that of the Roman Church should not discern that the rival claim assailed its fundamental position, but it is regrettable that an institution possessing the sacramental system should have disturbed itself about a direct communication of the kind attempted by Ceremonial Magic. If it be said that the Church discerned the possibility behind the veil of vain observance, then it was not so acute as would seem, for behind that veil there is no danger to the sacramental system.

that the devil assists the magicians to perform a mathematical impossibility, or its qualified form, that the circle can be squared indifferently by those who invoke the angel Cassiel of the hierarchy of Uriel and those who invoke Astaroth. We shall see very shortly, as already indicated in the preface, that we are dealing with a bizarre literature, which passes, by various fantastic phases, through all folly into crime. We have to account for these characteristics.

The desire to communicate with spirits is older than history; it connects with ineradicable principles in human nature, which have been discussed too often for it to be necessary to recite them here; and the attempts to satisfy that desire have usually taken a shape which does gross outrage to reason. Between the most ancient processes, such as those of Chaldean Magic, and the rites of the Middle Ages, there are marked correspondences, and there is something of common doctrine, as distinct from intention, in which identity would more or less obtain, underlying them both. The doctrine of compulsion, or the power which both forms pretended to exercise even upon superior spirits by the use of certain words, is a case in point. In approaching the Ceremonial Magic of the Middle Ages, we must therefore bear in mind that we are dealing with a literature which, though modern in its origin, embodies some elements of antiquity.[1] It is doubtful whether the presence of these elements can be accounted for on the principle that mankind in all ages works unconsciously for the accomplishment of similar intentions in an analogous way; a bizarre intention, of course, tends independently to be fulfilled in a bizarre manner, but in this case the similarity is so close that it is more easily

[1] The Ceremonial Magic of certain Græco-Egyptian papyri offers the closest analogies with the process of the Kabbalistic school, but they are the channel, and not the source. We must look beyond history, certainly far beyond the documents of Leyden, and even the "Ritual of the Dead," for the origin of Ceremonial Magic.

explained by the perpetuation of an antique tradition, for which channels could be readily assigned. There is one upon the face of the literature, and that is the vehicle of Kabbalistic symbolism.

There are two ways of regarding the large and still unknown literature which embodies the Kabbalah of the Jews, and these in turn will give two methods of accounting for the spurious and grotesque processes which enter so extensively into Ceremonial Magic. It is either a barren mystification, a collection of supremely absurd treatises, in which obscure nonsense is enunciated with preternatural solemnity, or it is a body of symbolism. The first view is that which is formed almost irresistibly upon a superficial acquaintance, and there is not any need to add that it is the one which obtains generally in derived judgments, for here, as in other cases, the second-hand opinion issues from the most available source. The alternative judgment is that which prevails among the real students of the literature. From the one it would follow that the Ceremonial Magic which at a long distance draws from the Kabbalah, reproduces its absurdities, possibly with further exaggerations. Two erroneous views have issued from the other—an exaggerated importance attributed to the processes in question on the ground of their exalted connections, and—this, however, is rarely met with—an inclination to regard them also as symbolical writing.

There is no ground for the criticism of the first inference, which follows legitimately enough, and is that which will be most acceptable to the majority of readers. Those who value Kabbalistic literature as a symbolism, the inner sense of which is or may be of importance, but see nothing in the processes of Ceremonial Magic to make them momentous in their literal sense or susceptible to interpretation, will be tempted to dismiss them as mediæval and later impostures, which must be carefully distinguished from the true symbolical tradition. In either case the ceremonial literature is disdainfully rejected.

There is, however, yet another point of view, and it is of some moment, as it connects with that question of the Mystics about which it has been already observed that very little has transpired. All students of occultism are perfectly well aware of the existence in modern times of more than one Mystical Fraternity, deriving, or believed to derive, from other associations of the past. There are, of course, many unaffiliated occultists, but the secret Fraternities exist, and the keys of mystic symbolism are said to be in their possession. From a variety of isolated statements scattered up and down the works of professed occultists in recent years, it is possible to summarize broadly the standpoint of these bodies in respect of Ceremonial Magic. There is no extant Ritual, as there is no doctrine, which contains, or can possibly contain, the secret of mystical procedure or the essence of mystic doctrine. The reason is not because there is, or can reasonably be, any indicible secret, but because the knowledge in question is in the custody of those who have taken effectual measures for its protection; and though, from time to time, some secrets of initiation have filtered through printed books into the world at large, the real mysteries have never escaped. The literature of Magic falls, therefore, under three heads: (*a.*) The work of adepts, stating as much as could be stated outside the circle of initiation, and primarily designed to attract those who might be ripe for entrance. (*b.*) The speculations of independent seekers, who, by thought, study, and intuition, sometimes attained valuable results without assistance. (*c.*) Travesties of mystic doctrine, travesties of mystic intention, travesties of mystic procedure, complicated by filtrations from the superior source.[1]

Most Ceremonial Magic belongs to the third class; the first, by its nature, is not represented; the second only slightly. In a word, Ceremonial Magic reflects mainly the egregious ambitions and incorporates the mad processes of mediæval sorcery—of the Sabbath above all. The additional elements are debased applications of certain Kabbalistic methods, seering processes current among country people, and fantastic attempts to reduce magical legends to a formal practice.

Whichever of the above views the reader may prefer to adopt, it will be seen that the net result as regards the Rituals is not generically different, that they are of literary and historical interest, but nothing further. For the occultist they will possess, from their associations, an importance which will be of no moment to another student. It is desirable that they should not be undervalued because they have exercised an influence, and they are memorable as curiosities of the past; but it is more desirable still that the weak and credulous should be warned against acting like fools.

[1] In this connection, the author may be permitted to quote a general statement on the subject which he has received from a correspondent who seems to claim some connection of an unattached kind with the sources of secret knowledge. "Practical Magic is the science of the economy of spiritual dynamics, and is concerned with those Theurgic processes whereby he who has trained himself for the purpose can, by virtue of powers inherent in man's spiritual constitution (but undeveloped in the majority of mankind), enter into relations with the unseen intelligences to whom are assigned, in due order, the control of what are called natural forces. 'Ceremonial Magic'" (presumably not that of the Ceremonial Literature) "is Official Magic, in which the Magician, in connection with one or more assistants, acts as the delegate of an occult Fraternity, who, for some very important end, wish to communicate with beings of a higher order than usual. For this purpose there is a recognized ceremonial, or rather there are two—the 'ceremonial of approach' and the 'ceremonial of the presence.' It is chiefly in the former that lights, fumigations, symbolic figures and numbers, and incantations occur, all of which have their use, either as credentials of authority or as weapons of attack and defense in the intermediate hostile region between the material and spiritual universe."

The Antiquity of Magical Rituals

§ 2. *The Distinction between White and Black Magic.*

Having considered the possible stand-points from which the Rituals may be regarded, we come now to the distinctions that are made between them, and, first and foremost, to that instituted between White and Black Magic. The history of this distinction is exceedingly obscure, but there can be no question that in its main aspect it is modern, that is to say, in so far as it depends upon a sharp contrast between Good and Evil Spirits. In Egypt, in India, and in Greece, there was no dealing with devils in the Christian sense of the expression; Typhon, Juggernaut, and Hecate were not less divine than the gods of the over-world, and the offices of Canidia were probably in their way as sacred as the peaceful mysteries of Ceres.

Each of the occult sciences was, however, liable to that species of abuse which is technically know as Black Magic. Astrology, or the appreciation of the celestial influences in their operation upon the nature and life of man, could be perverted in the composition of malefic talismans by means of those influences. Esoteric Medicine, which consisted in the application of occult forces to the healing of disease in man, and included a traditional knowledge of the medicinal properties resident in some substances disregarded by ordinary pharmacy, produced in its malpractice the secret science of poisoning, and the destruction of health, reason, or life by unseen forces. The transmutation of metals by alchemy resulted in their sophistication. In like manner, Divination, or the processes by which lucidity was supposed to be induced, became debased into witchcraft, and Ceremonial Magic into dealing with devils. White Ceremonial Magic is, by the terms of its definition, an attempt to communicate with Good Spirits for a good, or at least an innocent, purpose. Black Magic is the attempt to communicate with Evil Spirits for an evil purpose.

The contrasts here established seem on the surface perfectly clear. When we come, however, to compare the ceremonial literature of the two classes, we shall find that the distinction is by no means so sharp as might be inferred from the definitions. In the first place, Theurgic Ceremonial, under the pretence of White Magic, usually includes the Rites for the invocation of Evil Spirits. Supposing that they are so invoked for the enforced performance of works contrary to their nature, the issue becomes complicated at once, and White Magic must then be defined as the attempt to communicate with Good or Evil Spirits for a good, or at least for an innocent purpose. This, of course, still leaves a tolerably clear distinction. Yet the alternative between a good and an innocent object contains all the material for a further confusion. It will be made clear as we proceed that the purposes and ambitions of Magic are commonly very childish, so that we must distinguish really between Black and White Magic, not as between the essentially good and evil, but as between that which is certainly evil and that which may only be foolish. Nor does this exhaust the difficulty. As will also be made evident in proceeding, White Ceremonial Magic seems to admit of a number of intentions which are objectionable, as well as many that are frivolous. Hence it must be inferred that there is no very sharp distinction between the two branches of the Art. It cannot be said, even, that Black Magic is invariably, and White Magic occasionally evil. What is called Black Magic is by no means black invariably; it is almost as much concerned with harmless and stupid processes as the White variety with those of an objectionable kind. Thus, the most which can be stated is that the literature falls chiefly into two classes, one of which usually terms itself black, but that they overlap one another.

In what perhaps it may be permissible to term the mind of Magic, as distinct from the effects which are proposed by the Rituals, there has always been a clear contrast between the two branches corresponding to Magus and Sorcerer, and the fact that the ceremonial literature tends to the confusion of the distinction stamps it immediately as garbled. But this is not to tay that it has been tampered with in the sense of having been perverted by editors. White Magic has not usually been written down into Black; Goetic Rituals have not been written up in celestial terms. They are, for the most part, naturally composite, and it would be impossible to separate their elements without modifying their structure.

Modern occultism has taken up the distinction and developed it. Appealing to the secret traditional knowledge behind the written word of Magic, to that unmanifested science which it believes to exist behind all science, and to the religion behind all religion, it affirms that the spiritual life has been entered by two classes of adepts, sometimes somewhat fantastically distinguished as the Brothers of the Right and the Brothers of the Left, transcendental good and transcendental evil being their respective ends, and in each case something altogether different from what is understood by either White or Black Magic. As might be expected, the literature of the subject does not bear out this development, but, by the terms of the proposition, this is scarcely to be regarded as an objection. For the rest, if recent revelations lead us to concede, within certain limits, that there may have been some recrudescence of diabolism in more than one country of Europe, some attempt at the present day to communicate formally with the Powers of

Darkness, it must be said that this attempt returns in its old likeness, and not invested with the sublimities and terrors of the modern view. Paris Diabolism, for example, in so far as it may be admitted to exist, is the Black Magic of the Grimoire, and not the sovereign horror of the Brothers of the Left Hand Path, wearing their iniquity like an aureole, and deathless in spiritual evil.

§ 3. *The Unprinted Literature of Ceremonial Magic*

For the purposes of the present inquiry it will be convenient to consider the Rituals under the three heads of Transcendental, Composite, and Black, subject, as regards the first, to some important qualifications which will appear in the second chapter. So far as may be possible, the antiquity of individual Rituals will be determined in the course of their examination, but as this inquiry is based, with a single exception of undeniable importance, upon the printed literature, because it is that only which has exercised a real influence, it may be well, as a conclusion to this introductory part, to give some information regarding magical processes which have remained in MS., and are to be found only, or can at least be consulted only, in the public libraries of Europe. Almost without exception, the source of their inspiration is the work mentioned in the preface, namely, "The Key of Solomon," and they are consequently of later date. The Library of the Arsenal at Paris has a reputation for being especially rich in Magical MSS., but there is also a large collection in the British Museum which may be regarded as typical. There is nothing of earlier date or more importance among the French treasures, and, to determine the question of antiquity in a few words, there is nothing among our own that is much anterior to the beginning of the fourteenth century.

The numerical strength of the treatises, late and early combined, is in itself considerable, but, setting aside the codices made use of by the English editor of "The Key of Solomon," the interest of which has been exhausted by the appearance of that work, there are only three small classes or cycles to which special importance attaches in connection with the present inquiry. The first may be termed the group of Honorius, comprising three MSS.; the second is that of the Sepher Raziel, of which there are two forms; the third includes the English codices of the "Lemegeton." The chief MS. of the first group is also one of the most ancient treatises dealing with Magic in the library. This is Sloane 313, a Latin MS. on vellum, in a bad state of preservation. The close writing and abbreviations make it very difficult to read. It is interesting, however, because it connects with the Grimoire of Honorius, one of the most important Rituals of Black Magic, being the work of some person bearing that name. It belongs to the fourteenth century, has no title or other determinate name, but it appears from the text that it was understood to be the "Sworn Book of Honorius." The introduction or prologue to the work is somewhat obscurely worded in the initial pages, but it seems to account for the condemnation of magic by the prelates of the Church on the ground that they have been deceived by demons. The result was the convocation of all the "masters of Magic," to the number of 811, all of whom seem to have come out of Naples, Athens, and a place entitled Tholetus. Among these a species of spokesman was chosen, whose name was Honorius, the son of Euclidus, Master of the Thebans. He was deputed to work for the rest, and he entered into council with an angel called Hochmel or Hocroel, (? Hochmael), and thereby wrote seven volumes of Magic Art, "giving the kernel to us and the shells to others."

From these books he seems afterwards to have extracted ninety-three chapters containing a summary of the art, and made them into a volume which "we term the sacred or sworn book." In the meantime, the princes and prelates, having burned "certain fables or trifles," concluded that they had completely destroyed the art, and were therefore pacified. The magicians, however, took an oath among themselves to preserve the masterpiece of Honorius in the most secret and careful manner, making three copies at the most, the possessor of any example being bound over to bury it before his decease, or otherwise insure its interment in his own grave, unless there was some trusty and worthy person to whom it could be transmitted. The important point about this MS. is that it fixes the source of the mendacious tradition which ascribes a Grimoire of Black Magic to a Pope of the name of Honorius, as will be seen at length later on. The "Sworn Book" is not, of course, the Grimoire, but the existence and reputed authorship of the one enables us to understand the attribution of the other. Honorius the sorcerer was identified with Honorius the Pope, firstly by the confused mind of magical legend, and secondly by conscious imposture, much after the same manner that Raymond Lully, the "illuminated doctor" of Majorca, was identified with Lully the alchemist, by tradition at the inception, and not long afterwards by the help of forged treatises. The "Sworn Book" is in other respects exceedingly remarkable, and has been most unaccountably overlooked by writers on Ceremonial Magic; it may be taken to indicate that an association of magicians was most probably in corporate existence during or before the fourteenth century. While it is clearly of Christian origin, it derives from the supposed works of Solomon, and would appear to indicate that the Solomonic cycle was at that time only in course of formation, as also that the earliest elements approximate not to the Grand Clavicle, but to the Little Key, otherwise, the Lemegeton. As to its operations, they are those of White and Black Magic, undiscriminated, without, however, any trace of the conventional "dealing with the devil." The MS. under notice need not, of course, be regarded as the original; as to this there is no means of knowing. The British Museum possesses also a later transcript, belonging to the sixteenth century, and a most valuable English translation, written on vellum in beautiful Gothic characters. It is referred to the fifteenth century.

The second group comprises two MSS., both in the Sloane collection, and both containing, among other treatises, the important and curious work attributed to Solomon under the title of Sepher Raziel. That numbered 3826 belongs to the sixteenth century. It is an English translation of a Latin original which in this form is unknown to the present writer; the first line of this original is usually given at the beginning of each section. It is divided into seven books, and purports to have been sent to Solomon by a prince of Babylon who was greater and more worshipful than all men of his time, his name being Sameton, while the two wise men who brought it were called Kamazan and Zazant. The Latin title of the treatise is said to be *Angelus Magnus Secreti Creatoris;* it was the first book after Adam, written in the language of Chaldea and afterwards translated into Hebrew. It is a noticeable fact that in this work the first section is entitled *Clavis,* and if we may regard the Sepher Raziel as antedating the Claviculæ, it explains why a Key was attributed to Solomon. The *Clavis* in question is, however, concerned with the magical influences of the stars, "without which we can effect nothing." The second book is called *Ala;* it treats of the virtues of stones, herbs, and beasts. The third is *Tractatus Thymiamatum,* the use of which term connects it with the "Sworn Book" of Honorius; it treats of suffumigations. The fourth sets out the times of the year, day, and night which are disposed to operation; the fifth embodies the laws regarding cleanness and abstinence; while the sixth, called Samaim, expounds the nature of the heavens, of the angels, and of the operations of each. The seventh and last book is concerned with the virtues of names. A Latin version of the Sepher Raziel occurs in Sloane MS. 3853, ascribed to the same period. It differs greatly from the former, being much shorter, and full of rear magical symbols.

The MSS. of the third group are all in English, and all of late date.

Sloane 2731 is a very neat MS., begun on January 10, 1676, and containing the entire "Lemegeton, or Lesser Key of Solomon," in English. Some account of this celebrated work, which has so unaccountably escaped publication, will be found in the third chapter of this part. Sloane 3648 is another manuscript of the "Lemegeton," also in English, together with the *Ars Notoria,* a book of invocations and prayers attributed to Solomon, of which there are many examples extant in England and on the Continent.[1] It is a work which connects with Magic without being itself magical, and, in fact, stands in much the same relation to the Key or Clavicle as the "Enchiridion of Pope Leo" to the "Isagoge" of the Arbatel. Lastly, the same MS. contains the "Magical Archidoxies" of Paracelsus, but seems to be quite distinct from the treatise so entitled in the Geneva folio, containing the collected writings of the German adept.[2]

[1] The English translation of Robert Turner is well known to collectors.

[2] The genuine "Archidoxies" are concerned with the alchemical separation of elements, with transcendental Medicine and the Quintessence, with Magisteries and Elixirs. The first complete translation is in "The Hermetic and Alchemical Writings of Paracelsus," edited by Arthur Edward Waite, 2 vols. 4to 1910 (Published by, Messrs. de Laurence, Scott & Co.)

In either case, it is not a work of Ceremonial Magic. Sloane 3805 is a quarto MS., chiefly alchemical and medical, comprising a translation of the forged epistles of Sendivogius, and towards the end the "Lemegeton," started by the writer apparently with the intention of transcribing all the works attributed to Solomon under the heading of this angelic name. It breaks off, however, at the end of the offices of the thirteenth spirit of the Infernal Hierarchy.

It should be added that the three groups contain materials which are common to all. The independent treatises which follow the Sepher Raziel in Sloane 3826 extract matter from the "Sworn Book," while that entitled *Liber Lunæ*, concerning the intelligences of the mansions of the moon, the squares of the planets, their seals, rings, and so forth—which, by the way, is in this form unknown to modern critics—has given material to other and later collections.

The unprinted literature of Ceremonial Magic offers a vast field of bibliographical research, and may be the subject of a future inquiry. Among the miscellaneous MSS. in the British Museum, it is here only necessary to notice two, as they contain materials connected with the present design. Sloane 3884 includes a process in Necromancy—how to call the ghost of a dead body—the invocation of spirits into a crystal—the form for summoning spirits within a circle—and a method of exorcism in the Tuscan language,—all impudently attributed to the author of the "Nullity of Magic," Roger Bacon. In the second part of this work a special chapter is devoted to Infernal Necromancy, and the MS. here mentioned will be useful for purposes of reference. Sloane 3850 is a MS. of the seventeenth century, which contains transcripts from the fourth book of Cornelius Agrippa and from the Heptameron of Peter de Abano in Latin. There is also a "Good and Proved Experiment" for evocation, which uses the *Pater, Ave, Credo,* and Litany of the Saints as magical formulæ. There are also processes, mostly in Latin, but some in English, for the discovery of things lost, the recovery of things stolen, for the spirits of the dead who cannot rest in their graves, and for persons possessed by evil spirits. The treatise *De Novem Candariis Salomonis,* containing curious figures and sigils, deserves particular mention, as it seems unknown to students. Its attribution notwithstanding, it is the work of a Catholic writer.

CHAPTER II

The Rituals of Transcendental Magic

§ 1. *The Arbatel of Magic.*

THE term transcendental must not be interpreted in any exalted or philosophical sense when it is used, informally enough, in such a connection as the present. It has not been adopted because it is more than tolerably appropriate, but rather in the absence of a better word of definition, and because also it has been previously admitted in the same connection. It is perhaps loosely equivalent to the *Haute Magi* of Eliphas Lévi, which has been rendered "Transcendental Magic," not as an identical equivalent, but because there is no current or admitted expression which corresponds more closely. When due allowance has been made for the conceptions which may be presumed to underlie it, it must be admitted that in Ceremonial Magic there is little true Transcendentalism. Whatever may be claimed for the intelligences with whom communication is sought to be established, they reveal themselves by their offices, which are mostly either fantastic or frivolous. In such an association it should be understood that material interests are to be included in the second class; in the first would be comprised those which are outside realisation by reason of their extravagance, and at the same time are quite unconnected with spiritual aspiration.

There is scarcely anything in Practical Magic which interlinks, for example, with a true Mystic Purpose.[1] Hence, by Rituals of Transcendental Magic there must not be understood a collection of processes by which the Divine in Man is sought to be united with the Divine in the Universe. The works of St. John of the Cross, of Ruysbroeck, of Eckart, of Molinos, of Saint-Martin, even the Imitation of St. Thomas a Kempis, these contain the grand processes of true Transcendental Magic, were it fitting to apply a term which has become almost ridiculous to treasures which might be disparaged by the association. There must be understood simply those processes of so-called Theurgic Ceremonial, in which there is at least no explicit connection with Black Magic, which not only contain no dealings with evil spirits for evil purposes, but appear to eschew all such communication, for whatever purpose. An exception—which, properly understood, is, however, an exception only on the surface—should be made in favour of the procedure adopted by the Church for the expulsion of diabolical powers from persons in the flesh, not because the phenomena of possession are necessarily other than pathological, even in those cases which would appear to be marked and obstinate, but because, on the terms of the ecclesiastical assumption, the Rite of Exorcism is a far more exalted Rite than most which obtain in Transcendental Magic. In this matter, as in many other cases of much higher importance, sufficient justice has not been done to the position of the Catholic Church. It should be observed in addition, that while Ceremonial Magic is concerned with a variety of processes which may obviously tend to produce in unwary operators the phenomena which characterise possession, there is scarcely a single pro-

[1] By Practical Magic is here intended not the transcendent science said to be imparted by initiation, and to be totally distinct from childish attempts to discover hidden treasure, to obtain the ring of invisibility, and so forth; the reference is intended solely to the Magic of the Ceremonial Literature.

cess in any one of the Rituals—White or Black, Composite or Transcendental—which makes any pretence of relieving persons so afflicted.[1] There is, therefore, no reason to doubt on which side of hallucination the apparatus of the Rituals has been developed, and the sympathies of reasonable students will be with the honourable institution which condemned the practices and sought to liberate the victims, leaving possesssion itself as an open question, and in this sense as a side-issue.

Even with the qualification which we have registered, the Transcendental Rituals are exceedingly few. There is—1. The Enchiridion of Pope Leo the Third. 2. The Arbatel of Magic. 3. The Celestial Magic of an anonymous German mystic, entitled "Theosophia Pneumatica," which must be held to represent and to save enumeration of one or two similar handbooks. Of these, the first is included among the Rituals of Ceremonial Magic by the invincible ignorance of almost every person who has undertaken to class it. On the other hand, the third borrows all its importance from the second, in which, upon both counts, the interest evidently centres. As regards its origin, its authorship, and even its scope,

TALISMAN OF ARBATEL.

[1] There are, of course, innumerable processes for destroying spells and enchantments; among them one occasionally meets with an exorcism to be used in a case of possession. There is one in the edition of the "Grimoire of Honorius" published at Rome in 1760. It is supposed to be efficacious both for men and animals afflicted by Satan. In the edition of 1800 there is another process, which prescribes holy water for aspersion in the case of a human being, and in that of an animal salt exorcised with blood drawn from the bewitched creature.

there is, however, considerable mystery. Within the knowledge of the present writer, there are no copies in manuscript, or none at least which are prior to the end of the sixteenth century. It appeared in a tiny volume at Basle and bore the date 1575.[1] Back-dating and imputed authorship are the two crying bibliographical sins of Grimoires and magical handbooks, and the antiquity of the "Arbatel" rests under a certain suspicion on account of its literary connections; at the same time it would require the knowledge of an expert in typography to pronounce certainly on the reliability of the date indicated. The text is in Latin, but there is a slender possibility in favour of its being the work of an Italian.[2] It makes a reference to Theophrastic Magic, which indicates the influence of Paracelsus, and, although it is difficult to speak with any certainty, seems to hint at an early period of that influence, the period, in fact, of Benedictus Figulus, slightly antedating Rosicrucian enthusiasm, and thus accounting for the omission of all Rosicrucian references, which, in view both of matter and manner, might have been irresistibly expected had the work been posterior to the year 1610.

It should be observed that the Arbatel has no connection with the cycle, hereinafter considered, of the Keys of Solomon, and it is permeated with Christian ideas. The authorship is completely unknown. Arbatel, is probably not an assumed name, but indicative of an instructing or revealing

[1] Arbatel, *De Magia Veterum*, Basileæ, 1575. The mottoes on the title are *Summum Sapientiæ Studium* and *In omnibus consule Dominum, et nihil cogites, dicas, facias, quod tibi Deus non consuluerit.*

[2] The possibility is warranted by references in the 30th and 31st Aphorisms to some obscure points of Italian history. It is said that by a judgment of the Magicians it was decreed that no Italian should reign over the kingdom of Naples; now the monarch at the time was an Italian, and he was dethroned in due course. To restore the national dynasty the decree must be annulled by those who made it. A magiciau of greater power might be able to enforce this, and also the restitution of a certain Book, Jewel, and Magic Horn, of which the Treasury of Magic has been despoiled. The mastery of the whole world would pass into the hands of their possessor.

Angel. The use of this Hebrew term is, however, peculiar in connection with the fact that the references to the Old Testament are few and unimportant, while the sayings of Christ, and the New Testament narrative generally, are subjects of continual citation. Solomon, moreover, is not mentioned in the frequent enumerations of adepts and wise men.

So far concerning the origin, authorship, and date of the book. It remains to say that it is incomplete. Of the nine "Tomes" into which it purports to be divided, we possess only one. It is not unlikely that the rest were never written, because the author has left us a plan of his entire proposal, and it is evident that his first book more than once overlaps what should have followed. As it stands, the "Arbatel of Magic" is concerned with the most general precepts of Magic Art—in other words, with the Institutions. It is entitled "Isagoge," which means essential or fundamental instruction. The missing books are those of Microcosmical Magic, or Spiritual Wisdom; Olympic Magic, that is, the evocation of the Spirits of Olympus; Hesiodiacal and Homeric Magic, being the operations of Caco-daimones; Roman or Sibylline Magic, concerning Tutelary Spirits; Pythagorical Magic, dealing with the Genii of the Arts; the Magic of Apollonius, giving power over the enemies of mankind; Hermetic or Egyptian Magic; and that, finally, which depends solely on the Word of God, and is called Prophetical Magic.

It is an open question whether all of these books could have been completed without a proportion of that dangerous instruction which makes for Black Magic. The *Isagoge,* however, must be exempted from any such charge; the Seven Septenaries of aphorisms of which it consists contain many moral and spiritual exhortations, which, if they are not exactly unhackneyed, are at least quite unexceptionable, and must indeed rank among the more exalted of their kind. The initial groups of these aphorisms serve to introduce the Ritual of the Olympic Spirits, dwelling in the firmament and in the stars of the firmament, between whom the government of the world is distributed. There are 196[1] Olympic Provinces in the entire universe, so that Aratron has 49, Bethor 42, Phaleg 35, Och 28, Hagith 21, Ophiel 14, and Phul 7. These provinces are termed visible, but even as the Seven Septenaries of Arbatel cover the whole ground of Transcendental Magic, so these seven successive multiples of the same mystical number may most probably be taken to indicate powers and offices. It is further said that the Olympic Spirits rule alternately, each for 490 years, which would be mere confusion were separate assemblages of spheres permanently assigned to them.

The powers possessed by these Intelligences are very curiously set forth. They rule naturally over certain departments and operations of the material world, but outside these departments they perform the same operations magically. Thus Och, the prime of Solar things, presides over the preparation or development of gold naturally in the veins of the earth—that is to say, he is the Mineralogist in Chief of Nature; he presides also over the quicker preparation of the same metal by means of chemical art—that is, he is the Prince of Alchemists; and, finally, he makes gold in a moment by Magic. It is in this way that Ceremonial Magic connects with while it assumes to transcend Hemetic Art.

There is another curious instruction, with regard to the

[1] The original edition of the Arbatel reads 186, and ascribes 32 provinces to Bethor, which breaks the progression of the septenary and is probably a printer's mistake. It is followed, however, by the English and German translators.

names and characters of the Spirits. In opposition to much of the traditional doctrine of Magic, it is affirmed that there is no power in the figure of any character or in the pronunciation of any name, except in so far as there is a virtue or office ordained by God to both. The names, moreover, are not definite, final or real names, whence they differ with different writers accordingly as these have received them. The only effectual names are those which are delivered to an operator by the Spirits themselves, and even then their efficacy seldom endures beyond forty years. It is, therefore, better for the student, says the "Arbatel," to work only by the offices of the Spirits, without their names; should he be pre-ordained to attain the Art of Magic, the other parts of that Art will offer themselves of their own accord.

The sources of occult wisdom, it proceeds, are, firstly, in God; secondly, in spiritual essences—that is to say, the Angelical Hierarchy; thirdly, in corporal creatures, the reference being probably to the *signatura rerum* of Paracelsus; forthly, in Nature—that is to say, in a knowledge of the secret virtues of natural things, as, for example, herbs and precious stones; fifthly, but after a long interval, in the apostate spirits reserved to the last judgment;[1] sixthly, in the ministers of punishments in hell, which seems to connect with the classical conception of avenging infernal gods; seventhly, in the people of the elements, that is, the Salamanders, Sylphs, Undines, and Pigmies.

The secrets deriving from these sources range from the highest achievements of mystical science[2] to the bourgeois

[1] This reference, taken in connection with the matters proposed to be treated in the seventh book, points conclusively to the intention of including the government of Evil Spirits in the scheme of the "Arbatel."

[2] It should be observed that the mystical achievements are barely mentioned, and that their attainment is imparted by a spirit possessing the office, which is quite opposed to Mysticism. The author of the "Arbatel," however, considers it good enough Mysticism, as does Eliphas Lévi, to cause oneself "to be worshipped as a god," in virtue of the sigil of Och.

ambitions of daily life, from the Regeneration of Enoch and the Knowledge of God, Christ, and His Holy Spirit, wherein is the perfection of the Microcosm, to the attainment of honours and dignities, the ingathering of much money, the foundation of a family, good fortune in mercantile pursuits, and successful housewifery both in town and country. The prolongation of life, the transmutation of metals, and the talismanic cure of all diseases, with other "paradoxes of the highest science," also figure in the list.

Meditation, inward contemplation, and the love of God are the chief aids to the acquisition of Magic Art, together with great faith, strict taciturnity, and even justice in the things of daily life. Finally, a true magician is brought forth as such from his mother's womb; others who assume the function will be unhappy.[1]

The powers and offices of the Seven Olympic Spirits are as follows; ARATRON governs those things which are ascribed astronomically to Saturn. He can convert any living organism, plant, or animal into stone, and that in a moment of time; he can also change coals into treasure, and treasure into coals; he gives familiars, and reconciles subterranean spirits to men; he teaches Alchemy, Magic, and

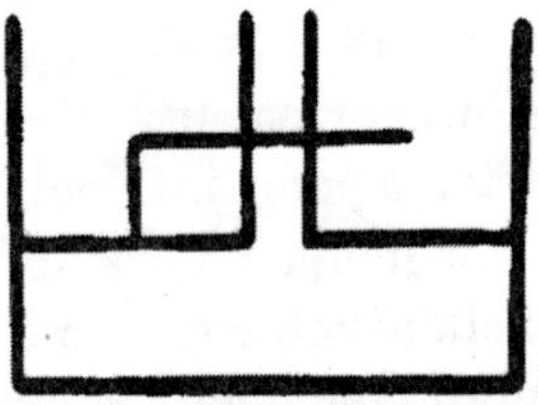

THE CHARACTER OF ARATRON.

[1] When his highest authorities disagree, the occult student is liable to get at the truth, and will find occasionally that it is not at either end, nor yet in the middle. It is edifying to compare this express statement of a ruling ceremonial process with another, not less express, which we owe to the reconstruction of all the processes and the reputed recoverer of the true practice of Magic. "Furthermore, certain physical organizations are better adapted than others for the revelations of the occult world; there are sensitive and sympathetic natures, with whom intuition in the astral light is, so to speak, inborn; certain afflictions and certain complaints

Medicine, imparts the secret of invisibility, makes the barren fruitful, and, lastly, confers long life. He should be invoked on a Saturday, in the first hour of the day,[1] making use of his character, given and confirmed by himself.

The affairs of Jupiter are administered by BETHOR, who responds quickly when called. The person dignified by his character may be exalted to illustrious positions, and obtain large treasures. He reconciles the Spirits of the Air to man, so that they will give true answers, transport precious stones, and compose medicines having miraculous effects. Bethor also grants familiars of the firmament, and can prolong life to seven hundred years, subject to the will of God.

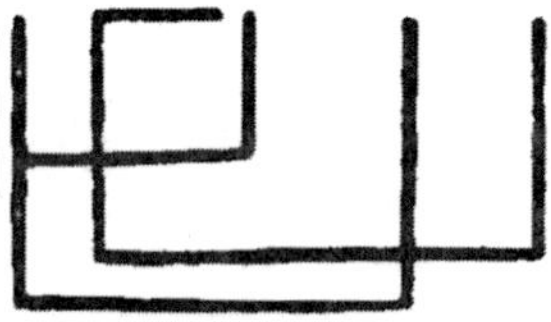

THE CHARACTER OF BETHOR.

PHALEG governs the things which are attributed to Mars. The person who possesses his character is raised by him to great honour in military affairs.

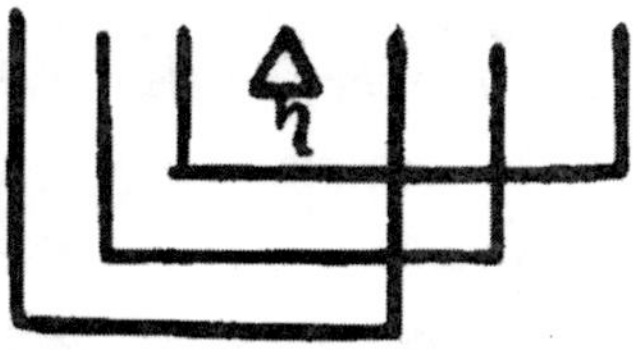

THE CHARACTER OF PHALEG.

can modify the nervous system, and, independently of the concurrence of the will, may convert it into a divinatory apparatus of less or more perfection; but these phenomena are exceptional, *and generally magical power should, and can, be acquired by perseverance and labour.*"—"Doctrine and Ritual of Transcendent Magic," by Eliphas Lévi, English translation by A. E. Waite, p. 196. In this case the genius of enlightened differentiation rests entirely upon the later adept. As a matter of fact, occult writers have always recognized that there is the Natural Magician and the Magician according to Art. *Vel sanctum invenit, vel sanctum facit* has been said of Magic, and so also magical knowledge means magical power; where it does not find it, it brings it. But such knowledge is not of Rituals or Grimoires, of *Arbatel* or another.

[1] See Part II, c. 6.

Solar interests are administered by OCH, who prolongs life to six hundred years with perfect health, imparts great wisdom, gives excellent (familiar) spirits, composes perfect medicines, converts any substance into the purest of metals, or into precious stones, also bestows gold and a purse, quaintly described by the English translator of the "Arbatel" as "springing with gold." He causes the possessor of his character to be worshipped as a god by the kings of the whole world.

THE CHARACTER OF OCH.

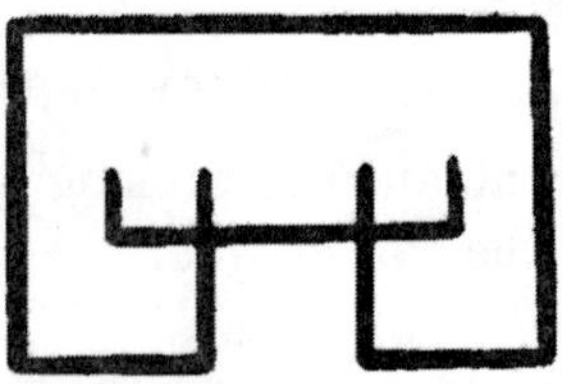

THE CHARACTER OF HAGITH.

The government of Venereal concerns is entrusted to HAGITH, and the person possessing his character is adorned with all beauty. He converts copper into gold in a moment and gold instantaneously into copper; he also gives faithful serving spirits.

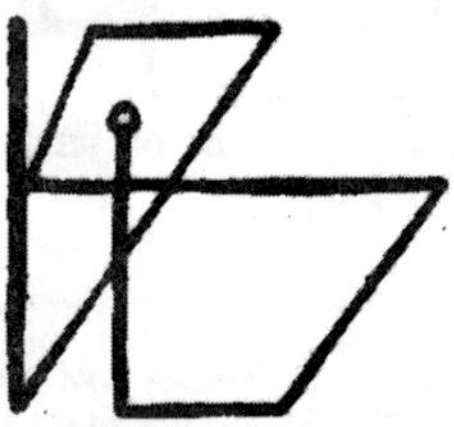

THE CHARACTER OF OPHIEL.

OPHIEL is the ruler of those things which are attributed to Mercury; he gives familiar spirits, teaches all arts, and enables the possessor of his character to change quicksilver immediately into the Philosopher's Stone.

Lunary concerns are under the government of PHUL,

who truly transmutes all metals into silver, heals dropsy, and provides Spirits of the Water, who serve men in a corporal and visible form; he also prolongs life to three hundred years.

THE CHARACTER OF PHUL.

Legions of inferior spirits are commanded by each of the Governors, who also have Kings, Princes, Presidents, Dukes, and Ministers ruling under them. Ceremonial Magic usually administers the hierarchies upon a colossal scale. The invocation of the Governors is simple. It is performed in the day and hour of the planet which is in correspondence with the Olympic Intelligence by means of the following:—

Prayer.

O Eternal and Omnipotent God, who hast ordained the whole creation for Thy praise and Thy glory, as also for the salvation of man, I beseech Thee to send Thy Spirit N., of the Solor Race,[1] that he may instruct me concerning those things about which I design to ask him [or that he may bring me medicine against the dropsy, &c.]. Nevertheless, not my will, but Thine be done, through Jesus Christ, Thine only-begotten Son, who is our Lord. Amen.

Unless the Spirit, in the words of Robert Turner, be "familiarly addicted" to the operator, he should not be detained above one hour, and should in either case be "licensed to depart" as follows:—

[1] There is merely a typical form subject to variations according to the spirit who is evoked.

Michael
Machen
Och
Gabriel
Shamain
Phul
Samael
Machon
Phaleg
Raphael
Raquie
Ophiel
Sachiel
Zebul
Bethor
Anael
Sagun
Hagith
Cassiel
Aratron

THE DISCHARGE.

Forasmuch as thou camest in peace and quietness, having also answered unto my petitions, I give thanks unto God, in whose Name thou camest. Now mayst thou depart in peace unto thine own order, but return unto me again, when I shall call thee by thy name, or by thine order, or by thine office, which is granted from the Creator. Amen. [Then add:] Be not rash with thy mouth, and let not thine heart be hasty to utter anything before God: for God is in heaven, and thou art upon earth; therefore let thy words be few. For a dream cometh through the multitude of business, and a fool's voice is known by multitude of words.—Eccles. v. 3, 4.

§ 2. *Theosophia Pneumatica.*

In the year 1686, the "Arbatel" was translated into German, and in the same year—possibly in the same volume—appeared, also in German, a work entitled "The Little Keys of Solomon" or *Theosophia Pneumatica.*[1] There are no examples of these editions in the British Museum, and inquiry has failed to elicit any particulars concerning them. Both are reprinted, together with other specimens of Ancient Magical Literature, to illustrate the Faust legend, in the third volume of Scheible's *Das Kloster.*[2] The translation of the "Arbatel" makes no reference to the previous edition in Latin, and *Theosophia Pneumatica* nowhere states that it is an adaptation of the earlier work. The attribution to Solomon is, of course, wholly contrary to the spirit of the Ritual, and betrays so far the hand of ignorance.

[1] Claviculæ Salomonis vel Theosophia Pneumatica.

[2] J. Scheible, *Das Kloster. Weltlich und Geistlich. Meist aus der Altern Deutschen Volks-Literatur*, 12 vols., Stuttgart, 1845-49.

The adapter had, however, been subject to other occult influences besides the "Arbatel." He applies the term Talmid [1] to the magical aspirant, and this is not used by the original. The adaptation has been well executed and makes for additional clearness. The transcendental portions are slightly accentuated; it is said in one place that the exaltation of prayer is the end of the whole Mystery, and that such exaltation will never be denied to the true seeker, who is recommended on no account to undervalue his own prayers. This is better mysticism than the corresponding passage in the "Arbatel" itself. There is also an addendum on Transcendental Medicine, which, so far as can be known, is original, and it is as curious as anything in the literature with which we are dealing.[2]

[1] There is a curious history attaching to this word, but it can be elucidated only by a Hebrew scholar. It seems to be of late introduction, though it derives from the verb *to learn*. It represents a stage of initiation in certain mystical societies of Islam.

[2] As it is unlikely that *Theosophia Pneumatica* will ever be printed in English, it may be well to give a summary of its appendix, that is to say, of the only section of this work which differs generically from the "Arbatel." Affirming that all things are threefold, from the Divine Triad of Father, Son, and Holy Ghost, to man, who is composed of the fleshly body, the sensitive soul, and the rational spirit, it defines the human principles as follows; The body is of earth; the sensitive soul is of the four elements, but derives through the stars, and is the seat of understanding and genius for arts and sciences; the rational spirit is from God absolutely; the sphere of its activity is celestial and divine, and divine inspiration and influence pass through it to the material body. The body is a house wherein soul and spirit abide and perform their functions, having been married therein by God. At the same time they strive daily with one another, till the spirit overcomes the soul, and thus attains regeneration. There are two kinds of death—that which results from the destruction of vital physical organs by disease or injury, and that which results from the destruction of the sensitive soul by envenomed astral influences. Physical disintegration and flight of the divine spirit follow in either case. The spirit may also be recalled by the direct action of the will of God, without disease or injury. Man is therefore poised upon three pillars: if one of them fall or break, the man dies. He should preserve and embalm his body against infectious diseases, for the living organism can be embalmed better than a corpse. He should also combat the venomous influences of baleful stars, for Elohim has gifted men with the power to compose characters that will destroy such influences. It is impossible, however, to cure those diseases with which God in His unsearchable compassion may Himself scourge mankind; vain are the best medicines and vain the highest arcana, vain is *p. ex. unicorn.*, vain is the potent *aurum*, vain the *spiritus auri*, vain the *quinta essentia*; Azoth itself is useless; the *lapis philosophorum* is made void. The skilled physician will immediately discover such a case in a patient. All other diseases deriving from the planets, from the natural corruption of the earth, or from neglect, may be cured by natural remedies

§ 3. *The Enchiridion of Pope Leo.*

We come now to the "Enchiridion of Pope Leo III., which, as already indicated, is not a book of Ceremonial Magic; it is necessary, however, to include it in this notice, and to analyze it at some length, so as to establish its true character. Misconceptions and mistakes upon a subject so obscure as Magical Rituals are, speaking generally, excusable enough, but in this case they are found where they are not excusable, namely, among those persons who have undertaken to give account of the work. Catholic bibliographers of the occult sciences, or at least the anonymous author of the occult encyclopædia in Migne's great series, are very angry at the pontifical attribution, and stigmatise the "Enchiridion" as an infamous storehouse of Black Magic. Eliphas Lévi, who may possibly have read it—because occasionally he seems to have glanced at his authors—magnifies its occult importance by stating that it has never been printed with its true figures. In the absence of all evidence on this point, it is impossible to entertain it seriously. The "Enchiridion" is assuredly not a book of Black Magic, nor does it lend itself to the introduction of other figures than those which appear in it, and these are few and simple. Finally Alfred Maury, in *La Magic et l'Astrologie dan' l'Antiquité et au Moyen Age,* describes the "Enchiridion" as a work on Sorcery, bearing traces of Neo-Platonic, and even older, influences. He also evidently had not read it, and is a personage of sufficient consequence to deserve severe censure for following such an evil principle of criticism.

—by herbs, balms, spices, oils, metals, or preparations of alchemy. When natural diseases become incurable, it is through the ignorance or indocility of man. This Appendix of *Theosophia Pneumatica* not only indicates the influence but reproduces the terminology of Paracelsus.

The legend of the "Enchiridion" is as follows. When Charlemagne was leaving Rome after his coronation by Leo III., that pontiff presented him with a memorial of the visit in the shape of a collection of prayers to which wonderful virtues were attributed. Whosoever bore the little work upon his person with the respect due to Holy Scripture, and recited it daily to the honour of God, would never be overcome by his enemies, would pass unscathed through all perils, and the Divine protection would abide with him to the end of his days. These things took place in the year 800. In the year 1523 the "Enchiridion" is supposed to have been printed at Rome for the first time. Thus broadly outlined, there is nothing in this legend to offend possibility or to raise very serious objection to the authorship. The reputed connection with occult science would indeed seem the chief presumption against it, because there never was a literature so founded in forgery as that of Magic, except the sister science of Alchemy. When we come, however, to examine the work at first hand, the case against it assumes a different aspect, and it is condemned out of its own mouth. While it is not a Ritual of Magic, it is also certainly not a simple collection of devotions designed to fortify the person making use of them against dangers of body and soul by the operation of Divine grace; it is rather a collection of charms cast in the form of prayers, and is quite opposed in its spirit to the devotional spirit of the Church; furthermore, it is concerned with worldly advantages far more than with those of a spiritual kind. The work opens by pointing out that of all the sovereign princes of past ages there was none more fortunate than Charlemagne, and the source of his great prosperity is acknowledged by him in a letter of thanks addressed to Pope Leo, the original of which, it is affirmed, may still be seen in the Library of the Vatican, written with the monarch's own hand. He states therein that since his reception of a little volume entitled "Enchiridion," filled with special prayers and mysterious figures, sent by His Holiness as a precious gift, he has never ceased to be fortunate, and that of all things in the universe which are capable of harming man, not one has shown any malignity against him, in gratitude for which he proposes to devote himself and all that is his to the service of his benefactor. The letter is in Latin; the monarch styles himself Carolus Magnus, which appears highly unlikely, and he terms the pontiff Summus Antistitum Antistites, but this is not in itself improbable, as the Papal claim to Episcopal supremacy was fully developed at the beginning of the ninth century.

It is needless to say that there is no such document preserved in the Vatican Library; furthermore, there are no letters of Charlemagne extant, and, despite the encouragement he gave to men of learning and the Academy mentioned by Alcuin, it is not at all certain that he could either read or write. Lastly, while it is quite true that his empire included Germany, as it did also Holland, Belgium, Switzerland, and part of Italy, after his coronation it is much more probable that he would have styled himself Emperor of the Romans. There is, in fact no colourable pretence of genuineness about the so-called autograph letter.

This fact being established, we may proceed to the consideration of the alleged date of publication—Rome, 1523. This edition is mentioned by Pierre Christian in his *Histoire de la Magie,* and he defends the authenticity of the "Enchiridion" on the ground, among others, that it passed unchallenged in the Eternal City during such a pontificate as that of Clement VII. A second edition is said to have been printed at Rome in 1606; between 1584 and 1633 it appeared four times at Lyons and once at Mayence. In 1660 it was published for the last time at Rome. Unfortunately for the purposes of this criticism, the examples of 1633 and 1660 have been alone available. The first claims to be *nuperrime mendis omnibus purgatum,* but it has been evidently in the hands of a Grimoire maker, and it appears to have been edited and extended in the Grimoire interest.[1] This is certain, but it is impossible to say how much beyond the "Seven Mysterious Orisons" connected with the name of Pope Leo are to be found in the original, or whether the original was antedated. Outside these Orisons the modern accent of the work is unmistakable, and it is difficult to understand how any instructed person, much less a bibliophile like M. Christian, could have been deceived by it.

The work itself, as already said, is simply a collection of religious charms, effectual against all the perils to which every sort and condition of men are made subject on land, on water, from open and secret enemies, from the bites of wild and rabid beasts, from poisons, from fire, from tempests. While it thus ensures against evil, it gives happiness in domestic matters and in the enterprises which contribute to prosperity and to the pleasures of a contented life, "only the instructions must be followed as accurately as human weakness will allow." Fortunately they are more simple than the Grimoires. When a copy of the book has been secured, it must be placed in a small bag of new leather, so that it may be kept clean. A vow must be made to carry it as far as practicable on one's person, and to read with at-

[1] This appears more evidently in the last Roman edition, which pretends to be based on all those which preceded it, including impressions published at Parma, Ancona, and Frankfort, which are now generally unknown. The editor has, moreover, altered and rearranged, omitted and added at choice. He has supplied also a Key to the whole work, which is a short process for the government of evil spirits.

tentive devotion at least one page daily. If a specific danger be apprehended, a page suitable to its nature should be selected. Reading must be done upon the knees, with the face turned to the east; "so did Charlemagne invariably." Furthermore, works of piety must be performed in honour of the celestial genii whose benign influence it is desired to attract; alms also must be given to the poor, "as this is of all things most pleasing unto such spirits, for thereby we become their coadjutors and friends, the economy of the universe being committed to them by the Creator."

Here we have the magical doctrine concerning planetary intelligences which connects the "Enchiridion" with the "Arbatel," and the hint of "secondary deities" which connects it with Trithemius.[1]

The *In Principio,* or first chapter of the Gospel according to St. John, is declared to be the most potent of all the devotions in the book, and it is to be recited the most frequently. The mysterious figures are said to have been extracted from the rarest manuscripts which antiquity has committed to us, and their virtue is not only highly efficacious, but so easily put in motion, that it is enough for this purpose to carry the work reverently on one's person. "Experience will remove any doubt which may be felt in this respect, while the scruples which may be occasioned by the idea that there is Magic or superstition herein will be banished by a slight exercise of reason."

As to this latter point, it is said that a little reflection upon the infinite number of secret sympathies and antipathies found in different beings here below will explain how it is that such figures may be in sympathy with the Celestial Intelligences which govern this vast universe.

[1] Joannis Tritemii, Abbatis Spanheymensis, *De Septem Secundiis, id est, Intelligentiis, sive Spiritibus, Orbes post Deum Moventibus, &c.* Coloniæ, 1567. The treatise is well known, or at least much talked of, and this is the original edition, belonging to the date claimed for it.

It will scarcely be necessary to observe that the doctrine of sympathies and antipathies is the very essence of Natural Magic, and connects it with the higher branches. The mysterious figures referred to were originally nine in number, and in most cases recur several times. The most conspicuous is the Labarum of Constantine and the Tau symbol, which Levi connects with the Tarot.

The apparently unmeaning enumeration of various Divine Names is a special characteristic of Ceremonial Magic, and certainly makes the "Enchiridion" interlink with a cycle of literature from which it is otherwise distinct. There is, indeed, little specific difference between the prayers which incorporate them and the Invocations which swarm in the Rituals. It may be added that the use of such Divine Names is supported by reference to the Angelical Theology of Dionysius.

The prefatory matter ends at this point. The prose of the Gospel of St. John follows, with versicles and a prayer. Next come the Seven Penitential Psalms, with the Litany of the Saints, after which are the "Mysterious Prayers of Pope Leo," followed by a multitude of others not less mysterious, and prevailing against human fragility, and so forth. There are prayers for voyages, prayers addressed to the Cross, and then under the Tau symbol, commencing with the curious exclamation, *Per signum* ✠ *Domine Tau, libera me,* there follows a long conjuration, as express as anything in Magic, designed to prevent the petitioner from injury by any steel weapons whatsoever. Forming part of this ceremony is the the pseudo-epistle addressed by Jesus Christ to King Abgar, explaining why our Saviour could not come Himself to that monarch, and promising to send His disciple Thaddeus when He had fulfilled the work given Him by His Father. It goes on to say that Christ has writ-

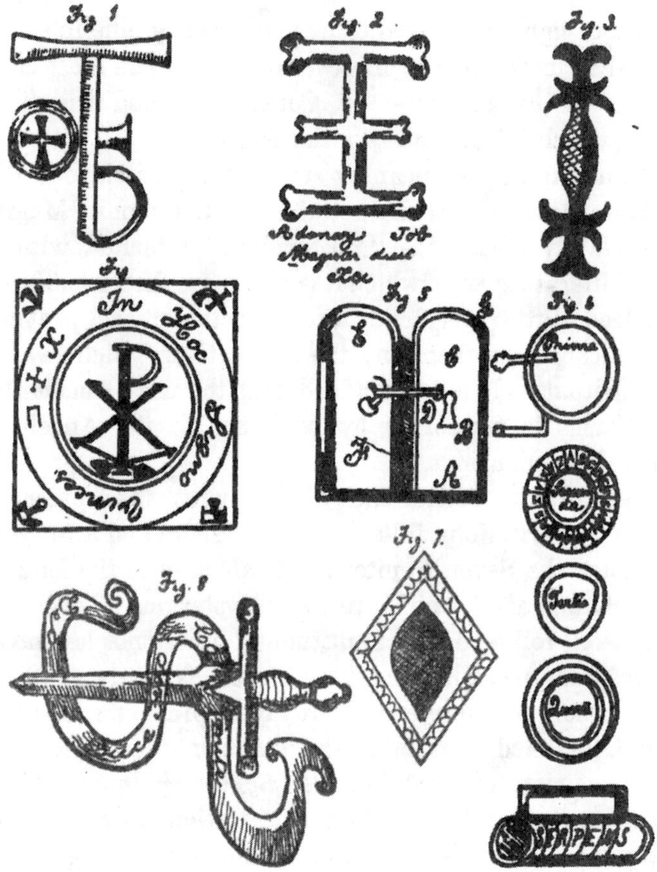
Fig. 1
Fig. 2
Adonay Job
Fig. 3
In Hoc Signo Vinces
Fig. 5
Fig. 6
Prima
Fig. 7
Fig. 8
SERPENS

ten it with His own hand, and that wheresoever the recipient shall be, in house or field, by sea or stream, *sive in præ lio Paganorum seu Christianorum* (!) his enemy shall never prevail over him.[1] The king recived the epistle with many tears and prayers, all which being duly described, the conjuration of the *baculi, gladii, lanceæ, enses, cultelli, sagittæ, claves, funes, et omnia alia genera armorum,* is continued.

As it is difficult to say where the original "Enchiridion" actually begins, so it is uncertain where it ends. A variety of miscellaneous prayers are, however, attributed to well-known saints quite outside the Carlovingian period, and to Innocent IV. and John X., without prejudice to a further orison of the great Pope Leo himself. Then come the "curious secrets"—to conciliate and discover one's proper genius, to become invulnerable, to prevent a gun from going off, to behold a future husband or wife, all effected by means of formal prayers—a kind of royal road to the chief ends of Magic, without apparently exceeding the devotional discipline of the Church.

To complete the analysis of this curious collection, its most important practical part is here added, namely:—

§ 4. *The Seven Mysterious Orisons.*

Sunday.

Pater noster, &c. Deliver me, O Lord, I beseech Thee, me even, thy creature, N., from all evils past, present, and to come, whether of body or soul; grant me peace and health in Thy goodness; incline favourably unto me Thy creature, by the intercession of the Blessed Virgin Mary and of Thy holy apostles, Peter, Paul, Andrew, and of all the saints.

[1] For this legend, see Fabricius, *Cod. Apoc. N.T.*, I., p. 317.

Vouchsafe peace unto Thy creature, and health during all my life, so that, strengthened by the mainstay of Thy mercy, I may never be the slave of sin, nor go in fear of any trouble, through the same Jesus Christ Thy Son, our Saviour, who, being truly God, liveth and reigneth in the unity of the Holy Spirit for ever and ever, Amen. May the peace of the Lord be always with me, Amen. May that peace, O Lord, which Thou didst leave to Thy disciples abide ever with power in my heart, standing always between me and my enemies, both visible and invisible, Amen. May the peace of the Lord, His countenance, His body, His blood, assist, console, and protect me, Thy creature, N., in my soul and my body, Amen. Lamb of God, who didst deign to be born of the Virgin Mary, who didst cleanse the world from its sins upon the Cross, have pity on my soul and my body. O Christ, Lamb of God, immolated for the salvation of the world, have pity on my soul and my body. Lamb of God, by whom all the faithful are saved, give unto me Thy peace, to remain with me for ever, both in this life and that which is to come, Amen.

Monday.

O great God, by whom all things have been set free, deliver me also from all evil. O great God, who hast granted Thy consolation unto all beings, grant it also unto me. O great God, who hast succoured and assisted all things, aid me also, and succour me in all my necessities and miseries, my enterprises and dangers; deliver me from all the hindrances and snares of my enemies, both visible and invisible, in the Name of the Father who created the whole world ✠, in the Name of the Son who hath redeemed it ✠, in the name of the Holy Ghost who hath accomplished the entire law in its perfection. I cast myself utterly into Thine arms, and place myself unreservedly under thy holy protection, Amen. May the blessing of God the Father Almighty, of the Son, and of the Holy Ghost, be always with me ✠, Amen. May the blessing of God the Father, who by His only Word hath made all things, be with me for ever ✠, Amen. May the blessing of our Lord Jesus Christ, Son of the great living God, be with me for ever ✠, Amen. May the blessing and seven Gifts of the Holy Ghost be with me for ever ✠, Amen. May the blessing of the Virgin Mary, and of her Son, be with me for ever, Amen.

Tuesday.

May the blessing and consecration of the bread and of the wine, which our Lord Jesus Christ made when He gave them to His disciples and said unto them: Take and eat ye all of this, for this is My Body which shall be delivered for you, in remembrance of Me and for the remission of all sins, be with me for ever ✠. May the blessing of the Holy Angels, Archangels, Virtues, Powers, Thrones, Dominations, Cherubim and Seraphim, be with me for ever ✠, Amen. May the blessing of the patriarchs and prophets, apostles, martyrs, confessors, virgins, and of all the saints of God, be with me for ever ✠, Amen. May the blessing of all the heavens of God be with me for ever ✠, Amen. May the majesty of God Omnipotent sustain and protect me; may His eternal goodness lead me; may His boundless charity inflame me; may His supreme divinity direct me; may the power of the Father preserve me; may the wisdom of the Son enliven me; may the virtue of the Holy Ghost stand always between me and my enemies, both visible and invisible. Power of the Father, strengthen me; wisdom of the

Son, enlighten me; consolation of the Holy Ghost, comfort me. The Father is peace, the Son is Life, the Holy Ghost is the consoling and saving remedy, Amen. May the Divinity of God bless me, Amen. May His piety warm me; may His love preserve me. O Jesus Christ, Son of the living God, have pity upon me a poor sinner.

Wednesday.

O Emmanuel, defend me against the malignant enemy, and against all my enemies, visible and invisible, and deliver me from all evil. Jesus Christ the King hath come in peace, God made man, who hath suffered patiently for us. May Jesus Christ, the gentle King, stand always for my defence between me and my enemies, Amen. Jesus Christ triumphs, Jesus Christ reigns, Jesus Christ commands. May Jesus Christ deliver me from all evils for ever, Amen. May Jesus Christ vouchsafe me grace to triumph over all my adversaries, Amen. Behold the Cross of our Lord Jesus Christ. Fly, therefore, O my enemies, at the sight thereof; the Lion of the Tribe of Juda and of the Race of David hath conquered. Alleluia, Alleluia, Alleluia. Saviour of the world, save and succour me. Thou who hast purchased me by Thy Cross and Thy Blood, succour me, I conjure Thee, my God. O Agios, O Theos, Agios, Ischyros, Agios, Athanatos, Elieson, Himas, Holy God, Strong God, Merciful and Immortal God, have pity upon me Thy creature, N. Sustain me, O Lord; forsake me not, reject not my prayers, O Thou, the God of my salvation. Do Thou assist me always, O God of my salvation.

THURSDAY.

Enlighten mine eyes with true light, that they may never be closed in eternal sleep, lest mine enemy should say: I have prevailed over him. So long as the Lord is with me I will not fear the malice of my enemies. O most sweet Jesus, preserve me, aid me, save me; at the name of Jesus let every knee bow, in heaven, on earth, and in hell, and let every tongue confess openly that Jesus Christ is in the glory of His Father, Amen. I know beyond doubt that in what day soever I shall call upon the Lord, in the same hour shall I be saved. O most sweet Lord Jesus Christ, Son of the great living God, thou hast performed most mighty miracles by the sole power of Thy most precious name, and hast enriched the poor most abundantly, so that by force thereof the demons flee away, the blind see, the deaf hear, the lame walk erect, the dumb speak, the lepers are cleansed, the sick cured, the dead raised up; for wheresoever the most sweet Name of Jesus is pronounced, the ear is ravished and the mouth is filled with pleasant savour; at that one utterance, I repeat, the demons take flight, every knee is bent, all temptations, even the worst, are scattered, all infirmities are healed, all disputes and conflicts between the world, the flesh, and the devil are ended, and the soul is filled with every heavenly delight; for whosoever invoketh or shall invoke this holy Name of God is and shall be saved, this holy Name pronounced by the angel even before His conception in the womb of the Holy Virgin.

FRIDAY.

O sacred Name, Name which strengthens the heart of man, Name of life, of salvation, of joy, precious Name, resplendent, glorious, agreeable Name, which fortifies the sinner, Name which saves, conserves, leads, and rules all. May it please Thee, therefore, most precious Jesus, by the power of this same (Name of) Jesus, to drive away the demon from me; enlighten me, O Lord, for I am blind; remove my deafness; set me upright, who am lame; give me speech, who am dumb; cleanse my leprosy; restore me to health, who am sick; raise me up, for I am dead; give me life once more, and enrich me in all my parts, within and without, so that, furnished and fortified by Thy holy Name, I may abide always in Thee, praising and honouring Thee, because all is due to Thee, and Thou only art worthy to be glorified, the Lord and eternal Son of God, in whom all things rejoice, and by whom all are governed. Praise, honour, and glory, be given Thee for ever and ever, Amen. May Jesus be always in my heart and in my breast, Amen. May our Lord Jesus Christ be ever within me, may He establish me for ever, may He be around me and preserve me; may He be before me and lead me; may He be behind me and guard me; may He be above me and bless me; may He be within me and give me life; may He be near me and rule me; may He be beneath me and fortify me; may He be always with me and deliver me from all the pains of eternal death, who liveth and reigneth for ever and ever, Amen.

Saturday.

Jesus, Son of Mary, salvation of the world, may the Lord look favourably upon me, with mildness and propitiation; may He give me a holy and willing spirit, to respect and honour Him only, who is the Liberator of the world. On Him could no one lay hand, for His hour was not yet come— He who is, who was, who shall remain, God and man, the beginning and the end. May this prayer which I offer unto

Him deliver me eternally from my enemies, Amen. Jesus of Nazareth, King of the Jews, honourable title, Son of the Virgin Mary, have pity upon me, a poor sinner, and lead me, according to Thy loving-kindness, in the way of eternal salvation, Amen. Now Jesus, knowing what things must come to pass concerning Him, came forward and said unto them: Whom seek ye? They answered Him: Jesus of Nazareth. But Jesus said unto them: I am He. And Judas, who was to deliver Him, was with them. As soon then as He had said unto them: I am He, they fell backward upon the earth. Then asked He them again: Whom seek ye? And they said: Jesus of Nazareth. Jesus answered: I have told you that I am He; if therefore ye seek Me, let these go their way (speaking of His disciples). The lance, the nails, the cross ✠, the thorns, the death which I have endured, prove that I have effaced and expiated the crimes of the unfortunate. Preserve me, O Lord Jesus Christ, from all afflictions of poverty and from the snares of my enemies. May the five wounds of our Lord be unto me an everlasting remedy. Jesus is the Way ✠, Jesus is the Life ✠, Jesus is the Truth ✠, Jesus has suffered ✠, Jesus has been crucified ✠, Jesus, Son of the living God, have pity on me ✠. Now, Jesus passing went through the midst of them, and no one could place his murderous hand upon Jesus, because His hour was not yet come.

While these prayers are in some respects curious enough, they compare quite unfavourably with the simple good sense which characterises those of the Roman Liturgy; they are inexact in their references and confused in their method, and no person who seriously considers them will sustain the early date which is claimed for them. Their period is subsequent to the Renaissance, and the ignorance of liturgical formulæ which they show, in common with all similar forgeries, makes it doubtful whether they are the work of an ecclesiastic at all. In any case they are clumsy imitations, the product of an unskilful hand.

§ 5. *Summary of Transcendental Magic.*

This concludes our examination of the Rituals of Transcendental Magic, comprising all those to which any currency has been given. There are no doubt other treatises which exist only in manuscript and possess no literary history, but they scarcely come within the scope of the present inquiry. Such possibly is the "Book of Sacred Magic" in the Library of the Arsenal, Paris, while a few others which connect partially with the higher branches of ceremonial practice have been noted briefly in the first chapter.

The general conclusion which must follow from the examination is not of a favourable kind. As premised at the outset, the Rituals with which we have been dealing are not worthy of the name Transcendental. We have, on the one hand, a collection of prayers, falsely attributed and modern in their origin, to which no occult significance can be reasonably attached. Devotionally they are innocent enough; applied after the manner of a charm, they are offices of vain observance. On the other hand, we have a bald rite for the Invocation of Olympic Spirits, which, despite the grandiloquent claims of the unknown author, is rather childish than exalted, for it may be assumed that no person is naive enough at the present day to take the angelical offices literally, and to believe, for example, that by the evocation of Aratron the contents of his coal-cellar will be transformed into real treasures. Transcendental Magic is, therefore, hyperbolical in its promises, while these from the mystical standpoint would be frivolous if they could be construed

Fig 1
Formation
Reformation
Transformation
Fig 2
IN
VINCE
HOC
Fig 3
Fig 4
Fig 5
Fig 6
Fig 7
Fig 8
Fig 9

literally. The occult student will derive no light from such processes, but the subject is at the same time a very curious and fantastic branch of bibliographical research, in which we have been able, moreover, to clear up some doubtful points, and in this sense it has been worth prosecuting.

CHAPTER III

Composite Rituals

§ I. *The Key of Solomon the King.*

BY far the most important class of Magical Rituals is that which incorporates elements both of Black and White procedure. For convenience of treatment these are here termed Composite. At the head of all, and, within certain limits, the inspiration and the source of all, stands the "Key of Solomon," with its complement, in many respects more important than itself, the "Lemegeton, or Lesser Key," sometimes attributed to Solomon Rabbi; the Rabbi and the monarch are, however, one and the same. The other Rituals which will be treated in this class are the so-called "Fourth Book of Cornelius Agrippa" and the "Magical Elements" of Peter of Abano. The occult student has been taught to regard these works as dealing exclusively with White Magic, and it is part of the present design to indicate for the first time the mixed character of their proceedings. The innumerable Rituals of Magic which remain in MS. and are never likely to be printed, belong also, with few exceptions, to the composite class, but, setting the "Lemegeton" aside, to which every prominence should be given, they have had little influence, and being, therefore, of no moment to the history of the occult sciences, will not demand further consideration than has already been accorded some of them in the slight sketch at the close of the first chapter.

The existence of Mr. Mathers' admirable edition of the "Key of Solomon,"[1] which is still in print, although costly, and therefore not so readily accessible, must be held to remove the necessity for entering into a detailed account of the contents of that curious work. So far as it has been incorporated by the later makers of Grimoires, it will be found, with its Goëtic variations, in the Second Part. We have here only to consider the question of its antiquity and to establish its true character.

The "Key of Solomon" proper is familiar to scholars in Latin, French, Italian, and one or two German MSS. The oldest codex used by the English editor is in contracted Latin, and belongs to the sixteenth century. It is preserved in the British Museum. It is possible that older MSS. may exist in Continental libraries, but those of the Bibliotheque Nationale and of the Arsenal at Paris are of later date.[2] The majority of known MSS. are in the French language. It is, however, claimed that the work was written originally in Hebrew. In this claim there is nothing essentially improbable, and, assuming that it is well founded, it is not unlikely that the original may still exist. The large Hebrew literature of the Middle Ages has been only imperfectly explored, especially in that part which connects with practical Magic. The knavish methods which have ruled in the manufacture of most magical books largely discount the probability with which we are dealing, and the mere affir-

[1] "The Key of Solomon the King *(Clavicula Salomonis)*, now first translated and edited from ancient MSS. in the British Museum." By S. Liddell Macgregor Mathers. With plates, George Redway. 1889.

[2] As regards the Arsenal, they are all of the eighteenth century. *Les Clavicules de Rabbi Salomon*, 2346 (72 S.A.F.), claims to be literally translated from the Hebrew text into French. 2348 (75 S.A.F.) is entitled *Livre de la Clavicule de Salomon, Roy des Hébreux;* it is said to have been translated from the Hebrew into Italian by Abraham Colorno, and thence into French. 2349 (77 S.A.F.), reads, *Les Vrais Clavicules du Roy Salomon,* traduitte *(sic)* de l'Hébreux par Armadel. 2350 (78 S.A.F.) is entitled *Le Secret des Secrets, autrement La Clavicule de Salomon, ou le véritable Grimoire.* Finally, there is the *Livre Second de la Clavicule de Salomon* 2791 (76 S.A.F.).

mation in an MS. cannot, under such circumstances, be regarded as evidence. No Hebrew scholar is acquainted at the present day with such an original, and three hundred years back the matter, according to P. Christian, was involved in precisely the same uncertainty, for at the end of the sixteenth century the learned Jesuit, Gretser, states that it was unknown, but that there was a Greek translation in the library of the Duke of Bavaria. The present whereabouts of this highly important MS. we have failed to trace. In the eighteenth century the Abbe d'Artigny mentions various examples in Latin, and also an edition printed in 1655, which is not only unknown to Mr. Mathers, but seemingly to all modern bibliographers.[1]

Leaving the language of the original an open question, it is clear that, in either case, there is no ground for attributing to the "Key of Solomon" in its present form a higher antiquity than the fourteenth or fifteenth century, at which

[1] Christian's reference is, however, a mere travesty of some information found in the *Nouveaux Mémoires d'Histoire, de Critique, et de Littérature*, par M. l'Abbé d'Artigny, 7 vols., Paris, 1749-1756. The fourth article in the first volume is entitled, "Concerning some pretended Books of Magic, with an Extract from the Clavicles of Solomon." It enumerates three works which, under this title, were current at the time in the French language, and a fourth in Latin, *Clavicula Salomonis ad Filium Roboam*. A *Liber Pentaculorum* is also mentioned, in a way which leaves it to be inferred that it is the Key of Solomon under another title, but it is probably the Latin version of the Sepher Raziel. Whether any of these works were printed does not explicitly appear, and the Abbé, like Christian himself, knew very little of his subject. It is he, however, who supplies the information concerning Gretser, but it reads very differently. "Perhaps this (*Liber Pentaculorum*) is the same as the treatise *De Necromantia ad Filium Roboam*, which Father Gretser, a learned German Jesuit, had seen written in Greek in the library of the Duke of Bavaria." The collected works of Gretser are in seventeen folio volumes, and there are limits to research. It may be affirmed, however, that the *Catalogus Codicum Manuscriptorum Bibliothecæ Regiæ Bavariæ, auctore Ignatio Hardt, ejusdem bibliothecæ subpræfecto*, 5 vols., Manarchii, 1806, does not mention such a work. The reference to the printed edition of the Clavicle occurs at pp. 36, 37 of D'Artigny's article, and describes it as consisting of 125 pp. in quarto, without name of place or printer. The frontispiece (? title) reads "Clavicle of Solomon," with a cross within a circle beneath, and below this symbol the date 1655. The whole work is divided into twelve paragraphs, of which D'Artigny transcribes part of No. 9, an Exorcism of the Spirits of the Air, which most certainly does not occur in any known edition of the "Grand Clavicle," and is apparently adapted from the "Lemegeton."

time Hebrew literature was developing at a rapid rate.[1] If it were first written in Latin, it is, at any rate, permeated with late Jewish ideas, and the corrupt state of the Hebrew in the conjurations and talismans—which is much the same, and that as bad as it can be, in all existing copies—could scarcely have been attained in less than two centuries of careless and ignorant transcription. We may therefore fix the date of its manufacture, or otherwise of its translation, about the period which has been mentioned.

The attribution of the work to Solomon is obvious enough; it could not fail to have suggested itself to a compiler with Kabbalistic leanings, and it is quite consistent with a literature which has done nothing but ascribe falsely. That it should be taken seriously by any well-equipped person at the present day seems, of course, quite inscrutable, but as it is the case, it must be accounted for in one of two ways:—by a predisposition to accept statements on the faith of occult tradition following upon a conviction as to the reality of occult science; or, alternatively, by a knowledge derived from the traditions of initiation. The first is regrettable because it is open to abuse, but is not the less readily to be understood in particular instances; the second is not likely to exist, because it is injurious to the intelligence of the King of Israel to suppose that he wrote the Clavicle.

So far concerning the antiquity of the work and the sovereign mystification of its authorship. It remains now to say something of its character. The "Key of Solomon" can scarcely be judged accurately in the light of its English version, for the translator, sincerely regarding it as a highly

[1] A bibliography of Papus appended to his "Methodical Summary of the Kabbalah" enumerates forty-seven separate Kabbalistic treatises which appeared in Hebrew between the middle of the thirteenth and the close of the sixteenth century. These are only the most noted, and extra-Kabbalistic literature was far larger.

honourable memorial of lawful magic, has excised as much as possible the Goëtic portions, on the ground that they are later interpolations. He still retains, however, what is generally stigmatised as one of the distinctive marks of Black Magic; the Ritual is permeated with the bloody sacrifice, which Mr. Mathers rightly condemns, but has not seen his way to reject. His version also includes various references to the performance of works of hatred and destruction—that is, works betraying an evil purpose, or a purpose directly connecting with Black Magic. The chapter detailing the method of effecting such objects is omitted, but it is found in five out of the seven codices upon which the version is based. Furthermore, where the intention is not evil, it is frivolous, hyperbolical, or paramountly foolish. It is (*a.*) frivolous in such experiments as the detection of stolen goods, by which it is placed on the same level as the pedlar's literature of fortune-telling; it is (*b.*) hyperbolical and fantastic in the experiment of invisibility, in the composition of the Magic Garters and the Magic Staff; it is (*c.*) foolish in such chapters as that on preventing a sportsman from killing any game. M. Papus, the mouthpiece of the French occultists, distinguishes between the Keys of Solomon and the impostures of *colportage;* but in what respect, it may be asked, are these processes superior to the chapbooks of *colporteurs?*

The highest ambition of the Clavicles is identical with that of the Grimoires—to become master of a treasure possessed by spirits. It should also be observed that experiments which have for their object an interference with the freewill of another person, such as that of seeking favour and love, are essentially evil experiments.

We have now enumerated all the processes which are set forth in this "fountainhead and storehouse of Kabbalistical

Magic"; it is for such trumpery purposes that the Magus is directed to undertake his laborious preparation, and for such also to put in motion the powers believed to be inherent in Divine Names, in long pages of pretentious prayers, and in "stronger and more powerful" conjurations. However much the justice of the critic may be tempered by the mercy of the transcendentalist towards a memorial of occult science which has been unduly honoured—that is, honoured otherwise than as a literary curitosity—it must be concluded that the "Key of Solomon" is a grotesque combination of the pompous and ridiculous; it is, in fact, the old story of the mountain and the mouse, but so great is the travail that, in this case, the mouse is brought forth dead.[1]

§ 2. *The Lesser Key of Solomon.*

The "Lemegeton, or Lesser Key of Solomon," Rabbi and King, is a work of a far more exalted pretensions, which deploys all the hierarchies and evokes spirits by milliards. About its antiquity there is no need for serious dispute; it claims to be translated from the Hebrew, but its earliest perfect examples are in French of the seventeeth century, and no one has heard of the original. It must have existed, however, in a much earlier form; it is the subject of continual reference by demonologists like Wierus, under the style of the sorcerer's *Liber Spirituum,* and it is from this source that the scornful sceptic who was the pupil of Agrippa, derived his *Pseudo-Monarchia Damonum,* with, however, significant variations from the known copies.

The "Lemegeton" is divided into four parts, which control the offices of all spirits at the will of the operator, from

[1] It should, however, be observed that Mr. Mathers, tacitly, it is true, but almost certainly, accepts the work as in the main of literary or archæological importance.

whom the ordinary conditions are exacted.[1] With the exception of the first part, which gave materials to Wierus, this remarkable, and in many respects attractive, work has never been printed, although it has been taxed surreptitiously for contributions by most makers of Rituals and Grimoires. It deals, as we have said, with the evocation of all classes of spirits, evil, indifferent, and good; its opening Rites are those of Lucifer, Bel, Astaroth, and the whole cohort of Infernus; it is entitled *Goetia,* which sufficiently explains itself,[2] and contains the forms of conjuration for seventy-two chief devils and their ministers, with an account of their powers and offices. The second part, or *Theurgia Goetia,* deals with the spirits of the cardinal points and their inferiors. These are mixed natures, some good and some evil. The third book is called the "Pauline Art," for the significance of which name we are unable to account. It concerns the Angels of the Hours of the Day and Night and of the Zodiacal Signs. The fourth part, or *Almadel,* enumerates four other choirs of spirits in a somewhat obscure manner. There is one significant point about the entire work—the powers resident in the offices of Infernal Spirits are minutely set forth, but the Ritual is almost silent as to the special benefits which may be expected from intercourse with the higher classes of intelligence; it is, therefore, obvious to whom the magician would have recourse if he had a definite end in view. It is, indeed, by no means improbable that the first or Goetic portion constitutes the true "Lemegeton," and that the others, apparently unknown to Wierus, are additions of a later date. This division, in either case, is not only expressly connected with Black Magic, or rather exclusively devoted to

[1] See Part ii. c. I.
[2] It is a Greek word meaning, Witchcraft.

it, but it indubitably divides with the so-called Greater Key the forbidding honour of having been the chief inspiration of all the later handbooks of infernal ceremonial. Devoid of any doctrinal part, it has nothing which calls for citation in this place, but as no Grimoire can pretend to completeness without it, all its hierarchic tabulations and all its evoking processes will be given in the Second Part.

§ 3. *The Fourth Book of Cornelius Agrippa.*

It is a matter now almost of general knowledge that a Fourth Book of "Occult Philosophy" is attributed to Cornelius Agrippa, and that it is rejected as spurious. The authenticity of the famous three books has never been questioned, and is indeed beyond challenge; the fourth is perhaps less interesting from the nature of its contents than from this question of its authorship. It is, at the same time, a much more skilful performance than the common run of magical impostures; it connects with and arises out of the genuine work in a very curious manner; and, having regard to the special magical complexion of the latter, there is no inherent reason why it should not have been the production of Agrippa. The difficulties concerning it may be reduced to three heads. One is of time; it appeared after the death of the restless speculating philosopher of Nettersheim. Now, a posthumous publication is not necessarily open to suspicion unless it is a treatise on Magic, but a treatise on Magic of the period concerned, not appearing in the lifetime of its writer, is open to the gravest suspicion, because of the scandalous company to which is belongs. The second difficulty is internal, and it is just possible that it can be overridden. It is to a considerable extent a *rechauffé* of various portions of the three undisputed books, and, even in the days of Agrippa, it is not likely that any author would have so liberally reproduced himself. The third difficulty is that it was rejected as a forgery by Wierus, the pupil of Agrippa, who must have had a good opportunity of knowing; its rejection by later writers simply follows the lead of Wierus, and is therefore of no moment. The strength of the case against it lies mainly in the third difficulty, and even that is not quite conclusive. If not the work of Agrippa, it was evidently produced in immediate proximity to his period.

The book itself, which is quite informally written, falls into several divisions. There is, firstly, an elaborate treatise on the method of extracting the names of the good and evil spirits referred to the seven planets. This is a further development of a subject treated at some length in the third book of "Occult Philosophy." The method is of no importance to our inquiry, but those who have sought to unravel it confess that they have been baffled. Possibly Agrippa and his successor were only fooling their readers, and did not disclose the secret. The treatise on Names is followed by one upon Characters, and depending as it does from the first, is also not readily intelligible. Then comes a formal tabulation of all the known shapes familiar to the spirits of the planets, after which there is a disquisition upon Pentacles and Sigils, another upon the consecration of instruments used in magical ceremonies, as also of fire, water, and so forth. The work concludes with methods for the invocation of good and evil spirits and a short process in Necromancy. As we shall have occasion to cite it frequently in the Second Part, the analysis may here be confined to establishing its connection with diabolism, and the kind of manifestations which are supposed to be obtained by its processes.

Like the "Lemegeton," it gives specific directions for

communicating with evil spirits, and there is no question whatever as to the lawful nature of the experiment. Refinements of this kind were evidently outside the magic of the fifteenth century. In the following citation we shall depart from our usual custom of translating at first hand, and make use, with some needful prunings, of the version of Robert Turner, which is quite faithful, and has, morever, the pleasant flavour of antiquity.

Concerning the Invocation of Evil Spirits.

If we would call any evil Spirit to the circle, it first behoveth us to consider and to know his nature, to which of the planets it agreeth, and what offices are distributed to him from the planet. This being known, let there be sought out a place fit and proper for his invocation, according to the nature of the planet and the quality of the offices of the same Spirit, as near as the same may be done. For example, if his power be over the sea, rivers, or floods, then let a place be chosen on the shore, and so of the rest. In like manner, let there be chosen a convenient time, both for the quality of the air—which should be serene, clear, quiet, and fitting for the Spirits to assume bodies—and for the quality and nature of the planet, and so too of the Spirit, to wit, on his day, noting the time wherein he ruleth, whether it be fortunate or unfortunate, day or night, as the stars and spirits do require. These things being considered, let there be a circle framed at the place elected, as well for the defence of the invocant as for the confirmation of the Spirit. In the circle itself there are to be written the Divine general names, and those things which do yield defence unto us; the Divine names which do rule the said planet, with the offices of the Spirit himself; the names, finally, of the good Spirits which bear rule, and are able to bind and constrain that Spirit which we intend to call. If we would further fortify our circle, we may add characters and pentacles agreeing to the work. So also, and within or without the circle, we may frame an angular figure,[1] inscribed with such numbers as are congruent among themselves to our work. Moreover, the operator is to be provided with lights, perfumes, unguents, and medicines compounded according to the nature of the planet and Spirit, which do partly agree with the Spirit by reason of their natural and celestial virtue, and partly are exhibited to the Spirit for religious and superstitious worship. The operator must also be furnished with holy and consecrated things, necessary as well for the defence of the invocant and his fellows as to serve for bonds which shall bind and constrain the Spirits. Such are holy papers, lamens, pictures, pentacles, swords, sceptres, garments of convenient matter and colour, and things of the like sort. When all these are provided, the master and his fellows being in the circle, and all those things which he useth, let him begin to pray with a loud voice and a convenient gesture and countenance. Let him make an oration unto God, and afterwards entreat the good Spirits. If he will read any prayers, psalms, or gospels for his defence, they should take the first place. Thereafter, let him begin to invocate the Spirit which he desireth, with a gentle and loving enchantment to all the coasts of the world, commemorating his own authority and power. Let him then rest a little, looking about him to see if any Spirit do appear, which if he delay, let him repeat his invocation as before, until he hath done it three times. If the Spirit be still pertinacious and will not appear, let him begin to conjure him with Divine power, but in such a way that all the conjura-

[1] Compare the figures of the "Lemegeton," Part ii. c. 4.

tions and commemorations do agree with the nature and offices of the Spirit himself. Reiterate the same three times from stronger to stronger, using objurgations, contumelies, cursings, punishments, suspensions from his office and power, and the like.

After all the courses are finished, again cease a little, and if any Spirit shall appear, let the invocant turn towards him, receive him courteously, and earnestly entreating him, let him require his name. Then proceeding further, let him ask whatsoever he will. But if in anything the Spirit shall show himself obstinate or lying, let him be bound by convenient conjurations, and if you still doubt of any lie, make outside the circle, with the consecrated sword, the figure of a triangle or pentacle, and compel the Spirit to enter it. If you would have any promise confirmed upon oath, stretch the sword out of the circle, and swear the Spirit by laying his hand upon the sword. Then having obtained of the Spirit that which you desire, or being otherwise contented, license him to depart with courteous words, giving command unto him that he do no hurt. If he will not depart, compel him by powerful conjurations, and, if need require, expel him by exorcism and by making contrary fumigations. When he is departed, go not out of the circle, but stay, making prayer for your defence and conservation, and giving thanks unto God and the good angels. All these things being orderly performed, you may depart.

But if your hopes are frustrated, and no Spirit will appear, yet for this do not despair, but, leaving the circle, return again at other times, doing as before. And if you shall judge that you have erred in anything, then you shall amend by adding or diminishing, for the constancy of reiteration doth often increase your authority and power, and striketh terror into the Spirits, humbling them to obedience.

Hence some do use to make a gate in the circle, whereby they go in and out, which they open and shut as they please, and fortify it with holy names and pentacles. This also we are to take notice of, that when no Spirits will appear, but the Master, being wearied, hath determined to cease and give over, let him not therefore depart without licensing the Spirits, for they that do neglect this are very greatly in danger, except they are fortified with some sublime defence. Oftentimes also the Spirits do come, although they be not visible (for to cause terror to him that calls them), either in the thing which he useth or in the operation itself. But this kind of licensing is not given simply, but by a kind of dispensation with suspension, until they shall render themselves obedient.

When we intend to execute any effect by evil Spirits where an apparition is not needful, this is to be done by making the required instrument or subject of the experiment itself, whether it be an image, a ring, or a writing, any candle, character, or sacrifice, or anything of the like sort. The name of the Spirit is to be written thereon, with his character, according to the exigency of the experiment, either writing with blood or using some perfume agreeable to the Spirit, making also frequent prayers to God and the good angels before we invocate the evil Spirit, and conjuring him by the Divine power.

Over and above the formal diabolism of this process, there are instructions for composing a book of evil spirits, to be prepared ceremoniously, according to their name and order. By means of a "holy oath," the ready obedience of the Spirit whose name is written therein is supposed to be insured. The book itself must be formed of most pure and clean paper which has never been used previously—a stipulation which may have been of moment in the days of the palimpsest, but is, of course, unnecessary in our own. The image of the Spirit must be drawn on the left side, and his character on the right, preceded by the oath containing the name of the Spirit, with his dignity, place, office, and power. The operation must be performed on the day and in the hour of the planet to which the Spirit is attributed. When the book has been composed, it must be well bound and emblazoned, being furnished also with markers and seals, for to open it at random after its consecration might endanger the operator. It should be kept reverently and free from profanation, for otherwise it will lose its virtue. Its consecration is a matter of some difficulty, as every Spirit whose name appears therein must be called before the circle, the bonds read over in his presence, and each in succession must be compelled to impose his hand where his respective image and character are drawn, and to "confirm and consecrate the same with a special and common oath." In a word, the document must be regularly and legally delivered as the act and deed of each. During this ceremony the book must be laid within a triangle described outside the circle.

There can be no doubt that these directions are the work of a writer well acquainted with the "Lemegeton," or that the *Liber Spirituum* in question is identical with that mentioned by Wierus. The forms assumed by the evoked Spirits differ somewhat from those of the "Lesser Key," which, moreover, at least in its Goëtic portion, has no planetary attribution. According to pseudo-Agrippa, the Spirits of Saturn usually appear with a tall and lean body and an angry countenance, having four faces, of which one is in the usual position, another at the back of the head, and two, with beaks, on either side. They have also a face on each knee, of a shining black. Their motion is like that of the wind, and it is accompanied with a kind of earthquake. Their sign is white earth, "whiter than any snow." Their particular forms are a bearded king riding on a dragon; an old bearded man; an old woman leaning on a staff; a boy; a dragon; an owl; a black garment; a hook or sickle; a juniper-tree. How the three last manifestations are provided with the six visages is a perplexity which must be surrendered to occult commentators.

The Spirits of Jupiter appear with a sanguine and choleric body; they are of middle stature; their motion is "horrible and fearful," but they are mild of countenance, and gentle in speech. They are of iron colour, which ought to have connected them with Mars; their motion is that of flashing lightnings, and withal thunderous; their sign is the apparition of men about the circle who seem to be devoured by lions. Their particular forms are a king with drawn sword riding on a lion; a mitred personage in a long vestment; a maid crowned with laurel and adorned by flowers; a bull; a stag; a peacock; an azure garment; a sword; a box-tree.

The Spirits of Mars have a tall body and a choleric, filthy countenance, brown, swarthy, or red in colour; they have horns like the hart, claws like a griffin, and they bellow like wild bulls. They have the motion of burning fire, and their sign is thunder and lightning about the circle. Their particular forms are an armed king riding on a wolf; an armed man; a woman holding a buckler on her thigh; a she-goat; a horse; a stag; a red garment; wool; a cheestip. Wool of a choleric disposition is perhaps a Goëtic form of gun-cotton.

The Spirits of Venus have a body of medium height and limb, sanguine, gross, and of a gold colour tinctured with blood—which recalls Mrs. Browning's pomegranate. Their motion is that of lightning; their sign is to produce sweat

Fig. 1.
Fig. 2
Fig. 3
Fig. 4.
Fig. 5.
Fig. 6
Fig. 7.
Fig. 8.
Fig. 9
Fig. 10.
Fig. 11
Fig. 12
Fig. 13.
Fig. 14.
Fig. 15.
Fig. 16.
Fig. 17.
Fig. 18
Fig. 19
Fig. 20.
Fig. 21
Fig. 22
Fig. 23.
Fig. 24.
Fig. 25.
Fig. 26.
Fig. 27.

in the operator, which might, however, be the normal property of all these stellar nondescrips of the world infernal. Their particular forms are a sceptred king riding on a lion; a crowned king; a queen with a sceptre; a bird—not otherwise described, but anything probably except that of paradise; a lion; a cock; a golden garment; a sceptre; and lastly, something which Robert Turner wisely left untranslated—*caudatus, i.e.,* tailed.

The Spirits of Venus have a body of medium height and a pleasant visage, of which the upper part is golden and the lower white or green. Their motion is like that of a brilliant star. Their sign is the semblance of maids sporting about the circle, and luring the Magician to join them. Their particular forms are a sceptred king riding on a camel; a naked maid; a she-goat; a camel—probably the atrocious demon of Cazotte; a dove; a white or green garment; the herb savine.

The Spirits of Mercury appear commonly with a body of middle stature, cold, liquid, moist, which sounds redundant, but the reference is to the properties of quicksilver—that is to say, the Mercury of the philosophers was supposed not to wet the hand, but the Mercurial spirits of the sorcerer apparently did. They are withal fair, affable in speech, of human shape, and like unto armed knights. They are like silver-coloured clouds in their motion. Their sign is that they cause horror and fear to the operator. Their special shapes are a king riding on a bear; a comely youth; a woman holding a distaff—it is difficult to understand how such an apparition can be like an armed knight, an observation which, if it were worth while, might apply to the remaining modes of manifestation; a dog; a she-bear; a magpie; a garment of many changing colours; a rod; and a little staff.

Finally, the Spirits of the Moon have a large, soft, phlegmatic body, like a dark cloud in colour. Their countenance is swollen, their head bald, their eyes are red and rheumy, their teeth like those of a wild boar. Their motion is like that of a great tempest sweeping the sea. Their sign is a heavy shower of rain about the circle. Their particular shapes are a king like an archer riding on a doe; a little boy; a huntress with bow and arrows; a cow; a small doe; a goose; a green or silver-coloured garment; an arrow; a many-footed creature—perhaps a centipede.

The imbecility of this muddled tabulation places the forged Fourth Book in a more absurd light than it otherwise deserves. It really reproduces the manner of Agrippa's treatise with a fidelity which is not unskilful, and has quite as much claim to be taken seriously as any of the composite Rituals.

§ 4. *The Heptameron.*

The Fourth Book of Cornelius Agrippa was much too informal, and left too much to the discretion of the operator to be satisfactory for a science so exact as that of Ceremonial Magic. A form of procedure which bequeathed nothing to the imagination and asked no other skill than the patient exactitude of the rule of thumb was necessary to the weakness of the ordinary sorcerer. The "Heptameron, or Magical Elements" of Peter de Abano is an attempt to supply the want, and to offer to the neophyte a complete wizard's cabinet. Cornelius Agrippa, says the introduction, seems to have written for the learned, for the well-experienced in this art; he does not treat specially of the ceremonies, but mentions them in a general way. Those who have not "tasted magical superstitions" may here find them ready to their hand. "In brief, in this book are kept the principles of magical conveyances." It may be conceded at once that the undertaking is scrupulously fulfilled; what the operator must do and how he should perform it, so as to "draw spirits into discourse," are matters set forth so plainly that the wayfaring man need not err therein. Assuming the sacerdotal office of the operator, or a priest for an accomplice, it is all so simple that failure could not well be ascribed to a blunder on his part.

It would be invidious to suppose that the "Heptameron" is more authentic as regards its attribution than the work to which it is professedly a sequel; its real authorship is involved in much the same kind of obscurity as that of pseudo-Agrippa. As there is no grave reason why the pupil of Trithemius should not have written the spurious Fourth Book, so Peter of Abano is not at all an unlikely personage to connect with the "Magical Elements." The one professedly wrote upon Magic, the other upon Astrology and Geomancy, unless his works in these departments of occult science are also forgeries. But the "Heptameron" was never heard of for nearly two hundred years after the death of its reputed author, which occurred in 1316, and it is too obviously late in its tone, too obviously a sequel [1] to a much more recent work, for it to have been possibly a memorial of the fourteenth century.

Peter of Abano, a town in the vicinity of Padua, was born in 1250, and was a learned physician of his period, who attempted to conciliate the different medical systems, and is supposed to have been the first European who quoted Averroes. He established himself at Paris, but at the in-

[1] A sequal, moreover, which contains direct references, as, for example: "But after what manner they appear has been described already in the former book of magical ceremonies."—*The Conjuration of the Lord's Day*. This recurs with slight variations throughout the "Heptameron."

stigation of jealous professional brethren he was accused of heresy, and fled to his native place. At Padua a chair of medicine was created for him, but the accusation followed him; by some he was charged with denying the existence of demons, by others with obtaining his knowledge from seven imps whom he kept in a bottle. However this may be, the Inquisition commenced its process, but the intended victim was delivered by death—as some say, on the eve of his execution. The intervention infuriated the Tribunal, though the testament left behind him by Peter of Abano affirmed his belief in the orthodox faith. The magistrates of the city were ordered, on pain of excommunication, to exhume his body, but it was removed by a faithful servant and buried secretly in another church. The Inquisition clamoured for the punishment of the offender, but was content in the end to burn the dead physician in effigy. As a counterpoise, a century later his bust was placed in the town-hall of Padua. His undoubted works, which are frankly unreadable, betray no acquaintance with the occult sciences beyond a belief in astrology, which in those days was catholic as Rome and powerful as the Holy Tribunal. He remains, however, one of the moral martyrs of Magic, *faussement accusé,* as Gabriel Naudé has it. His accusation and the mode of its prosecution remain also among the lesser glories of the Holy Office.

Accepting the "Heptameron" as a work belonging to the period of its first publication, it is here placed among the Rituals of a composite character, not because it professedly deals with devils, but because the nature of its angels and spirits is indicated by the manner of their conjuration; in a word, they are described as angels and threatened as demons.

The procedure is divided into two parts—a general

method for the evocation of the Spirits of the Air, who are undoubtedly demons, and a set of angelical conjurations proper to each day of the week. The second presumably belongs to the department of White Magic, as the intelligences concerned are said to be good and great, but their offices are mixed and confusing, including the discovery of treasures, the detection of secrets, fomenting war, opening locks and bolts, procuring the love of women, inclining men to luxury and sowing hatred and evil thought. Obviously, White Magic of this kind is much blacker than it is painted. Though the entire "Heptameron" appears under one attribution, the first part only is ascribed in the text to Peter de Abano. Therein the personal preparation of the operator corresponds to that given in the Second Part of the present work, and the ceremonial itself, which, if cited at all, would have to be printed *in extenso,* as it contains no detachable portions, is much too elaborate to be inserted in this place, more especially as that of the "Lemegeton" will provide later on a fairly complete notion of the scope and purpose of the Composite Rituals.

CHAPTER IV

The Rituals of Black Magic

§ 1. *The Grimorium Verum.*

THE four specific and undisguised handbooks of Black Magic, all in the French language, but in three cases, like so much of the Ceremonial literature, possessing Italian connections, real or imputed, are:—

GRIMORIUM VERUM, or the Most Approved Keys of Solomon the Hebrew Rabbin, wherein the Most Hidden Secrets, both Natural and Supernatural, are immediately exhibited, but it is necessary that the Demons should be contented on their part.[1] Translated from the Hebrew by Plaingiére, a Dominican Jesuit,[2] with a Collection of Curious Secrets. Published by Alibeck the Egyptian. 1517.[3]

TRUE BLACK MAGIC, or the Secret of Secrets, an MS. found at Jerusalem in the Sepulchre of Solomon, containing: 1. Forty-five Talismans with their representation, as

[1] This is only a conjectural translation. It is impossible to render such a passage as *modo operator per necessaria et contenta facit scia tamen oportit Damonum potentia dum taxat per agantur.*

[2] It will be scarcely necessary to advise the reader that a Dominican Jesuit is an absurdity, which might be paralleled by "secular monk," "unordained priest," and so forth. The Order of St. Benedict and the Society of Jesus are totally distinct. A Catholic critic might almost be justified in observing that so gross a blunder would be possible only to a Jew or a heretic; certainly he would have more reason than would be discoverable in the hypothesis of Papus, that priests are the authors of the Grimoires.

[3] On the reverse of the title:—"The True Clavicles of Solomon. Memphis. Published by Alibeck the Egyptian."

also the manner of using them, together with their Marvelous Properties. 2. All Magical Characters known unto this day.[1] Translated from the Hebrew of the Magus Iroe-Grego.[2] Rome. In the year of grace, 1750.

THE GRAND GRIMOIRE, with the Powerful Clavicle of Solomon and of Black Magic; or the Infernal Devices of the Great Agrippa for the Discovery of all Hidden Treasures and the Subjugation of every Denomination of Spirits, together with an Abridgment of all the Magical Arts. (In its earliest edition, without place or date.)

THE CONSTITUTION OF POPE HONORIUS THE GREAT, wherein may be found the Arcane Conjurations which must be used against the Spirits of Darkness. With a Collection of the Most Rare Secrets. Rome, 1670.

They are all tiny volumes, nominally in duodecimo, but much smaller according to modern measurements.

The date specified in the title of the *Grimorium Verum* is undeniably fraudulent; the work belongs to the middle of the eighteenth century, and Memphis is Rome. The "Grand Grimoire" is not of higher antiquity. That of Honorius is said to have appeared originally in 1629, but it has been sometimes referred erroneously to the same period of the previous century.

As indicated by the authorship which is attributed to it, the *Grimorium Verum* is based to some extent upon the "Key of Solomon," the main points of resemblance being in the description of the magical instruments, and in some of the forms of prayer. It distinguishes plainly the powers

[1] That is, mystic characters for engraving on magical instruments, vessels, and vestments. The statement is utterly untrue, for the characters given by the Grimoire are few in number, and exceedingly imperfect as well.

[2] Mr. Mathers reads Iohé Grevis. Iroe Gecis is another variation. It is a corruption in any case.

which it is proposed to invoke by the name of Devils.[1] At the same time it refers them nominally to the four elements, which would connect them with the Sylphs, Salamanders, and so forth, but the classification in question, somewhat incidentally made, does not really obtain. There is an account of the Hierarchy of Spirits, with Lucifer, Beelzebuth, and Astaroth, as potentates in chief.[2] A portion of this account is drawn from the "Lemegeton," perhaps through the *Pseudo-Monarchia* of Wierus. The work purports to be divided into three sections, containing:—(*a.*) The Characters and Seals of the Demons, with the forms for their Evocation and Dismissal. (*b.*) A description of the Natural and Supernatural Secrets which can be operated by the power of the Demons, and that without any deception. (*c.*) The Key of the work, and the proper application thereof. Passing over typographical errors, the MS. from which it has been printed must have been in a most confused state; there are not in reality any distinct divisions, and the little volume abounds in Latin passages which often defy translation, as, for example, *sic pro ratione voluntas; ut illud sit hoc in opere inclusum minimo clerum in doctis; quia amicus fiet capitalis, fiet inimicus.* So also we have *Sanctum Regum* throughout for *Sanctum Regnum.* There are two folding plates of Characters and Seals, of which many have no reference to the text, while others essential to the processes are missing, the deficiencies being supplied in the modern Italian versions, which probably follow another edition, also Italian, and the source of the French translation, but

[1] "Here beginneth the *Sanctum Regnum*, called the Royalty of Spirits, or the little Keys of Solomon, a most learned Hebrew nigromancer and Rabbin, containing various combinations of characters whereby the Powers, Spirits, or, more correctly, Devils are invoked, so that they are forced to appear whensoever you may determine, each one according to his faculty, and are compelled to bring whatsoever you may require of them, causing you no kind of annoyance, provided only that they are contented on their part, for these sorts of creatures give nothing for nothing."

[2] See Part ii. c. 3.

unknown to the present writer, as indeed to most bibliographers. The work, as it stands, is really in two parts only, the *Grimorium Verum* proper, and certain "Rare and Astounding Magical Secrets." The first may be analysed as follows:—(*a.*) Directions for the preparation of the Operator, all of a personal kind, and analogous to those of the Clavicle. (*b.*) Instructions for the manufacture of the magical instruments required in the work, also analogous to the Clavicle. (*c.*) The composition of the virgin parchment on which the characters and seals are to be inscribed, showing distinct variations from the Clavicle. (*d.*) The processes of evocation and the discharge. Beyond the fact that the evoked Spirits are Lucifer, Beelzebuth, Astaroth, and the inferiors and ministers of these, this first and chief part is not more repulsive, as it is indeed scarcely more unintelligent, than most of the processes in its prototype.

The second part contains the usual curiosities common to all the later Grimoires, including the "Admirable Secrets" of the pretended Albertus Magnus, the "Little Albert," &c. In so far as it presents any considerable variations, such variations are usually in the direction of Black Magic. Some are venereal in the objectionable sense of the term, others merely revolting, while yet others, as that of the Magic Garters, are derived from the Clavicle. Finally, there are certain processes which are obviously those of White Magic,[1] and are concerned with the ceremonial induction of simple clairvoyance.

We may therefore conclude that the *Grimorium Verum* proper is not more diabolical than the first part of the "Lemegeton," which indeed contains the ceremonial for the evocation of precisely the same spirits.

[1] See Part ii. c. 8, §§ 6, 7, and 8.

§ 2. *True Black Magic.*

The Grimoire entitled "True Black Magic" is simply an adapted version of the "Key of Solomon," with the same preambles, the same ritual, the same talismans, and characters which are analogous when they are not identical. With the intelligible and careful presentation of Mr. Mathers it of course compares very badly; like the *Grimorium Verum,* it is exceedingly confused, and is rendered almost unmeaning by the omission of all the practical part. Its malicious or diabolical element consists, however, solely in its introduction of the chapter upon works of hatred and destruction, which, as already seen, and as more fully established later on, should undoubtedly be regarded as an integral portion of the original work.

§ 3. *The Grand Grimoire.*

The "Grand Grimoire" is the most fantastic of the cycle, and is introduced with great pomp by its pretended editor, Antonio Venitiana del Rabina, a personage whose name indicates the Italian origin of the work. By reason of its rarity and the great request in which it is, we are informed that it must be regarded as the veritable *Magnum Opus*—a view which may appear inconsequential, but for which the authority of Rabbinical writers is cited. It is to these authors that we owe the priceless treasure which innumerable charlatans have endeavored to counterfeit, but have never succeeded in discovering. The copy made use of by Antonio in preparing his edition was transcribed from the genuine writings of the mighty King Solomon, which were obtained by pure chance. "Of a truth, what other man, save this invincible genius, would have had the hardihood to reveal the withering words which God makes use of to strike terror into the rebellious angels and compel them into obedience? Having soared into the celestial altitudes that he might master the secrets and learn the omnipotent words which constitute all the power of a terrible and venerable Deity, the essence of those innermost arcana, made use of by an infinite Divinity, was extracted by this grand king, who passed all the days of his life in the most laborious researches, and in pursuit of the most obscure and hopeless secrets. He succeeded ultimately in all his undertakings, penetrating into the most remote haunts of spirits, whom he bound, one and all, and forced them to obey him by the power of his Talisman or Clavicle. Therein he has discovered unto us the stellar influences, the constellation of the planets, and the method for the evocation of all hierarchies of spirits, by the recitation of the sublime Appellations, as they are hereafter set down for you in this book, as well as the true composition and effects of the dreadful Blasting Rod, which causes the spirits to tremble; which God also used to arm his Angel when Adam and Eve were driven out of the Earthly Paradise; wherewith, finally, he smote the rebellious Angels, precipitating their ambitions into the most appalling gulfs by the power of this very Rod—of this Rod which collects the clouds, disperses tempests, averts the lightning, or precipitates each and all upon any portion of the earth at the pleasure of its director."

Such is the preamble of the "Grand Grimoire." The work is divided into two parts, the first containing the evocation of Lucifuge Rofocale [1] by means of the Blasting Rod, the second what Antonia inscrutably regards as the *Sanc-*

[1] This alteration of the fallen Light-Bearer into Fly-the-Light does not seem to occur in magical literature preceding the Grand Grimoire. It was afterwards adopted by Lévi, by whom it has been made popular among occultists, who are for the most part, quite unaware of its source.

tum Regnum, namely, the Rite of making Pacts; but one of the most notable characteristics of all the Grimoires is not their diabolical malice, but their unconscious ingenuousness, and the devout, almost laudable, character of all the operations seems to have been quite sincerely held.

The "Grand Grimoire" is, however, regarded as one of the most atrocious of its class; it has a process in Necromancy which is possible, say occult writers, only to a dangerous maniac or an irreclaimable criminal. It must be admitted that the Rite is highly unreasonable, but in dealing with such literature it seems unsafe to advance the objection, for it applies much too widely. As to its criminality, this centres in the creation of a disturbance at midnight Mass on Christmas Eve. There is further an account of a poison entitled "The Composition of Death, or Philosophical Stone," which is supposed to indicate an advanced degree of diabolism. Eliphas Lévi says that it pretends to be the Powder of Projection, the great Mystery of the Sages, but it is really the Powder of Consecution—as to the significance of which a vague image can alone be invoked. It may, in any case, be added that it cannot well be either, seeing that the composition is a liquid. For the rest, it is simply a stupid recipe, and as no unlawful application is suggested, it is not diabolical at all, unless toxicology, as such, is Satanic simply because it does not deal in anodynes.

There is, of couse, no question that the "Grand Grimoire" is a book of Black Magic, and it is contrary to the nature of things that a book of Black Magic should be otherwise than diabolical. The most objectionable works are not those which openly announce that they are evil, but those which teach evil under the pretence of excellence. The noticeable point, as regards the "Grand Grimoire" and works of its class, is that the diabolism of the confessedly diabolical is often so exceedingly thin, and that the angelical element in Rituals assumed to be angelical should often border so perilously on the Satanic. The first part of the "Grand Grimoire," just like the *Grimorium Verum*, is simply a process for the evocation of evil spirits to obtain the enforced surrender of hidden treasure. In the second part the magician is certainly expected to give himself, body and soul, to the demon who serves him meanwhile, and there can be no hesitation in admitting that this creates a sharp distinction, not only between the "Grand Grimoire" and all the Composite Rituals, but also between the "Grand Grimoire" and the other Liturgies of Black Magic. It is only a palliation to say that the compact is worded as a subterfuge, and in reality gives nothing to the demon, who here, as so frequently in folk-lore, is bamboozled, receiving the shadow in place of the substance.[1]

§ 4. *The Grimoire of Honorius.*

Despite the iniquities of the *Pacta Conventa Dæmonum*, the "Grand Grimoire" has failed, however, to invoke upon itself such severe condemnation as the "Grimoire of Honorius the Great," otherwise Honorius the Third. It is scarcely too much to say, that almost every accusation preferred against this remarkable work is false generally and specifically, the chief distinction between them being that some are the misrepresentations of ignorance, and others the false interpretations of prejudgment. The French occultist, Papus, alone seems to take the middle view, though he speaks with some vagueness when he says that the sorcery

[1] Compare the droll history of the Devil and his Dam, and that concerning the course of Black Magic delivered by the Prince of Darkness at the University of Salamanca.

of this Grimoire is more dangerous for weak experimentalists than for the enemies of the sorcerer. Eliphas Lévi observes that the work is not without importance for the students of occult science.[1] At first sight it seems to be nothing but a tissue of repulsive absurdities, but for those who are initiated in the signs and secrets of the Kabbalah, it becomes a veritable monument of human perversity. There was seldom a statement for which there was less foundation; there was never a magical work which less connected with Kabbalism; the connection in so far as it exists, and it is confined to a few words which occur in the Conjurations, is common to all Ceremonial Magic, and this is the one Grimoire which most is permeated with Christian elements. Those, however, who are well acquainted with the principles of interpretation which obtain in the writings of Lévi, will not take a charge seriously which depends upon the significance of Kabbalistic words or signs, for it is notorious that with the French occultist they meant many things according to his humour. But Eliphas Lévi was not contented with the general impeachment; in a later work[2] he elaborated a more particular charge. In common with the "Key of Solomon" and all the Grimoires, the work of Honorius prescribes the sacrifice of a virgin kid, with the object of ensuring the possession of a virgin parchment by the operator. Now Lévi affirms that when the "abominable author" mentions a kid, he means really a human child. In this interpretation he had not even the excuse of the humorous analogy which has been instituted in vulgar English, for his acquaintance, had he any, with our language was exceedingly slight. There is not a particle of foundation for the charge; the sacrifice in the case

[1] *Histoire de la Magic*, p. 307.
[2] *La Clef des Grands Mystères.* See also "Thaumaturgical Experiences of Eliphas Lévi" in "The Mysteries of Magic," by A. E. Waite, second edition.

of the "Grimoire of Honorius" means, and can mean, no more than in the case of the "Key of Solomon." There was a defined purpose in connection with the slaughter of the victim, which was the same in both instances.

So far concerning the misinterpretations of writers who pretend to some first-hand acquaintance with the work under notice. Others who have mentioned it within recent years have been content to follow the French authority without examination. Thus it is that we find Mr. J. H. Slater, in a paper read before the Bibliographical Society, and printed in its Transactions,[1] describing the Grimoire as an advocate of murder and all kinds of crimes. Furthermore, he confuses it throughout with the "Grand Grimoire."

Taking the work at first hand, the initial question concerning it is the attribution of the authorship. From what we know of magical literature, to say nothing of pontifical dignity, it is antecedently unlikely that it is the work of a Roman Bishop, more especially of such a bishop as Honorius. Eliphas Lévi, who rightly sought to vindicate the Church of his childhood, assailed, in the person of one of its sovereign pontiffs, by an unintelligent accusation, but vindicated it badly as usual, took a glance at the history of the time, and discovered that during the pontificate of Honorius there was an anti-pope set up by Henry IV. of Germany, and that he was a man of evil life. He immediately conjectured that this personage was the likely author of the objectionable Grimoire. Again there is not a particle of evidence for such a surmise, and it is *un bien vilain procédé,* as M. Papus might say, to increase, without good reason, the responsibility resting upon the memory of the wicked prelate in question.

[1] "Some Books on Magic." Transactions of the Bibliographical Society, Vol. iii. Part 2.

If we come to the facts, they are these. The first edition of the Grimoire is said to have appeared in 1629, and it is not likely that it was forged much earlier than the end of the sixteenth century, being, roughly, nine hundred years after the death of its supposed author. The Pope, it must be confessed, was a voluminous writer; his sermons and his vast correspondence have appeared in two large volumes at Paris,[1] under auspices which were unlikely to admit even a contemptuous reference to the forged constitution. There is none, accordingly, which is to be regretted from the standpoint of bibliography. But the editor has also excluded with the same silence another work much more reasonably attributed, and to which no odium can attach. It is one also which is important to our inquiry, and it is entitled *Honorii Papæ adversus tenebrarum Principem et ejus Angelos Conjurationes ex originale Romæ servato,* Rome, 1529. The authenticity of this work is evidently questioned by its exclusion, and it is impossible to speak certainly concerning it, as, on account of its extreme rarity, few public libraries, none apparently in England, possess an example. But it is evidently the formularies of exorcism, a rite of the Church, and possessing a considerable body of literature, to which even a Pope of past ages might not inconceivably have contributed. However this may be, the attribution in the one case will account for it in the other. The book of Black Magic may be merely a perversion of the orthodox conjurations, and if not that, is a reprisal; it is Sorcery revenging herself on a Pope who casts out devils by representing him as the prince of those who dealt with them.

Having said something to justify the Grimoire from groundless condemnation, it is necessary now to add, on the authority of its own evidence, that it is a malicious and

[1] Horoy's *Bibliotheca Patristica, Honorii III. Opera Omnia.* Paris, 1879, 8 vo.

clever imposture, which was undeniably calculated to deceive ignorant persons of its period who may have been magically inclined, more especially ignorant priests, since it pretends to convey the express sanction of the Apostolical Seat for the operations of Infernal Magic and Necromancy. The entire claim is set forth most curiously at the beginning of the pseudo-constitution, and must be cited at considerable length to convey its full force.

The Holy Apostolic Chair, unto which the keys of the Kingdom of Heaven were given by those words which Christ Jesus addressed to St. Peter: I give unto thee the Keys of the Kingdom of Heaven, and unto thee alone the power of commanding the Prince of Darkness and his angels, who, as slaves of their Master, do owe him honour, glory, and obedience, by those other words of Jesus Christ: Thou shalt worship the Lord thy God, and Him only shalt thou serve—hence by the power of these Keys the Head of the Church has been made the Lord of Hell. But seeing that until this present the Sovereign Pontiffs have alone possessed the power of using invocations and commanding Spirits, His Holiness Honorius the Third, being moved by his pastoral care, has benignly desired to communicate the methods and faculty of invoking and controlling Spirits to his venerable Brethren in Jesus Christ, adding the Conjurations which must be used in such case, the whole being contained in the Bull which here follows.

HONORIUS.

Servant of the Servants of God, unto all and each of our venerable Brethren of the Holy Roman Church, Cardinals, Archbishops, Bishops, Abbots; unto all and each of our sons in Jesus Christ, Priests, Deacons, Subdeacons, Acolytes,

Exorcists, Cantors, Pastors, Clerks both Secular and Regular, Health and Apostolic Benediction. In those days when the Son of God, Saviour of the World, generated in the fulness of time, and born, according to the flesh, of the Race of David, did live on this earth, whose Most Holy Name is Jesus, before which the heavens, earth, and hell do bend the knee; we have seen with what power He commanded demons, which power was also transmitted to St. Peter by that utterance: Upon this rock I will build my Church, and the Gates of Hell shall not prevail against it. These words were addressed to St. Peter as the Head and Foundation of the Church. We then, who, by the mercy of God, and despite the poverty of our merit, have succeeded to the Sovereign Apostolate, and, as lawful successor of St. Peter, have the Keys of the Kingdom of Heaven committed to our hands, desiring to communicate the power of invoking and commanding Spirits, which hath been reserved unto us alone, and our possessors did alone enjoy; wishing, I repeat, by Divine inspiration, to share it with our venerable Brethren and dear sons in Jesus Christ, and fearing lest in the exorcism of the possessed, they might otherwise be appalled at the frightful figures of those rebellious angels who in sin were cast into the abyss, lest also they should be insufficiently learned in those things which must be performed and observed, and that those who have been redeemed by the blood of Jesus Christ may not be tormented by any witchcraft or possessed by the demon, we have included in this Bull the manner of their invocation, while same must be observed inviolably. And because it is meet that the ministers of the Altar should have authority over the rebellious Spirits, we hereby depute unto them all powers which we possess, in virtue of the Holy Apostolic Chair, and we require them by our Apostolic authority to observe what follows inviolably, lest by some negligence unworthy of their character they should draw down on themselves the wrath of the Most High.

The *Grimorium Verum* has once been reprinted in the French language.[1] Of the Italian version there have been two modern editions, both poorly produced.[2] The book of "True Black Magic" is known only by the edition of 1750. The "Grand Grimoire" reappeared at Nismes in 1823, and is, moreover, in all respects identical with the work entitled the "Red Dragon," of which there are several editions.[3] The "Grimoire of Honorius" is exceedingly rare in the original, but is better known by the reprints of 1660 and 1670, though these also are scarce. There is, finally, an edition dated 1760, and this even commands a high price among collectors. It remains to state that the Abbé d'Artigny was presented about the middle of the last century with an MS. copy of this Grimoire, which was much more complete than the printed editions. He gives no satisfactory account of it, nor can it be traced at this day. Possibly it represented the transition of the "Sworn Book of Honorius" into the spurious Papal Constitution.

§ 5. *Minor and Spurious Rituals of Black Magic.*

To distinguish in a mass of forged literature certain books as more spurious than others, seems at first sight a

[1] *Les Véritables Clavicules de Salomon. Trésor des Sciences Occultes, suivies d'un Grand Nombre des Secrets, et notamment de la Magie du Papillon Vert.* N.D.

[2] *La Vera Clavicola del Re Salomone, Tesoro delle Science Occulie con molti Altri Segreti e principalmonte La Cabala della Farfalla Verde tradotte dalla Lingua Straniera alla Lingua Italiana da Bestetti.* Milano, 1868. Also, with slight variations, Firenze, Armato Muzzi editore, 1880.

[3] For example, *Le Dragon Rouge, ou l'Art de Commander les Esprits célestes, aériens et infernaux.* A Milan, chez Gaspard Buffanelli. And, *Le Vóritable Dragon Rouge, plus la poule Noire, edition augmentée des secrets de la Reine Cleopatre, secrets pour se render invisible, sécrets d'Artephius, &c.* This is a reprint of the rare so-called edition of 1521, and is possibly still in print.

needless ingenuity of criticism. There are, however, some Rituals of Black Magic which are merely the knavish speculations of catchpenny booksellers, and there are others, anterior to the period, and foreign to the centres, of *colportage,* which have never exercised any influence, and are, in fact, generally unknown. Both classes neither possess a history nor have contributed anything to their subject. Yet it does not follow that they offer no points of curiosity or interest, and some account of them must be given in this place.

The *Verus Jesuitarum Libellus,* or "True Magical Work of the Jesuits, containing most powerful conjurations for all evil spirits of whatever state, condition, and office they are, and a most powerful and approved conjuration of the Spirit Uriel;[1] to which is added Cyprian's Invocation of Angels, and his Conjuration of the Spirits guarding Hidden Treasures, together with a form for their dismissal," —purports to have been published at Paris in the Latin tongue, and in the year 1508. It was reprinted by Scheible at Stuttgart in 1845, forming part of the curious collection of Faust documents already mentioned. Finally, in the year 1875, the late Major Herbert Irwin made an English translation, which remains in MS. The date placed on the title-page of the original edition at once betrays the imposture. It will be almost needless to say that in the first decade of the sixteenth century there were no Jesuits; the Society originated with St. Ignatius, who died in 1556, being two years after the confirmation of the Society by Pope Paul III. The Conjurations are excessively curious. The first is addressed to a spirit whose name is not indi-

[1] The modern reprint of Scheible reads *Usiel* throughout, as does also the MS. English translation. Supposing the latter to have followed the original edition, it would seem conclusive that the blunder—for such it evidently is—occurs also in that.

cated, but he is supposed to have been obedient to Abraham and Isaac, and is directed to bring the magician out of the depths of the sea so many millions—the number is not specified, and depends upon the cupidity of the operator—of the best Spanish gold; otherwise, says the Conjuration, I will condemn thy body (*sic*) and thy soul. In the second formula, the spirit is cited by the knowledge and exorcising power of Agrippa,[1] which again puts a definite limit to the antiquity of the collection, were it otherwise necessary. The third Invocation is addressed to the spirit Zayariel, who is conjured by Agla Scheffert and the great Jehova Podashocheia. The remainder, to the number of seven in all, are nearly identical in character and quite in purpose, the demon being invariably required to bring that which is desired by the operator from the depths of the sea, or from the abyss of the waters, or from the spiritual abyss. The Discharge or Absolution which concludes the series is really an additional conjuration.

The "Citation of St. Cyprian" is presumably an experiment in White Magic, seeing that it is addressed to an Angel who was the guest of Lot and Abraham. As the object is "help in need," it is apparently appropriate for every strait in life, and should be, therefore, noted for reference by those who may think it work while; it is too cumbrous and tedious for these pages. A similar observation would apply only too truly to the "Process for the Magical Acquisition of Hidden Treasures," but it is much more complete than the rest, and has so much connection with the *Summum Bonum,* the desire of the eyes of all Ceremonial Magic, that it is necessary to give it. It is, however, an operation of Necromancy, and will be found in its proper place in the Second Part.[2] The *Verus Jesuitarum Libellus*

[1] Cornelius Agrippa died in 1535.
[2] Part II. c. 9.

closes with a fuliginous conjuration of the entire hierarchy of Infernus, which continues for many pages, and contains more unintelligible words than several combined Grimoires. In the absence of all knowledge of its original edition, it is impossible to throw any light upon this singular emposture.

The *Praxis Magica Fausti,* or "Magical Elements of Dr. John Faust, Practitioner of Medicine," claims to have been printed from the original MS. in the Municipal Library of Weimar, and is dated 1571, at which period it must be respectfully affirmed that there was no Municipal Library in the birthplace of Goethe. Furthermore, the existing collection does not include the MS. Whether the original edition was antedated cannot be certainly affirmed, as it is exceedingly scarce, and we are acquainted with it only in the reprint of Scheible, and in an unprinted transcript by Major Irwin. The work consists of a few curious plates, in the manner of the seventeenth century, and a few unintelligible conjurations, all exceedingly brief. The third of these exhorts the Evil Spirit on the quaint ground that now it is the time of the Great Name Tetragrammaton. The purpose of citation is not indicated; the formulæ are Christian, broken up by innumerable crosses, and by names and terms which defy conjecture as to their significance. The hierarchy of the spirit is determined by the closing words: "I command thee, O Spirit Rumoar, even by Lucifer, thy mighty sovereign."

§ 6. *The Black Pullet.*

"The Black Pullet," the "Druid of Menapienne," "Red Magic, or the Cream of the Occult Sciences," with derivatives from the first of these works, such as the "Queen of the Hairy Flies," the "Green Butterfly," &c., form a class by themselves, and, with one exception, are quite unserious publications, which can scarcely be called spurious, as they are almost without pretence.[1] They belong to the late end of the eighteenth century. Dr. Encausse, the head of the French Martinists, suggests that they were all fabricated at Rome, and thence goes on to infer that we owe them to the industry of priests, which seems to follow somewhat loosely from the evidence, and is indeed of much the same value as the statement in "Isis Unveiled," that the habitual practice of Black Magic at the Vatican could be "easily proved."

The "Black Pullet" is far the most curious of its class, and there is indeed sufficient merit in its narrative to lift it much above the paltry impostures with which it connects. Its chief occult interest centres in the series of talismanic rings which it incorporates with the text, itself a species of magical romance. It makes no claim to antiquity, except that it embodies its wisdom, and it does not appeal to Solomon. In a book of Black Magic, as it certainly is, though the Goëtic intention is disguised, such modesty makes for virtue. Many of the Talismans seem to be original devices, at least they connect with nothing in occult symbolism known to the present writer. At the same time they are constructed in accordance with the rules laid down by the Fourth Book attributed to Cornelius Agrippa as regards infernal signatures.

The "Black Pullet" reappeared during its own period at various dates, with slight alterations—once as the "Treasure of the Old Man of the Pyramids," when it was fol-

[1] Much depends, however, on the point of view of the critic. A work which, even in its own country, seems almost unknown, *Le Triple Vocabulaire Infernal*, a Manual of Demonomania, by Finellan, defines the Cabala as the art of communicating with elementary spirits, and adds that among the Grand Cabalas are included (1) That called the Green Butterfly; (2) That of the Black Pullet; (3) That of the Queen of Hairy Flies; and (4) That of the Black Screech Owl. The works containing these mysteries are, it is said, exceedingly rare.

lowed by a sequel or companion under the title of the "Black Screech Owl." It has been reprinted within recent years at Paris in an edition intended for bibliophiles, but bearing no indications of bibliographical research. Though modest in the claims which have been specified, the title of the original edition is portentous enough, namely, "The Black Pullet, or the Hen with the Golden Eggs, comprising the Science of Magic Talismans and Rings, the Art of Necromancy and of the Kabbalah, for the Conjuration of Aerial and Infernal Spirits, of Sylphs, Undines, and Gnomes, for the acquisition of the Secret Sciences, for the Discovery of Treasures, for obtaining power to command all beings, and to unmask all Sciences and Bewitchments. The whole following the Doctrines of Socrates, Pythagoras, Zoroaster, Son of the Grand Aromasis, and other philosophers whose works in MS. escaped the conflagration of the Library of Ptolemy. Translated from the Language of the Magi and that of the Hieroglyphs by the Doctors Mizzaboula-Jabamía, Danhuzerus, Nehmahmiah, Judahim, and Eliaeb. Rendered into French by A. J. S. D. R. L. G. F." The place of publication is Egypt, which probably stands for Rome, and the date is 740, meaning 1740, which, however, is untrue, as we shall see. It may be said at once that there is no pretence in the text to fulfil the magnificent assurances of the title.

The preface entreats that the "Black Pullet" may not be confounded with the collections of reveries and errors which so many have sought to accredit by announcing supernatural effects. This request, after due consideration, most readers will find it impossible to grant. The work, it has been said, is a romance, and the first thing which it makes clear is that even the addition of a thousand years to the date in the title is insufficient.[1] It is the narrative of a man who "formed part of the expedition to Egypt," and was "an officer in the army of the genius." The reference is, of course, to Napoleon, and the date of composition is less than a century ago. While in Egypt, the narrator was sent upon an expedition to the Pyramids, accompanied by some mounted chasseurs. They lunched under the shadow of the grand colossus, when they were attacked by a horde of Arabs of the desert, the comrades of the writer were slain, and he himself was left for dead upon the ground. On returning to consciousness, he surrendered himself to mournful reflections in the immediate anticipation of his end, and delivered a valedictory address to the setting sun, when a stone was rolled back in the Pyramid, and a venerable man issued forth, who was proclaimed to be a Turk by his turban. This personage did not fail to discover the corpses which strewed the desert, nor to identify their nation. When the officer in his turn was examined, he manifested life by kissing the hand of the ancient man, who, superior to all prejudices which might have been dictated to the ordinary Mussulman by patriotism or religion, took pity on him, revived him by a wonderful liqueur which put the wounded man upon his feet, and he followed his preserver into the Pyramid, which was the home of the ancient man, and withal a house of Magic. There were vast halls and endless galleries, subterranean chambers piled with treasures, apparitions of blazing lamps, ministering spirits innumerable, magic suppers; above all things there was the Black Pullet. In a word, diurnal life was illustrated throughout by the supernatural; it was a methodised version of Aladdin with an inner meaning by Astaroth. The sage himself proved to be sole heir of the Magi and the

[1] It is not impossible that the middle of the nineteenth century may be the period to which it should be assigned.

makers of those Egyptian hieroglyphics which are the "despair of the learned," and, not least, he was himself in quest of an heir, for he felt that he was about to pass away. In fine, the French officer, having acquired the Turkish language by means of a grammar which had its root in sorcery, and being thus enabled to communicate with his protector, which on the whole seems superfluous, seeing that his protector possessed a talisman which communicated immediate proficiency in all tongues, was instructed in the powers and wonders of twenty-two talismanic figures and the rings corresponding, as well as in the secret of the manufacture of the Black Pullet, which possessed more skill in gold-finding than the divining rod in the discovery of water. After these instructions, in spite of many prayers, and the ministries of the genius Odous, the just man expired upon a sofa, while the fortunate kinsman in philosophy swooned at the feet of his benefactor. In due course, accompanied by the genius who had been transferred to his service, the French officer managed to depart from Egypt, laden with treasures, and with the ashes of the sage in a costly urn. He took ship for Marseilles, stilled the tempest on the voyage, and returned to his native country. He made his abode in Provence, spending his days in experiments with the Black Pullet, or in study, meditation, and rambling. He undertook at length to write this memorial of his good fortune, in which he threatens the publishers of any pirated edition to adorn them, by means of a talisman, with ears six inches longer than those of Midas. But this does not seem to have prevented the publishers.

The Black Pullet disclaims all connection with Black Magic, and duly connects therewith, firstly by its characters, and secondly by their pretended power over evil spirts; though it should be observed that the infernal beings mentioned in the title are not devils, but Salamanders—that is to say, elementary Spirits of Fire. But while it transcends Black Magic it is not superior to plagiarism, and incorporates many pages of the *Comte de Gabalis*.

For the evocation of the genii who served the Old Man of the Pyramid it suffices to say: THOMATOS, BENESSER, FLIANTER. You are then liable to be encompassed by thirty-three several intelligences. To obtain their respect say: LITAN, IZER, OSNAS, and they will bow down before you, individually remarking: NANTHER. The words SOUTRAM, UBARSINENS will cause them to transport you through the air wheresoever you are inclined. Upon the utterance of the one word RABIAM they will return you to your own abode. It is necessary, however, to be fortified by the talismans and rings of the master, but they can be obtained by a cheap process. In the cabinet of the Old Man of the Pyramid they were formed of the precious metals and were resplendent with gems, but they will answer all practical purposes if the rings are composed of bronzed steel and the talismans of satin, in strict accordance with the description which here follows.

TALISMAN I.
The characters should be graven on the inner side of the Ring.

§ 7. *Talismans of the Sage of the Pyramids.*

I. Serves for the conjuration of celestial and infernal powers. It should be embroidered in silver upon sky-blue satin. The evoking words are

SIRAS, ETAR, BESANAR, at which multitudes of spirits will appear.

II. Gives the love and complaisance of the entire female sex. It should be embroidered in silver on black satin. The evoking words are NADES, SURADIS, MANINER, pronounced with the ring, which should be on the middle finger of the left hand, pressed against the lips. They ensure the mani-

TALISMAN II.

The characters should be graven on the inner side of the Ring.

festation of a genius with rose-coloured wings, who, if addressed with the words SADER, PROSTAS, SOLASTER, will traverse all space to transport you the lady of your heart, though she were the queen of the Caliph's seraglio. At the words MAMMES, LAHER, she will be removed by four slaves.

III. Discovers all treasures and ensures their possession. The figure of the talisman should be embroidered in gold upon green satin. The words ONAIM, PERANTES, RASONASTOS, will cause the appearance of seven genii *au teint bazane*, each of whom will pour out golden ducats from great bags

TALISMAN III.

The characters should be graven on the inner side of the Ring.

of hide at the feet of the sorcerer, the operations of this Grimoire being performed upon a huge scale. *Item,* a black hooded bird will be perched upon the shoulder of each spirit.

IV. Discovers the most hidden secrets and enables its

possessor to penetrate everywhere unseen. The talisman should be of violet satin, with the figures embroidered in silver. It should be held in the left hand, on which also the ring should be worn, and should be placed close to the ear, pronouncing the words Nitrae, Radou, Sunandam, when a distinct voice will utter the desired secret.

Talisman IV.

The characters should be graven on the outer side of the ring.

Talisman V.

The characters should be graven on the outer side of the ring.

V. Will make the most taciturn man bosom himself to its possessor, whose enemies will also be forced to confess all their machinations. The talisman should be of gold-coloured satin with the figures embroidered in gold. By placing the ring on the little finger of the left hand, the talisman against the right ear, and pronouncing the words Noctar, Raiban, the most discreet man will be compelled to unveil his most secret thoughts. The addition of the word Biranther will force the enemies of the possessor to declare their projects aloud.

VI. Sets to work enough genii for the immediate achievement of any work which the possessor may desire to undertake, and for the stoppage of any which may oppose him. The talisman should be of lilac satin with the figures embroidered in shaded silk. The magical words are ZORAMI, ZAITUX, ELASTOT.

TALISMAN VI.

The characters should be graven on the outer side of the ring.

TALISMAN VII.

The characters should be graven on the inner side of the Ring.

VII. Has the power to destroy everything; to cause the fall of hail, thunderbolts, and stars of heaven; to occasion earthquakes, storms, and so forth. At the same time it preserves the friends of the possessor from accidents. The figure of the talisman should be embroidered in silver upon poppy-red satin. The magic words are: (1) DITAU,

HURANDOS, for works of destruction; (2) RIDAS, TALIMOL, to command the elements; (3) ATROSIS, NARPIDA, for the fall of hail, &c.; (4) UUSUR, ITAR, for earthquake; (5) HISPEN, TROMADOR, for hurricanes and storms; (6) PARANTHES, HISTANOS, for the preservation of friends.

TALISMAN VIII.

The characters should be graven on the outer side of the Ring.

VIII. Gives invisiblity, even to the eyes of genii, so that God alone shall witness the actions of the possessor. It is accompanied by the power of penetrating everywhere and passing through brick walls. The magic words are BENATIR, CARARKAU, DEDOS, ETINARMI. For each operation the ring must be placed upon a different finger of the right hand. The talisman is of yellow satin embroidered with black silk.

IX. Transports the possessor to any part of the world,

and that without danger. The potent words are RADITUS, POLASTRIEN, TERPANDU, OSTRATA, PERICATUR, ERMAS. The talisman is of puce-coloured satin embroidered with gold.

TALISMAN IX.

The characters should be graven on the inner side of the Ring.

TALISMAN X.

The characters should be graven on the outer side of the ring.

X. Opens all locks at a touch, whatever precautions have been taken to secure them. The magic words are SARITAP, PERNISOX, OTTARIM. The talisman is of deep blue satin embroidered with silver.

XI. Sets the possessor in any desired house without the preliminary of entering, and reads the thoughts of all persons, so that they can be helped or harmed at pleasure. The talisman is of light grey satin embroidered with gold. To know thoughts, place it on your head, breathe upon the ring, and say: O TAROT, NIZAEL, ESTARNAS, TANTAREZ. To serve those who deserve it: Nista, Saper, Visnos, and they will forthwith enjoy every kind of prosperity. To punish your enemies or evil persons: Xatros, Nifer, Roxas, Tortos, and they will be immediately delivered to frightful torments.

Talisman XI.

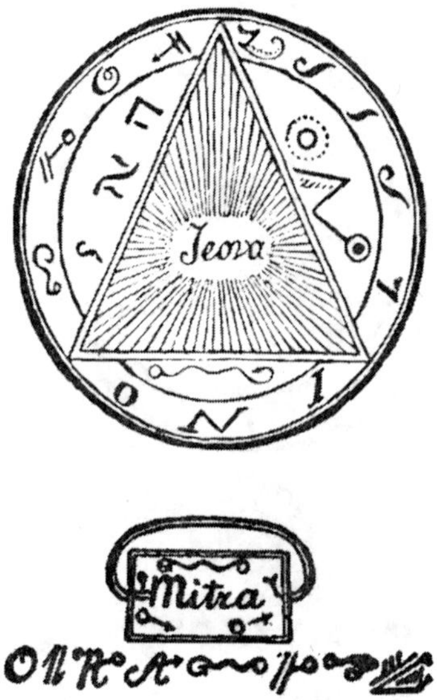

The characters should be graven on the outer side of the ring.

Talisman XII.

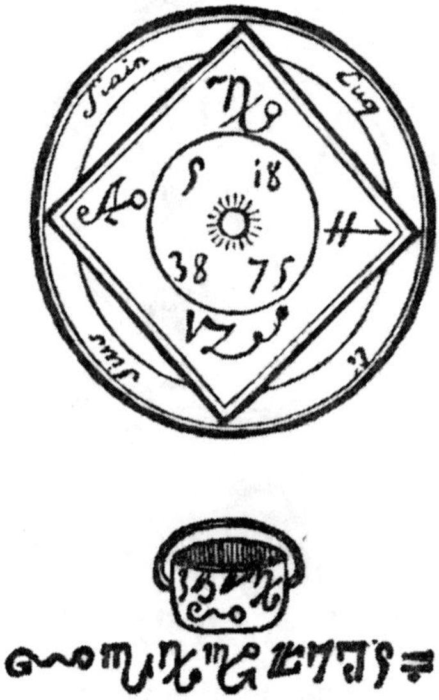

The characters should be graven on the inner side of the Ring.

XII. Destroys all projects formed against the possessor and compels rebellious spirits. The talisman is of rose-coloured satin embroidered with silver. It should be placed upon a table, the left hand imposed upon it; the ring should be on the middle finger of the right hand, and the operator, with bent head, should repeat in a low voice the words: Senapos, Terfita, Estamos, Perfiter, Notarin.

XIII. Endows the possessor with every virtue and talent, as well as with the desire to do good. All substances of evil quality can be rendered excellent by means of it. For the first advantage, it is sufficient to raise up the talisman, having the ring upon the first joint of the third finger of the right hand, and to pronounce the words: TURAN, ESTONOS, FUZA. For the second say: VAZOTAS, TES-

TALISMAN XIII.

The characters should be graven on the outer side of the ring.

TALISMAN XIV.

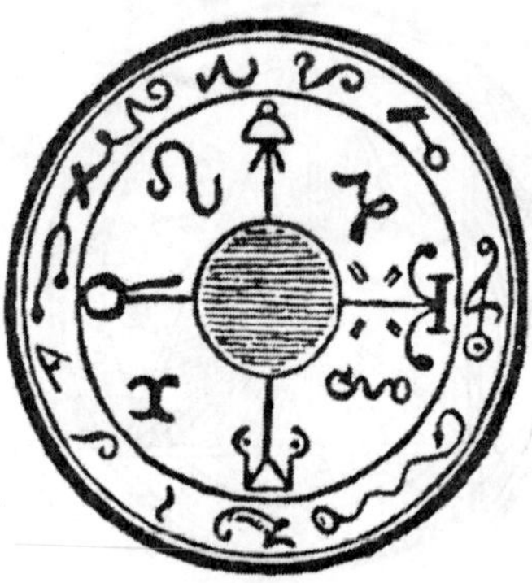

The characters should be graven on the outer side of the ring.

TANAR. The talisman should be of saffron-coloured satin embroidered with silver.

XIV. Gives the knowledge of all minerals and vegetables, with their virtues and properties; gives also the universal medicine, and the faculty of healing all sick persons. The talisman is of orange-coloured satin embroidered with silver. It should be worn upon the breast, and the ring in a locket (kerchief) round the neck by means of a ribbon of flame-coloured silk. The operative words are: RETER-REM, SALIBAT, CRATARES, HISASTER.

XV. Gives immunity from the most ferocious animals; gives the means of overcoming them; gives the knowledge of their language; and drives mad animals away. The talisman should be of deep green satin embroidered with gold.

TALISMAN XV.

The characters should be graven on the outer side of the ring.

TALISMAN XVI.

The characters should be graven on the outer side of the ring.

For the first three objects say: HOCATOS, IMORAD, SURATER, MARKILA. For the last: TRUMANTREM, RICONA, ESTUPIT, OXA.

XVI. Gives discernment for the good or bad intentions of any person. The talisman is of black satin embroidered with gold. It should be placed upon the heart, and the ring on the little finger of the right hand. The words are: CROSTES, FURINOT, KATIPA, GARINOS.

XVII. Gives all talents and a profound knowledge of all arts, so that the possessor will outshine their professors. The talisman, which must be carried on the person, should be of white satin embroidered with black silk. The operative words are: RITAS, ONALUN, TERSORIT, OMBAS, SERPITAS, QUITATHAR, ZAMARATH, specifying the art which it is desired to possess.

TALISMAN XVII.

The characters should be graven on the inner side of the Ring.

TALISMAN XVIII.

The characters should be graven on the inner side of the Ring.

XVIII. Gives good fortune in any lottery. The talisman is of cerise-coloured satin, embroidered with gold and silver. It should be bound upon the left arm by means of a white ribbon, and the ring must be on the little finger of the right hand. The words are: ROKES for a winning number, PILATUS for an ambes-ace, ZOTOAS for a denary, TULITAS for a quaternary, XATANITOS for a quinary, being careful to pronounce all the words at the quine. At cards they should be repeated when shuffling for self or partner. Before beginning, touch your left arm with your right hand in the neighbourhood of the talisman, and kiss the ring. These little contrivances can be effected, says the honest Grimoire, without exciting the notice of your opponent.

XIX. Gives the power of directing all the infernal hosts

TALISMAN XIX.

The characters should be graven on the outer side of the Ring.

TALISMAN XX.

The characters should be graven on the outer side of the Ring.

against the enemies of its possessor. The talisman is of greyish white satin shaded. It may be worn in any manner, and the words are: OSTHARIMAN, VISANTIPAROS, NOCTATUR.

XX. Gives the knowledge of the counsels of Infernus and the means of rendering its projects abortive. The talisman is of red satin, with the center embroidered in gold, the border in silver, and the figures in black and white silk. It should be worn upon the breast, and the ring on the first joint of the little finger of the left hand. The words are: Actatos, Catipta, Bejouran, Itapan, Marnutus.

The range of human ambition recognized by Ceremonial Magic being always somewhat restricted, it is not surprising that the offices of these talismans frequently overlap one another, or that some of them correspond very closely to the powers ascribed to the Magus by the transcendental science of the "Arbatel." The talismans are preceded in the original by the figure of a magical rod, stained, says the letter-press which accompanies it, with the blood of a lamb, and having the form of a serpent. The Description is somewhat obscure, but the wand can be apparently bent, and the mouth and tail joined by means of a golden chain, so as to form a circle. The wand should be six feet long, and when bent can be used as a circle of evocation. There is also a figure of the grand magical circle, but it is not described in the text. There are thus twenty-two figures in all, and the inclusion of the word Tarot in the list of evoking terms is not without

THE MAGIC ROD ACCORDING TO THE BLACK PULLET.

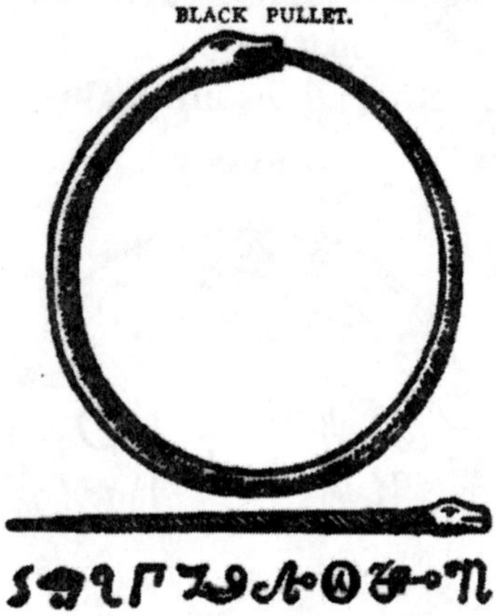

These characters should be inscribed upon the Rod with Chinese Ink.

THE GOETIC CIRCLE OF THE BLACK PULLET.

significance in this connection. A certain correspondence between the talismans and the Tarot trumps is indeed unmistakable, at least in some instances, and seems to indicate that the work has a more serious occult aspect than would appear at first sight.

§ 8. *The Gold-Finding Hen.*

We must hasten, however, to the incubation of the gold-finding hen, which is the head and crown of the proceedings. The grand Oromasis, the father of Zoroaster, was the first person who possessed one of these marvellous fowls, which are hatched from an egg in the following manner. Take aromatic woods, such as aloes, cedar, orange, citron, laurel, iris-root, with rose-leaves dried in the sun. Place them in a golden chafing-dish; pour balsamic oil over them; add the finest incense and clear gum. Next say: Athas, Solinam, Erminatos, Pasaim; set a glass over the chafing-dish; direct the rays of the sun thereon, and the wood will kindle, the glass will melt, a sweet odour will fill the place, and the compost will burn speedily to ashes. Place these ashes in a golden egg while still red-hot; lay the egg upon a black cushion; cover it with a bell-glass of faceted rock-crystal; then lift up your eyes and stretch your arms towards heaven and cry: O Sanataper, Ismai, Nontapilus, Ertivaler, Canopistus. Expose the glass to the most fierce rays of the sun till it seems enveloped in flame, the egg ceases to be visible, and a slight vapour rises. Presently you will discern a black pullet just beginning to move, when if you say: Binusas, Tespipas, it will take wings and nestle in your bosom.

While this is the true process of the Pyramids, and easy no doubt to an heir direct of Oromasis, it is obvious that it has its difficulties to those born merely under the common moon of sorcery, and, merciful, like all its companions, to human limitations, the Grimoire provides an alternative method suitable to persons of small means. Take an unspotted egg; expose it to the meridian rays of the sun; then select the blackest hen you can meet with; if it have any coloured feathers, pluck them. Should the Society for the Prevention of Cruelty to Animals not intervene opportunely, contrive to hood this bird with a kind of black bonnet drawn over the eyes so that it cannot see. Leave it the use of its beak. Shut it up in a box also lined with some black material, and large enough to hold it comfortably. Place the box in a room where no light of day can penetrate; give food only in the night to the fowl; see that no noise disturbs it, and set it to hatch the egg. As every thing will be black to the bird, its imagination, which is likely enough, will be overwhelmed by the sense of blackness, and if it should survive the incarceration, it will ultimately incubate a perfectly black chicken, provided only that the operator by his wisdom and virtue is worthy to participate in such sacred and divine mysteries. It does not appear how or why a fowl incubated after this uncomfortable fashion should have a particular instinct for detecting the places wherein gold is hidden, but such is the faculty attributed to it, and it can only be concluded that the "Black Pullet" is a degree more foolish than its idle company of Grimoires.

The simplified process did not, however, in the opinion of sorcery, seem the last word which it was possible to say upon the subject. Despite the threatened vengeance of the heir of Oromasis, the mystery was adapted by the later editors of the "Red Dragon," and reappears as the Grand Cabala, without which no other can succeed. In this, its last transformation, it becomes a recipe for evoking the devil which seems to breathe the true spirit of Goetic genius. Its success, it may be premised, will depend upon a recollected and devotional spirit in the operator, together with a clean conscience; otherwise, in place of commanding the evil spirit, the latter will command him. This understood, the process itself is simple. You have merely to secure a black hen which has never been crossed by the male bird,

THE APPARITION OF THE GRAND CABALA.

and to do this in such a manner that it shall not cackle; it is best therefore to seize it in its sleep, clutching it by the neck, but not more than is necessary to prevent it from crying. You must repair to the highroad, walk till you come to a cross-way, and there, on the stroke of midnight, describe a circle with a cypress rod, place yourself in the midst thereof, and tear the bird in twain, pronouncing three times the words, *Eloim, Essaim, frugativi et appellavi.* Next turn to the east, kneel down, recite a prayer, and conclude it with the Grand Appellation, when the Unclean Spirit will appear to you in a scarlet surcoat, a yellow vest, and breeches of pale green. His head will resemble that of a dog, but his ears will be those of an ass, with two horns above them; he will have the legs and hoofs of a calf. He will ask for your orders, which you will give as you please, and as he cannot do otherwise than obey you, you may become rich on the spot, and thus the happiest of men. Such at least is the judgment of the Grimoire. Whether the victim of the process is to be torn in pieces alive does not explicitly appear, but may be inferred from the initial precaution.

SOLVE
COAGULA
ELIPHAS
LEVI DEL

PART II

THE COMPLETE GRIMOIRE

CHAPTER I

The Preparation of the Operator

§ 1. *Concerning the Love of God.*

THE rites of Transcendental Magic are divine and religious rites, and the counsels, spiritual and moral, which are found in its instructions are, in their way, the counsels of perfection, whatever element of puerility may radically obtain in its experiments.[1] The Composite Rituals, despite the result of their analysis, also partake largely of the nature of religious observances, at times Judaistic, at times Christian. In both cases this fact is readily intelligible; to communicate with the fabled Spirits of the Firmament, and to practise an art which offers to its adepts the regeneration of Enoch, King of the Inferior World,[2] "who was not, for God took him," may well demand a high degree of sanctity from its candidates; while to dominate the so-called Spirits of the Elements, the Kabbalistic Klippoth and the Evil Demons, it is reasonable to assume that the Magus must be free from common weak-

[1] The Analysis of the "Arbatel of Magic" in Part I. establishes this point, but the following passages may be cited in support of the statement. "In all things call upon the Name of the Lord, and without prayer unto God, through His only-begotten Son, do not thou undertake to do or to think anything." Aph. 2. "Let the word of God never depart from thy mouth." *Ib.* Aph. 3. "Look unto God in all things." *Ib.* Aph. 4. "Desire from God alone." *Ib.* Aph. 11. "Before all things, be watchful in this, that your name is written in Heaven." *Ib.*

[2] The secret of this regeneration is promised to the adept in "Arbatel," Aph. 24.

ness, from common vice,[1] and must be fortified by the grace and favour of the superior world. Given the magical standpoint in each case, the conditions essential to operation seem, in this respect, above challenge. But it will assuredly appear at first sight a most bizarre anomaly that Black Magic should involve also religious observances and should exact similar conditions, both inward and outward, from those who would undertake its enterprises. It is not, as generally supposed, either Christianity *a rebours* or a reversed religion of Israel; it is not the intentional profanation of religious ritual and observance; it is something less outrageous but logically more insensate; so far as it has recourse to such ritual and such observance, it is not to do outrage to God in the interests of diabolism, but to derive power and virtue from above for the more successful control of Evil Spirits, and this obtains indifferently whether the purpose of the operator be otherwise lawful or not.

The Divine Love, says the book of "True Black Magic,"[2] must precede the acquisition of the Scenece of Solomon, son of King David, who said: The beginning and Key of my Wisdom are the fear of God, to do Him honour, to adore Him with great contrition of heart, and to invoke His aid in all our intentions and aspirations; which fulfilling, God will lead us into the good way.[3]

To account for this anomaly it is insufficient to say that the book of "True Black Magic" is simply the "Key of Solomon" adapted to Goetic intentions. In the first place, as already seen, it is impossible to read the Goetic intention out of either of the Clavicles; and, in the second place, the

[1] "To overcome and subjugate the elementary spirits, we must never yield to their characteristic defect. . . . In a word, we must overcome them in their strength without ever being overcome by their weaknesses."—ELIPHAS LEVI, *Rituel de la Haute Magie*, c. 4.

[2] Book I. c. 1.

[3] An adapted rendering of "The Key of Solomon," Book I. c. 1.

same characteristics are found in the Grimoires which derive least of all from the Clavicles, namely, that of Honorius, and that called the "Grand Grimoire." To meditate continually on the undertaking and to centre every hope in the infinite goodness of the Great Adonay, is the rule established by the latter as the first principle of success.[1]

Nor does the insensate nature of the processes of Black Magic offer explanation by itself. The attempt to propitiate the Deity by means of prayers, sacrifices, and abstinence, and thus obtain the Divine assistance for the successful consummation of hideous offences and preposterous or impossible undertakings, is, of course, madness; for the God acknowledged and invoked by Goetic Magic is not the Principle of Evil, as the myth of Modern Satanism supposes,[2] but the servance followed in reality from the interpretation placed by "terrible and venerable Deity" who destroyed the power of the rebellious angels, the Jehovah of the Jewish rituals and the Trinity of the Christian magical cycle. The insane observance followed in reality from the interpretation placed by Goëtic Theurgy on the fundamental doctrine of practical magic, namely, the power of Divine words to compel the obedience of all spirits to those who could pronounce them.[3] Collections of these words and names were recited as invoking and binding forms, and,

[1] Grand Grimoire, Book I. c. I.

[2] To do evil because it is pleasing to the Prince of Evil did not enter into the conception of Sorcery. Refinements of this kind are of late date, and mostly of French invention. The sorcerer who sought to do evil and had recourse for assistance to Satan was actuated by no recondite motive; he ministered merely to his own propensities for lust, wealth, or revenge. He used Satan as an instrument treated him and his inferiors as slaves, and always reckoned ultimately to elude the dangers of such dealings.

[3] The doctrine is summarized in a sentence by Eliphas Lévi, when he declares that the virtue of things has created words. Cornelius Agrippa refers it to Platonic teaching, affirming that a certain power or life belonging to the idea underlies the "form of the signification," that is, the voice or word, whence he also says that Magicians regard words as the "rays of things." *De Occulta Philosophia*, Book I. c. 70. Compare also his rendering of the Platonic doctrine that the form comes first from the idea. *Ibid.*, c 13.

incorporated into a suitable setting of official prayers, were used in all magical ceremonies. Black Magic was simply their application to unlawful purposes. The utterance of the Divine Name, which was supposed to make the devils tremble and place them at the will of the Magus, was at least equally powerful, it was argued, to enforce their obedience for a purpose in consonance with their own nature. Then seeing that prayer to God and the invocation of the Divine Names presuppose a proper Spirit of reverence, devotion, and love as the condition upon which prayer is heard, it became a condition in Goetia. The first impossibility required of the adept in Black Magic is therefore that he should love God before he bewitches his neighbour; that he should put all his hopes in God before he makes pact with Satan; that, in a word, he should be good in order to do evil.

§ 2. *Concerning Fortitude.*

The spiritual intention of the operator being thus determined, his next step was the acquisition of the mental attitude appropriate to his future work. We may picture him in the traditional state of the sorcerer—poor, proscribed, envious, ambitious, and having no capacity for legitimate enterprises. Unable to earn money, he hankers after hidden treasures, and haunts those spots up and down the countryside which are reputed to conceal them. He has done this presumably for a long time before determining to betake himself to Magic, but the earth will not yield up her hoards, for the gnomes and the Earth-Spirits, the Alastors and the Demons of the Solitudes, stand guard over the secrets of dead misers when the human ghost has ceased to walk in the neighbourhood. He does not long hesitate when he learns that the Grimoires of Black Magic are full of darksome rites and fell, mysterious words which compel or expel those guardians. The Church and State may threaten him with a fire for his flesh and a fire for his soul, but by watchfulness and secresy he hopes to elude the one, and the other is a distant danger. Obviously, however, in order to reach his determination, he must arm himself with intrepidity and prudence, and this is the first counsel of his guides to the sanctum Regnum of Goëtia.

"O men! O impotent mortals!" cries the author of the "Grand Grimoire,"[1] "tremble at your own temerity when you blindly aspire to the possession of a science so profound. Lift up your minds beyond your limited sphere, and learn of me that before you undertake anything it is necessary that you should become firm and immovable, besides being scrupulously attentive in the exact observation, step by step, of all things whatsoever that I shall tell you, without which precautions every operation will turn to your disadvantage, confusion, and total destruction; while, on the contrary, by following my injunctions with precision, you will rise from your meanness and poverty, achieving a complete success in all your enterprises. Arm yourselves, therefore, with intrepidity, prudence, wisdom, and virtue, as qualifications for this grand and illimitable work, in which I have passed sixty-and-seven years, toiling night and day for the attainment of success in this sublime object."[2]

§ 3. *Concerning Continence and Abstinence.*

The Fourth Book of Occult Philosophy, referred to Cornelius Agrippa, but composite in character and spurious in attribution, as already seen, gives an exceedingly curious explanation of the rule of sanctity prescribed by all forms

[1] Book I. c. 2.
[2] The speaker is pseudo-Solomon.

of Ceremonial Magic. The instruments used in the Art are ineffective without consecration. The act of consecration is the act by which virtue is imparted to them, and this virtue derives from two sources, the power of sanctification residing in Divine Names and in the prayers which incorporate them, and the power of sanctification residing in the holiness of the person consecrating.[1] An indispensable part of this holiness was the preservation of chastity for a defined period preceding operation, and a fast of graduated severity. In their directions concerning these points the Rituals of Black Magic differ little from their prototypes, the earlier Keys of Solomon, the work of pseudo-Agrippa,[2] or "The Magical Elements" of Peter de Abano. Here is the direction of the Neophyte which occurs in the "Grand Grimoire": "You must abstain during an entire quarter of the moon from the society of females, so as to protect yourself from the possibility of impurity. You must commence your magical quarter at the same moment with that of the luminary itself, by a pledge to the Grand Adonay, who is the Master of all Spirits, to make no more than two collations daily, that is to say, in every twenty-four hours of the said quarter of the Moon, which collation should be taken at noon

[1] Here the Fourth Book of Occult Philosophy merely reproduces the instruction of the genuine work. "Consecration is a lifting up of experiments, by which a spiritual soul, being drawn by proportion and conformity, is infused into the matter of our works according to the tradition of Magical Art rightly and lawfully prepared, and our work is vivified by the spirit of understanding. The efficacy of consecration is perfected by two things especially, viz., the virtue of the person himself consecrating, and the virtue of the prayer itself. In the person is required holiness of life and a power to consecrate. The former, nature and desert perform; the latter is acquired by imitation and dignification." Book III. c. 62. The virtue of prayer derives from its institution by God, the ordinance of the Church, or the commemoration which it may make of sacred things.

[2] So also in the Third Book *De Oculta Philosophia*, which is especially devoted to Ceremonial Magic, the student is directed to abstain "from all those things which infect either mind or spirit," and above all from idleness and luxury, "for the soul being suffocated by the body and the lust thereof, can discern nothing that is celestial," c. 55. The fourth book merely says: "Let the man who would receive an oracle from the good spirits be chaste, pure, and confessed." Compare Peter de Abano: "The operator should be clean and purified for the space of nine days before beginning the work; he should be confessed also, and

and midnight, or, if it better please you, at seven o'clock in the morning and at the corresponding hour in the evening, using the following prayer previously to each repast during the whole of the said quarter:—

PRAYER.

I implore Thee, O Thou Grand and Powerful ADONAY, Master of all Spirits! I beseech Thee, O ELOIM! I implore Thee, O JEHOVAM! O Grand ADONAY, I give unto Thee my soul, my heart, my inward parts, my hands, my feet, my desires, my entire being! O Grand ADONAY, deign to be favourable unto me! So be it. Amen.

Then take your repast, disrobe as seldom and sleep as little as possible during the whole of the said period, but meditate continually on your undertaking, and centre all your hopes in the infinite goodness of the Great Adonay.[1]

The "Grimoire of Honorius," which is exclusively intended for persons in Holy Orders, restricts the period of fasting to three days, as will be seen later on, and makes no condition of continence in those who are devoted to celibacy. The *Grimorium Verum* prescribes a similar period, and adds that the fast should be most austere, that human society and human communications must be avoided as much as possible, but that of women especially. The "Book of True Black Magic" varies the instruction as follows:[2] If the Priest-Exorcist would succeed in operation, he must, when all things else are prepared, abstain from every labour of soul and body, from much eating and drinking, from all luxury, from all vice, and he must meditate on those things which he is about to put in practice for nine complete days

[1] Grand Grimoire, Book I. c. 2.
[2] An adaptation of the "Key of Solomon," Book II. c. 4.

before beginning the work; his assistants—if any—must do in like manner, so that all may be truly fulfilled. Let them begin by the following prayer, which should be recited twice in the night and once in the day.

PRAYER.

O Lord God Almighty, be Thou favourable unto us, though unworthy to lift our eyes to Heaven by reason of the multitude of our offences! O God all-merciful, who willest not the death of a sinner, but rather his true conversion, bestow Thy grace on us! O Lord, O God, full of compassion, aid us in this work which we are about to perform, that Thy Name may be blessed for ever! Amen.[1]

The last days of the fast should be additionally strict, the meals being limited to bread and water, with abstinence from all sin and repetition of the above prayer.

§ 4. *Concerning the External Preparation of the Operator, and firstly Concerning Ablution.*

The rite of lustration being the sacramental mark of inward cleanliness, is prescribed in all magical ceremonies, and is equally important in Goetic art. The ordinary daily ablution itself becomes symbolical. When the operator rises in the morning during the preparatory triduum prescribed by the *Grimorium Verum*, his hands and face must

[1] The following is added in the Clavicle, *loc. cit.*: "O Lord God, Father Eternal! O Thou who are seated upon Cherubim and Seraphim, who beholdest the earth and the sea! Unto Thee do I lift up my hands, and beseech Thine aid alone—Thou who art the fulfillment of good works, who givest rest unto those who toil, who humblest the proud, who art Author of all life and Destroyer of death. Our rest art Thou, Protector of those who call upon Thee; do Thou guard and defend me in this undertaking, O Thou who livest and reignest for ever and ever. Amen.

be sponged with a clean white cloth, using water which has been previously exorcised according to the indications of the Ritual [1] and reciting the

PREPARATORY PRAYER.

Lord God ADONAY, who hast formed man out of nothing to Thine own image and likeness, and me also, unworthy sinner as I am, deign, I pray Thee, to bless ✠ and sanctify this water, that it may be healthful to my body and soul, that all delusion may depart from me. O Lord God, Almighty and Ineffable, who didst lead forth Thy people from the land of Egypt, and didst cause them to pass dryshod over the Red Sea! Grant that I may be cleansed by this water from all my sins, and may appear innocent before Thee. Amen.

The "Book of True Black Magic" observes that the bath is most necessary for Magical Art,[2] and that it must be taken on the final day of the fast, when the exorcisor has been cleansed from all sins, when he has written with the pen of the Art, upon virgin paper or parchment, all the conjurations and exorcisms required in the practice, and has performed all the other preparatory ceremonies. From the crown of his head to the soles of his feet, he must purify himself with warm exorcised water, saying as he does so: "O Lord Adonay, who hast formed me in Thine image and in Thy likeness, deign to bless and sanctify this water, so

[1] From these indications it follows literally that such water would hold quicklime in solution. The passage stands thus: "Warning: The said water must be that which was previously exorcised, wherein thy lime was put"—namely, for the dressing of the lambskin. But water consecrated at the same time as most probably intended.

[2] The statement is adapted from the "Key of Solomon," Book II. c. 5, but the analogy ends with the prescription of warm water; the prayers differ, and the whole ceremony is simplified in the Goëtic ritual.

so that it may become unto me the salvation of my soul and body, and that no wickedness may ever find place upon me." The Psalms *Dominus illuminatio mea* and *Dixit insipiens in corde suo* should be added.[1] Then he shall dry himself.

The prayer following must be repeated—five times during the day and four times during the night—for the space of three days: ASTROSCHIO, ASATH, *a sacra* BEDRIMUBAL, FELUT, ANABOTOS, SERABILEM, SERGEN, GEMEN, DOMOS. O Lord God, who art seated above the heavens, who beholdest the depths, grant me, I pray Thee, that those things which I conceive in my mind may also be executed by me, through Thee, O Great God, who livest and reignest for ever and ever! Amen.

§ 5. *Concerning the External Preparation of the Operator, and secondly Concerning the Vestments.*

The use of special garments in the ceremonies of Magic follows reasonably enough from the religious character ascribed to these operations. Peter de Abano recommends a priest's garment if possible, by which an alb may be understood.[2] "The Book of Black Magic," following the "Key of Solomon," and representing the Jewish rite, prescribes an outer vestment like that of the Levites, with the

[1] These Psalms are numbered 13 and 26 in the Vulgate. They were possibly selected on account of the symbolism attaching to these numbers. Thirteen refers to death and resurrection into new life; it thus connects with the regeneration typified by the bath. Twenty-six is the number of Jehovah. In the Authorized Version these Psalms appear as 14 and 27.

[2] A long garment of white linen, close before and behind, covering the whole body even to the feet, and cinctured by a girdle—such is the ordinance of pseudo-Agrippa.

following characters embroidered in red silk upon the breast:—

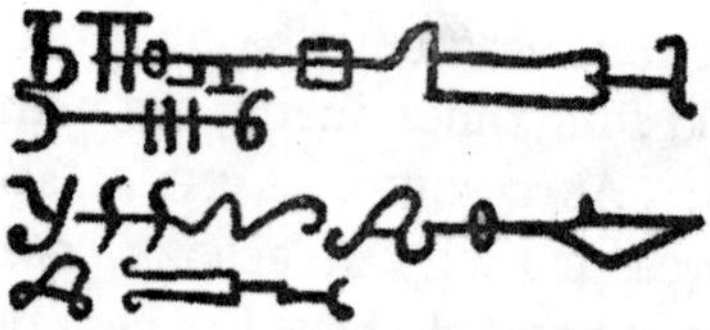

All garments, even to the shirt, must be of linen cloth,[1] and when assuming them these words should be recited: ANTON, AMATOR, EMITES, THEODONIEL, PONCOR, PAGOR, ANITOR[2]; by the virtue of these most holy Angelic Names do I clothe myself, O Lord, in my Sabbath garments, that so I may fulfil, even unto their term, all things which I desire to effect through Thee, Most Holy ADONAY, whose kingdom and rule endure for ever and ever. Amen.

The shoes and hat should be of white leather, bearing the same characters[3] written in cinnabar diluted with gum-water, the pen of the Art being used. The following names must be written about the hat:[4] JEHOVAH, behind; ADONAY, on the right hand; ELOY on the left; and GIBOR,[5] on the front.

[1] According to the "Key of Solomon" the thread of which they are made should be spun by a young maiden.

[2] The "Key of Solomon" renders these names differently, namely, Amor, Amator, Amides, Ideodaniach, Pamor, Plaior, Anitor, and for Sabbath garments substitutes Vestments of Power.

[3] Special characters are given for the garment and the shoes by the Clavicle. They bear no analogy to those of the Grimoire.

[4] For the hat or bonnet a crown is prescribed in the Clavicle, and it should be made of virgin paper.

[5] In place of these words the "Key of Solomon" substitutes El and Elohim.

CHAPTER II

The Initial Rites and Ceremonies

§ 1. *Concerning the Virtues of the Planets.*

THE "Key of Solomon the King" is the only Magical Ritual which regulates the operations of Magical Art in accordance with a formal attribution of certain hours in the day and night to the rule and influence of certain planets, and the Book of "True Black Magic" is the only Goetic Grimoire which follows the Clavicle closely in this as in other respects.[1] The directions given are, however, exceedingly confused. The common attribution of the seven days to the seven planets obtains in both cases, and is set out in the Grimoire as follows:[2]—

Soldey . .	= Saturn . .	= ♄ . .	= Saturday.
Zedex . .	= Jupiter . .	= ♃ . .	= Thursday.
Madime . .	= Mars . .	= ♂ . .	= Tuesday.
Zemen . .	= Sol . .	= ☉ . .	= Sunday.
Hogos . .	= Venus . .	= ♀ . .	= Friday.
Cocao . .	= Mercury . .	= ☿ . .	= Wednesday.
Zevenc . .	= Moon . .	= ☽ . .	= Monday.

But as there is inequality in the length of the days, says the Grimoire, that is to say, the comparative duration of day

[1] It should be observed, however, that favourable days and hours are occasionally mentioned, but there is no attempt at a systematic salutation of the times and seasons suitable to different operations.

[2] The apparently barbarous names given in the table are corruptions of Hebrew words, and the English editor of "The Key of Solomon" has restored their proper orthography, as follows:—Shabbathai, Tzedek, Madim, Shemesh, Nogah, Cochab, Lebanah.

and night varies in accordance with the times of sunrise and sunset, so also the hours of the planets are unequal. When the day is, say, fifteen hours, to ascertain how many minutes compose an hour of the planet, multify the fifteen hours by five; the result is seventy-five, and as many minutes will form the hour of the planet of that day. The corresponding hours of the night are nine; these multiplied by five produce forty-five, and as many minutes will form the hour of the planet of the night. The same method may be followed through all seasons of the year.

But in any given day of twenty-four hours the number of minutes is 1440, as against 1530 in the above computation, and the method is therefore absurd.[1] The attribution accepted by all writers on Natural Magic, and corresponding with the angelical succession in Peter de Abano, will be found in the following:—

TABLE OF PLANETARY HOURS COMPUTED FROM MIDNIGHT TO MIDNIGHT

HOURS OF THE DAY

	Sunday.	Monday.	Tuesday.	Wednesday.	Thursday.	Friday.	Saturday.
1.	Sun	Moon	Mars	Merc.	Jup.	Venus	Sat.
2.	Venus	Sat.	Sun	Moon	Mars	Merc.	Jup.
3.	Merc.	Jup.	Venus	Sat.	Sun	Moon	Mars
4.	Moon	Mars	Merc.	Jup.	Venus	Sat.	Sun
5.	Sat.	Sun	Moon	Mars	Merc.	Jup.	Venus
6.	Jup.	Venus	Jup.	Sun	Moon	Mars	Merc.
7.	Mars	Merc.	Sat.	Venus	Sat.	Sun	Moon
8.	Sun	Moon	Mars	Merc.	Jup.	Venus	Sat.
9.	Venus	Sat.	Sun	Moon	Mars	Merc.	Jup.
10.	Merc.	Jup.	Venus	Sat.	Sun	Moon	Mars
11.	Moon	Mars	Merc.	Jup.	Venus	Sat.	Sun
12.	Sat.	Sun	Moon	Mars	Merc.	Jup.	Venus

[1] It offers no analogy with the system set forth in the Clavicle, nor can it be definitely traced to any magical authority within the knowledge of the writer.

HOURS OF THE NIGHT

1.	Jup.	Venus	Sat.	Sun	Moon	Mars	Merc.
2.	Mars	Merc.	Jup.	Venus	Sat.	Sun	Moon
3.	Sun	Moon	Mars	Merc.	Jup.	Venus	Sat.
4.	Venus	Sat.	Sun	Moon	Mars	Merc.	Jup.
5.	Merc.	Jup.	Venus	Sat.	Sun	Moon	Mars
6.	Moon	Mars	Merc.	Jup.	Venus	Sat.	Sun
7.	Sat.	Sun	Moon	Mars	Merc.	Jup.	Venus
8.	Jup.	Venus	Sat.	Sun	Moon	Mars	Merc.
9.	Mars	Merc.	Jup.	Venus	Sat.	Sun	Moon
10.	Sun	Moon	Mars	Merc.	Jup.	Venus	Sat.
11.	Venus	Sat.	Sun	Moon	Mars	Merc.	Jup.
12.	Merc.	Jup.	Venus	Sat.	Sun	Moon	Mars

It will be seen from this table that there is a recurring rule of the planets in unbroken succession through the whole week, after which the sequence recommences in the same order, each planet during the first and the eighth of the day hours and the third and the tenth of the night hours of the day referred to that planet. These constitute the planetary hours.

The "Book of Black Magic," still following and confusing the statements of the Clavicle,[1] lays down that the hours of Saturn, Mars, and Venus are good for communion with spirits; the hour of Saturn serves for invoking souls in hell, and to have news of those who have died naturally. The souls of those who have been slain should be invoked in the hour and also on the day of Mars. It adds that experiments made faithfully and with great diligence, observing all that is laid down, will be invariably verified, but to fail over the smallest part will void perfection in any.

The hours of Saturn and of Mars are also good for preparation on those days when they are in conjunction with the Moon, or indeed with one another.[2] In a contrary or

[1] In the version which follows, which condenses and summarises the original, there is an attempt to reduce them to order, and to make them consistent, if not intelligible.

[2] The "Key of Solomon" says that the hours of Saturn and of Mars, and also the days in which the Moon is in conjunction with these planets, are admirable for experiments of hatred, enmity, and discord.

quadrate aspect they are good for experiences of hatred, lawsuits, enmities, discords, and so forth. The hours of the Sun, Jupiter, and Venus, especially their planetary hour, are favourable both to ordinary and extraordinary experiments not included in those already mentioned. Those of the Moon are especially suited to the conjuration of spirits, works of necromancy, and the finding of stolen goods; but the luminary must be collocated and in a terrestrial sign—that is to say, (in conjunction) with Mercury for love, favours, and invisibility; for works of hatred and discord in a sign belonging to the fiery triplicity—Aries, Leo, Sagittarius; for extraordinary experiences in an aquatic sign—Cancer, Scorpio, or Pisces. Should, however, the observation of these rules seem over-difficult, do this only—see that the Moon waxing is in an equal number of degrees with the Sun; it is then very good for the performance of the above experiments. When the full Moon is in opposition to the Sun, it is excellent for warlike, riotous, and discordant experiments; in its last quarter it favours works which deal directly with operations of destruction and ruin. The best time for the experiences of death and invisibility is when the Moon is almost deprived of light.

When the Moon is in conjunction with the Sun nothing must be undertaken, because it is an unfortunate time and all things fail therein; but when in its crescent period, actuated with light, any experiences may be prepared and any writings and operations accomplished, especially for conversing with spirits. It must, however, be the day of Mercury and in the hour of that planet, the Moon being in an earthly or aërial sign, as above said, and in a pair number with the Sun.[1]

[1] The attribution in the original is throughout this portion not only erroneous, but seems to involve impossible positions. It has been corrected partially, in accordance with the Clavicle.

§ 2. *A General Instruction concerning the Instruments required for the Art.*

Most Goëtic rituals specify with considerable minuteness the instruments which are required for the operations, and in these respects, but with variations peculiar to themselves, and distinguishing them also from one another, they follow the authority of the "Key of Solomon." Peter de Abano tells us nothing concerning them, nor yet pseudo-Agrippa, with the one exception of the sword, which, following a physical analogy, seems to be universal in practical magic. In the Grimoires, however, though sometimes the first weapon to be mentioned, its position is comparatively insignificant, as the knife is a readier instrument, and, speaking generally, there is little in the literature to justify the complex modern elaborations of Eliphas Lévi and of Christian.

Among the necessary properties mentioned by the Book of "True Black Magic" are the sword, the staff, the rod, the lancet, the arctrave or hook, the bolline or sickle, the needle, the poiniard, a white-handled knife, and another knife with a black handle used to describe the circle. The most important to make is that called the bolline; it must be forged on the day and in the hour of Jupiter, taking a small piece of unused steel. Set it thrice in the fire and extinguish it in the blood of a mole mixed with the juice of the pimpernel.[1] Let this be done when the Moon is in her full light and course. On the same day and in the hour of Jupiter, fit a horn handle[2] to the steel, shaping it with a new sword forged

[1] Or, according to the "Key of Solomon," in the day and hour of Mercury, and substituting the blood of the magpie and the juice of the herb Mercury, the French *Foirole*, from which a so-called Elixir of Long Life was formerly made.

[2] The "Key of Solomon" substitutes white boxwood; it omits the planetary influence, leaving it to be inferred that it should be done in the hour that the steel is forged, which must also be sunrise.

thrice as above in the fire. When made and perfected, recite over it this

PRAYER OR CONJURATION.

I conjure Thee, O form of this instrument, by the authority of God the Father Almighty, by the virtue of Heaven and the stars, by the virtue of the Angels, by that of the elements, by that of stones and herbs, and in like manner by the virtue of snowstorms, thunder, and winds, that thou receive all power unto the performance of those things in trickery, falsehood, or deception, by the command of God, Creator of the ages and Emperor of the Angels. Amen.

The ensuing salutations must then be pronounced over the instrument: *Domine, Deus meus, in te speravi; Confitetor tibi, Domine, in toto corde meo: Quemadmodum desiderat cervus ad fontes aquarum,*[1] &c., adding the following words: DAMAHII, LUMECH, GADAL, PANCIA, VELOAS, MEOROD, LAMIDOCH, BALDACH, ANERETHON, MITATRON, most holy Angels, be ye warders of this instrument, because I shall make use of it for several necessary works.

Place it in a new wrapper of red silk, making suffumigation with odoriferous perfumes, as will be hereinafter set forth. Take care not to perfect the instrument otherwise than on the day of Venus, and in the hour thereof, when also the needle and other like instruments may be prepared.

Subsequently, on the day of Venus, the Moon being in the sign of Capricorn, or otherwise of the Virgin,[2] if the same be possible, thou shalt make the first knife, and steep

[1] Psalms vii., cx., and xli., according to the computation of the Vulgate.
[2] According to the "Key of Solomon," it should be on the day and in the hour of Mercury, when Mars is in Aries or Scorpio.

it in the blood of the mole[1] and the juice of the pimpernel. Let the Moon be in an acute time of course and light, the operation beginning in the first hour of Venus and ending at the ninth hour of the same day. Fit the knife with a handle of white wood cut at a single blow with a new sword or knife, and on this handle engrave the following characters:—

Fumigate as before, and with this knife do all things needful to the Art, the circle excepted. But if such a knife be too difficult to manufacture, procure one of the same form ready made; steep it in the blood and juice as above; fit thereto the same handle bearing the same characters, and upon the blade, proceeding from point to handle, write with a male goose-quill the words: AGLA, ON. Perfume as before, sprinkle with exorcised water, and place in the silken wrapper already mentioned.

That with the black handle, destined to describe the circle and intimidate the spirits, and for performing other similar things, must be made in every respect like the first, except as regards the day and hour, which should be those of Saturn. The steel should be extinguished in the blood of a cat[2] and the juice of hemlock, while the handle should be of sheep's horn. The poniard or stiletto and the lancet should be made after the same manner on the day and in the hour of Mercury, and the steel extinguished in the blood of a mole and the juice of the herb Mercury. They should

[1] Of a gosling, says the Clavicle.

[2] Of a black cat, says the Clavicle, and the weapon when finished should be wrapped in a cloth of black silk, which, however, contradicts Book ii. c. 20, of the same work.

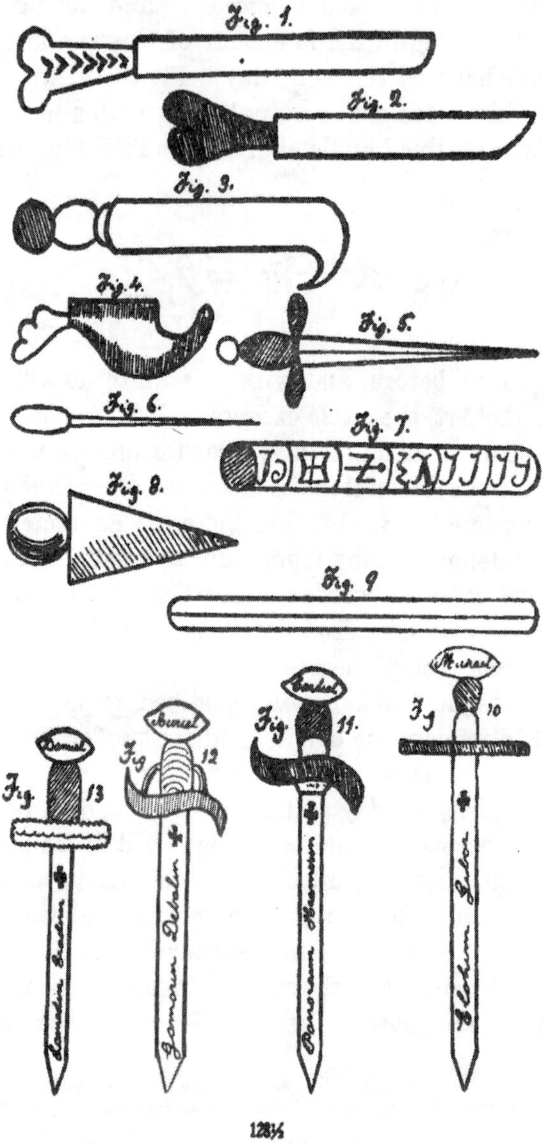
Fig. 1.
Fig. 2.
Fig. 3.
Fig. 4.
Fig. 5.
Fig. 6.
Fig. 7.
Fig. 8.
Fig. 9
Fig. 10
Fig. 11.
Fig. 12
Fig. 13

be fitted with horn handles,[1] shaped with a new sword in the day and hour of Mercury, and should bear these char-

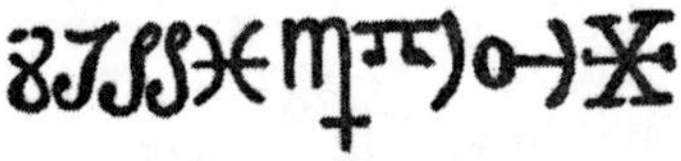

acters upon the said handles. Fumigate as before, and use in their proper place as required.

The *Grimorium Verum,* which makes for simplicity, reduces the steel instruments to three, namely, knife, graver, and lancet. The two first should be made on the day and in the hour of Jupiter, with the waxing Moon in the ascendant, which is at issue with the previous authority. When finished, the following Prayer or Conjuration must, in each case, be recited over them. The knife should be large enough to sever the neck of a kid at one blow; it should be fitted with a haft of wood, made on the same day and in the same hour, and graven with magic characters. The instrument should then be sprinkled, fumigated, and preserved for use as required.

CONJURATION.

I conjure thee, form of the instrument, N., by God the Father Almighty; by the virtue of Heaven and by all the stars which rule; by the virtue of the four elements; by that of all stones, all planets, and all animals whatsoever; by the virtue of hailstorms and winds; to herein receive such virtue that we may obtain by thee the perfect issue of all our desires, which also we seek to perform without evil, without deception, by God, the Creator of the Sun and the Angels. Amen.

[1] White boxwood is prescribed by the "Key of Solomon."

Recite the Seven [Penitential] Psalms, and add these words: DALMALEY, LAMECK, CADAT, PANCIA, VELOUS, MERROE, LAMIDECK, CALDULECH, ANERETON, MITRATON, most pure Angels, be ye guardians of these instruments, which are needful for many things.

The lancet, which is mentioned but not described in the Book of "True Black Magic," should, according to the *Grimorium Verum,* be made in the day and hour of Mercury, the Moon waxing, and conjured after the same manner as the knife and graver. Should assistants accompany the operator, each must be provided with his knife, and the like rule obtains concerning the Sword of the Art, which should be polished on the day of Mercury, from the first to the third hour of the night.[1] That designed for the Master or chief operator should bear the words ELOHIM JITOR,[2] proceeding from point to hilt. For that of the first disciple, write the name CARDIEL upon the handle, and upon the blade REGION, proceeding from point to hilt. It should appear on both sides transversely, but add on the one PANORAIM ✠, and on the other HEOMESIM ✠. On the sword of the second disciple write URIEL, SARAION, GAMERIN ✠, DEBALIIN, in the manner before described. On that of the third disciple write DANIEL, IMETON, LAMEDIIN ✠, ERADIN and fit the same with a handle of white bone.[3]

The following Conjuration must be recited secretly over the swords:—I conjure you, O sword, by the three Holy

[1] The first or the fifteenth hour is the reading of the "Key," but there is more reason in the longer period, having regard to the nature of the operation.

[2] *ie.,* Elohim Gibor. The "Key of Solomon" prescribes other Divine Names for the Sword of the Master.

[3] These instructions are terribly confused. Compare the English version of the "Key of Solomon," wherein the passage is thus restored:—"The first sword should have on the pommel the name Cardiel or Gabriel; on the Lamen of the Guard, Region; on the blade, Panoraim Heamesin. The second should have on the pommel the name Auriel; on the Lamen of the Guard, Sarion; on the Blade, Gamorin Debalin. The third sword should have on the pommel the name Daniel or Raphael; on the Lamen of the Guard, Yemeton; on the Blade, Lamedin Eradim."

Names, ALBROT, ABRACADABRA, JEOVA! Be thou my fortress and defence against all enemies, visible and invisible, in every magical work. By the Holy Name SADAY, which is great in power, and by these other names, CADOS, CADOS, CADOS, ADONAY, ELOY, ZENA, OTH, OCHIMANUEL, the First and the Last, Wisdom, Way, Life, Virtue, Chief, Mouth, Speech, Splendour, Light, Sun, Fountain, Glory, Mountain, Vine, Gate, Stone, Staff, Priest, Immortal, MESSIAH, Sword, do thou rule in all my affairs and prevail in those things which oppose me. Amen.

§ 3. *Concerning the Rod and Staff of the Art.*

The great mystery of practical magic is supposed to be centred in the Magic Rod, and Eliphas Lévi, who claims to have reconstructed the primitive ceremonial, but seems rather to have over-edited his materials, supplies a highly sensational account of its powers and an elaborate method of its preparation. For him it is the sign of the transmission of the magical priesthood, which has never ceased since the darksome origin of transcendent science. The operator is overwhelmed with precautions concerning the secrecy which must be maintained in regard to it, and dejected by the difficulties of its consecration. In view of such imputed importance it is curious that De Abano and pseudo-Agrippa omit all mention of this tremendous instrument, and the "Key of Solomon" dismisses it in a few lines of easy instruction. It would appear, however, that a staff and rod are both necessary, especially in Goëtic operations, though their distinctive provinces are in no case described. According to the Book of "True Black Magic," the staff should be of cane and the wand or rod of hazel, both virgin

—that is, having no branches or offshoots.[1] They must be cut and trimmed on the day and in the hour of the Sun, while the following characters must be inscribed upon the staff, but on the day and in the hour of Mercury:[2]—

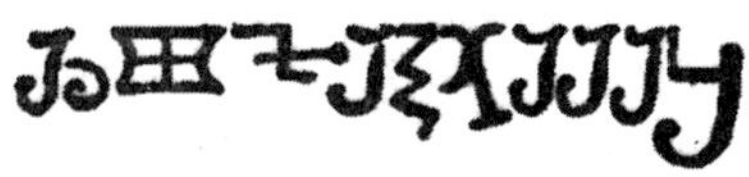

If engraved with the sacred instrument, it will be so much the better.[3] In either case, let the following words be recited when the writing is finished:—O ADONAY, most Holy and most Powerful, vouchsafe to consecrate and bless this Staff and this Rod, so that they may possess the required virtue, O most Holy ADONAY, to whom the honour and glory for ever and ever. Amen.

Lastly, the two instruments should be asperged, fumigated, and put away in the silken cloth.

The *Grimorium Verum* directs the operator to make two wands of wood which has never borne fruit. The first should be cut as a single stroke from an elder-tree on the day and in the hour of Mercury. The second should be of hazel, free from bud, and cut in the hour of the Sun.[4] The magic characters which should be engraved upon each have been omitted by the printer, but they are supplied in the modern Italian versions. They are, for the first, the seal or character of Frimost and that of Klippoth for the second (see Chap. III., Sec. 2). The prayer of consecration offers no variation of importance from that of "True Black Magic," and

[1] The definition of virgin wood differs in the "Key of Solomon," which says: In all cases the wood should be virgin—that is, of one year's growth only.

[2] According to the "Key of Solomon," both staff and rod should be cut on the day and in the hour of Mercury at sunrise, which limits the operation to the few days of the middle winter, when the sun rises about eight o'clock.

[3] Presumably, with the burin or graver.

[4] This variation appears to reconcile the "Book of True Black Magic" with the "Key of Solomon," and is probably the true reading.

does not need to be reproduced. Aspersion and fumigation are prescribed, as in the previous case.

The "Grand Grimoire" devotes an entire chapter to the true composition of the Mysterious Wand, otherwise the Destroying or Blasting Rod. It mentions no other instrument, and ascribes to it all power in diabolical evocations. It would seem to have supplied Eliphas Lévi with the first hint of his still more potent Verendum, to which, however, an allegorical significance may perhaps be attributed. On the eve of the great enterprise, says this Ritual, you must go in search of a wand or rod of wild hazel which has never borne fruit; its length should be nineteen and a half inches. When you have met with a wand of the required form, touch it not otherwise than with your eyes; let it stay till the next morning, which is the day of operation; then must you cut it absolutely at the moment when the sun rises; strip it of its leaves and lesser branches, if any there be, using the knife of the sacrifice stained with the blood of the victim.[1] Begin cutting it when the sun is first rising over this hemisphere, and pronounce the following words:—I beseech Thee, O Grand ADONAY, ELOIM, ARIEL, and JEHOVAM, to be propitious unto me, and to endow this Wand which I am cutting with the power and virtue of the rods of Jacob, of Moses, and of the mighty Joshua! I also beseech Thee, O Grand ADONAY, ELOIM, ARIEL, and JEHOVAM, to infuse into this Rod the whole strength of Samson, the righteous wrath of EMANUEL, and the thunders of mighty *Zariatnatmik*, who will avenge the crimes of men at the Day of Judgment! Amen.

Having pronounced these sublime and terrific words, and still keeping your eyes turned towards the region of the rising sun, you may finish cutting your rod, and may then carry

[1] See Chapter VI., Sec. 1.

it to your abode. You must next go in search of a piece of ordinary wood, fashion the two ends like those of the genuine rod, and take it to an ironsmith, who shall weld the steel blade of the sacrificial knife into two pointed caps, and affix them to the said ends. This done, you may again return home, and there, with your own hands, affix the steel caps to the joints of the genuine rod. Subsequently, you must obtain a piece of loadstone and magnetise the steel ends, pronouncing the following words:—By the grand ADONAY, ELOIM, ARIEL, and JEHOVAM, I bid thee join with and attract all substances which I desire, by the power of the sublime ADONAY, ELOIM, ARIEL, *and* JEHOVAM. I command thee, by the opposition of fire and water, to separate all substances as they were separated on the day of the world's creation. Amen.

Finally, you must rejoice in the honour and glory of the sublime Adonay, being convinced that you are in possession of a most priceless Treasure of the Light.[1]

§ 4. *Concerning the Pen and Ink of the Art.*

Preliminary magical ceremonial seems to have as its chief object the personal consecration of every article, great or small, indispensable or occasional, which is connected with the several processes. The pen and ink with which characters and names are written must both be specially prepared. Take a new quill, says the *Grimorium Verum;* asperge and fumigate it after the manner of the other in-

[1] Another method of preparing a Magic Rod ordains that it shall be a branch of the hazeltree put forth during the year of operation. It must be cut during the first Wednesday after the new moon, between 11 P.M. and midnight. The knife must be new and the branch severed by a downward stroke. The rod must then be blessed; at the stouter end must be written the word AGLA ✠, in the centre ON ✠, and towards the point TETRAGRAMMATON ✠. Lastly, say over it: *Conjuro te cito mihi obedire*—I conjure thee to obey me forthwith.

struments; when you hold it in your hand to shap it, say the following words:—ABABALOY, SAMOY, ESCAVOR, ADONAY: I have expelled all illusion from this pen, that it may retain efficaciously within it the virtue necessary for all things which are used in this Art, as well for operations as for characters and conjurations. Amen.

In like manner, a horn or ink-well must be bought on the day and in the hour of Mercury, and in the same hour the following names of God must be written about it:—JOD, HE, VAU, HE, METATRON, JOD,[1] CADOS,[2] ELOYM,[3] SABAOTH. It must then be filled with fresh ink which has been exorcised as follows:—

EXORCISM OF THE INK.

I exorcise thee, creature of Ink, by ANSTON, CERRETON, STIMULATOR,[4] ADONAY, and by the name of Him whose one Word created all and can achieve all, that so thou shalt assist me in my work, that my work may be accomplished by my will, and fulfilled with the permission of God, who ruleth in all things and through all things, everywhere and for ever. Amen.

BENEDICTION OF THE INK.

Lord God Almighty, who rulest all and reignest through all eternity, who dost fulfil great wonders in Thy creatures, grant unto us the grace of Thy Holy Spirit by means of this ink. Bless it ✠, sanctify it ✠, and confer upon it a peculiar virtue, so that whatsoever is said, whatsoever we desire to

[1] The "Key of Solomon" substitutes the Divine Name, Jah, thrice repeated.
[2] *i.e.*, Kadosch.
[3] *i.e.*, Elohim.
[4] The "Key of Solomon" reads Anaireton, Simulator.

do and to write herewith may succeed through Thee, Most Holy Prince Adonay. Amen.[1]

Then asperge, fumigate, and exorcise.

"The Book of True Black Magic," on the other hand, directs the operator to pluck the third feather from the right wing of a male goose,[2] and to say when extracting it: Abrachay, Abatoy, Samatoy, Scaver, Adonay! expel all evil from this feather, so that it may possess full power to write whatsoever I will.

Then shape it with the Knife of the Art, namely, that having a white handle; incense also and asperge it. Lastly, take a new earthen cornicle or inkhorn, made on the day and in the hour of Venus, and write about it these names with the exorcised lancet of the Art: Jod, He, Vau, He, Mitatron, Jae,[3] Jae, Jae, Cados, Eloyn, Zevao.[4] Then dip the pen therein, pronouncing the following words:—I exorcise thee, creature of the feather kind, by Etereton,[5] by Stimulation,[5] and by the name Adonay. Do thou aid me in all my works.

The instruction continues:—As it is sometimes necessary to write with coloured inks, have several horns containing white inks, in which infuse thy colours for the pentacles and characters. The colours must be diluted with the blessed water which we term exorcised, and with gum arabic. Lastly, perfume them. Let this be done with all devotion, humility, and faith, wanting which nothing can be accomplished, says the Grimoire.

[1] This prayer, like many others in the Grimoires which derive from the Clavicle, is the introduction of a Christian compiler. The "Key of Solomon" has no Trinitarian references and no crosses.

[2] This process is identical with that of the Clavicle, the names only being mutilated.

[3] *i.e.*, Jah.

[4] *i.e.*, Elohim Tzabaoth.

[5] As before, Anaireton and Simulator.

The same work gives particulars concerning the extraction of the sword-feather from the right wing of a swallow, preceding the action with the words *Sin re.* It should then be made into a pen by means of the Knife of the Art, and the name Anereton must be written on it with the goose-quill, after which the Psalms *Ecce quam bonum et quam jucundum* and *Laudate Dominum omnes gentes*[1] are to be recited over it, followed by aspersion and fumigation.

It is not to be supposed that any ordinary ink could be suitable for so serious a business as that of engrossing pacts. Even the consecrations previously given are inadequate in such a case. It is understood that the signature is written with the blood of the operator, but the form itself requires a special preparation, as follows:—Place river-water in a new, varnished earthenware pot, together with the powder hereinafter described. Then take sprigs of fern gathered on the Eve of St. John, and vine twigs cut in the full moon of March. Kindle this wood by means of virgin paper, and when the water boils the ink will be made. It must be changed each time that there is occasion to write, that is to say, whensover the appellation of a spirit is undertaken.

Powder for Pact-Ink.

Gall-nuts	10 oz.
Roman Vitriol or Green Copperas .	3 oz.
Rock Alum or Gum Arabic . .	3 oz.

Make an impalpable powder, and when you would compose the ink, use as above described.

The authorities for this process—which seems in itself sufficiently harmless—are not the Grimoires proper, but the collections of Magical Secrets which are sometimes appended to them, and sometimes form independent works.

[1] Psalms cxxxii. and cxvi. of the Vulgate.

§ 5. *Concerning Virgin Wax or Virgin Earth.*[1]

The candles used in evocation or in other magical experiences, and the images required for bewitchment, must be composed of virgin wax or virgin earth. That is to say, the substances in question must not have been applied previously to another purpose.[2] Before operating the following words must be recited over the material:—ENTABOR, NATABOR, *Si tacibor,* ADONAY, AN, LAYAMON, TINARMES, EOS PHILODES.[3] Angels of God, be ye present! I invoke you in my work, that I may obtain virtue by your mediation, and may be perfected very surely. Then recite the Psalms *Domine non est exaltatum cor meum* and *Dominus quis habitabit,*[4] adding these words: I exorcise thee, creature of wax [or earth], and, by the Creator and God Almighty, who created all things from nothing by His Most Holy Name, and by His angels, I ordain thee to receive virtue and benediction in His Name, that so thou mayst be sanctified and blessed, thus obtaining that virtue which we desire, by the Most Holy Name Adonay, which is the life of all creatures, Amen. Asperge the substance with the holy water of the Art, after which preserve it to make use thereof when needed. So doing, says "True Black Magic," thou shalt obtain a true result in all which thou undertakest.[5]

[1] This process is adapted from the "Key of Solomon," Book ii. c. 8.

[2] The virginity of the wax and the earth is more perfectly ensured by the directions of the "Key of Solomon," in accordance with which the operator must dig up the earth with his own hands, and reduce it to a paste, using no instrument in case of defilement. The wax must be taken from bees who have made it for the first time.

[3] These names differ from those in the "Key of Solomon," which, however, are, for the most part, equally unintelligible.

[4] Ps. cxxx. and Ps. xiv. in the Vulgate.

[5] The "Key of Solomon" directs that the earth should be freshly dug up on each occasion that it is required.

§ 6. *Concerning the Silken Cloth.*[1]

When all the instruments belonging to the Art have been properly consecrated and exorcised, they must be gathered into a costly cloth of silk, as Solomon ordains, whereby they may be preserved clean and pure, and may thus be more efficacious. So it be not black or brown, the colour is indifferent, but the following characters must be written upon it in pigeon's blood with the male goose-quill proper to the Art.

Add these names: ADONAY, AMMASTIUS, ANARETON, COSBOS, ELOYM. Then fumigate and asperge, saying subsequently the Psalms *Domine, Dominus noster, Deus Judicium tuum Regi da,* and *Ecce nunc dimittis.*[2] Place, lastly, all the magical instruments in this silken cloth. "So shalt thou use them at will, and shalt learn their effect," says the Magus, Iroë-Grego.

§ 7. *Concerning the Victim of the Art.*

It is usually supposed that the offering of a bloody sacrifice is an essential condition of success in Black Magic, and that the embrutement of the operator is the chief purpose of the ordination. It is true that such an offering is in most cases enjoined, but its object is simple and commonplace rather than diabolical or recondite, and the practice itself

[1] The process is adapted from the "Key of Solomon," Book ii. c. 20. There, however, the use of blood is omitted.

[2] Psalm viii. and Psalm lxxi. in the Vulgate, together with the Canticle of Simeon.

is based on the so-called White Magic of the "Key of Solomon." The Art has its victim, not because blood is required in the one case more than the other, but because it was customary for pacts and pentacles to be written on parchment or vellum, and, in view of that doctrine of personal consecration already explained, the Black Magician had, as far as possible, to dispense with outside labour, to be his own whitesmith, his own penmaker, and hence also his own tanner. *Alterius non sit qui suus esse potest* was the maxim of Paracelsus, and it was carried further in Goëtia than mere intellectual independence. Make yourself what you want; do not trust it to others; it will not only possess more of your personal virtue, but you will be sure of the article—such might be the commentary of the Grimoires upon the aphorism of the sage of Hohenheim, and there is the more reason in the counsel because even the accessible substances required by the operator had usually some awkward conditions attached to them, which might remain unfulfilled unless he himself was actively present in their preparation. A particular case in point is the parchment used in the Art. The magician was required to slay a lamb or kid with his own hands, not because there was any symbolical importance attached to the act of destruction—the Grimoires make no such ascription—not because the blood was used—for its use is seldom prescribed—but to insure that the animal was one from which virgin parchment or virgin vellum could be prepared.

That is called virgin, says the "Book of True Black Magic," which is made from animals that have never engendered, males above all,[1]—from which definition it is obvious that recourse to the professional tanner might jeopardise the

[1] The "Key of Solomon," Bk. ii. c. 17, distinguishes between virgin parchment and unborn parchment; the latter is obtained from an animal which has been taken before its time from the womb of its mother.

entire injunction. But seeing that every operation undertaken in the Art assumed a religious aspect, the slaughter of the animal became a sacrifice,[1] and had its accompanying ceremonies, prayers and invocations, each ritual possessing its own variants.

The preparation of the virgin parchment is given as follows in the *Grimorium Verum*:[2]—

CONCERNING THE VICTIM OF THE ART.[3]

Take your kid; place it on a block with the throat turned upward, so that it may be easier for you to cut it; be ready with your knife, and cut the throat at a single stroke, pronouncing the name of the Spirit whom you wish to invoke. For example, say: I slay thee, N., in the name and to the honour of N. Have a care that two blows be not needed, but let it die at the first; then skin it with the knife, and while skinning it make the following

INVOCATION.

ADONAY, DALMAY, LAUDAY, TETRAGRAMMATON, ANERETON,[4] and all ye holy angels of God, be ye here and deign to impart virtue unto this skin, that it may be properly conserved, and that all things there written may attain their perfection.

[1] It is fair to state that there is a form of evocation given in the *Vocabulaire Infernal* in which a sacrifice *per se* is prescribed. The source from which it is derived is not cited. "Whosoever would evoke the devil must sacrifice to him a dog, a cat, and a hen; these animals must be the property of the operator, who must also pledge himself to eternal fidelity and obedience, and must receive a special mark upon his body impressed by the devil himself. His recompense is an absolute control over three infernal spirts, respectively of earth, water, and air." Some obscure demonologist is most likely the authority for this process, which is unknown to the Grimoires. It should be added that the *Vocabulaire Infernal* was compiled in the Catholic interest.

[2] This preparation being one of the most important preliminaries of Goëtic Art, will be given with all its variations as they are found in the four chief Grimoires. For the sacrificial portions of the "Grand Grimoire" and that of Honorius, see Chapters VI. and VII.

[3] The process in the *Grimorium Verum* is an adaptation of that in the "Key of Solomon."

[4] The English edition of the Clavicle reads, Zohar, Zio, Talmai, Adonai, Shaddai, Tetragrammaton.

After the skinning take salt well pounded; stretch the skin; strew your salt upon it so as to cover the whole surface. But first let the salt be blessed in the following manner:—

Exorcism of the Salt.

I exorcise thee, creature of salt, by the living God, by the God of gods and the Lord of lords, that all illusions may depart from thee, and that so thou mayst serve to make the virgin chart.

Benediction of the Salt.

God of gods and Lord of lords, who hast created all things out of nothing, and hast specially designed salt for human health, bless ✠ and sanctify this salt, and may I so use it that all things which are in this circle may receive the required virtue for that effect which we desire. Amen.

This ended, place your salted skin in the rays of the sun for the space of one day. Then prepare a vessel of glazed clay, and write the characters of Guland and Surgat (Chap. III. Sec. 2) about it with the pen and ink of the Art. Set quicklime slaked with exorcised water in the pot, and while it is liquid place your skin therein, and so leave it till it peels of itself. When the hair is ready to fall at the touch of a finger, take it from the pot and peel it with a knife of hazel-wood, over which you have pronounced these words: Most Holy Adonay, be pleased to impart such virtue unto this wood that I may cleanse this skin therewith, through Thy Holy Name Agason. Amen.

This done, and the skin being also cleansed, stretch the same upon a board of new wood, and round about it set stones of the same length as the sides of the skin. But first say over them the prayer which here follows:—

PRAYER.

O ADONAY, most strong and powerful God, grant that these stones may stretch this skin, and do Thou remove from them all illusion, so that by Thy power they may possess the virtue which we desire. Amen.

This done, the skin may be left to dry, but before quitting it recite the following

PRAYER.

JE, AGLA, JOD, HEU, HE, EMMANUEL, be ye guardians of this parchment or skin, so that no phantoms may possess it.

This finished, leave it in the air until it be dried,[1] taking care that the place is clean, and has been asperged while reciting the following holy words: In the name of the immortal God, may God asperge thee and cleanse thee from all delusion and from all wickedness; so shalt thou be whiter than snow. Amen.

When the skin is dry, take it from the board, bless it with aspersion and fumigation, and preserve it for use. It must not be seen by women, especially in their times, for it will lose its virtue, and whosoever makes this parchment must be, in like manner, most pure and clean and chaste. Let him say a Mass of the Nativity, whether it be the day of the Feast or another day, and note that all the instruments must be generally on the Altar.[2]

"The Book of True Black Magic" reproduces with further variations the process of the genuine Clavicle:—Se-

[1] Which should be in the space of three days, according to the Clavicle.

[2] The *Grimorium Verum* exhibits the transition of the Rituals from the purely Jewish elements of the "Key of Solomon" to the purely Christian materials of the Grimoire of Honorius.

cure the animal which is to furnish the parchment in a secret place, where no one dwells or can behold it. Then take a virgin rod; shape it into the form of a knife with the white-handled Knife of the Art, paring it neatly of all branches. Over this say: I conjure thee, Rod, by the Creator of the Universe and the King of Angels, whose name is HELSADAY![1] Receive thou power and virtue to skin this animal for the making of the parchment, that so all things which I shall write thereon may prosper, by God Almighty, who liveth and reigneth for ever and ever. Amen. When shaping this knife recite the Psalm *Deus judicium tuum Regi da.*[2] Then write these words upon the Rod: Agla, Adonay, Eloe,[3] may the work of this wooden Knife be accomplished by you! Say also over it: Cara, cherna, sito, cirna.[4] Next, skin the animal with the same wooden knife, saying: ADONAY, DAHNAY, SADAY, TETRAGRAMMATON, ANERETON, ANERETON, CURETON,[5] Holy Angels of God, be ye present and give virtue to this parchment. May it be consecrated by you, and thus may all things which shall be written therein acquire the virtue needful for the attainment of the desired end. When you have skinned it, take salt, and say over it: God of gods, vouchsafe to bless and sanctify this salt, so that it may cleanse the parchment which I am about to prepare therewith, and that both may obtain virtue, power, and effect. Salt the skin, and set it in the sun for fifteen days; next take a pot of glazed clay, and write these characters

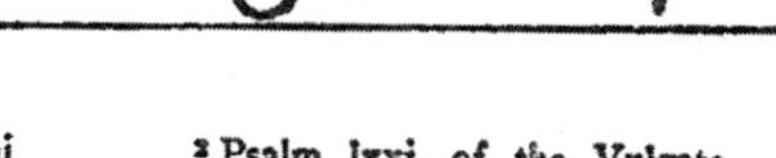

---

[1] *i.e.*, El Shaddai. [2] Psalm lxxi. of the Vulgate. [3] *i.e.*, Elohim.

[4] These words are peculiar to the Grimoire, and their significance is beyond conjecture.

[5] See Note on p. 141.

about it; place a large piece of quicklime with some blessed water in this vessel, and when the coal is extinguished steep the skin for the space of nine whole days therein, after which it must be extracted and scraped with a wooden knife to remove the hair. Let it dry for eight days in the shade, and when setting it to dry, asperge it and say: In the Name of the Great Eternal God, I asperge thee. Be thou cleansed from all vice and iniquity! [When dry] perfume it with sweet-smelling herbs; wrap it in the silken cloth with the other instruments of the Art; and take notice that if it be seen by a woman in her times, it will lose all its virtue.

But if this kind of parchment be too difficult to prepare,[1] take virgin parchment of any animal, exorcise it as before, place lighted coal in a new glazed pot, mix good perfumes therewith, and hold your parchment above the vessel to receive them. Before all, however, write these characters about the pot[2] with

the intruments of the Art.

So long as the fumigation goes on, say: Angels of God, be my help, and by you be my work accomplished! When it is finished say: LAZAY, SALMAY, DALMAY, ANEPATON, CENDRION, ANITOR, ENCHEION,[3] Holy Angels of God, be ye present and give virtue to this parchment, so that it may in turn acquire that of all characters with which it shall be clothed, by the help of the pious and merciful God. Recite the Psalms *Deus judicium tuum Regi da* and *Laudate Dominum omnes gentes,* adding the following

[1] The shorter process is not so good, says the Clavicle.

[2] The "Key of Solomon" provides characters for the parchment but not for the pot. They are, moreover, entirely different.

[3] The "Key of Solomon" reads: Zazaii, Zalmaii, Dalmai, Adonai, Anaphaxeton, Cedrion, Cripon, Prion, Anaireton, Elion, Octinomon, Zevanion, Alazaion, Zideon, Agla, On, Yod He Vau He, Artor, Dinotor.

CONJURATION.

I conjure thee, creature of parchment, by all the names of God, that nothing which shall be written within thee may ever be blotted from truth.

Lastly, asperge it and place it in the silken cloth, as above.

The *Grimorium Verum* indulges the weak pupil by a further simplification, as follows:—If you are unable to prepare the parchment yourself, buy a new one and conjure it; asperge also and fumigate it three times. The sacrifice, with its delays and unpleasantness, is thus abrogated, and the operator can proceed at once to the practical mystery of the *Sanctum Regnum*. It would also appear that parchment or vellum proper may be dispensed with in favour of:—(*a.*) the skin of some other animal, which would, however, involve a like process; or (*b.*) the caul of a new-born child, which would, of course, possess the requisite virgin character, and was simply consecrated according to the following instructions, as found in "True Black Magic."[1]

When you have succeeded in obtaining the caul of a new-born child, perfume the same with sweet odours and sprinkle it, after which say the following Psalms: *Domine, exaudi orationem meam,* and *Domine, Deus meus, respice in me,* with the conjuration here following:—BOSMELETIC, JEYSMY, ETH, HODOMOS, BELUREOS. O Lord, who didst make all things in wisdom; who didst choose Abraham, Thy first believer, and his seed hath multiplied like the stars of heaven; who didst appear unto Moses, Thy servant, surrounded with flaming fire, and didst make known to him Thy

[1] The "Key of Solomon" merely observes that the cauls of newly-born children, duly consecrated, may be used instead of virgin parchment, and that paper, satin, or silk may also be employed in operations of less importance.

names, which are HEIE, ACER, HEIE,[1] that is to say, I am that I am; who didst also lead forth Thy people dry-shod over the Red Sea; who unto Moses, Thy servant, didst give the Law of Salvation on Mount Sinai; who unto Solomon didst impart wisdom above the measure of men; I humbly adore Thy majesty and beseech Thy mercy, praying Thee to consecrate this skin by Thy virtue, O Most Holy ADONAY, whose reign endureth for ever. Amen.

Asperge the caul with the blessed water of the Art, place it in the silken cloth, and when working the exorcisms, the requisitions made to the spirits must be written on this skin, which should be fumigated with stinking odours.

§ 8.—*Concerning Aspersion and Fumigation.*

In the preparation of the instruments, as already abundantly evident, and in the more important works which follow it, the ceremonies of aspersion and fumigation, that is, of purifying and consecrating, are frequently enjoined. Sprinkling is performed with the Aspergillus, which, according to the *Grimorium Verum,* should be composed of mint, marjory, and rosemary, bound about with a thread woven by a virgin girl. It should be made on the day and in the hour of Mercury, the moon waxing. The ewer, according to "True Black Magic," should be a pot of glazed earth,[2] filled with fresh spring water, in which some salt has been cast. The following Psalms should be recited over it:—*Domine, ne in furore tuo arguas me,* and *Domine, exaudi orationem meam,*[3] with the addition of this

[1] The mutilations of the Divine Names in the Grimoires are part of the distinguishing characteristics of these works, and hence they are preserved in the text. It will be unnecessary to inform the student that the words mentioned should read AHIH, ASHR, AHIH.

[2] The "Key of Solomon" offers choice between a vessel of brass, of lead varnished within and without, and of earth.

[3] Psalm vi. and Psalm xlii. in the Vulgate.

PRAYER.

O Thou most powerful Lord, my God, my rest, and my life! Do Thou help me, Most Holy Father! In thee I place my hope, who art the God of Abraham, God of Isaac, God of Jacob, God of the Angels and Archangels, God of the Prophets, and God the Creator of all things. In all humility, and with the invocation of Thy Holy Name, I pray that Thou wilt vouchsafe to bless this water, that in whatsoever place it shall be cast it may sanctify our bodies and our souls, through Thee, Most Holy ADONAY, whose reign is without end. Amen.

The Aspergillus recommended by this Ritual differs somewhat from the former, being of vervain, periwinkle, sage, mint, valerian, ash, and basil, taking care not to use hyssop,[1] but rosemary in place thereof. It should be fitted with a handle of virgin hazel, three palms in length, and bound as before. The following characters should be engraved on one side of the said handle:—

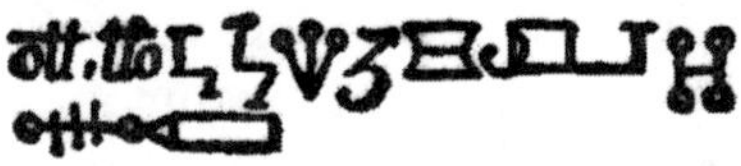

This Aspergillus may be used on all occasions with perfect assurance that all phantoms will be expelled from every place which shall be sprinkled thereby with water duly exorcised. The prayer to be used at sprinkling is thus given by the *Grimorium Verum*:—In the Name of God Immortal, may God asperge thee, N., and cleanse thee from all illusion and from all wickedness, and thou shalt be whiter than snow.

When asperging add also: In the Name of the Father ✠ and of the Son ✠ and of the Holy Ghost ✠. Amen.

[1] The plant here condemned is prescribed by the "Key of Solomon."

Concerning Incense and Fumigation.

The *Grimorium Verum* prescribes a cruse or chafing-dish for fumigation, adding somewhat redundantly that it should be filled with freshly kindled coal and fresh fire, the whole blazing. Place aromatics thereon, and perfume what you would, saying: Angels of God, be our help, and by you be our work fulfilled! ZAZAY, SALMAY, DALMAY, ANGERECTON, LEDRION, AMISOR, EUCHEY, OR! Great Angels! And do thou also, O ADONAY, be present and impart hereto such virtue that this creature may receive a form whereby our work may be accomplished! In the Name of the Father ✠ and of the Son ✠ and of the Holy Ghost ✠. Amen. Recite the Seven Psalms which follow *Judicium tuum Regi da* and *Laudate Dominum omnes gentes.*[1]

The perfumes are aloes wood and incense for most occasions, and mace for the fumigation of the circle. "The Book of True Black Magic" omits mace and substitutes benzoin and storax, and any others at choice, but without distinction as to the circle. The following Prayers, Exorcisms, and Benedictions to be said over the aromatic perfumes occur in the two Rituals, the first and third being common to both, and borrowed from the "Key of Solomon"; the second, also referable to the same source, is not found in the *Grimorium Verum*.

First Exorcism.

O God of Abraham ✠, God of Isaac ✠, and God of Jacob ✠, vouchsafe to bless and sanctify these creatures, of whatsoever species they may be, so that they may obtain

[1] As these Psalms, lxxi. and cxvi. in the Vulgate, are widely separated from each other, and so also in the Authorised Version, it is difficult to determine those which are referred to in the text.

virtue and power to discern good spirits from bad, even phantoms and enemies, through Thee O Adonay, who livest and reignest for ever and ever. Amen.

Second Exorcism.

I exorcise thee, O impure Spirit, who art the phantom of the Enemy. In the name of God Almighty, come out from this kind, with all thy falsehood and wickedness, so that it may become sanctified and exorcised, in the Name of God Almighty, that all virtues may inspire those who partake of this odour, that the Spirit of God may descend, and the virtue of the Lord manifest, in the burning of this species, and that no phantom may dare to accost it. Through the Ineffable Name of God Almighty. Amen.

Third Exorcism.

Deign, O Lord, to sanctify this creature, so that it may become a signal remedy for the human race, and the salvation of our souls and bodies, through the invocation of thy Most Holy Name, that so all creatures who inhale the smoke of this kind may have health of body and soul. Through that Lord who hast created the ages of ages. So be it.

This done, sprinkle the perfumes with exorcised water, and set them aside in the silken cloth for use as prescribed. When you would fumigate anything, take new coal which has not been kindled, set it alight, and while it is still black, exorcise it, saying:

Exorcism of the Lighted Coal.

I exorcise thee, O creature of Fire, by Him who hath made all things! Do thou expel from thee all phantoms, so that they may in no wise harm or trouble us in our work, by the invocation of the Most High Creator. Amen. O Saviour, Almighty and merciful, bless Thy creature of this kind, so that no harm may come to him who shall make use of it. Amen.

In concluding this portion of its ceremonial, "The Book of True Black Magic" states that there are occasions on which perfumes of a stinking or malodorous kind must be used; the same should be prepared, saying: ADONAY, LAZAY, DELMAY, AMAY, SADAY, ELOY,[1] by the invocation, O Saviour, of Thy Most Holy Name, vouchsafe us, through this kind, the help of Thy grace, and may it assist us in all things which we need to fulfil; may all malice pass out therefrom, and may it be blessed and sanctified in Thy most powerful Name. Amen.

Asperge the stinking perfume with exorcised water, place it in the silken cloth, and use it as needed, but always in the name of the Most Holy ADONAY. So doing, thou shalt obtain thy desire, says the "Manuscript discovered at Jerusalem in the Sepulchre of Solomon."[2]

§ 9. *Concerning the Time of Operation.*

When the sacrifice of the Art or its substitute has once been completed, the operator is in possession of all the materials he will require for the performance of the Goëtic works described in "The Book of Black Magic" or the *Grimorium Verum.* But as the first of these Rituals or-

[1] The names given in the "Key of Solomon" are Adonai, Lazai, Dalmai, Aima, Elohi.

[2] A short way to Magic by means of perfumes is given by Nyrauld in his work on Lycanthropy. To discern future events, fumigate yourself with linseed and seed of psellium, or with roots of violets and wild parsley. To drive away evil spirits and phantoms, make a perfume of calamon, peony, mint, and *palma Christi.* To attract serpents, burn the windpipe of a stag; to expel them, burn a horn of the same animal. Make a perfume with gall of cuttlefish, thyme, roses, and aloe wood. When kindled, sprinkle with water or blood, and presently the whole house will seem full of water or of blood, as the case may be. Add ploughed earth, and the ground will appear to tremble. The enumeration might be continued almost indefinitely.

dains that the preparation of the artist shall be made in accordance with certain planetary influences, so in like manner does it regulate the time of operation or accomplishment. As before, its instructions follow, and still in a confused manner, the authority of the Clavicle. It will be well to reproduce them here in a succinct analysis, though the piecemeal nature of the treatise attributed to Iroé-Grego leaves the rules without much practical value, and no attention is paid to them by other makers of Grimoires:—

An experiment of speaking with spirits or conjuring them should be operated in the day and hour of Mercury, which hour may be the first or the eighth, but the fifteenth or twenty-second of the same night will be still better, for spirits appear more easily in the silence of the dark hours. A certain atmospheric condition is also required for the experiment of calling spirits, and an obscure uninhabited place congruous to such an art is even more necessary, for so only will it be accomplished and educed. But if the experiment be concerned with a theft,[1] it should be performed in the hour of the Moon and on her day—if it be possible, in the crescent Moon—from the first to the eighth hour, or, failing this, at ten o'clock in the night. It is better, however, in the day, because the light has more correspondence to the intention, that is, to manifest hidden things. The experience of invisibility[2] should be operated when the Moon is in Pisces. Experiments of love, favour, and grace[3] should be accomplished on the day and in the hour of the Sun or Venus, from the first to the eighth hour, with the Moon in

[1] An experiment of this kind is reproduced by the Grimoire from the "Key of Solomon," but does not call for inclusion either by its connection with Black Magic—for there is no connection, or by any inherent interest—for there is again none.

[2] See Chapter VIII.

[3] See Venereal Experiments in Chapter VIII.

Pisces. Works of destruction, hatred, and desolation[1] should be performed on the day and in the hour of Saturn, from the first or eighth to the fifteenth or twenty-second hour of the night; they are then certain. Burlesque and amusing experiments are performed on the day of Venus, in the first and the eighth hour, or in the fifteenth and twenty-second hour of the night. Extraordinary experiences should be operated in corresponding hours on the day of Jupiter.[2]

[1] See Chapter VIII.

[2] The chapter on Extraordinary Experiments in the "Key of Solomon" is rendered useless by want of details. It reappears in the Grimoire, but is omitted from this translation for the reason indicated.

CHAPTER III.

Concerning the Descending Hierarchy

§ 1.—*The Names and Offices of Evil Spirits.*

IN all matters of ceremonial the inspiration of the Grimoires must be sought in the "Key of Solomon" proper, but for the names and offices of the demons it must be sought in the "Lesser Key." The hierarchy, according to the "Lemegeton," with its accompanying evoking processes, will be given in the fourth chapter, as there is no special reason for separating it from its practical context. We shall deal in this place with the simpler though later summaries, which will prevent these curious issues from being confused.

The Book of "True Black Magic," like its prototype the original Clavicle, gives no account of the nature of the Spirits with which it professes to deal, and, as already seen, it breaks off abruptly at the point where the conjuring formulæ should follow to complete the work. This "Secret of Secrets," as the Grimoires term the methods for raising and discharging spirits, being omitted, it may now be dismissed from consideration till we come to the minor processes of Ceremonial Magic, chiefly venereal and fantastic, which are grouped in the eighth chapter.

The "Grimoire of Honorius" mentions by name four kings referred to the cardinal points and seven lesser spirits to be invoked on the days of the week, but, as will appear later on, there is no explicit notice of the Descending

Hierarchy. These deficiencies are supplied by the *Grimorium Verum* and the "Grand Grimoire."

THE SEAL AND CHARACTERS OF LUCIFER.

THE SEAL AND CHARACTERS OF BEELZEBUTH

As regards spirits, says the former, some are superior and others inferior. The three superior are Lucifer, Beelzebuth, and Astaroth. According to the latter, Lucifer is Emperor; Beelzebuth, Prince; and Astaroth, Grand Duke. They must be invoked by means of the characters which they themselves have made known, and these characters must be written with the blood of the operator, or with that of a sea-tortoise. Failing this, they may be engraved on an emerald or ruby, for both these stones have great sympathy with spirits, especially with those of the solar race,

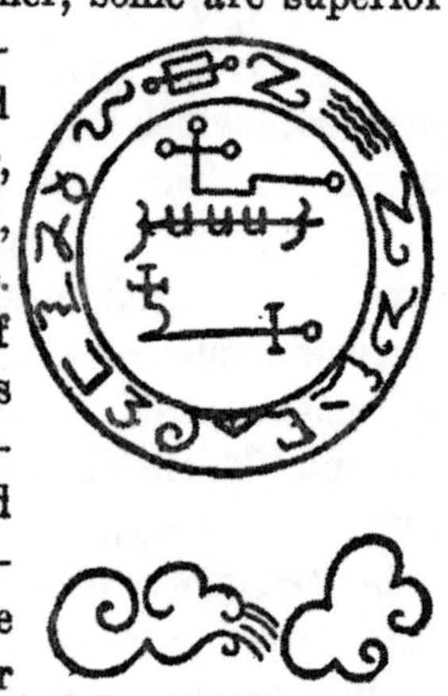

THE SEAL AND CHARACTERS OF ASTAROTH.

who are wiser, better, and more friendly than the rest.[1] The character must be worn upon the person; in the case of a male, it should be placed in the right pocket, but a female must carry it between the breasts, towards the left side, like a reliquary. It should be graven or written on the day and in the hour of Mars for both sexes, and apparently in the case of each of the three spirits.

The lord commands the servants, so the Grimoire proceeds, and these three spirits can do all things. But the operator is advised that he shall obey those who obey him, because the exalted and powerful spirits serve only their confidants and intimate friends. He is further grimly warned to keep upon his guard lest any spirit should seize him unawares. Each of the rules has two chief officers, who announce to the subjects all things which their lord hath commanded throughout the world, and ordain all that is to be done. The inferiors of Lucifer are Put Satanachia and Agaliarept; they inhabit Europe and Asia. Those of Beelzebuth are Tarchimache and Fleurety; they dwell in Africa. Those of Astaroth are Sargatanas and Nebiros, whose asylum is America.

The "Grand Grimoire" does not distribute the six subordinate spirits among the three rulers, but enumerates them somewhat differently, together with their dignities, as follows:[2]

---

[1] The attribution is somewhat confused; the ruby is a solar stone, but Albertus Parvus attributes the emerald to the Moon, which would establish its connection with evocation.

[2] The Hierarchy according to Wierus is at variance with both the Rituals, and may be worth quoting on account of its curious details:—

PRINCES AND GRAND DIGNITARIES.—*Beelsebuth*, Supreme Chief of the Infernal Empire, founder of the Order of the Fly. *Satan*, Leader of the Opposition. *Euronymous*, Prince of Death, Grand Cross of the Order of the Fly. *Moloch*, Prince of the Land of Tears, Grand Cross of the Order. *Pluto*, Prince of Fire. *Leonard*, Grand Master of Sabbaths, Knight of the Fly. *Baalberith*, Minister of treaties. *Proserpine*, Arch-she-devil, Sovereign Princes of Mischievous Spirits. MINISTERS.—*Adramelek*, Lord High Chancellor, Grand Cross of the Order of the Fly. *Astaroth*, Grand Treasurer. *Nergal*, Chief of the Secret Police. *Baal*, Commander-in-Chief of the Infernal Armies, Grand Cross of the Order of the Fly. AMBASSADORS.—*Belphegor*, in France, *Mammon* in England, *Belial* in Turkey,

Concerning the Descending Hierarchy

LUCIFUGE ROFOCALE.—Prime Minister.
SATANACHIA.—Commander-in-Chief.
AGALIAREPT.—Another Commander.
FLEURETY.—Lieutenant-General.
SARGATANAS.—Brigadier-Major.
NEBIROS.—Field-Marshal and Inspector-General.

It will be seen that the principalities of Infernus are chiefly represented in the light of a standing army, yet their interference in earthly matters is not of a military kind. LUCIFUGE ROFOCALE has the control, with which Lucifer has invested him, over all the wealth and treasures of the world. His subordinates are Baal,[1] Agares,[2] and Marbas.[3] The grand SATANACHIA has the power of subjecting all wives and maidens to his wishes, and of doing with them as he wills. His subordinates are Pruslas, Aamon,[4] and Barbatos.[5] AGALIAREPT has the faculty of discovering the arcane secrets in all the courts and council-chambers of the world; he also unveils the most sublime mysteries. He commands the Second Legion of Spirits, and his subordinates are Buer,[6] Gusoyn,[7] and Botis.[8] FLEURETY has the power to perform any labour during the night, and to cause hailstones in any required place. He controls a very con-

Rimmon in Russia, *Thamus* in Spain, *Hutgin* in Italy, *Martinet* in Switzerland. JUDGES.—*Lucifer*, Lord Chief Justice. *Alastor*, Commissioner of Public Works. ROYAL HOUSEHOLD.—*Verdelet*, Master of Ceremonies. *Succor Benoth*, Chief of the Eunuchs. *Chamos*, Lord High Chamberlain, Knight of the Fly. *Melchom*, Paymaster. *Misroch*, Grand Steward. *Behemoth*, Grand Cup-Bearer. *Dagon*, Grand Pantler, *Mullin*, First Gentleman of the Bedchamber. MASTERS OF THE REVELS.—*Kobal*, Stage Manager. *Asmodeus*, Superintendent of Casinos. *Nybbas*, Chief Mimic. *Antichrist*, Juggler and Mimic.

[1] Baal, is the first Spirit of the "Lemegeton," and a King ruling in the East.
[2] The second Spirit of the "Lemegeton."
[3] The fifth Spirit of the "Lemegeton."
[4] Possibly Paimon, ninth Spirit of the "Lemegeton."
[5] The eighth Spirit of the "Lemegeton."
[6] The tenth Spirit of the "Lemegeton."
[7] Eleventh Spirit of the "Lemegeton."
[8] The seventeenth Spirit of the "Lemegeton."

siderable army of spirits, and has Bathsin[1] (or Bathim), Pursan, and Eligor[2] as his subordinates. SARGATANAS has the power to make any person invisible, to transport them anywhere, to open all locks, to reveal whatsoever is taking place in private houses, and teach all the arts of the shepherds. He commands several Brigades of Spirits, and has Zoray, Valefar, and Faraii for his immediate inferiors. NEBIROS has the power to inflict evil on whomsoever he will; he discovers the Hand of Glory, and reveals every virtue of metals, minerals, vegetables, as also of all animals, both pure and impure. He possesses the art of predicting things to come, being one of the greatest Necromancers in all the Infernal Hierarchies; he goes to and fro everywhere and inspects all the hordes of perdition. His immediate subordinates are Ayperos, Naberrs, and Glassyalabolas.

It is added that there are millions of other spirits in subjection to those which have been mentioned, but their enumeration serves no purpose, as they are required only when it pleases the superiors to employ them in their own place, for the latter make use of all the inferior Intelligences like workmen or slaves.

The *Grimorium Verum,* however, mentions seventeen of the most important subordinate spirits, who seem to correpond with the ministers of the six great leaders mentioned above, but there is little unanimity among makers of magical rituals, whether white or black.

CHARACTER OF CLAUNECK.

CLAUNECK has power over goods and riches; he can discover hidden treasures to

[1] The eighteenth Spirit of the "Lemegeton."
[2] The fifteenth Spirit of the "Lemegeton."

him who makes pact with him; he can bestow great wealth, for he is well loved by Lucifer. He brings money from a distance. Obey him, and he will obey thee!

Musisin has power over great lords; he instructs them in all that passes in the Republics and those of the Allies.

CHARACTER OF MUSISIN.

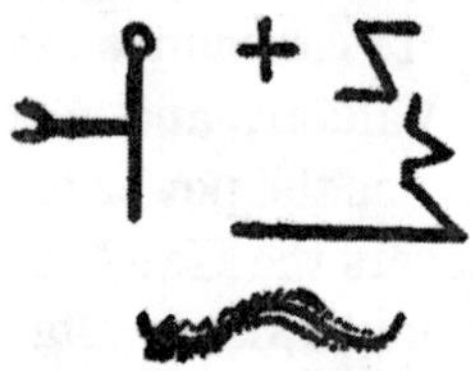

CHARACTER OF BECHARD.

Bechard has power over winds and tempests, over lightning, hail, and rain, by means of a charm with toads and other things of this nature, &c.

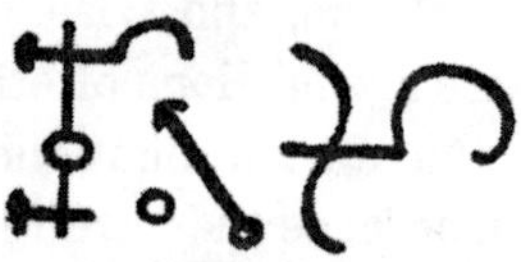

CHARACTER OF FRIMOST.

Frimost has power over wives and maids, and will help thee to enjoy them.

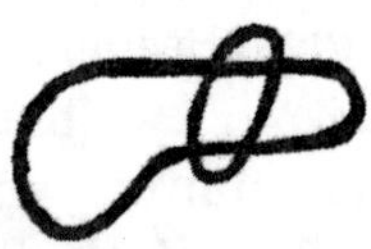

CHARACTER OF KHIL.

CHARACTER OF MERSILDE.

Khil occasions great earthquakes.

Mersilde can transport thee instantaneously wheresoever may be desired.

CLISTHERET makes day or night about thee at pleasure.

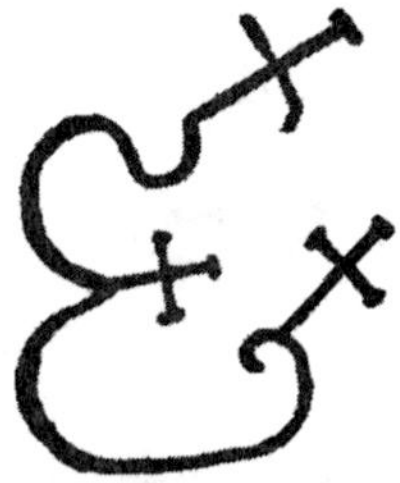

CHARACTER OF CLISTHERET.

SIRCHADE has power to show thee all kinds of animals, of whatsoever nature they may be.

CHARACTER OF SIRCHADE.

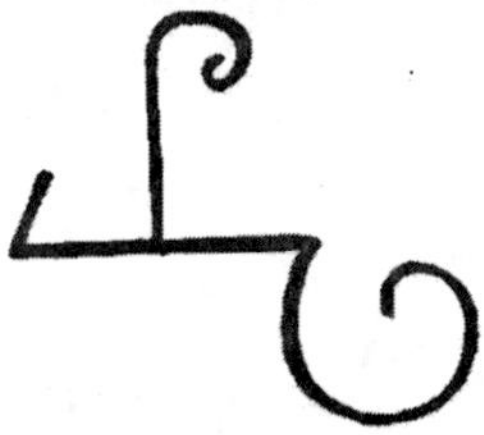

CHARACTER OF SEGAL.

SEGAL causes all manner of prodigies visibly, both natural and supernatural.

HIEPACTH will bring thee a distant person in an instant.

CHARACTER OF HIEPACTH.

CHARACTER OF HUMOTS.

HUMOTS can transport all manner of books for thy pleasure.

FRUCISSIERE brings the dead to life.

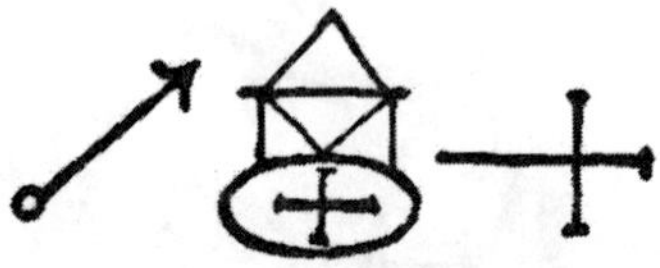

CHARACTER OF FRUCISSIERE.

GULAND can cause all varieties of disease

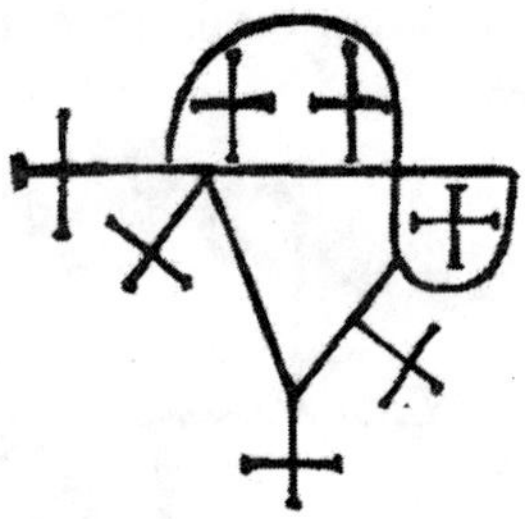

CHARACTER OF GULAND.

CHARACTER OF SURGAT.

SURGAT opens all locks.

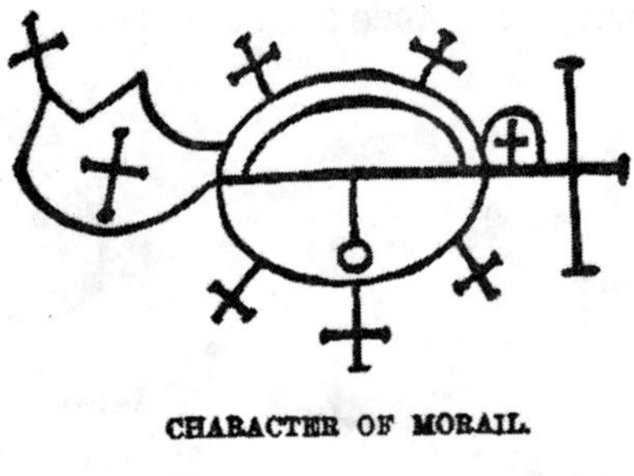

CHARACTER OF MORAIL.

MORAIL has the power to make everything in the world invisible.

FRUTIMIERE dights thee all kinds of festivals.

HUICTIIGARA occasions sleep and walking in some, and afflicts others with insomnia.

Satanachia and Satanicię govern forty-five, or , as some say fifty-four demons, four of whom are Sergutthy, Heramael Trimasel, and Sustugriel. Two of these rank as chief. The rest are of no great importance.

These are serviceable spirits, who act easily and quickly,

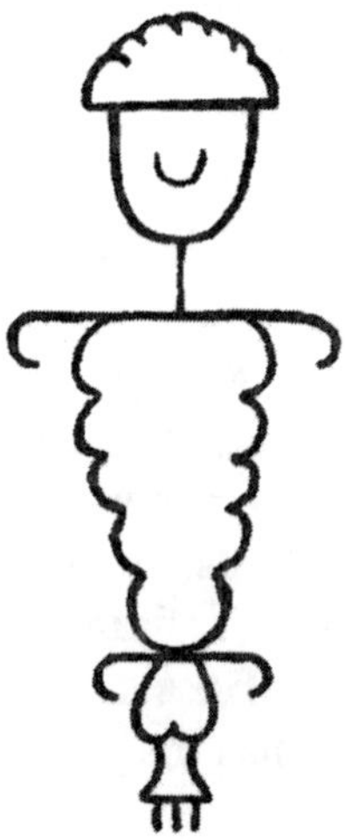

CHARACTER OF FRUTIMIERE.

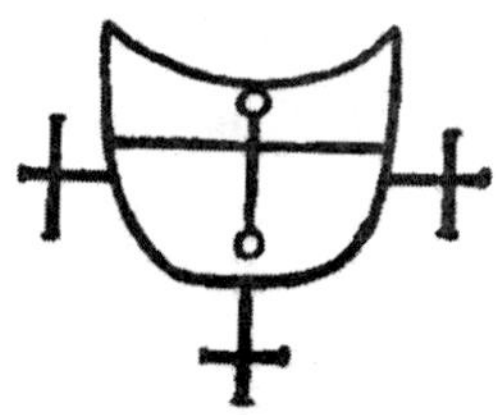

CHARACTER OF HUICTIIGARA.

provided that they are content with the operator. Serguthy has power over wives and virgins, when the occasion is favourable. Heramael teaches the art of medicine, gives perfect knowledge of all diseases, with their perfect and radical cure, makes known all plants in general, the places where they grow, and the times of their gathering, their virtues also and their composition for the attainment of a perfect cure. Trimasel, and Sustugriel. Two of these rank as chief. The parts the true secret for confecting the powder of projection which changes imperfect metals—lead, iron, pewter, copper, and quicksilver—into true good silver and good gold, namely, Sun and Moon, according to the ferment thereof. Only he must be satisfied with the operator, if the operator would be satisfied with him. Sustugriel teaches magical art; he gives familiar spirts for all things that can be desired, and furnishes mandragores.

Agalierept and Tarihimal govern Elelogap, whose power is over water. The two Nebirots rule Hael and Sergulath. Hael instructs in the art of writing all kinds of letters, gives an immediate power of speaking all kinds of tongues, and explains the most secret things. Sergulath furnishes all kinds of speculations, teaches tactics, and the breaking of hostile ranks. They have eight powerful inferiors. 1. Proculo, who gives sleep for twenty-four hours, with knowledge of the spheres of sleep. 2. Haristum, who gives the power of passing unsinged through the fire. 3. Brulefer, who makes one loved by women. 4. Pentagnony, who renders invisible and also beloved by great lords. 5. Aglasis, who transports through the whole world. 6. Sidragrosam, who makes girls dance stark naked. 7. Minoson, who insures winning in all games. 8. Bucon, who has the power to excite hatred and jealousy between the two sexes.

§ 2.—*Concerning the Forms of Infernal Spirits in their Manifestations.*

Having regard to the nature and antecedents of the intelligences with which Black Magic professes to be concerned, it must be highly important that the operator should know the kind of apparitions which may be expected, when, despite the incredulity of Horatio, the spirits from the vasty deep do respond to conjuration. The majority of the Grimoires leave it to be inferred from their silence that they come in human shape—possibly in "a neat surcoat and snow-white linen," like the Adonay of the sorcerer in the Thaumaturgic Experiences of Eliphas Lévi. With the Composite Rituals it is always a subject of apprehension, and a peaceable manifestation is earnestly bargained for.

According to the *Grimorium Verum,* the spirits do not invariably manifest under the same forms; being disengaged from all matter, they must of necessity borrow a body in order to appear before us,[1] and then they assume any form and figure which seems good to them. Beware, however, lest they affright thee! is another pregnant warning. Lucifer appears under the form and figure of a comely boy; when angered, he shows with a ruddy countenance, but there is nothing monstrous in his shape. Beelzebuth appears occasionally under monstrous forms, such as the figure of a misshapen calf, or that of a goat having a long tail; at the same time he manifests most frequently under the semblance of an enormous fly.[2] When angered, he vomits floods of water and howls like a wolf. Astaroth appears of a black and white colour, usually under a human figure, but occasionally in the likeness of an ass.

The subject of Infernal Manifestations is, however, fully treated in the next chapter. The indications in the present section are merely the later variants.

[1] A portion of this statement is derived from the "Key of Solomon"; but whereas it is put clearly in the Grimoire, it is incomplete and inconsequent in the original.
[2] A giant, a serpent, a woman, are also other modes of his manifestation, according to the discretion of certain demonologists.

CHAPTER IV.

The Mysteries of Goëtic Theurgy According to the Lesser Key of Solomon the King

§ I.—*Concerning the Spirits of the Brazen Vessel, otherwise called the False Monarchy of Demons.*

THE Goëtic Art of Solomon[1] gives instructions for the evocation of the seventy-two spirits whom the King of Israel, according to a well-known legend, shut up in a brass vessel and cast into a deep lake. When the vessel was discovered by the Babylonians, it was supposed to contain a great treasure, and was accordingly broken open. The spirits who were thus set at liberty, together with their legions, returned to their former places, Belial excepted, who entered into a certain image, and gave oracles to the people of the country in return for sacrifices and divine honours. Their names and offices are as follows:—

---

[1] Though a work of considerable length, this "Lesser Key," so far as it concerns our inquiry, admits of reduction into a manageable compass by the omission of tiresome and egregious particulars as to the number of spirits who are subject to a particular Lord, Prince, or Emperor, and are liable to appear in the company. It should be understood in a general way that there are hundreds and thousands and millions, according to the dignity of the hierarch, and they must have been a source of considerable inconvenience, and even of dismay, to the operator!

THE SEAL OF BAAL.

I. BAAL, a king ruling in the East who imparts invisibility and wisdom. He appears with a human head, or with that of a toad or cat,[1] but sometimes with all at once. He speaks with a hoarse voice.

II. AGARES, a duke ruling in the East, who appears in the form of a comely old man, ambling upon a crocodile and carrying a goshawk on his wrist. He makes those who run

THE SEAL OF AGARES.

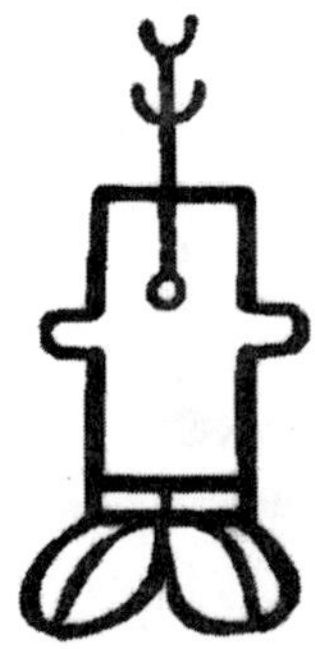

THE SEAL OF VASSAGO.

SEAL OF VASSAGO USED IN WHITE MAGIC.

stand still, brings back runaways, teaches all languages, destroys spiritual and temporal dignities, and causes earthquakes.[2] He is of the Order of the Virtues.[3]

III. VASSAGO, a mighty prince, of the nature of Agares,

[1] The cat is the traditional domestic favourite not only of those who diabolise, but of the diabolical world itself, which shows that after all there is a strong link with humanity in the cohorts of Lucifer. The reader will remember that the cat falls on its feet, not by natural good luck, but by the special dispensation of Mohammed, and that the favourite of the Prophet is in Paradise, no doubt on the best terms with the dog of the Seven Sleepers.

[2] According to the *Vocabulaire Infernal*, the special province of Agares is to put to flight the enemies of those whom he protects.

[3] That is to say, during the first estate of the Fallen Angels.

who declares things past, present, and future, and discovers what has been lost or hidden. He is good by nature.[1]

IV. Gamygyn, a great marquis, appearing in the form of a small horse or ass, but afterwards in human shape. He speaks hoarsely, teaching the liberal sciences, and giving news of souls who have died in sin.[2]

V. Marbas,[3] a president, who appears as a mighty lion, and then in human shape.[4] He answers truly concerning all

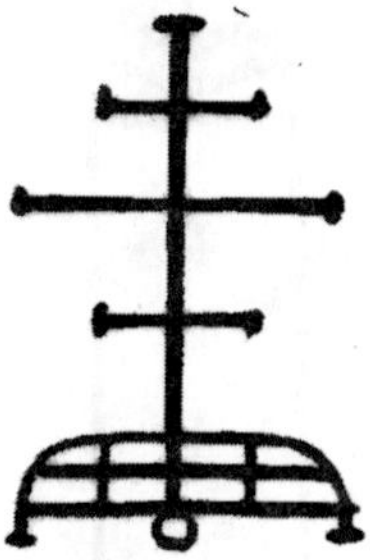

THE SEAL OF GAMYGYN.

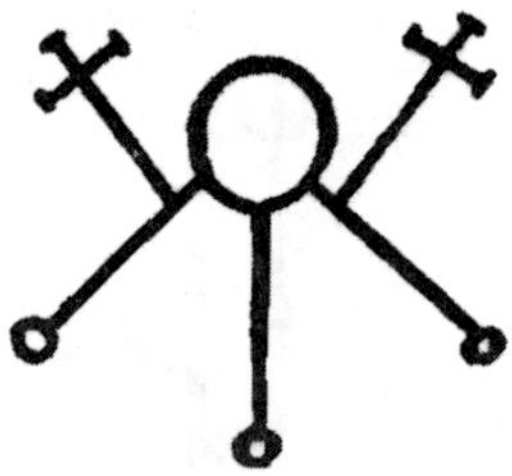

THE SEAL OF MARBAS.

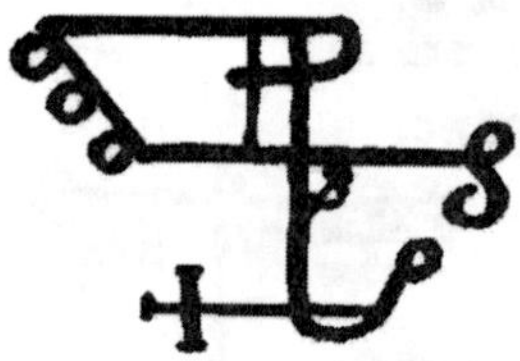

THE SEAL OF VALEFOR.

things hidden or secret, causes and cures diseases, imparts skill in mechanics, and changes men into various shapes.[5]

VI. Valefor,[6] a powerful duke, appearing as a many-headed lion.[7] He leads those with whom he is familiar into theft.

[1] This may account for his invocation, especially in Ceremonial Crystallomancy, by adepts of White Magic.

[2] According to Wierus, he summons into the presence of the exorcist the souls of drowned men, and of those detained in Purgatory, called magically Cartagra—that is, the affliction of souls. They assume an aërial body, are visible to sight, and reply to questions.

[3] Or Barbas.

[4] At the request of the operator (Wierus).

[5] He is the third spirit in the Hierarchy of Wierus.

[6] Or Malaphar.

[7] With the head of a hunter or a thief, says Wierus. He shows friendship to his familiars till they are caught in the trap.

VII. Amon, a strong and powerful marquis, who appears like a wolf with a serpent's head,[1] and vomiting flame. When so ordered, he assumes a human shape, but with the teeth of a dog. He discerns past and future, procures love, and reconciles friends and foes.

THE SEAL OF AMON.

VIII. Barbatos, a great count and duke, who appears when the sun is in Sagittarius with four noble kings and three companies of troops; he gives instruction in all the sciences, reveals treasures concealed by enchantment, knows the past and future, reconciles friends and those in power, and is of the Order of the Virtues.[2]

THE SEAL OF BARBATOS.

IX. Paimon, a great king, very obedient to Lucifer. He appears like a crowned man seated on a dromedary, preceded by all manner of musicians. He speaks with a roaring voice, teaches all arts, sciences, and secrets, gives and confirms dignities, makes men subject to the will of the Magician, provides good familiars. He is observed towards the north-west, and is of the Order of Dominions.[3]

THE SEAL OF PAIMON.

X. Buer,[4] a great president, who appears when the sun is in Sagittarius, and teaches philosophy, logic, the virtues

[1] *Cauda serpentis,* says Wierus.
[2] He also understands the songs of birds and the language of all other animals (Wierus).
[3] It appears from Wierus that the operator may fail to understand this spirit, in which case he must stretch forth the character belonging to him, and command him to speak clearly.
[4] The seventh spirit of the "Pseudo-Monarchia."

of herbs, &c., he heals all diseases and gives good familiars.

XI. GUSION,[1] a mighty duke, who appears like a cynocephalus, and discerns the past, present, and future, answers

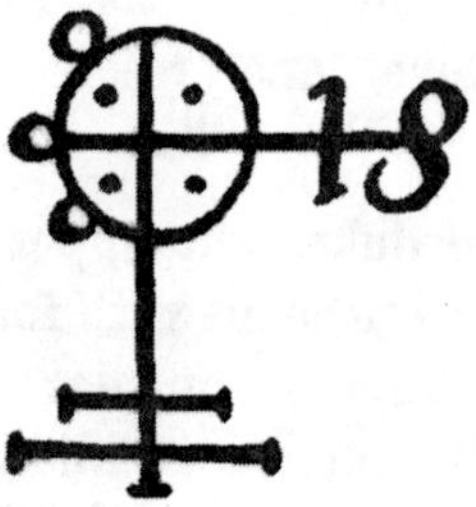

THE SEAL OF BUER.

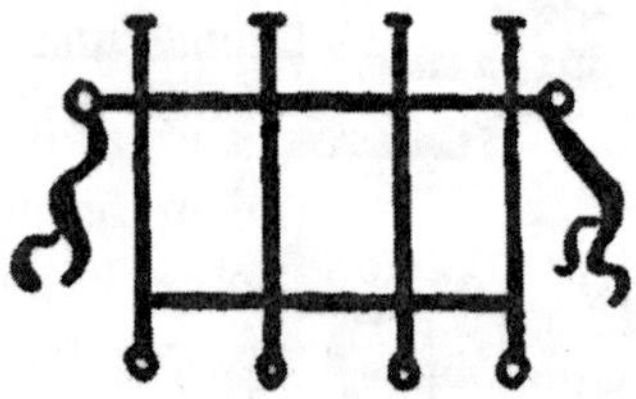

THE SEAL OF GUSION.

all questions, reconciles enemies, and gives honour and dignities.

XII. SYTRY, a great prince, who appears with a leopard's head, but assumes a human form at the Magician's command. He procures love between the two sexes, and causes women to show themselves naked.[2]

XIII. BELETH,[3] a terrible and mighty king, riding on a

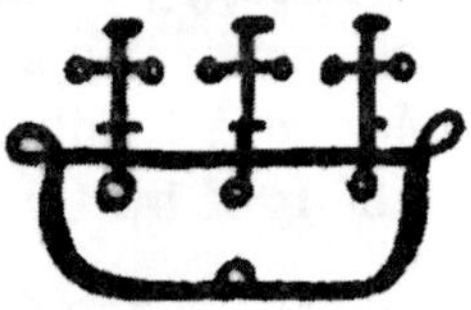

THE SEAL OF SYTRY.

THE SEAL OF BELETH.

pale horse, preceded by all manner of musicians. He is very furious when first summoned, and must be commanded into a triangle or circle with the hazel wand of the Magician

[1] Otherwise, Gusayn, the eighth spirit of Wierus.

[2] "Jussus secreta libenter detegit feminarum, eas ridens ludificansque ut se luxorise nudent."—*Wierus.*

[3] Otherwise, Byleth.

pointed to the south-east. He must be received courteously and with homage, but a silver ring must be worn on the middle finger of the left hand, which must be held against the face. He procures love between man and woman, and is of the Order of the Powers.[1]

XIV. Lerajie, a powerful marquis, coming in the like-

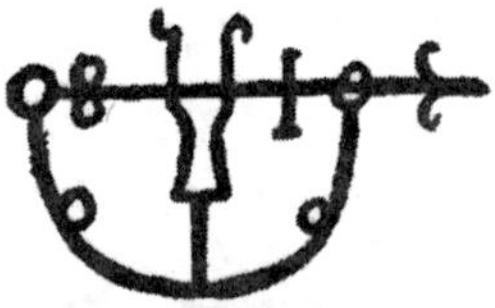

THE SEAL OF LERAJIE.

THE SEAL OF ELIGOR.

ness of an archer, clad in green, and bearing bow and quiver. He occasions battles and causes arrow-wounds to putrefy.

XV. Eligor, a great duke, appearing as a goodly knight carrying a lance, pennon, and sceptre. He discovers hidden things, causes war, marshals armies, kindles love and lust.

XVI. Zepar, a great duke, who appears in red apparel and armed like a soldier. He inflames women with love for

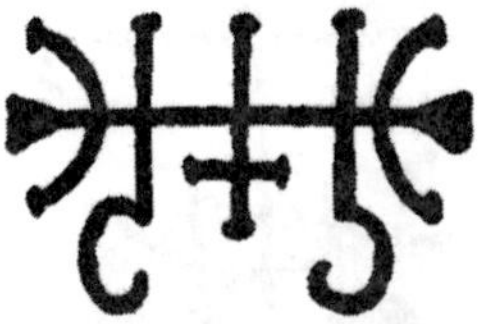

THE SEAL OF ZEPAR

THE SEAL OF BOTIS.

men, and can transform them into other shapes till they have been enjoyed by their lovers.[2]

XVII. Botis, a great president and earl, who appears

[1] He yet hopes to be restored to the Seventh Thrones.

[2] The last statement is on the authority of Wierus. According to another reading, Zepar makes women barren.

like a horrid viper, but, when commanded, assumes a human shape, with large teeth and horns. He bears a sharp sword in his hand, discerns past, present, and future, and reconciles friends and foes.

XVIII. BATHIN,[1] a mighty duke, who appears like a strong man with a serpent's tail, riding on a pale horse. He knows the virtues of herbs and precious stones, and can transport men swiftly from one country to another.

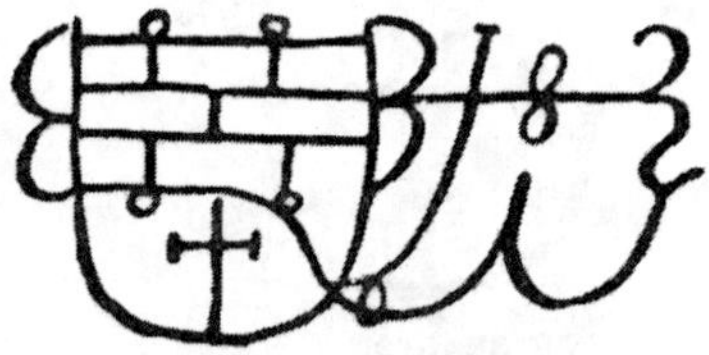

THE SEAL OF BATHIN.

XIX. SALEOS,[2] a great duke, who appears like a brave soldier, riding on a crocodile crowned. He promotes love between the sexes.

THE SEAL OF SALEOS.

XX. PURSON,[3] a great king, who appears like a lion-headed man, carrying a viper in his hand, and riding on a bear, preceded by many trumpeters. He conceals and discovers treasure, discerns past, present, and future, gives true answers concerning things human and divine, and provides good familiars.

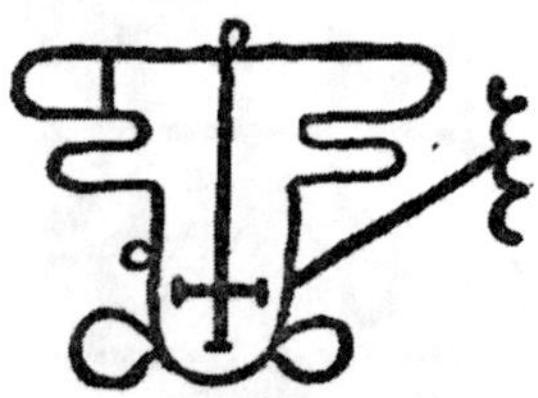

THE SEAL OF PURSON.

[1] Otherwise, Bathym or Marthim.
[2] Called also Zaleos.
[3] Otherwise, Curson.

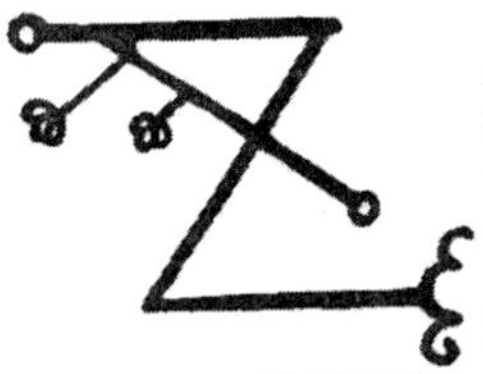

THE SEAL OF MORAX.

XXI. MORAX,[1] a great earl and president, who appears like a human-headed bull, and gives skill in astronomy and the liberal sciences, with good familiars. He knows the virtues of all herbs and precious stones.

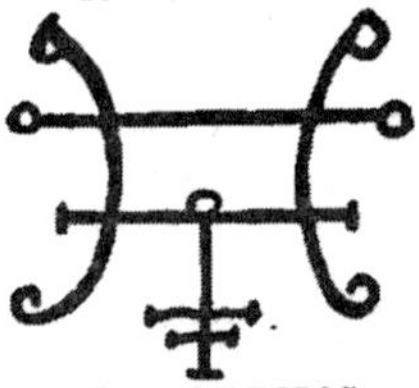

THE SEAL OF IPOS.

XXII. IPOS,[2] a mighty earl and prince, appearing as an angel with a lion's head,[3] the webbed feet of a goose, and a hare's tail. He knows the past and future, and imparts wit and courage.

XXIII. AINI,[4] a strong duke, who appears with the body of a handsome man and three heads, the first like a serpent, the second like a man with two stars on the forehead, and the third like a cat. He rides on a viper, and carries a blazing fire-brand, with which he spreads destruction. He imparts much cunning, and gives true answers concerning private matters.

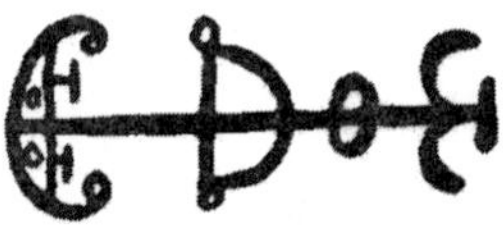

THE SEAL OF AINI.

XXIV. NABERIUS,[5] a valiant marquis, who appears in the form of a crowing cock and flutters about the circle. He speaks hoarsely, gives skill in arts and sciences, especially rhetoric, and restores lost dignities and honours.

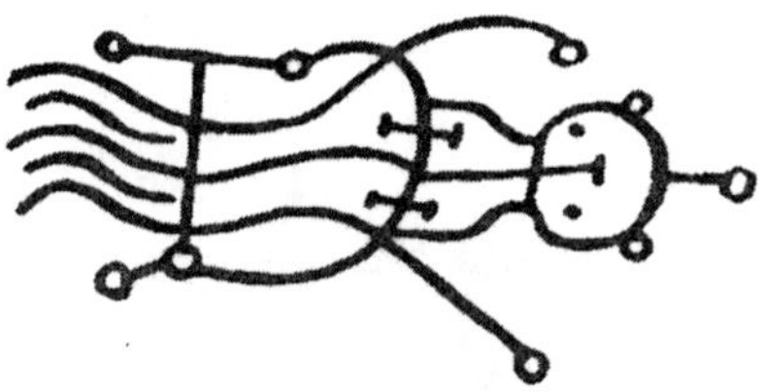

THE SEAL OF NABERIUS.

[1] This spirit is named Faraii by Wierus.
[2] Otherwise, Ipes and Aypeos.
[3] According to Wierus, sometimes in the form of an angel and sometimes in that of a crafty and evil lion.
[4] Called Aym or Halloryn by Wierus.
[5] *i.e.*, Cerberus.

XXV. Glasyalabolas,[1] a mighty president, who comes in the form of a dog, but winged like a griffin. He teaches all arts and sciences instantaneously, incites to bloodshed, is the leader of all homicides, discerns past and future, and makes men invisible.

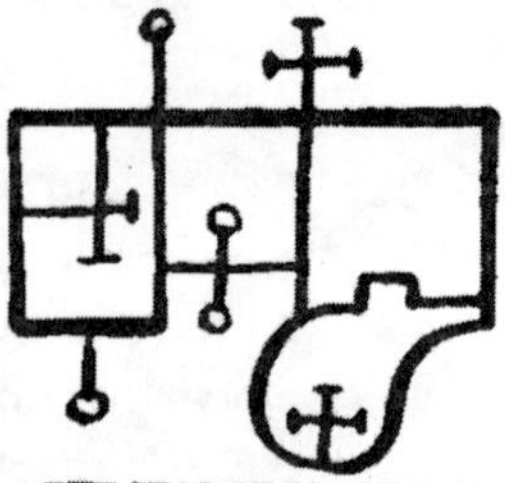

THE SEAL OF GLASYALABOLAS.

XXVI. Bune, a strong duke, who appears as a three-headed dragon, the heads being respectively those of a dog, griffin, and man. He has a pleasant voice; he changes the places of the dead, causes demons to crowd round sepulchres, gives riches, makes men wise and eloquent, answers questions truly.

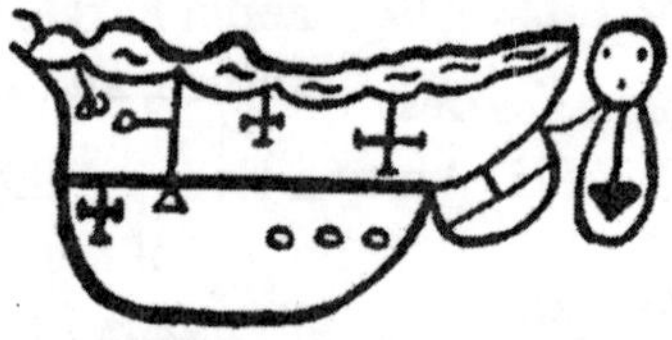

THE SEAL OF BUNE.

XXVII. Ronobe,[2] a great marquis and earl, appears in a monstrous form; he teaches rhetoric and the arts, gives a good understanding, the knowledge of tongues, and favour of friends and foes.

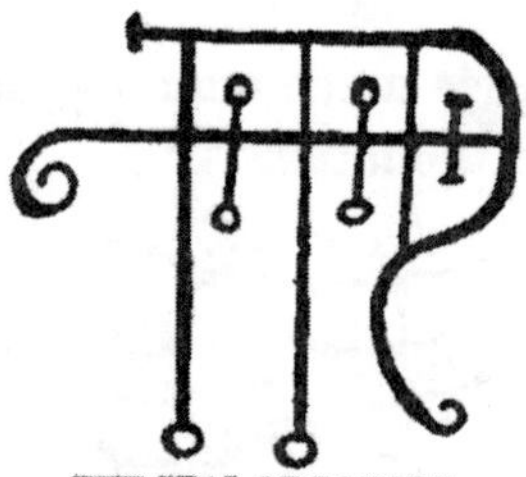

THE SEAL OF RONOBE.

XXVIII. Berith,[3] a terrible duke, appearing in the

[1] *Alias*, Caacrinolaas or Caassimola.
[2] Otherwise, Roneve.
[3] This spirit, says Wierus, is by some called Beal, but by the Jews Berith, and by necromancers Bofi.

form of a soldier in red apparel, with a golden crown, and bestriding a red horse. The ring used for Berith is required for his evocation. He gives true answers of things past, present, and to come, turns all metals into gold, gives and confirms dignities. He speaks in a clear and persuasive voice, but is a great liar, and his advice must not be trusted.

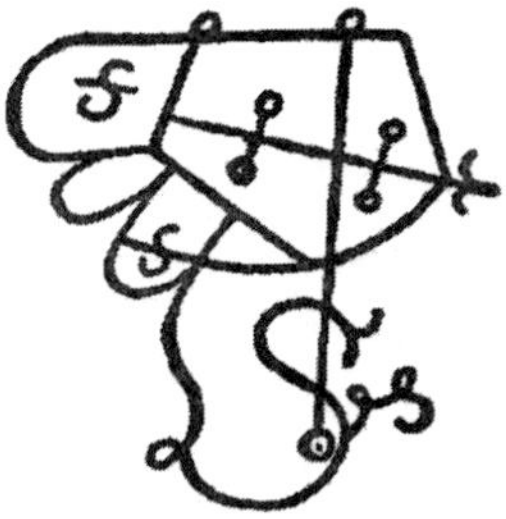

THE SEAL OF BERITH.

XXIX. ASTAROTH, a great and powerful duke, appears like a beautiful angel riding on an infernal dragon, and carrying a viper in his right hand. He must not be permitted to approach on account of his stinking breath, and the magician must defend his face with the magic ring. Astaroth answers truly concerning past, present, and future, discovers all secrets, and gives great skill in the liberal sciences. He will also discourse willingly concerning the fall of spirits.[1]

THE SEAL OF ASTAROTH.

XXX. FORNEUS, a great marquis, appears as a sea-monster. He teaches all arts and sciences, gives a good reputa-

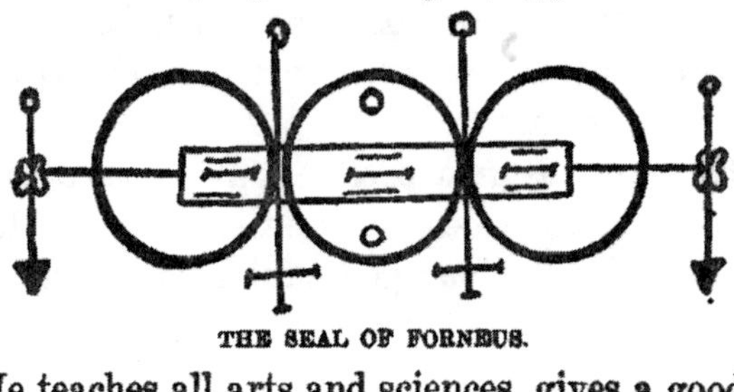

THE SEAL OF FORNEUS.

[1] But pretends that he himself was exempt from their lapse (Wierus).

tion and the knowledge of tongues, and causes men to be loved by their enemies even as by their friends.

XXXI. FORAS,[1] a great president, who appears in the form of a strong man, and teaches the virtues of all herbs and precious stones, as well as logic and ethics; he makes men invisible, imparts wit, wisdom, and eloquence, discovers treasures, and restores things lost.

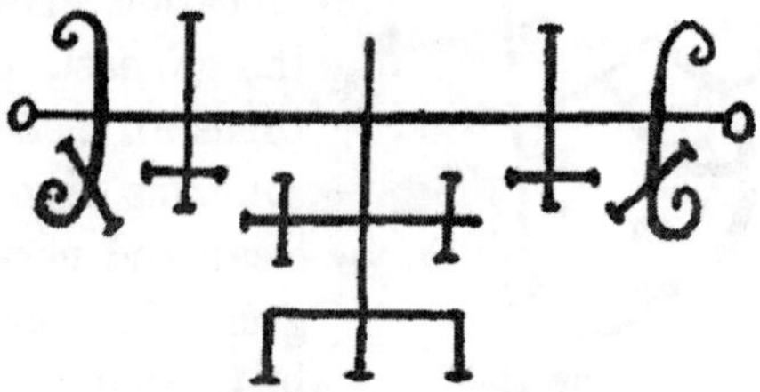

THE SEAL OF FORAS.

XXXII. ASMODAY,[2] a strong and powerful king, appears with three heads, the first like a bull, the second like a man, and the third like a ram. He has a serpent's tail, the webbed feet of a goose, and he vomits fire. He rides an infernal dragon, carries lance and pennon, and is the chief of the power of Amaymon. He must be invoked bareheaded,[3] for otherwise he will deceive. He gives the ring of virtues, teaches arithmetic, geomancy, and all handicrafts, answers all questions, makes men invisible, indicates the places of concealed treasures and guards them if within the dominion of Amaymon.

THE SEAL OF ASMODAY.

XXXIII. GAAP,[4] a great president and prince, appears when the sun is in the southern signs, coming in a human shape, and preceded by four powerful kings. He teaches

[1] Otherwise, Forcas.
[2] Called also Sydonay.
[3] And in a standing position (Wierus).
[4] *Alias*, Tap.

philosophy and the liberal sciences, excites love and hatred, makes men insensible, gives instruction in the consecration of those things which belong to the divination of Amaymon, his king, delivers familiars out of the custody of other Magicians, give true answers as to past, present, and future, transports and returns men speedily from place to place at the will of the exorcist.

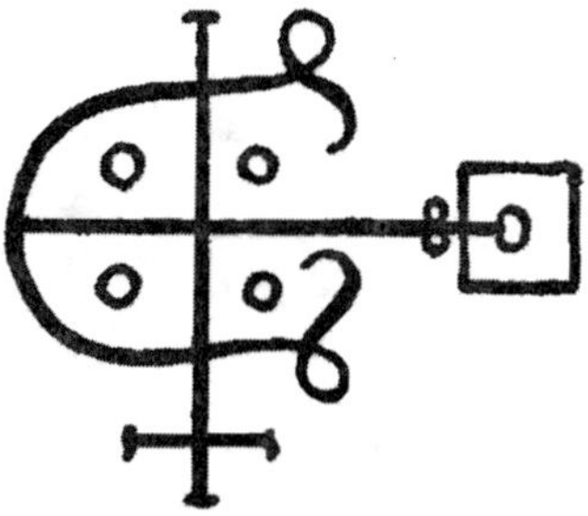
THE SEAL OF GAAP.

XXXIV. Furfur, a great earl, appears in the form of a hart with a fiery tail, and will not speak till compelled within the triangle.[1] He then assumes the form of an angel, speaking with a hoarse voice. He causes love between man and wife, raises thunder, lightning, and great winds, gives true answers about secret and divine things.

THE SEAL OF FURFUR.

XXXV. Marchosias, a mighty marquis, appears in the form of a wolf with the wings of a griffin, a serpent's tail, and fire issuing from his mouth. At the command of the operator he assumes a human form. He is strong in battle, gives true answers to all questions, and is ex-

THE SEAL OF MARCHOSIAS.

[1] According to Wierus, he will speak outside the triangle, but what he says will be false.

tremely faithful to the exorcist. He belongs to the Order of Dominations.[1]

XXXVI. SOLAS or STOLAS, a powerful prince, appears in the likeness of a raven and then as a man. He teaches the art of astronomy and the virtues of herbs and stones.

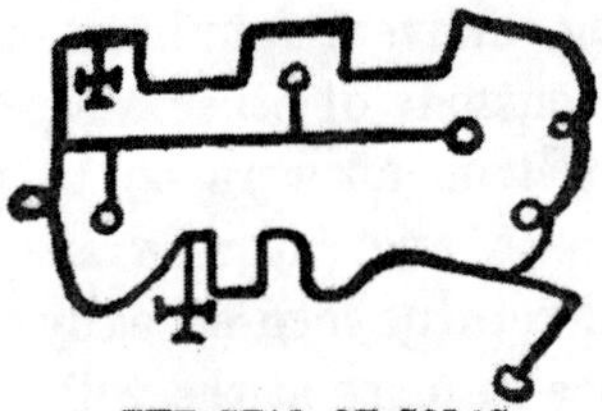

THE SEAL OF SOLAS.

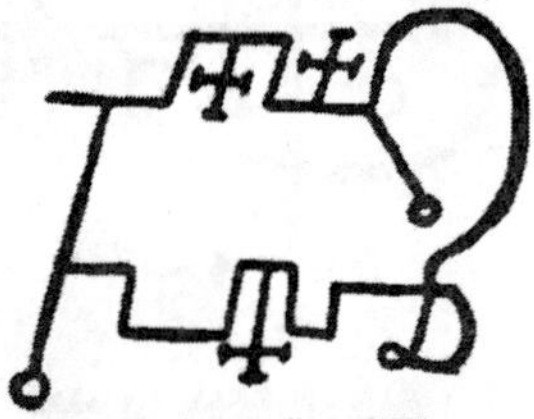

THE SEAL OF PHŒNIX.

XXXVII. PHOENIX, a great marquis, appears like the bird of that name, singing dulcet notes in a child's voice. When he assumes human shape at the will of the Magician, he speaks marvellously of all sciences, proves an excellent poet, and fulfils orders admirably. He hopes to return to the Seventh Thrones in 1200 years.

XXXVIII. HALPAS, a great earl, appears in the form of a stockdove, speaking wth a hoarse voice. He burns towns,[2]

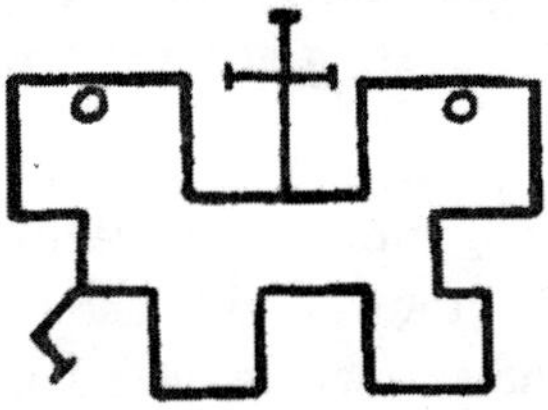

THE SEAL OF HALPAS.

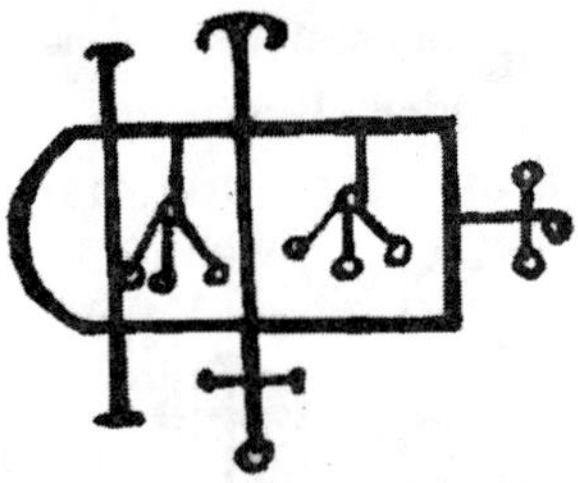

THE SEAL OF MALPAS.

visits the wicked with the sword, and can send men to fields of war or to other places.

XXXIX. MALPAS, a powerful president, appears at first

[1]And expects to return to the Seventh Thrones after 1200 years, but is deceived therein (Wierus).

[2]Or, according to Wierus, builds them and fills them with armed men.

like a crow, but afterwards, when so commanded, assumes a human form, speaking with a hoarse voice. He brings artificers swiftly from all parts of the world, destroys the desires and thoughts [1] of enemies, gives good familiars, and receives a sacrifice kindly, but will deceive him who offers it.

XL. RAUM,[2] a great earl, appears in the form of a crow, but assumes human shape when bidden. He steals treasure and carries it where commanded; he destroys cities and dignities; he discerns past, present, and future; he causes love between friends and foes. Finally, he is of the Order of the Thrones.

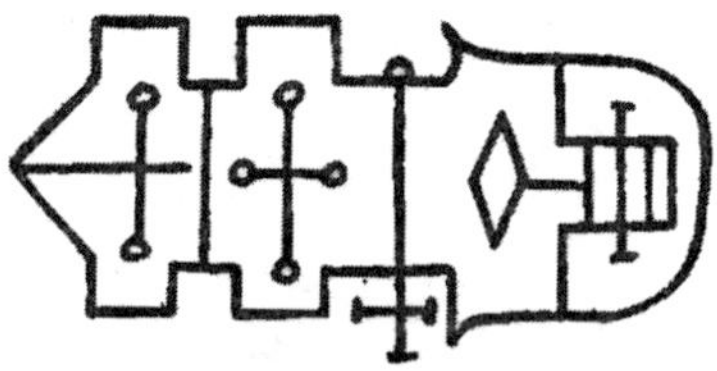

THE SEAL OF RAUM.

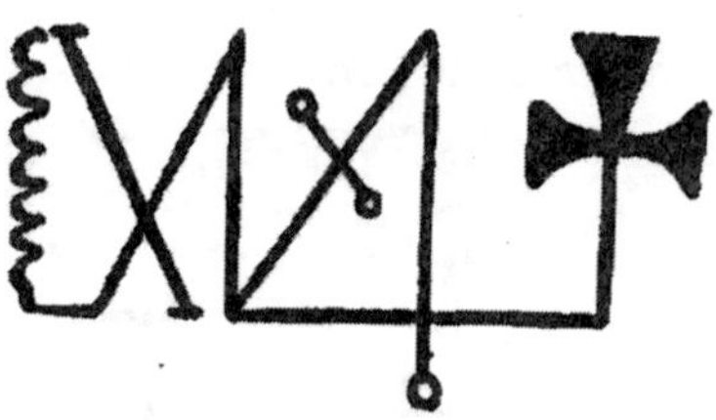

THE SEAL OF FOCALOR.

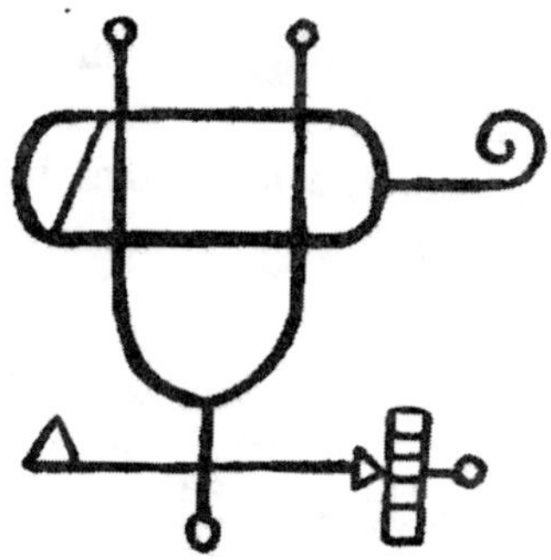

THE SEAL OF SABNACK.

XLI. FOCALOR, a strong duke, appears in the form of a man with the wings of a griffin. He drowns men, sinks warships, and has power over the winds and the sea, but he will hurt any one if commanded to forbear by the exorcist. He hopes to return to the Seventh Thrones in 1050 years.[3]

XLII. SABNACK,[4] a mighty marquis, appears in the form

[1] The reading of Wierus is preferable, *i.e.*, Temples and Towers.
[2] Or Raym.
[3] He is deceived, says Wierus.
[4] *Alias*, Saburac.

of an armed soldier, having a lion's head, and riding on a pale-coloured horse. He builds towers, camps, and cities, fortifies the same, torments men with wounds and putrid sores swarming with worms;[1] he gives good familiars.

XLIII. Vepar,[2] a great duke, appears as a mermaid. He guides the waters and battleships, and occasions storms at sea when so commanded by the Magician. He also causes the sea to seem full of ships, and occasions death in three days by means of putrefying sores and worm-eaten wounds.

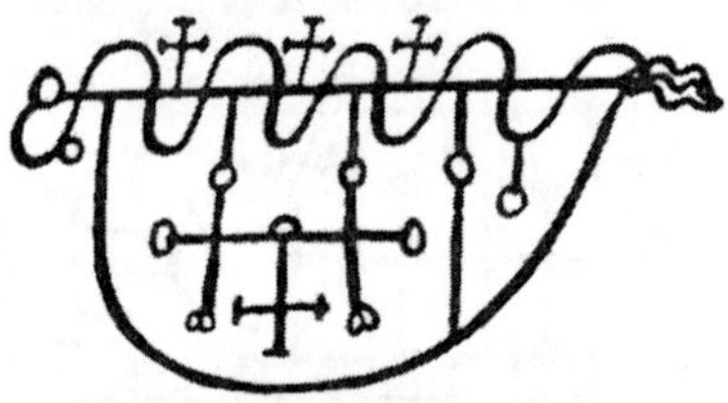

THE SEAL OF VEPAR.

XLIV. Shax,[3] a great marquis, comes in the form of a stockdove, speaking with a hoarse voice. He destroys the sight, hearing, and understanding of any man or woman at the will of the exorcist, steals money from the king's exchequer, and returns it in 1200 years. He will transport anything, but must first be commanded into the triangle; otherwise he will deceive the operator. He discovers all hidden things which are not in the keeping of wicked spirits, and gives good familiars.

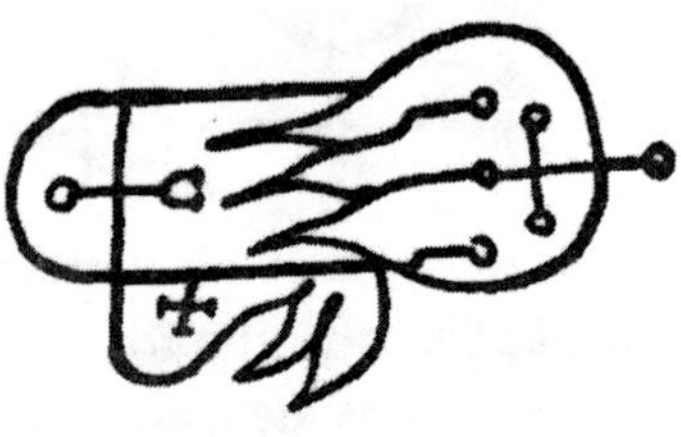

THE SEAL OF SHAX.

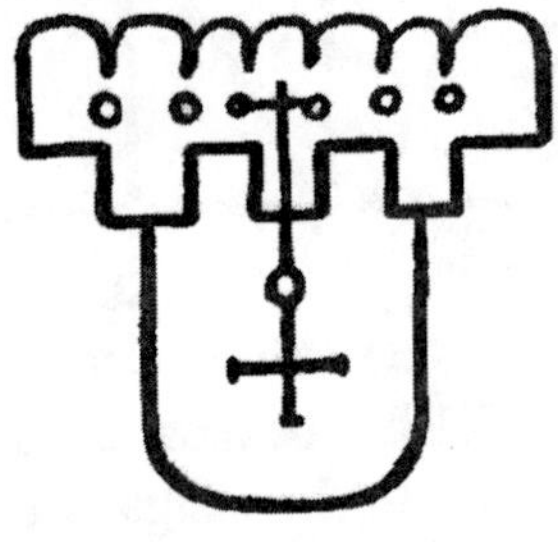

THE SEAL OF VINE.

XLV. Vine, a great king and earl, appears in a mon-

[1] At the command of the magician (Wierus).

[2] Otherwise, Separ.

[3] Also Chax or Scox.

strous form,[1] but assumes human shape when commanded. He discerns things hidden, reveals witches, and makes known the past, present, and future. At the command of the exorcist he will build towers, demolish walls, and make the waters stormy.

XLVI. Bifrons, a great earl, appears in a monstrous form, but assumes the human shape when commanded. He gives proficiency in astrology, geometry, and other mathematical arts; he teaches the virtues of herbs, precious stones, and woods; he changes dead bodies, puts them in other places, and lights phantom candles on their graves.

THE SEAL OF BIFRONS.

XLVII. Vual, a great duke, comes at first as an enormous dromedary, but afterwards assumes human form and speaks in the Egyptian tongue. He procures the love of women, discerns past, present, and future, and excites friendship even between foes. He was of the Order of the Powers.

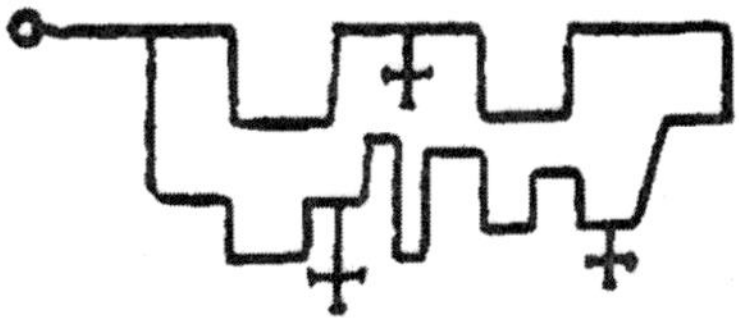

THE SEAL OF VUAL.

XLVIII. Hagenti, a great president, appears in the shape of a gigantic bull with the wings of a griffin, but will

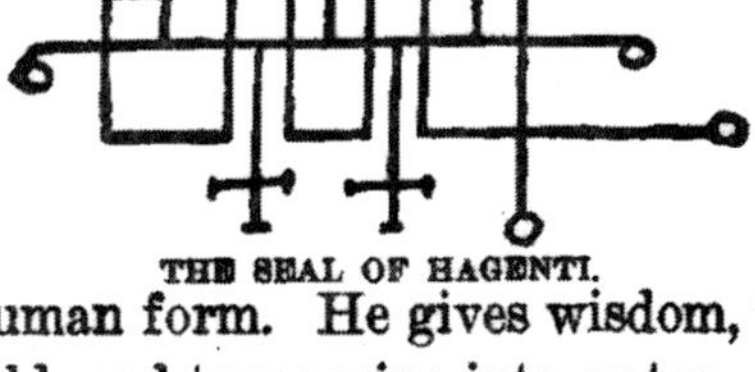

THE SEAL OF HAGENTI.

duly put on human form. He gives wisdom, transmutes all metals into gold, and turns wine into water.

[1] Or as a lion seated on a black horse and holding a viper in his hand.

XLIX. Procel[1] appears in the form of an angel, and is a great and strong duke. He speaks mystically of hidden things, teaches geometry and the liberal sciences, and at the command of the operator will make a great commotion like that of running waters; he also warms waters and tempers baths.[2] He was of the Order of the Powers before his fall.

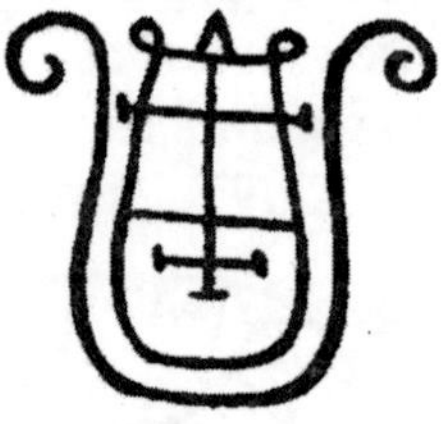

THE SEAL OF PROCEL.

L. Furcas, a great duke, appears in the form of a cruel old man, with long beard and hoary hair. He is seated on a pale horse, and has a sharp spear in his hand. He teaches philosophy, rhetoric, astronomy, logic, chiromancy, and pyromancy, perfectly in all their parts.

LI. Balam, a terrible and powerful king, appears with three heads, the first like that of a bull, the second like that

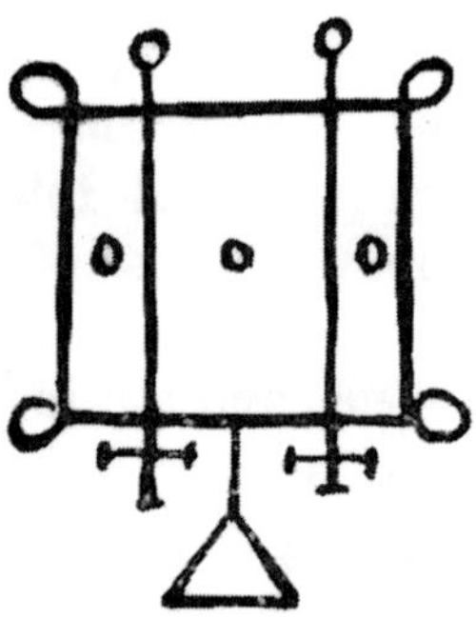

THE SEAL OF FURCAS.

THE SEAL OF BALAM.

of a man, and the third like a ram's. With the tail of a serpent and eyes flaming fire, he rides upon a furious bear, carrying a goshawk on his wrist, and speaking with a hoarse

[1] Otherwise, Pucel.
[2] *i.e.*, the thermal springs frequented by sick people.

voice. He gives true answers as to past, present, and future, makes men go invisible, and imparts wit.[1]

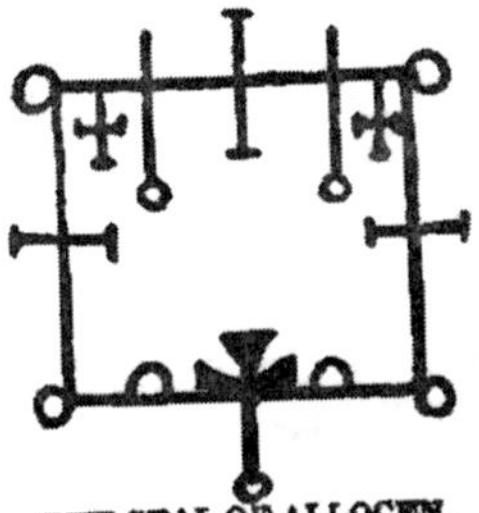

THE SEAL OF ALLOCEN.

LII. ALLOCEN,[2] a strong duke, appears in the form of a soldier, mounted on a great horse, his face like that of a lion, exceedingly red, his eyes flaming fire, his speech hoarse and loud. He teaches astronomy and the liberal sciences, and gives a good familiar.

LIII. CAIM, a great president, appears in the form of a thrush,[3] but afterwards in that of a man bearing a sharp sword, and seeming to answer in burning ashes. He is a keen disputant; he imparts to men the understanding of bird's songs, the lowing of cattle, the barking of dogs, and the voice of waters. He gives true answers concerning things to come, and was once of the Order of Angels.

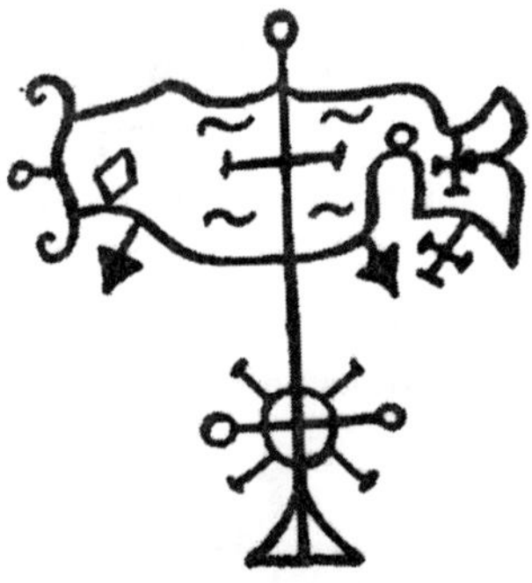

THE SEAL OF CAIM.

LIV. MURMUR, a great duke and earl, appears in the form of a soldier riding on a griffin, and having a duke's crown on his head. He is preceded by two ministers sounding trumpets. He teaches philosophy perfectly, and constrains the souls of the dead to appear and to answer questions. He was partly of the Order of Thrones and partly of Angels.

SEAL OF MURMUR.

1 He is of the Order of the Dominations.
2 Otherwise, Alloien.
3 Or of a blackbird.

LV. Orobas, a great prince, appears first like a horse, but when commanded, in human form. He discovers past, present, and future; he gives good dignities and advance-

THE SEAL OF OROBAS.

ments, with the favour of friends and foes; he will reply concerning the creation of the world and Divinity; he is very faithful to the exorcist, and defends him from temptation by any spirit.

LVI. Gomory, a powerful duke, appears like a beautiful woman, wearing a ducal crown.[1] He discovers past, pres-

THE SEAL OF GOMORY.

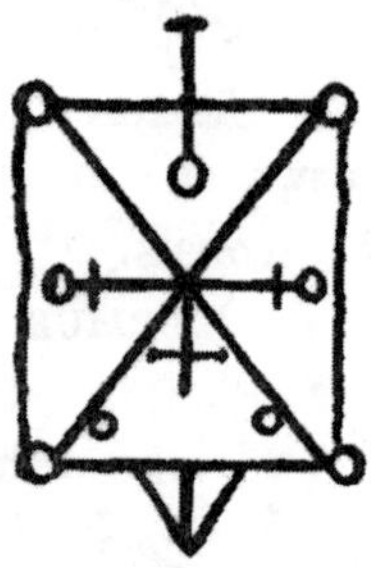

THE SEAL OF OSE.

ent, and future, as also the whereabouts of hidden treasures; he procures the love of women, and especially of girls.

LVII. Ose, a great president, appears at first like a leopard, and then in human shape. He gives skill in all liberal sciences, and true answers concerning divine and

[1] And riding on a camel (Wierus).

secret things. He can change men into any shape that the exorcist may desire, and he that is changed will not know it.[1]

LVIII. Amy, a great president, comes first as a great flaming fire and then as a man. He gives perfect knowledge

THE SEAL OF AMY.

of astrology and the liberal sciences, with good familiars, and can betray treasures that are kept by spirits.[2]

LIX. Orias, a great marquis, appears in the form of a

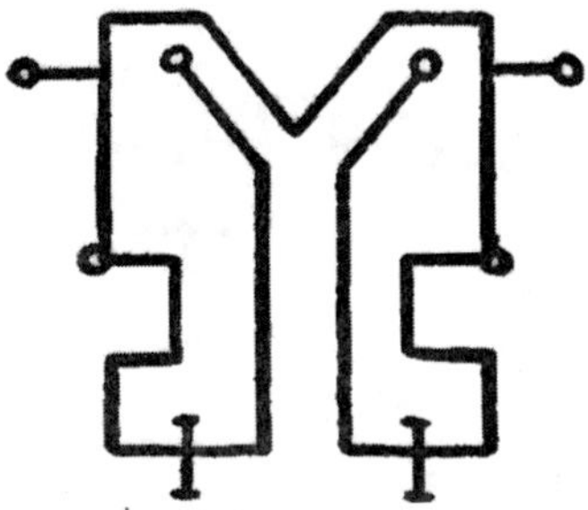

THE SEAL OF ORIAS.

lion bestriding a strong horse; he has a serpent's tail, and holds two enormous hissing snakes in his right hand. He teaches the virtues of the planets and the mansions thereof;

[1] He can also reduce them to such a state of insanity that they will believe their identity changed, that they are kings and so forth. The delusion, however, will only endure for one hour (Wierus).

[2] He is partly of the Order of the Angels and partly of that of the Powers. He hopes to return to the Seventh Thrones in 1200 years, which is incredible, says Wierus.

he transforms men, gives dignities, prelates, and confirmations, with the favour of friends and foes.

LX. Vapula, a strong duke, comes in the form of a lion

THE SEAL OF VAPULA.

with griffin's wings. He gives skill not only in manual professions but also in philosophy and the sciences.

LXI. Zagan, a great king and president, appears at first in the form of a bull with the wings of a griffin, and after in human shape. He makes men witty, turns water into wine, blood into oil, and oil into water; he can change any metal into coin of the realm and can make fools wise.

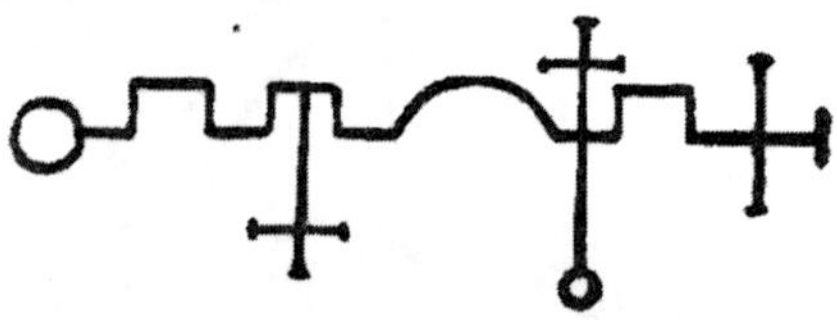

THE SEAL OF ZAGAN.

LXII. Valac, a great president, comes as a little boy with the wings of an angel and riding on a two-headed dragon. He gives true answers concerning hidden treasures, tells where serpents may be seen, and will deliver them helpless to the exorcist.

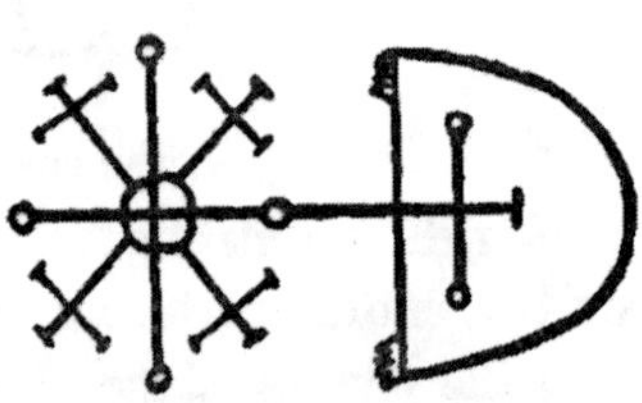

THE SEAL OF VALAC.

LXIII. ANDRAS, a great marquis, comes in the form of an angel, with the head of a black night-raven, riding upon a strong black wolf, and having a sharp bright sword gleaming in his hands. He sows discord, and will kill the unwary.

LXIV. FLAUROS, a great duke, appears at first like a terrible leopard, but at the command of the exorcist he puts on

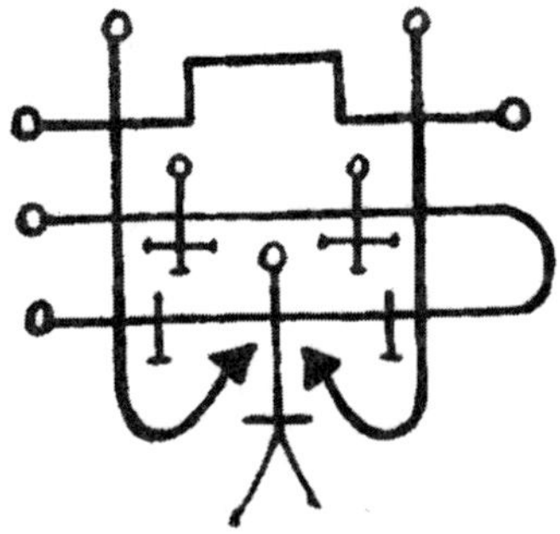

THE SEAL OF ANDRAS.

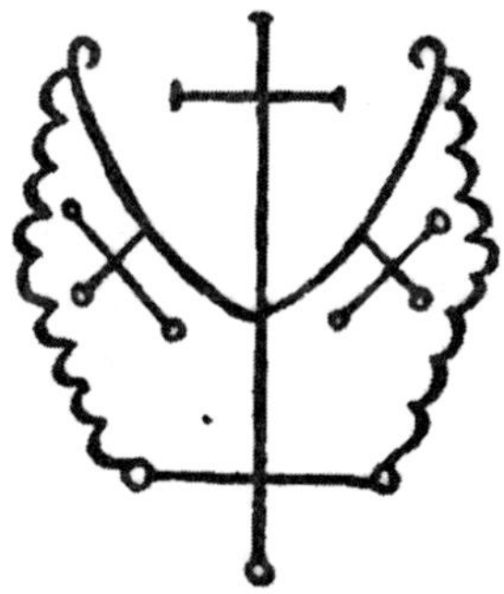

THE SEAL OF FLAUROS.

the shape of a man, with fiery eyes and terrible countenance. He gives true answers of things past, present, and future, but unless commanded into the triangle he will deceive the exorcist. He converses gladly of divinity and the creation of the world, as also of the fall of spirits, his own included. If desired, he will destroy and burn the enemies of the operator, nor will he suffer him to be tempted by spirits or otherwise.

THE SEAL OF ANDREALPHUS.

LXV. ANDREALPHUS, a mighty marquis, appears at first in the shape of a peacock, with a great noise, but after puts on human shape. He teaches geometry perfectly, and all that belongs to measurements, astronomy included. He can transform men into the likeness of a bird.

LXVI. Cimeries, a powerful marquis, appears like a valiant soldier on a black horse. He rules the spirits in the parts of Africa; he teaches grammar, logic, and rhetoric, discovers hidden treasures and things lost and hidden; he can make a man appear like a soldier of his own kind.

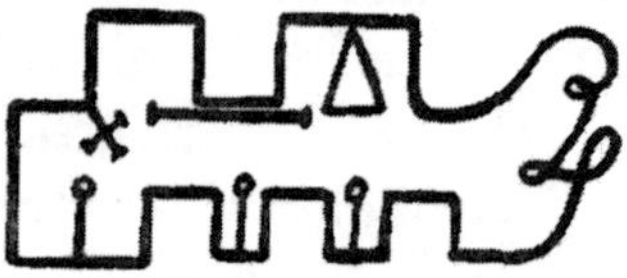

THE SEAL OF CIMERIES.

LXVII. Amduscias, a great duke, comes first like a unicorn, but will stand up at request in human shape, causing all manner of musical instruments to be heard but not seen. He makes trees fall at the will of the operator, and gives excellent familiars.

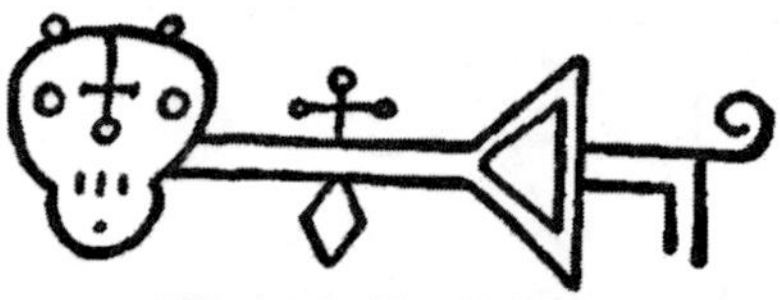

THE SEAL OF AMDUSCIAS.

LXVIII. Belial, a mighty king, created next after Lucifer, appears in the form of a beautiful angel seated in a chariot of fire, and speaking with a pleasant voice. He fell

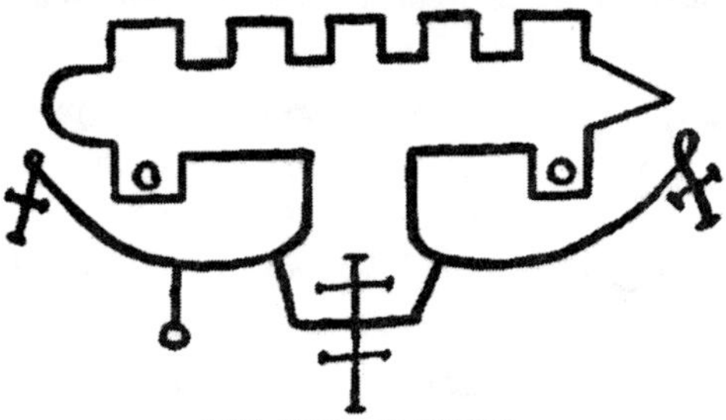

THE SEAL OF BELIAL.

first amongst the superior angels who went before Michael and other heavenly angels. He distributes preferences of senatorships, causes favours of friends and foes, and gives excellent familiars. He must have offerings and sacrifices made to him.[1]

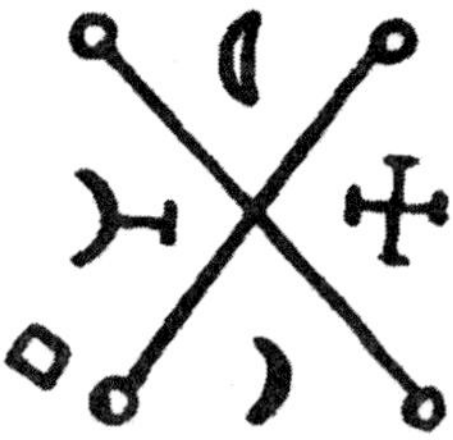

THE SEAL OF DECARABIA.

LXIX. DECARABIA, a marquis, comes in the form of a star in a pentacle, but puts on the image of man at command. He discovers the virtues of herbs and precious stones, makes birds seem to fly before the exorcist, and remain with him as familiars, singing and eating like other birds.

LXX. SEERE, a mighty prince under Amaymon, King of the East, appearing in the form of a beautiful man on a strong winged horse. He brings all things to pass suddenly, transports to any place in the twinkling of an eye, and discovers all thefts. He is indifferently good or bad, and will do the will of the operator.

THE SEAL OF SEERE.

LXXI. DANTALIAN, a mighty duke, appears in the form of a man with many faces of men and women, and has a book in his right hand. He teaches all arts and sciences, declares

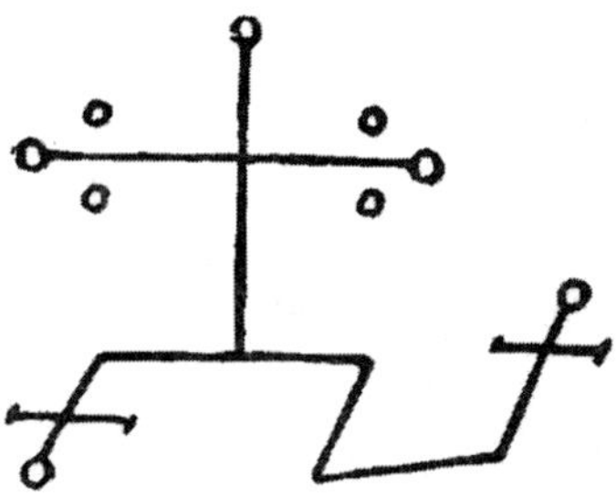

THE SEAL OF DANTALIAN.

[1] He is partly of the Order of the Virtues and partly of that of the Angels.

all secret counsels, for he knows all human thoughts, and can change them at his will. He kindles love, and shows the similitude of any person in a vision, wheresoever they may be.

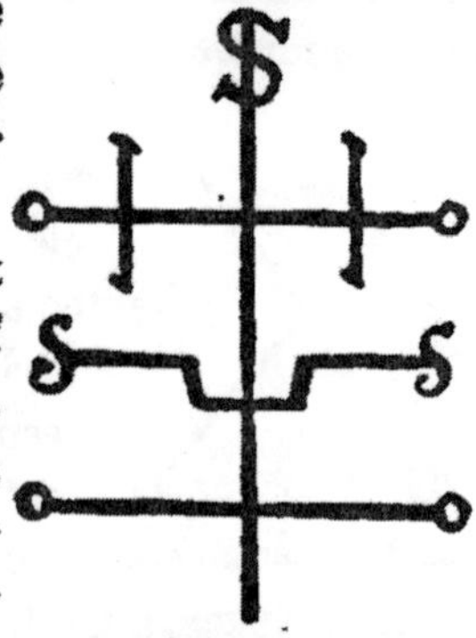

THE SEAL OF ANDROMALIUS.

LXXII. ANDROMALIUS, a great duke and earl, appears in the form of a man holding a serpent in his hand. He returns stolen goods and the thief, discovers all wickedness and underhand dealing, as also hidden treasures.

Such are the prime mysteries of Goetia according to the tradition of the "Lemegeton"; such is the work which has been described in the interest of White Magic as "distinct from the 'Key of Solomon,' but highly important and valuable in its own department." Viewed in the light of these two-and-seventy methods of accomplishing all abominations, it would seem that the three "analogical realms of occult philosophy" are the three kingdoms which we have known under other names from our childhood, "the world, the flesh, and the devil." It will be unnecessary after their enumeration to argue any longer upon the distinction between Black and White Magic as it appears in one of the oldest and best of the Rituals. There is no longer any need to inquire whether the operator is saved by his intention, for we are acquainted with the nature of the intentions which govern procedure in one of the most reputable memorials of White Magic which is now extant. The evocation of Lucifer and Astaroth, whatever the pretext, must be the first step towards Satanism; but here we have Satanism undiluted, *plus* all the mysteries of the impure Venus. To dismiss, therefore, the definition which no longer perplexes, let us establish that the distinction between White and Black Magic is the distinction between the "Lemegeton" and the "Grimoire of Honorius,"—in other words, between cipher and zero.

§ 2. *Concerning the Rite of Conjuration from the "Lemegeton."*

In communicating with the seventy-two spirits, the age of the Moon should be observed, for it is affirmed on the authority of Solomon that all days are profitable save the second, fourth, sixth, ninth, tenth, twelfth, or fourteenth of

THE TRIANGLE OF SOLOMON.

that luminary. The seals must be made of metals; those of the chief kings should be of gold; marquises, of silver; dukes, of copper; prelates, of tin or silver; knights, of lead; presidents, of fixed quicksilver;[1] and earls, of silver and copper in equal parts. The entire cohort is governed by

[1] Numerous experiments of the alchemists are concerned with congealing and fixing quicksilver, but there are also "cabalistic" processes by which this substance was prepared expressly for the construction of talismans, and these must not be confused with the more sober recipes of Hermetic Art. On this point see "Les Secrets du Petit Albert," Lyons edition, 1775, pp. 63-65.

AMAYMON, King of the East; CORSON, King of the West; ZIMINAR, King of the North; and GAAP, King of the South. These may be bound from 9 A.M. till noon, but, except on occasions of great importance, should not be invoked themselves, as they act commonly by their inferiors. Marquises may be bound from 3 to 9 P.M. and from sunset to sunrise; dukes from sunrise till noon in clear weather; prelates in any hour of the day; knights only from dawn till sunrise,

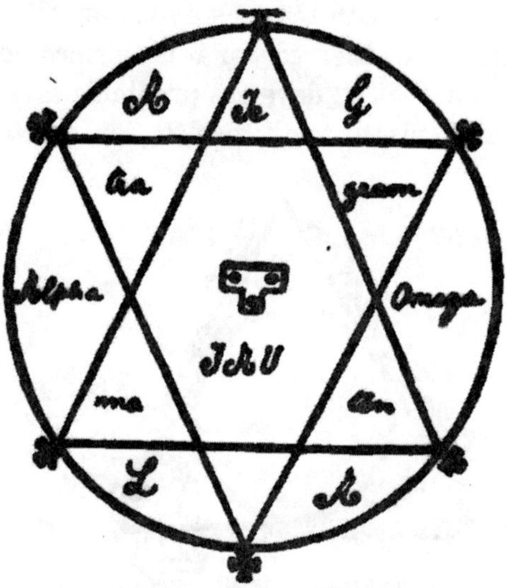

THE DOUBLE SEAL OF SOLOMON.

or from 4 P.M. till sunset; presidents in any daylight hour up to the evening twilight; counts and earls in any hour of the day, but it must be in the woods and forests, or in a place that is free from noise, and far from the resort of men. The ceremonial circle must be drawn towards that side to which the spirit who is to be called is attributed. The triangle into which Solomon summoned the rebellious demons must be made two feet outside this circle and three feet over it. The double seal and pentagram of Solomon must be drawn on a parchment of calf-skin, or otherwise on gold or silver, and worn upon the white vestment of the operator, together with the seal of the spirit, which must be exhibited on his appearance to compel obedience and assumption of the human form. In addition to these char-

THE PENTAGRAM OF SOLOMON.

acters the secret seal of Solomon must be drawn with the blood of a black cock that has never engendered, on virgin parchment, the operator himself being clean within and without, having abstained from sexual intercourse for the space of one month, and having obtained pardon for his sins by means of fasting and prayer. It is to be composed on a Tuesday or Saturday at midnight, with the Moon increasing in Virgo, and with burning of perfumes of aloes, resin, cedar, and alum.

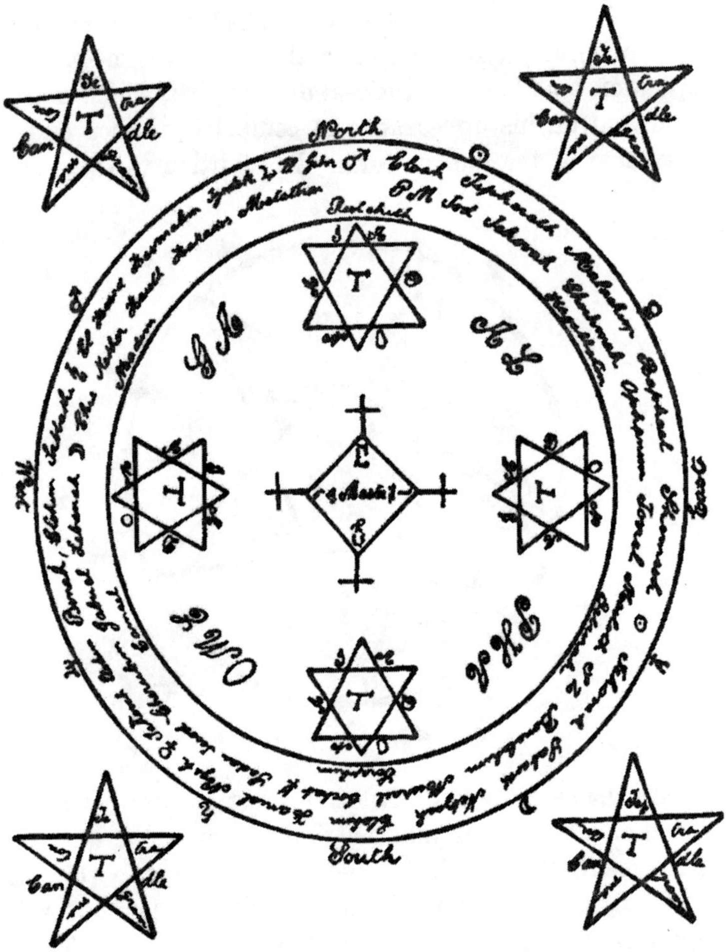
North
South

The other directions correspond broadly to those prescribed in the second chapter. There is the rod or sceptre; the sword; the mitre or cap; a long robe of white linen; a girdle of lion's skin, three inches wide and inscribed with the names which appear in the outer circle of practice; ma-

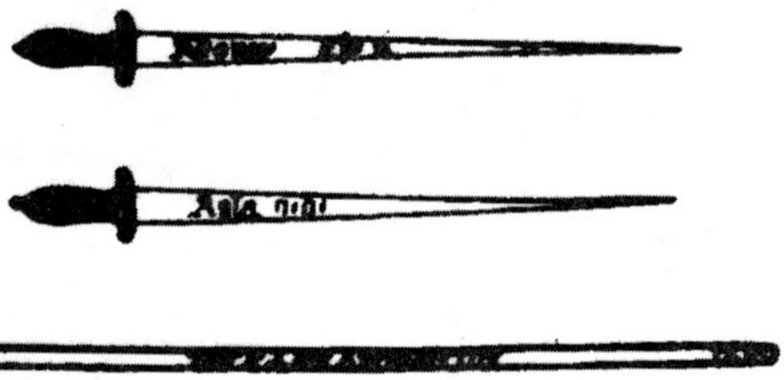

MAGICAL SWORDS AND WAND.

terial for the fumigations; oil to anoint the temples and eyes; and clean water for the ablution. The Prayer at Lustration is simply the versicle of David:—Thou shalt purge me with hyssop, O Lord, and I shall be cleansed; Thou shalt wash me and I shall be made whiter than snow.

Prayer at Vesting.

By the figurative mystery of this holy vestment, I will clothe me with the armour of salvation in the strength of the Most High, Ancor, Amicar, Amides, Theodonias, Anitor, that so the end which I desire may be effected, O Adonai, through Thy strength, to whom be praise and glory for ever and ever.

Prayers should be offered also in harmony with the intention of the operator before pronouncing the forms of evocation, as follows:—

FIRST CONJURATION.

I invoke and conjure thee, O Spirit N., and, fortified with the power of the Supreme Majesty, I strongly command thee by BARALAMENSIS, BALDACHIENSIS, PAUMACHIE,

THE SECRET SEAL OF SOLOMON.

APOLORESEDES, and the most potent princes GENIO, LIACHIDE, Ministers of the Tartarean Seat, chief princes of the seat of APOLOGIA in the ninth region; I exorcise and command thee, O Spirit N., by Him who spake and it was done, by the Most Holy and glorious Names ADONAI, EL, ELOHIM, ELOHE, ZEBAOTH, ELION, ESCHERCE, JAH, TETRAGRAMMATON, SADAI, do thou forthwith appear and show thyself unto me, here before this circle, in a fair and human shape, without any deformity or horror; do thou come forthwith, from whatever part of the world, and make rational answers to my questions; come presently, come visibly, come affably, and manifest that which I desire, being conjured by the Name of the Eternal, Living, and True God, HELIOREM; I conjure thee also by the particular and true Name of thy God to whom thou owest thine obedience, by the name of the King who rules over thee, do thou come without tarrying; come, fulfil my desire; persist unto the end, according to mine intentions I conjure thee by Him to whom all creatures are obedient, by this ineffable Name, TETRAGRAMMATON JEHOVAH, by which the elements are overthrown, the air is shaken, the sea turns back, the fire is generated, the earth moves, and all the host of things celestial, of things terrestrial, of things infernal, do tremble and are confounded together; speak unto me visibly and affably in a clear, intelligible voice, free from ambiguity. Come therefore in the name ADONAI ZEBAOTH, come, why dost thou tarry? ADONAI SADAY, King of kings, commands thee.

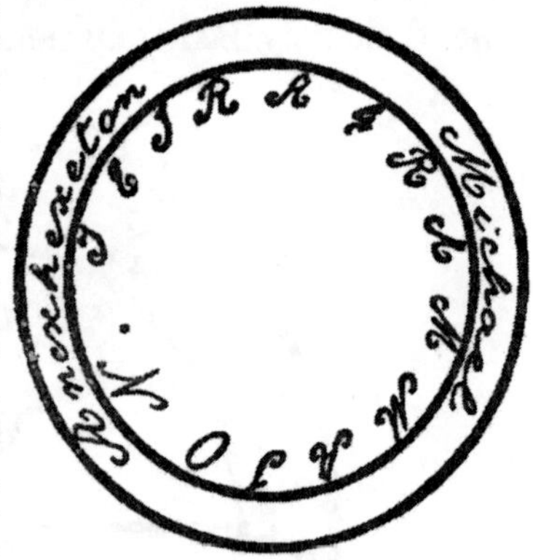

THE RING OF THE EXORCIST.

This being repeated frequently, if the spirit do not yet appear, say as follows:—

SECOND CONJURATION.

I invoke, conjure, and command thee, O Spirit N., to appear and show thyself visibly before this circle, in fair and comely shape, without deformity or guile, by the Name of ON; by the Name Y and V, which Adam heard and spake; by the Name of JOTH, which Jacob learned from the Angel on the night of his wrestling, and was delivered from the hands of his brother Esau; by the Name of God AGLA, which Lot heard and was saved with his family; by the Name ANEHEXETON, which Aaron spake and was made wise; by the Name SCHEMES AMATHIA, which Joshua invoked and the Sun stayed upon his course; by the Name EMMANUEL, which the three children, Shadrach, Meshach, and Abednego, chanted in the midst of the fiery furnace, and were delivered; by the Name ALPHA and OMEGA, which Daniel uttered, and destroyed Bel and the Dragon; by the Name ZEBAOTH, which Moses named, and all the rivers and waters in the land of Egypt brought forth frogs, which ascended into the house of the Egyptians, destroying all things; by the Name ESCERCHIE ARISTON, which also Moses named, and the rivers and waters in the land of Egypt were turned into blood; by the Name ELION, on which Moses called, and there fell a great hail, such as never was seen since the creation of the world; by the Name ADONAI, which Moses named, and there came up locusts over all the land of Egypt, and devoured what the hail had left; by the Name HAGIOS, by the Seal of ADONAI, by those others, which are JETROS, ATHENOROS, PARACLETUS, by the three Holy and Secret Names, AGLA, ON, TETRAGRAMMATON; by the dreadful Day of Judgment; by the changing Sea of Glass which is before the face of the Divine Majesty, mighty and powerful; by the four beasts before the Throne, having eyes before and behind, by the fire which is about the Throne, by the Holy Angels of Heaven, by the Mighty Wisdom of God; by the Seal of BASDATHEA, by this Name PRIMEMATUM, which Moses named, and the earth opened and swallowed Corah,

Dathan, and Abiram; do thou make faithful answers unto all my demands, and perform all my desires, so far as thine office shall permit. Come therefore peaceably and affably; come visibly and without delay; manifest that which I desire; speak with a clear and intelligible voice, that I may understand thee.

If he come not at the reheasing of these Conjurations, as without doubt he will, proceed as follows, it being a Constraint:—

Third Conjuration.

I conjure thee, O Spirit N., by all the most glorious and efficacious Names of the Great and Incomparable Lord the God of Hosts, come quickly and without delay, from whatsoever part of the world thou art in; make rational answers to my demands; come visibly, speak affably, speak intelligibly to my understanding. I conjure and constrain thee, O Spirit N., by all the aforesaid Names, as also by those seven other Names wherewith Solomon bound thee and thy fellows in the brazen vessel, to wit, Adonai, Prerai, Tetragrammaton, Anexhexeton, Inessensational, Pathumaton, and Itemon; do thou manifest before this circle, fufil my will in all things that may seem good to me. Be disobedient, refuse to come, and by the power of the Supreme Being, the everlasting Lord, that God who created thee and me, the whole world, with all contained therein, in the space of six days, by Eye, by Saray, by the virtue of the Name Primematum, which commands the whole host of Heaven, behold I will curse and deprive thee of thine office, thy joy, and thy place; I will bind thee in the depths of the bottomless pit, there to remain until the Day of the Last Judgment. I will chain thee in the Lake of Eternal Fire, in the Lake of Fire and Brimstone, unless thou come quickly, appearing before this circle, to do my will. Come, therefore, in the Holy Name ADONAI, ZEBAOTH, AMIORAM, come, ADONAI commands thee.

Should he still fail to appear, you may be sure that he has been sent by his King to some other place. Invoke, therefore, the King to despatch his servant as follows:—

INVOCATION OF THE KING.

O thou great and powerful King AMAYMON, who rulest by the power of the Supreme God, EL, over all Spirits, superior and inferior, but especially over the Infernal Order in the Dominion of the East, I invoke and command thee by the particular and true Name of God, and by the God whom thou dost worship, by the Seal of thy creation, by the most mighty and powerful Name of God, JEHOVAH, TETRAGRAMMATON, who cast thee out of Heaven with the rest of the Infernal Spirits, by all the other potent and great names of God, Creator of Heaven, Earth, and Hell, of all contained therein, by their powers and virtues, and by the Name PRIMEMATUM, which commands the whole host of Heaven. Do thou force and compel the Spirit N. here before this circle, in a fair and comely shape, without injury to myself or to any creature, that he may give me true and faithful answer, so that I may accomplish my desired end, whatsoever it be, provided that it is proper to his office, by the power of God, EL, who hath created and doth dispose of all things, celestial, aërial, terrestrial, and infernal.

Having twice or thrice invoked the King in this manner, again conjure the spirit, using the previous forms, and rehearsing them several times, whereupon he will come assuredly. Yet should he fail, be convinced that he is bound with chains in hell, and is not in the custody of his King. To set him free it is necessary to recite

THE CHAIN CURSE.

O thou wicked and disobedient N., because thou hast not obeyed or regarded the words which I have rehearsed, the glorious and incomprehensible Names of the true God, Maker of all things in the world, now I, by the power of these Names, which no creature can resist, do curse thee into the depths of the Bottomless Pit, to remain until the Day of Doom in the Hell of unquenchable fire and brimstone, unless thou shalt forthwith appear in this triangle, before this circle, to do my will. Come, therefore, quickly and peaceably by the Names ADONAI, ZEBAOTH, ADONAI AMIORAM. Come, come, ADONAI, King of Kings, commands thee.

Having read so far, if he come not, write his seal on parchment; put it in a black box, with brimstone, assafœtida, and other stinking perfumes; bind the said box with iron wire, hang it on the point of your sword, hold it over the fire of charcoal, which shall have been placed towards that quarter whence the spirit will come, and say first unto the Fire:—I conjure thee, O Fire by Him who made thee, and all other creatures in the world, to torment, burn, and consume this Spirit N. everlastingly.

TO THE SPIRIT.

Because thou art disobedient, and obeyest not my commandments nor the precepts of the Lord thy God, now I, who am the servant of the Most High and Imperial Lord

God of Hosts, JEHOVAH, having His celestial power and permission, for this thine averseness and contempt, thy great disobedience and rebellion, will excommunicate thee, will destroy thy name and seal, which I have in this box, will burn them with unquenchable fire, and bury them in unending oblivion, unless thou comest immediately, visibly and affably, here before this circle, within this triangle, assuming a fair and comely form, without doing harm unto myself or any creature whatsoever, but giving reasonable answer to my requests and performing my desire in all things.

If he appear not at this point, say as follows:—Thou art still pernicious and disobedient, willing not to appear and inform me upon that which I desire to know; now therefore, in the Name and by the power and dignity of the Omnipotent and Immortal Lord God of Hosts, JEHOVAH TETRAGRAMMATON, sole Creator of Heaven, Earth, and Hell, with all contained therein, the marvellous Disposer of all things visible and invisible, I do hereby curse and deprive thee of all thine office, power, and place; I bind thee in the depth of the Bottomless Pit, there to remain unto the Day of Judgment, in the lake of fire and brimstone, prepared for the rebellious Spirits. May all the Company of Heaven curse thee; may the Sun, the Moon, the Stars, the Light of the Hosts of Heaven, curse thee into fire unquenchable, into torments unspeakable; and even as thy name and seal are bound up in this box to be choked with sulphureous and stinking substances, and to burn in this material fire, so, in the Name of Jehovah, and by the power and dignity of the three Names, TETRAGRAMMATON, ANEXHEXETON, PRIMEMATUM, may all these drive thee, O thou disobedient Spirit N., into the Lake of Fire, prepared for the damned and accursed Spirits, there to remain until the Day of Doom, remembered no more before the face of that God who shall come to judge the quick and the dead, with the whole world, by fire.

Set the box in the flame, whereupon he will appear; when he comes, quench the fire, make sweet perfumes, give him good entertainment, shewing him the pentacle on the hem of your vestment covered with a linen cloth, and saying:—Behold thy confusion, if thou be disobedient. Behold the Pentacle of Solomon which I have brought into thy presence. Behold the person of the Exorcist, who is called OCTINIMOES, in the midst of the Exorcism, armed by God and fearless, potently invoking and calling. Make, therefore, reasonable answers to my demands, be obedient to me, thy Master, in the Name of the Lord BATHAL, rushing upon ABRAC, ABEOR, coming upon BEROR.

He will become obedient and bid you ask what you will, for he is made subject by God to your purpose. When he shows himself humble and meek, say:—Welcome, Spirit (or, most Noble King), welcome art thou unto me; I have called thee through Him who created Heaven, Earth, and Hell, with all contained therein, and thou hast obeyed also by the like power. I bind thee to remain affably and visibly before this circle, within this triangle, so long as I need thee, and to depart not without my license, till thou hast truly and faithfully fulfilled all that I shall require.

THE LICENSE TO DEPART.

O Spirit N., because thou hast diligently answered my demands, I do hereby license thee to depart, without injury to man or beast. Depart, I say, and be thou very willing and ready to come, whensoever duly exorcised and conjured by the Sacred Rites of Magic. I conjure thee to withdraw peaceably and quietly, and may the peace of God continue for ever between me and thee. Amen.

Go not out of the circle till he be gone, but make prayers to God for the great blessing He has bestowed upon you by thus granting your desires, and delivering you from the malice of the enemy.

For these verbose and tiresome conjurations the Latin version of Wierus substitutes one general form of citation, in the Name of the Christian Trinity, which is not really an anachronism, for the compiler of the "Lemegeton" was acquainted at least with the books of the New Testament. This is proved by the references in the Third Conjuration to the Living Creatures of the Apocalypse, and it leaves the attribution to Solomon in precisely that state which our respect for a prince in Israel would naturally desire.

CHAPTER V.

Concerning the Mystery of the Sanctum Regnum, or the Government of the Evil Spirits; being the Rite of Conjuration according to the Grimorium Verum

THE preparations of the operator prescribed by the *Grimorium Verum* are fully represented in the earlier chapters, but they may be summed here as follows:—1. An austere fast of three days; 2. Retreat or isolation from human society; 3. Abstinence from sexual intercourse; 4. The recitation of certain prayers and the performance of certain ablutions; 5. The composition of the required instruments. He must further devote himself to the invocations, lest memory fail him at the moment of operation, and to insure mastery of the practice. He should also recite the following prayer daily [1]—at Prime once, at Tierce twice, at Sext three times, at Nones four times, at Vespers five times, and six times before going to rest. It is explained that these hours are planetary and unequal.[2] Prime is reckoned at the rising of the sun, Tierce at three hours after, Sext at mid-day, Nones at three in the afternoon, and vespers at sunset.

[1] This portion of the process offers some analogy with the "Key of Solomon," Book ii. c. 2.

[2] *i.e.*, they are governed by the times of sunrise and sunset. Sext and Nones would not, however, be variable.

PRAYER.[1]

ASTRACHIOS, ASACH, ASARCA, ABEDUMABAL, SILAT, ANABOTAS, JESUBILIN, SCIGIN, GENEON, DOMOL, Lord God, who dwellest above the heavens, whose glance searchest the abyss; grant me, I pray Thee, the power to conceive in my mind and to execute that which I desire to do, the end of which I would attain by Thy Help, O God Almighty, who livest and reignest for ever and ever. Amen.

These things being done, says the Grimoire, it remains only to follow the invocations and to compose the characters, to which end the operator shall proceed as follows:—On the day and in the hour of Mars, the Moon waxing, and at the first hour of the day, which begins fifteen minutes before the rising of the Sun, a piece of virgin parchment must be prepared, containing all the characters and invocations of the spirits whom it is desired to invoke. On the day and in the hour aforesaid, let the operator bind the little finger of the (left) hand, which is the finger of Mercury, with a thread woven by a virgin girl; let him pierce that finger with the lancet of the Art, so as to draw blood, and form therewith the character of Scirlin, from whom all other spirits depend, since he is their messenger, and can compel them to appear despite themselves, because he has the power of the Emperor. His invocation, which must be written, is as follows:—

THE INVOCATION OF SCIRLIN.

HELON ✠, TAUL ✠, VARF ✠, PAN ✠, HEON ✠, HOMONO-

[1] This Prayer is similar to that of the "Key of Solomon," Book ii. c. 2, with the exception of the names, which are much mutilated in the Grimoire; these should read:—Herachio, Asac, Asacro, Bedrimulael, Tilath, Arabonas, Ierahlem, Ideodoc, Archarzel, Zophiel, Blautel, Baracata, Edoniel, Elohim, Emagro, Abragateh, Samoel, Geburahel, Cadato, Era, Elohi, Achsah, Ebmisha, Imachedel, Daniel, Dama, Elamos, Izachel, Beal, Segon, Gemon, Demas. But the majority of these are unintelligible.

REUM ✠, CLEMIALH ✠, SERUGEATH ✠, AGLA ✠, TETRAGRAMMATON ✠, CASOLY ✠.

With the confusion so common in the Grimoires, the character of Scirlin is not given, whence the operator who followed the instructions of this Ritual must have had recourse to one of the superior spirits. The instructions, however, are not described *ad clerum,* and it is scarcely possible to extract from them an intelligible method of procedure. The name and surname of the operator must apparently be written below the character of the spirit, following a prescribed manner, which is also omitted; the conjuration of the spirit must be added, and incense burnt in his honour.

CONJURATON TO LUCIFER.

LUCIFER ✠, OUYAR ✠, CHAMERON ✠, ALISEON ✠, MANDOUSIN ✠, PREMY ✠, ORIET ✠, NAYDRUS ✠, ESMONY ✠, EPARINESONT ✠, ESTIOT ✠, DUMOSSON ✠, DANOCHAR ✠, CASMIEL ✠, HAYRAS ✠, FABELLERONTHON ✠, SODIRNO ✠, PEATHAM ✠, Come ✠, LUCIFER ✠. AMEN.

CONJURATION FOR BEELZEBUTH.

BEELZEBUTH ✠, LUCIFER ✠, MADILON ✠, SOLYMO ✠, SAROY ✠, THEU ✠, AMECLO ✠, SEGRAEL ✠, PRAREDUN ✠, ADRICANOROM ✠, MARTIRO ✠, TIMO ✠, CAMERON ✠, PHORSY ✠, METOSITE ✠, PRUMOSY ✠, DUMASO ✠, ELIVISA ✠, ALPHROIS ✠, FUBENTRONTY ✠, Come, BEELZEBUTH ✠. AMEN.

CONJURATION FOR ASTAROTH.

ASTAROTH ✠, ADOR ✠, CAMESO ✠, VALUERITUF ✠, MARESO ✠, LODIR ✠, CADOMIR ✠, ALUIEL ✠, CALNISO ✠, TELY ✠, PLEORIM ✠, VIORDY ✠, CUREVIORBAS ✠, CAMERON ✠,

VESTURIEL ✠, VULNAVII ✠, BENEZ ✠, MEUS CALMIRON ✠, NOARD ✠, NISA CHENIBRANBO CALEVODIUM ✠, BRAZO ✠, TABRASOL ✠, Come ✠, ASTAROTH ✠. AMEN.

Having repeated seven times the conjuration addressed to one of these superior spirits, the same will forthwith manifest to perform whatsoever shall be desired. NOTE.—Such conjuration must have been written on virgin paper or parchment before invoking the spirits. These, having been satisfied, may be dismissed by using the following

DISCHARGE.

Go in peace unto your places; may peace be with you, and be ye ready to come whensoever I shall call upon you, In the Name of the Father ✠ and of the Son ✠ and of the Holy Ghost ✠. Amen.

CONJURATION FOR INFERIOR SPIRITS.

O SURMY ✠, DELMUSAN ✠, ATALSLOYM ✠, CHARUSIHOA ✠, MELANY ✠, LIAMINTHO ✠, COLEHON ✠, PARON ✠, MADION ✠, MERLOY ✠, BULERATOR ✠, DONMEO ✠, HONE ✠, PELOYN ✠, IBASIL ✠, MEON ✠, ALYMDRICTELS ✠, PERSON ✠, CRISOLSAY ✠, LEMON SEFLE NIDAR HORIEL PEUNT ✠, HALMON ✠, ASOPHIEL ✠, ILNOSTREON ✠, BANIEL ✠, VERMIAS ✠, ESLEVOR ✠, NOELMA ✠, DORSAMOT ✠, LHAVALA ✠, OMOT ✠, FRANGAM ✠, BELDOR ✠, DRAGIN ✠, Come.

The name of the required spirit must here be added on the parchment, when he will duly appear, and will grant what is desired of him, after which he may be dismissed by the previous Discharge.

The characters should be burnt in each case, as they avail once only.

Another Conjuration.

I conjure thee, N., by the great living God, the Sovereign Creator of all things, to appear under a comely human form, without noise and without terror, to answer truly unto all questions that I shall ask thee. Hereunto I conjure thee by the virtue of these Holy and Sacred Names.

CHAPTER VI

The Mysteries of Infernal Invocation according to the Grand Grimoire

§ 1. *The Rite of Lucifuge.*

THE "Grand Grimoire" divides with the "Grimoire of Honorius" the darksome honour of an intelligible and unmutilated Ritual of Black Magic. Each after its own kind is indeed an exceedingly curious work. In the first is contained what is probably the only printed method of making pacts; the second is remarkable, firstly, on account of its pretended origin and the elaboration with which it is set forth, secondly, for the ecclesiastical complexion of its process, which can scarcely have failed to impose upon innumerable credulous sorcerers. Both deserve to be printed almost *in extenso,* and, setting aside their preliminary portions, already adequately dealt with, they are given practically verbatim in the chapters which here follow.

It will be remembered that the operator, or Karcist, as he is termed in the "Grand Grimoire," is recommended continence, fasting, and similar privations for an entire quarter of the moon, such quarter coinciding with that of the luminary. On the morning which succeeds the first night of the quarter, he must repair to a druggist's, and purchase a bloodstone, called *Ematille,* which must be carried continually about him for fear of accident, and in expectation that the spirit whom it is proposed to compel and bind will henceforth do all in his power to overwhelm the operator with terror, so as to incite him to abandon the enterprise, hoping in this manner to escape from the wiles which are beginning to be woven about him.

The next operation is the purchase of a virgin kid, which must be decapitated on the third day of the moon. Previously to the sacrifice, a garland of vervian must be wound about the neck of the animal, immediately below the head, and secured by means of a green ribbon. The sacrifice must be offered on the scene of the coming evocation, a forlorn and isolated spot free from all interruption. There, with the right arm bared to the shoulder, having armed himself with a blade of fine steel, and having kindled a fire of white wood, the Karcist shall recite the following words in a hopeful and animated manner:—

Initial Offering.

I immolate this victim to thee, O grand Adonay, Eloim, Ariel, and Jehovam, to the honour, glory, and power of thy Name, which is superior to all Spirits. O grand Adonay! vouchsafe to receive it as an acceptable offering. Amen.

Here he must cut the throat of the kid, skin it, set the body on the fire, and reduce it to ashes, which must be collected and cast towards the rising of the sun, at the same time repeating the following words:—It is to the honour, glory, and dominion of thy name, O grand Adonay, Eloim, Ariel, Jehovam, that I spill the blood of this victim! Vouchsafe, O thou gread Adonay, to receive its ashes as an acceptable sacrifice.

While the victim is being consumed by the flames, the operator shall rejoice in the honour and glory of the grand

ADONAY, ELOIM, ARIEL, and JEHOVAM, taking care to preserve the skin of the virgin kid to form the round or grand Kabbalistic circle in which he must himself stand on the day of the grand enterprise.

The sacrifice of the victim is followed by the selection and composition of the Blasting Rod, of which a description has been given. From the purpose for which it is intended, and from the silence of the Grimoire, it may be inferred that the preparation of the goatskin is exceedingly simple and does not involve the removal of the hair.

When the night of action has arrived, the operator shall gather up his rod, goatskin, the stone called Ematille, and shall further provide himself with two vervian crowns, two candlesticks, and two candles of virgin wax, made by a virgin girl and duly blessed. Let him take also a new steel and two new flints, with sufficient tinder to kindle a fire, likewise half a bottle of brandy, some blessed incense and camphor, and four nails from the coffin of a dead child. All these must be carried to the place chosen for the great work, where everything hereinafter laid down must be scrupulously performed, and the dread Kabbalistic circle must be described in an accurate manner. Lastly, it must be carefully borne in mind that there should be either one or three taking part in the ceremony, the Karcist included, who is the person appointed to address the spirit, holding the Destroying Rod in his hand. The evoking process may be given in the actual words of the Grimoire.

CONCERNING A TRUE REPRESENTATION OF THE GRAND KABBALISTIC CIRCLE.

You must begin by forming a circle with strips of kid's skin fastened to the ground by means of your four nails. Then with the stone called Ematille you must trace the triangle within the circle, beginning at the eastern point. A large A, a small E, a small A, and a small J, must be drawn in like manner, as also the sacred name of Jesus between two crosses. By this means the spirits will have no power to harm you from behind. The Karcist and his assistants may then fearlessly proceed to their places within the triangle, and regardless of any noises, may set the two candlesticks and the two vervian crowns on the right and left sides of the triangle within the circle. This being done,

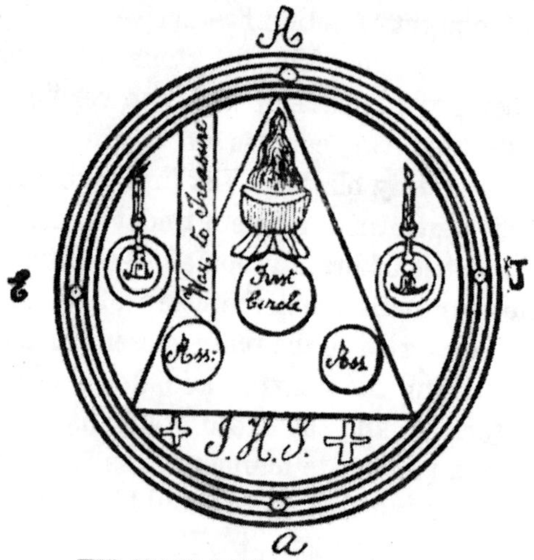

THE GRAND KABBALISTIC CIRCLE.

the two candles may be lighted, taking care that there is a new brazier in front of the Karcist, plied with newly consecrated charcoal. This must be kindled by the Karcist casting a small quantity of the brandy therein and a part of the camphor, the rest being reserved to feed the fire periodically, in proportion to the length of the business. Having punctually performed all that is mentioned above, the chief operator may repeat the following prayer:—I present thee, O great ADONAY, this incense as the purest I can obtain; in like manner, I present thee this charcoal prepared from the most ethereal of woods. I offer them, O grand and omnipotent ADONAY, ELOIM, ARIEL, and JEHOVAM, with my whole soul and my heart. Vouchsafe, O grand ADONAY, to receive them as an acceptable holocaust. Amen.

You should also be careful, says the Grimoire, to have no alloyed metal about your person, except a gold or silver coin wrapped in paper, which you must fling to the spirit when he

THE CIRCLE OF WHITE MAGIC.

appears outside the circle, so as to prevent him from harming you. While he is picking up the coin, begin promptly the following prayer, fortifying yourself with courage, energy, and prudence. Be, also, especially careful that the Karcist is the sole speaker; the assistants must preserve a determined silence, even if they are questioned or menaced by the spirit.

FIRST PRAYER.

O great and living God, subsisting in one and the same person, the Father, the Son, and the Holy Ghost; I adore

Thee with the deepest veneration, and I submit with the liveliest confidence to Thy holy and sufficient protection. I believe with the most sincere faith that Thou art my Creator, my Benefactor, my Preserver, and my Lord, and I testify to Thy sovereign Majesty that my sole desire is to belong to Thee through the whole of eternity. So be it. Amen.

Second Prayer.

O great and living God, who hast created man to enjoy felicity in this life, who hast adapted all things for his necessities, and didst declare that everything should be made subject to his will, be favourable to this my design, and permit not the rebellious spirits to be in possession of those treasures which were formed by Thine own hands for our temporal requirements. Grant me, O great God, the power to dispose of them by the potent and terrific names in Thy Clavicle: Adonay, Eloim, Ariel, Jehovam, Tagla, Mathon, be ye propitious unto me. So be it. Amen.

Offertory.

I offer Thee this incense as the purest which I have been able to obtain, O sublime Adonay, Eloim, Ariel, and Jehovam; vouchsafe to receive it as an acceptable holocaust. Incline to me in Thy power, and enable me to succeed in this great enterprise. So be it. Amen.

First Conjuration.

Addressed to the Emperor Lucifer.

Emperor Lucifer, Master and Prince of Rebellious Spirits, I adjure thee to leave thine abode, in whatsoever quarter of the world it may be situated, and come hither to communicate with me. I command and I conjure thee in the Name of the Mighty living God, Father, Son, and Holy Ghost, to appear without noise and without any evil smell, to respond in a clear and intelligible voice, point by point, to all that I shall ask thee, failing which, thou shalt be most surely compelled to obedience by the power of the divine ADONAY, ELOIM, ARIEL, JEHOVAM, TAGLA, MATHON, and by the whole hierarchy of superior intelligences, who shall constrain thee against thy will. Venité, Venité! Submiritillor Lucifuge, or eternal torment shall overwhelm thee, by the great power of this Blasting Rod. *In subito.*

SECOND CONJURATION.

I command and I adjure thee, Emperor Lucifer, as the representative of the mighty living God, and by the power of Emanuel, his only Son, who is thy master and mine, and by the virtue of His precious blood, which He shed to redeem mankind from thy chains, I command thee to quit thine abode, wheresoever it may be, swearing that I will give thee one quarter of an hour alone, if thou dost not straightway come hither and communicate with me in an audible and intelligible voice, or, if thy personal presence be impossible, despatch me thy Messenger Astarot in a human form, without either noise or evil smell, failing which I will smite thee and thy whole race with the terrible Blasting Rod into the depth of the bottomless abysses, and that by the power of those great words in the Clavicle—By ADONAY, ELOIM, ARIEL, JEHOVAM, TAGLA, MATHON, ALMOUZIN, AROIS, PITHONA, MAGOTS, SYLPHAE, TABOTS, SALAMANDRAE, GNOMUS, TERRAE, COELIS, GODENS, AQUA. *In subito.*

Notice.—Before uttering the third Conjuration, should the spirit refuse to comply, read what follows in the Clavicle, and smite all the spirits by plunging both the forked extremities of your rod into the flames, and be not alarmed in so doing at the frightful howls which you may hear, for at this extreme moment all the spirits will manifest. Then, before reading the Clavicle, and in the midst of the commotion, recite the third Conjuration.

Third Conjuration.

I adjure thee, Emperor Lucifer, as the agent of the strong living God, of His beloved Son, and of the Holy Ghost, and by the power of the Great Adonay, Eloim, Ariel, and Jehovam, to appear instantly, or to send thy Messenger Astarot, forcing thee to forsake thy hiding-place, wheresoever it may be, and warning thee that if thou dost not manifest this moment, I will straightway smite thee and all thy race with the Blasting Rod of the great Adonay, Eloim, Ariel, and Jehovam, &c.

At this point, should the spirit still fail to appear, plunge the two ends of your rod a second time into the flames, and recite the following potent words from the grand Clavicle of Solomon:—

Grand Conjuration.

Extracted from the Veritable Clavicle.

I adjure thee, O Spirit! by the power of the grand Adonay, to appear instanter, and by Eloim, by Ariel, by Jehovam, by Aqua, Tagla, Mathon, Oarios, Almoazin, Arios, Membrot, Varios, Pithona, Majods, Sulphae, Gabots, Salamandrae, Tabots, Gingua, Janna, Etitnamus, Zariatnatmix, &c. A. E. A. J. A. T. M. O. A. A. M. V. P. M. S. C. S. J. C. G. A. J. F. Z. &c.

After a second repetition of these sublime and powerful words, you may be sure that the spirit will respond after the ensuing manner.

Of the Manifestation of the Spirit.

Lo, I am here! What dost thou seek of me? Why dost

LUCIFUGE ROFOCALE.

thou disturb my repose? Smite me no more with that dread rod!

LUCIFUGE ROFOCALE.

Reply to the Spirit.

Hadst thou appeared when I invoked thee, I had by no means smitten thee; remember, if the request which I make thee be refused, I am determined to torment thee eternally.

SOLOMON.

The Spirit's Answer.

Torment me no further. Say, rather, what thou dost require at my hands. LUCIFUGE ROFOCALE.

The Requisition.

I require that thou shalt communicate two several times on each night of the week, either with myself or with those who are entrusted with my present Book, the which thou shalt approve and sign; I permit thee the choice of those hours which may suit thee, if thou approvest not those which I now enumerate. To wit:

On Monday at nine o'clock and at midnight.

On Tuesday at ten o'clock and at one in the morning.

On Wednesday at eleven o'clock and at two in the morning.

On Thursday at eight and ten o'clock.

On Friday at seven in the evening and at midnight.

On Saturday at nine in the evening and at eleven at night.

Further, I command thee to surrender me the nearest treasure, and I promise thee as a reward the first piece of gold or silver which I touch with my hands on the first day of every month. Such is my demand. SOLOMON.

The Spirit's Reply.

I cannot comply with thy request on such terms, nor on any others, unless thou shalt give thyself over to me in fifty years, to do with thy body and soul as I please.

LUCIFUGE ROFOCALE.

Rejoinder to the Spirit.

Lo, will I smite thee and thy whole race, by the might

of great Adonay, if, on the contrary, thou dost not comply with my request.

Notice.—Here plunge the points of the Blasting Rod into the fire and repeat the Grand Conjuration of the Clavicle till the spirit surrenders himself to your will.

Answer and Compliance of the Spirit.

Smite me no further; I pledge myself to do what thou desirest two several times on every night of the week. To wit:

On Monday at ten o'clock and at midnight.

On Tuesday at eleven o'clock and at one in the morning.

On Wednesday at midnight and at two in the morning.

On Thursday at eight and at eleven o'clock.

On Friday at nine o'clock and at midnight.

On Saturday at ten o'clock and at one in the morning.

I also approve thy Book, and I give thee my true signature on parchment, which thou shalt affix at its end, to make use of at thy need. Further, I place myself at thy disposition, to appear before thee at thy call when, being purified, and holding the dreadful Blasting Rod, thou shalt open the Book, having described the Kabalistic circle and pronounced the word Rofocale. I promise thee to have friendly commerce with those who are fortified by the possession of the said Book, where my true signature stands, provided that they invoke me according to rule, on the first occasion that they require me. I also engage to deliver thee the treasure which thou seekest, on condition that thou keepest the secret for ever inviolable, art charitable to the poor, and dost give me a gold or silver coin on the first day of every month. If thou failest, thou art mine everlastingly.

LUCIFUGE ROFOCALE.

IMPRIMATUR.

Reply to the Spirit.

I agree to thy conditions.

SOLOMON.

INVITATION OF THE SPIRIT.

Follow me, and come lay thy hands on the treasure.

Thereupon the Karcist, armed with the Blasting Rod and the stone called Ematille, shall issue from the circle at that point where the door of mighty Adonay is figured, and shall follow the spirit, but the assistants shall not stir one step from the circle, but shall remain firm and immovable within it, whatever reports they hear, and whatever visions they see. The spirit shall then conduct the Karcist to the vicinity of the treasure, when it may befall that the Karcist shall behold the apparition of a large and fierce dog with a collar as resplendent as the sun. This will be a Gnome, which he can drive off by the point of his rod, when the apparition will make off towards the treasure. The Karcist must follow, and on reaching the treasure, will be astonished to discover the person who has hidden it, who will endeavor to grapple with him, but will be unable so much as to approach him. The Karcist must be provided with a sheet of virgin parchment inscribed with the grand conjuration of the Clavicle. This he must cast upon the treasure, grasping one of its coins at the same moment as a pledge and a surety, and previously flinging down a piece of his own money bitten by his own teeth, after which he may retire, walking backwards, and carrying away what he can of the treasure. The rest cannot escape him after the above precautions. He must, however, take heed not to turn round, whatever noise he may hear, for at this critical moment it will truly seem as if all the mountains in the world were being precipitated upon him. He must for this cause be fortified with special intrepidity, must take fright at nothing, and keep perfectly firm. So acting, he will be led back by the Spirit to the entrance of the circle. Then shall the Karcist recite the following discharge of the Spirit.

Conjuration and Discharge of the Spirit.

O Prince Lucifer, I am, for the time, contented with thee. I now leave thee in peace, and permit thee to retire wheresoever it may seem good to thee, so it be without noise and without leaving any evil smell behind thee. Be mindful, however, of our engagement, for shouldst thou fail in it, even for a moment, be assured that I shall eternally smite thee with the Blasting Rod of the great Adonay, Eloim, Ariel, and Jehovam. Amen.

Act of Thanksgiving.

O Omnipotent God, who hast created all things for the service and convenience of men, we return Thee most humble thanks for the benefits which, in Thy great bounty, Thou hast poured out on us during this night of Thine inestimable favours, in which Thou hast granted us according to our desires. Now, O Almighty God, have we realised all the scope of Thy great promises when Thou didst say to us: Seek and ye shall find, knock and it shall be opened unto you. And as Thou hast commanded and warned us to succour the poor, we promise Thee, in the presence of the great Adonay, Eloim, Ariel, and Jehovam, to be charitable and to pour out on them the beneficent beams of the Sun with which those four potent divinities have enriched us. So be it. Amen. Vale.

The Mysteries of Infernal Evocation

§ 2. *Concerning the Genuine Sanctum Regnum, or the True Method of Making Pacts.*

There are two kinds of pacts, says the *Grimorium Verum,* the tacit and the manifest; but know at the same time that among the several kinds of spirits there are some which bind and some which do not bind, save only in a very light manner. As to the first, they are those which require something personally belonging to you whensoever a pact is agreed. Against these you must be on your guard, because the guileful friend becometh an open enemy.[1] The *Grimorium Verum* does not, however, entertain more largely the question of a compact with Satan or his ministers, though it may perhaps be inferred from its pages that all

[1] Catholic theologians who have concerned themselves with the question of the pact have so extended the sphere of its operation that it includes the mere process of communicating with spirits. In his "Theological Dictionary" Bergier defines the pact as an express or tacit agreement made with the demon in the hope of accomplishing things which transcend the powers of Nature. It is express and formal when the operator himself invokes and demands the help of the demon, whether that personage really appears in response, or the sorcerer believes that he beholds him, that is to say, is hallucinated. It is also express and formal when the demon is invoked by the mediation of some one supposed to be in relation with him; in other words, the consultation of a sorcerer is equivalent to a compact with Satan. The performance of any act with the expectation of a result from the demon is another compact of this kind. The pact is tacit or equivalent when an act is performed with a view to some effect which cannot naturally follow, while the intervention of God is not to be expected. There remains only the fiend. For example, should any one cure a disease by uttering certain words, this could only take place by the operation of the Infernal Spirit, because the words do not themselves possess the required virtue, and God is not likely to infuse it. Hence all theologians conclude that not only every species of Magic, but every kind of superstition involves at least a tacit and equivalent compact with the demon. St. Augustine and St. Thomas are said to have taken this view. It is by precisely such judgments as these that the theology of the Middle Ages brought itself to a by-word, and it is also for this reason that sorcery most flourished when such doctrines ruled, because a power which condemns everything to the same penalty condemns nothing effectually, and that which is over-judged is always vindicated in the eyes of the people. We have come to see that horse-stealing is not murder, and we no longer avenge it by the gallows; so also, with due respect to the masters of Theology, the follies of a village maiden who believes in a sooth-saying gipsy, and the trickeries of a quack-doctor who is absurd enought to take *Abracadabra* seriously, are not the crime of Faust. But the learned Bishop of Hippo and the Angel of the Schools produced Goethe as their ultimate antithesis; when the girl who draws lots for her lover is given over to Satan, the apotheosis of Faust is certain.

commerce with evil spirits is founded on a law of exchange.[1] They can be bent to the intention of the operator, but it is on the express understanding that they are satisfied for their part, because these kinds of creatures give nothing for nothing.

With the author of the "Grand Grimoire" the pact is a concession to the poverty of the operator's resources. In Black Magic, as in some other processes, the necessitous must be ready to sacrifice, and the sorcerer who is insufficiently equipped must pay a higher price in the end. The genuine *Sanctum Regnum* of the Grand Clavicle, otherwise termed the *Pacta Conventa Dæmonum,* is explained by the "Grand Grimoire," for the information of those who are desirous to bind spirits, but are devoid of the requisite resources for composing the Blasting Rod and the Kabbalistic circle. Such persons, it is affirmed, will never succeed in evoking spirits unless they perform, point by point, all that is detailed hereinafter concerning the manner of making pacts with any spirit whatsoever, whether the object in view may be the possession of treasures concealed in the earth, the enjoyment of women or girls, and for obtaining any desired favour at their hands, whether for the discovery of the most hidden secrets in all Courts and Cabinets of the world, whether for the revelation of the most impenetrable mysteries, whether for engaging a spirit to perform one's work in the night, whether to cause a fall of hail or a storm in any appointed place, whether to open seals, to behold what is passing in private houses, and learn all the skill of the shepherds, whether to obtain the Hand of Glory, and discern all the qualities and virtues of metals, minerals, and vegetables, and of animals both pure and impure, and to perform things so astounding that no person in existence

[1] But Lucifer, in ordinary cases, is contented with a cat.

can fail to be in a condition of utter bewilderment to see that by means of a pact with certain spirits one can discover the grandest secrets of Nature, which are hidden from the eyes of all other men.

It is to the Clavicle of the great King Solomon, says the Grimoire, that we owe the discovery of the genuine method of making pacts, which he also made use of himself for the acquisition of his immense riches, for the pleasure of such innumerable women, and for the revelation of the most impenetrable arcana of Nature, whereby every species of good and evil may be accomplished.

With the highest potentates of Infernus, with Lucifer, Beelzebuth, and Astaroth, it does not seem possible to enter into a binding compact. The sorcerer must be content with some one among the six governors,[1] who will generally work by their agents; an invariable covenant of the pact should bargain for service by one of the three superiors among such special subordinates.

Having determined to make a pact, continues the "Grand Grimoire," you must begin on the previous evening by cutting with a new and unused knife a rod of wild hazel, which has never borne fruit, and shall be similar to the Blasting Rod, as it has been previously described.

This must be done precisely at the moment when the sun appears upon our horizon. The same being accomplished, arm yourself with the stone called Ematille, and with two blessed candles, and proceed to select a place for the coming operation, where you will be wholly undisturbed; you may even make the pact in some isolated room, or in some subterranean part of an old ruinous castle, for the spirit has the power to transport the treasure to any required place.

[1] See c. iii. sec. 1.

This having been arranged, describe a triangle with the stone called Ematille—this is exclusively needed on the first occasion of making a pact.

Then set the two blessed candles in a parallel position on either side of the Triangle of Pacts, inscribing the Holy Name of Jesus below, so that no spirits can injure you after any manner. You may now take up your position in the middle of the triangle, holding the mysterious rod, together with the grand Conjuration of the Spirit, the Clavicle, the Requisition you mean to make, and the Discharge of the Spirit.

Having exactly fulfilled what things soever have been above described, begin by reciting the following Conjuration with decision and hopefulness:—

Grand Conjuration of Spirits with whom it is sought to make a Pact.

Taken from the Grand Clavicle.

Emperor Lucifer, Master of all the revolted Spirits, I entreat thee to favour me in the adjuration which I address to thy mighty minister, Lucifuge Rofocale, being desirous to make a pact with him. I beg thee also, O Prince Beelzebuth, to protect me in my undertaking. O Count Astarot! be propitious to me, and grant that to-night the great Lucifuge may appear to me under a human form, and free from evil smell, and that he may accord me, in virtue of the pact which I propose to enter into, all the riches which I need. O grand Lucifuge, I pray thee to quit thy dwelling, wheresoever it may be, and come hither to speak with me, otherwise will I compel thee by the power of the strong living God, His beloved Son, and the Holy Spirit. Obey promptly, or thou shalt be eternally tormented by the power of the

ASARADEL
AKIBECC
BERKAIAC
AMASARAC

potent words in the grand Clavicle of Solomon, wherewith he was accustomed to compel the rebellious spirits to receive his compact. Then straightway appear, or I will persistently torture thee by the virtue of these great words in the Clavicle.

AGLON, TETRAGRAM, VAYCHEON STIMULAMATON EZPHARES RETRAGRAMMATON OLYARAM IRION ESYTION EXISTION ERYONA ONERA ORASYM MOZM MESSIAS SOTER EMANUEL SABAOTH ADONAY, *te adoro, et te invoco.* AMEN.

You may rest assured that the recitation of these potent words will be followed by the appearance of the spirit, who will say:—

Manifestation of the Spirit.

Lo, I am here! What dost thou seek of me? Why dost thou disturb my repose? Answer me.

LUCIFUGE ROFOCALE.

Reply to the Spirit.

It is my wish to make a pact with thee, so as to obtain wealth at thy hands immediately, failing which I will torment thee by the potent words of the Clavicle.

The Spirit's Reply.

I cannot comply with thy request except thou dost give thyself over to me in twenty years, to do with thy body and soul as I please. LUCIFUGE ROFOCALE.

Thereupon throw him your pact, which must be written with your own hand on a sheet of virgin parchment; it should be worded as follows, and signed with your own blood:—I promise the grand Lucifuge to reward him in twenty years' time for all treasures he may give me. In witness whereof I have signed myself. N.N.

Reply of the Spirit.

I cannot grant thy request.

LUCIFUGE ROFOCALE.

In order to enforce his obedience, again recite the Supreme Appellation, with the terrible words of the Clavicle, till the spirit reappears, and thus addresses you:—

Of the Spirit's Second Manifestation.

Why dost thou torment me further? Leave me to rest, and I will confer upon thee the nearest treasure, on condition that thou dost set apart for me one coin on the first Monday of each month, and dost not call me oftener than once a week, to wit, between ten at night and two in the morning. Take up thy pact; I have signed it. Fail in thy promise, and thou shalt be mine at the end of twenty years.

LUCIFUGE ROFOCALE.

Reply to the Spirit.

I agree to thy request, subject to the delivery of the nearest treasure which I can at once carry away.

Follow the spirit without fear, cast your pact upon the hoard, touch it with your rod, remove as much as you can, return into the triangle, walking backwards, place the treasure in front of you, and recite the Discharge of the Spirit, as given in the preceding Rite.

It will be seen from the wording of the compact that it is designedly evasive, and the final response of the supposed spirit seems to recognize that it can obtain only by neglect on the part of the sorcerer. There were apparently more binding contracts, for in the year 1678 the Abbé Eynatton published a "Manual of Exorcisms" which contains the following formal process for forcing the Demon to return any writing which constitutes an agreement with him:—

EXORCISM.

O most merciful God, whose power hath no limit, whose dominion is supreme over all beings, so that nothing can possibly be estreated from Thy rule by apostasy; behold, we have sinned against Thee, we have provoked Thy most just wrath, when we have failed to obey Thy commands, above all when, forsaking Thy rule and Thy friendship, we have abjured Thee and have consorted with the impious demons, nor yet contented with Thy denial, have bound ourselves in writing to those demons, surrendering the document of our voluntary obligation against Thee into their custody. But Thy mercies are without number, O Lord of loving-kindness, and it is Thine to spare and to pardon; Look, therefore, with compassion upon this Thy creature, who, having formerly denied Thee and given himself in writing to the demons, but now, having returned to himself by the help of Thine infinite goodness, doth abhor his impiety, doth desire to be restored unto Thee his true Lord, and to be received with contrite heart into Thy favour. We know, O Lord, that a contrite and humble heart Thou wilt not desipse, nor can any writing be an impediment in the way of Thy mercy; we beseech Thee, therefore, that, by the abundance of Thy clemency, not only may the heinousness of this sin be blotted out with the Blood of Thy Son our Lord Jesus Christ, but that the demon, by the word of Thy power, may be compelled to restore the deed, and obligation, and delivery, lest he glory in his tyranny, and pretend to any right over the man whom we pray may be delivered through Thy Son from his bonds. Through the same Jesus Christ, Thy Son, our Lord, &c.

The propitiation of offended Deity is followed by a citation of the demon who is required to disgorge his prey.

EXORCISM.

I exorcise thee, O impious Satan, who, when thy power has passed away, dost still pretend to impose a tyrant yoke on man. I exorcise thee by Jesus Christ, who came into this world for the salvation of sinners; I conjure thee to remove thy yoke immediately from this creature, who, deceived by thy wiles, formerly delivered himself unto thee. Abandoning thee henceforth, he commits himself to the Divine mercy, seeking His service unto whom he alone is owing, who also promises the reward of eternal life to those who follow Him. I exorcise thee by the precious Blood of Jesus Christ by which the deed of judgment against us hath been blotted out, so that when Jesus receiveth the sinner into His favour, thou shalt dare not to advance anything against him, and shalt not fail to restore the deed by which this creature bound himself unto thee, when cancelled by the Blood of Jesus Christ.

Hear, therefore, accursed Satan, who art powerless over a servant of God, when encouraged by his true Lord, he turneth unto another service; in vain dost thou boast of this deed; I command thee to restore it in the name of the Lord, as a proof before the whole world that when God receiveth a sinner, thou hast no longer any rule over his soul. I abjure thee, by him who expelled thee from thy stronghold, bereft thee of the arms which thou didst trust in, and distributed thy spoils. Return therefore this deed, whereby this creature of God foolishly bound himself to thy service; return it, I say, in His name by whom thou art overcome; when thy power has come to nothing, presume not longer to retain this useless document. By penitence already hath this creature of God restored himself to his true Lord, spurning thy yoke hoping in the Divine mercy for defence against thine assaults, and assisted by the most holy and glorious virgin Mary, Mother of God, by whose intercession he shall obtain from Jesus Christ, His Son, that which he himself is not worthy to expect. Through the same Christ our Lord.

Whether this process was supposed to insure the visible and material return of the incriminating document, or, failing this, was held to cancel it formally, does not certainly appear, and will matter little; for what with the subtleties of the sorcerer and the assistance of the Church in the revocation of such acts and deeds, there was little chance for Infernus,[1] and the reluctance of Lucifuge Rofocale to enter into the tricky contract is, on the whole, exceedingly intelligible.

[1] But contracts with Infernus could apparently be repudiated with even greater facility. "If you are disposed to renounce the devil after having entered into a compact with him," says the *Vocabulaire Infernal,* "spit three times on the ground, and he will have no further power over you,"—in which case Black Magic with all its grim theatricals is the Art of exploiting lost Angels with impunity.

CHAPTER VII

The Method of Honorius

The "Grimoire of Honorius" is perhaps the most frankly diabolical of all the rituals connected with Black Magic, and yet, as we have already seen, its enormities have been much exaggerated. Its most obvious objections are: 1. Profanation of the mysteries of religion. 2. A bloody sacrifice, characterised by details of a monstrous kind. A less obvious objection is the superstitious nature of some of its ordinances. It must be confessed that such a charge seems fantastic, having regard to the innumerable offices of vain observance with which we have been dealing. But a vain observance, it should be remembered, is not necessarily superstitious. To assume that a virtue is resident in parchment prepared from the skin of an animal which has not engendered, and that such virtue is wanting in the skin of one which has reproduced its species, may have no foundation in fact, and may be eminently foolish, but it is not a superstitious assumption. It has been well

MYSTIC FIGURES FROM THE TITLE-PAGE OF THE "GRIMOIRE OF HONORIUS."

pointed out by Eliphas Lévi that the term superstition signifies survival; that is to say, it is the sign surviving the idea. Thus, the Catholic doctrine of Transubstantiation may or may not be true doctrine, but in neither case can the worship of the consecrated elements be superstitious, because such worship draws directly from the idea which has created the outward sign. If a time could be supposed when the Elements should continue to be worshipped after the doctrine itself had passed away, that would be a superstitious observance. But the etymological conception of superstition connects also with the idea of redundance. Thus, a double consecration of the Eucharistic elements would be a superstitious observance, as well as blasphemously absurd, because the first consecration is effectual by the theological hypothesis. But the repetition of the Angelical Salutation in the devotion of the Holy Rosary is not superstitious, because the first recitation is not necessarily effectual by the devotional hypothesis. So also the magical practice which consists with the magical hypothesis will not be superstitious though it may not consist with reason. The slaughter of a kid with a view to securing a virgin parchment is not a superstitious but a precautionary measure. The conversion of this slaughter into a sacrifice is not superstitious, because it has a purpose which consists with the magical hypothesis, namely, the increase of virtue by the consecration of the religious motive. The importation into such sacrifice of ceremonies which are not precautionary, and do not, by the hypothesis, increase the virtue, are redundant and so far superstitious. Such offices do not occur in the Grimoires, with the exception of that of Honorius, in which Ritual they are further characterised by brutal features. The slaughter of a black cock, and the extraction of the eyes, tongue, and heart, which must be reduced into powder, and that powder subsequently sprinkled on the lambskin, is a redundant and monstrous observance. We should say therefore that the "Grimoire of Honorius" must be avoided, were it necessary at the present day to warn any one against practices to which no one is likely to resort, which belong to the foolish mysteries of old exploded doctrines, and are interesting assuredly, but only as curiosities of the past. It should be added that the profanations of the mysteries of religion prescribed by the "Grimoire of Honorius" are not intentional profanations, and may be condoned to that extent. Their purpose is not outrage, but increase of efficacy.

Having made these initial provisions, the substance of this exceedingly curious Ritual may now be offered to the student in the words of its writer. It will be remembered that the person who desires to invoke the perverse "Spirits of Darkness" according to the method of Honorius must observe a three days' fast; he must also confess and approach the Holy Altar. After these three days, upon the morrow, and at the hour of sunrise, he shall recite the Seven Gradual Psalms, with the accompanying Litanies and Prayers,[1] the whole on his knees; further, he must drink no wine and eat no meat on that day. Next, he shall rise at midnight on the first Monday of the month,[2] and a priest shall say a Mass of the Holy Ghost.[3] After the consecration, taking the Host in his left hand, he shall recite the following prayer on his knees:—

[1] The reference is probably to the Litany of the Saints and the various orations which follow it.

[2] The three days' fast must therefore have been regulated so that it expired on the previous Saturday.

[3] The Mass of Pentecost, except the Epistle, which should be that of the Tuesday after Pentecost, and Gradual, for which there are special verisicles.

The Method of Honorius

PRAYER.

My Sovereign Saviour Jesus Christ, Son of the living God! Thou who for the salvation of all mankind didst suffer the death of the Cross; Thou who, before being abandoned to Thine enemies, by an impulse of ineffable love didst institute the Sacrament of thy Body; Thou who hast vouchsafed to us miserable creatures the privilege of making daily commemoration thereof; do Thou deign unto thine unworthy servant, thus holding thy Living Body in his hands, all strength and ability for the profitable application of that power with which he has been entrusted against the horde of rebellious spirits. Thou art their true God, and if they tremble at the utterance of Thy Name, upon that Holy Name will I call, crying Jesus Christ! Jesus, be Thou my help, now and for ever! Amen.

After sunrise a black cock must be killed, the first feather of its left wing being plucked and preserved for use at the required time. The eyes must be torn out, and so also the tongue and heart; these must be dried in the sun and afterwards reduced to powder. The remains must be interred at sunset in a secret place, a cross of a palm in height being set upon the mound, while at each of the four corners the signs which here follow must be drawn with the thumb:—

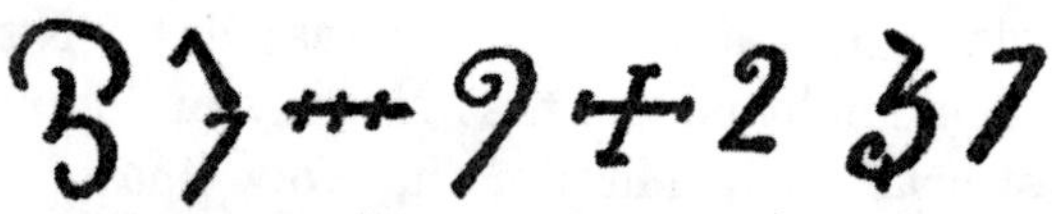

A later edition substitutes the following signs:—

On this day also the operator should drink no wine and abstain from eating meat.

On Tuesday, at break of day, let him say a Mass of the Angels,[1] placing the feather taken from the bird upon the altar, together with a new penknife. The signs hereinafter represented must be inscribed on a sheet of clean paper with the consecrated wine which is the Blood of Jesus Christ:—

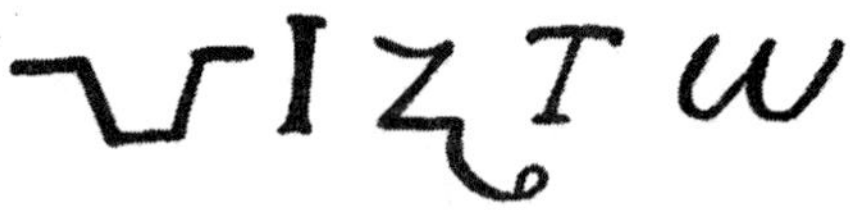

In an edition *circa* 1800 the following signs are substituted:—

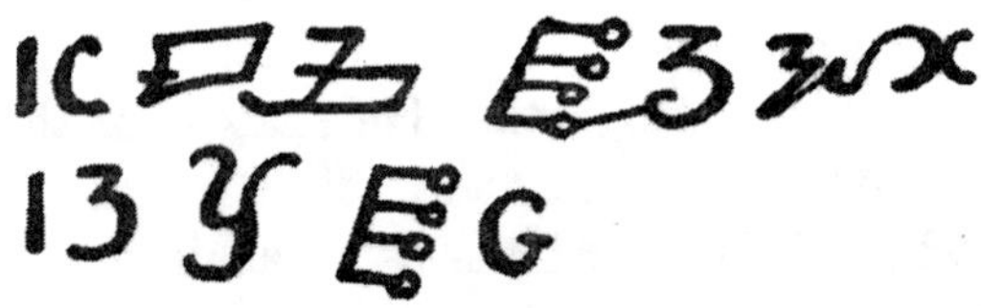

They should be written upon the altar, and at the end of the Mass the paper should be folded in a new veil of violet silk, to be concealed on the morrow, together with the oblation of the Mass and a part of the consecrated Host.

On the evening of Thursday the operator must rise at midnight, and, having sprinkled holy water about the chamber, he must light a taper of yellow wax, which shall have been prepared on the Wednesday and pierced in the form of a cross. When it is lighted he shall recite Psalm lxxvii.[2] —*Attendite, popule menus, legem meam*, &c.—without the

[1] The Mass for the Apparition of St. Michael, May 8, with a special Epistle, Gospel, Commemoration, &c.

[2] This Psalm is numbered lxxviii. in the Authorised Version.

Gloria Patri. He shall then begin the "Office of the Dead" with *Venite exultemus Domino,* &c. He shall recite Matins and Lauds, but in place of the versicle of the ninth Lesson[1] he shall say: Deliver us, O Lord, from the fear of hell. Let not the demons destroy my soul when I shall raise them from the deep pit, when I shall command them to do my will. May the day be bright, may the sun and moon shine forth, when I shall call upon them. Terrible of aspect are they, deformed and horrible to sight; but do Thou restore unto them their angelic shapes when I shall impose my will upon them. O Lord, deliver me from those of the dread visage, and grant that they shall be obedient when I shall raise them up from hell, when I shall impose my will upon them.

After the "Office of the Dead" the operator shall extinguish the taper, and at sunrise shall cut the throat of a male lamb of nine days, taking care that the blood does not gush forth upon the earth. He shall skin the lamb, and shall cast its tongue and heart into the fire. The fire must be freshly kindled, and the ashes shall be preserved for use at the proper time. The skin of the lamb shall be spread in the middle of a field, and for the space of nine days shall be sprinkled four time every day with holy water. On the tenth day, before the rising of the sun, the lambskin shall be covered with the ashes of the heart and tongue, and with the ashes also of the cock. On Thursday,[2] after sunset, the flesh of the lamb shall be interred in a secret place where no bird can come, and the priest with

[1] This is extremely confused; the Office of the Dead does not begin with the *Venite Exultemus.* The ninth Lesson belongs to the third Nocturne of the Matins. The prayer given in the Grimoire is based on the verses which it replaces.

[2] The days on which the various operations should be performed have been confused, after the prevailing manner of the Grimoires.

his right thumb shall inscribe on the grave the characters here indicated:—

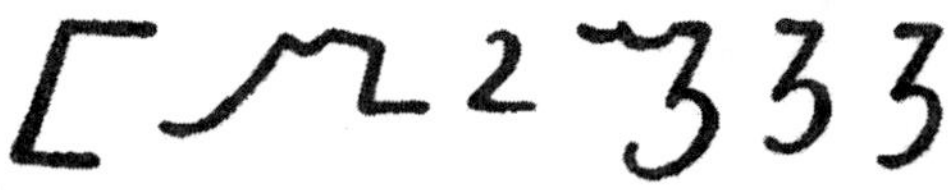

In the edition already cited the signs are varied thus:—

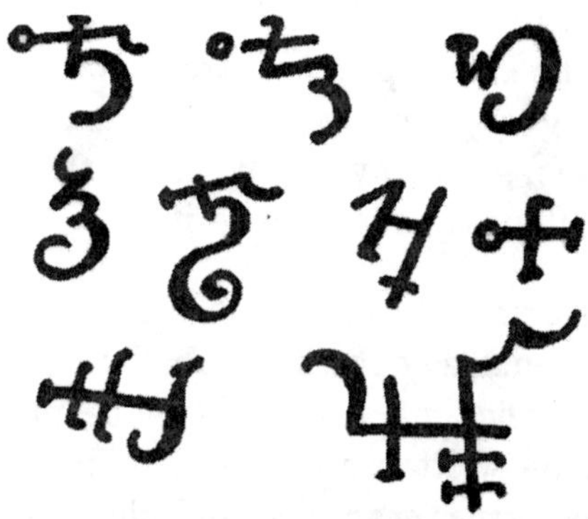

Moreover, for the space of three days he shall sprinkle the four corners with holy water, saying: Sprinkle me, O Lord, with hyssop, and I shall be cleansed! Wash me, and I shall be made whiter than snow!

After the aspersion let him recite the following prayer, kneeling with his face towards the east:—

PRAYER.

Christ Jesus, Redeemer of men, who, being the Lamb without spot, wast immolated for the salvation of the human race, who alone wast found worthy to open the Book of Life, impart such virtue to this lambskin that it may receive the signs which we shall trace thereon, written with Thy blood, so that the figures, signs, and words may become efficacious; and grant that this skin may preserve us against the wiles of the demons; that they may be terrified at the sight of these figures, and may only approach them trembling. Through Thee, Jesus Christ, who livest and reignest through all ages. So be it.

The Litanies of the Holy Name of Jesus must then be repeated, but instead of the *Agnus Dei,* substitute: Immolated Lamb, be Thou a pillar of strength against the demons! Slain Lamb, give power over the Powers of Darkness! Immolated Lamb, grant favour and strength unto the binding of the Rebellious Spirits. So be it.

The lambskin shall be stretched for eighteen days, and on the nineteenth day the fleece shall be removed, reduced into powder, and interred in the same place. The word *vellus* shall be written above it with the finger, together with the following character and the words: May this which hath been reduced into ashes preserve against the demons through the name of Jesus.

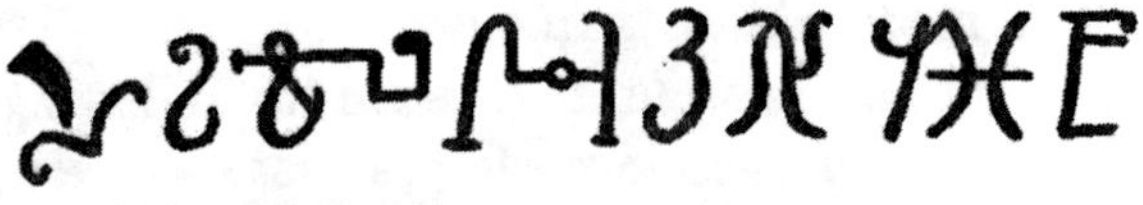

Or, according to the later edition:—

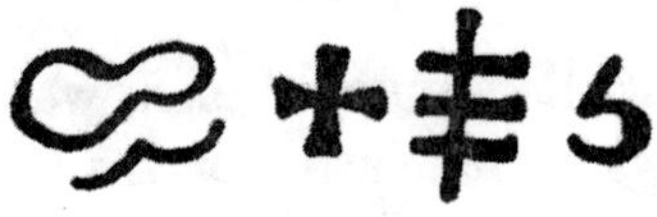

Add also these signs:—

Or, according to the later edition:—

Lastly, on the eastern side, the said skin must be set to dry in the sun for three days, the ensuing characters being cut with a new knife:—

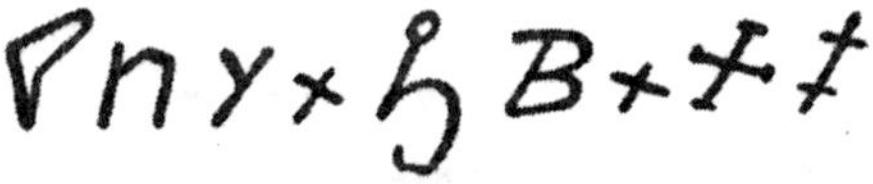

This being accomplished, recite Psalm lxxi., *Deus, judicium tuum regi da*, &c., and cut the following characters:—

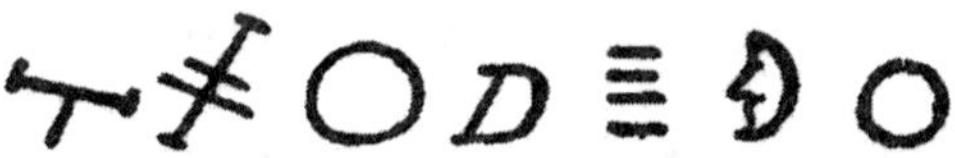

The figure being thus far completed, recite the verses *Afferte Domino, patriæ gentium,* occurring in Psalm xcv.: *Cantate Domino Canticum novum,* of which the seventh versicle is: *Offerte Domino, Filii Dei,* &c., and cut subsequently these characters:—

Next recite Psalm lxxvii.: *Attendite, populi meus, legem meam,* and compose the following figure:—

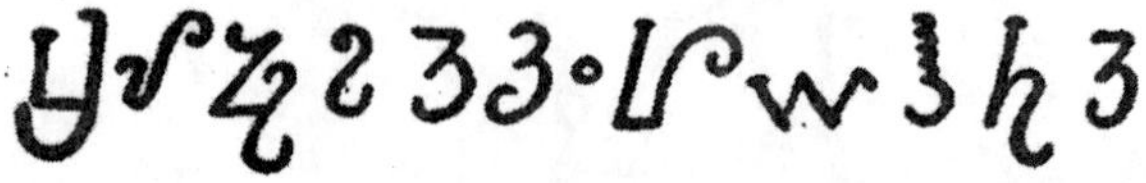

Which being accomplished, recite Psalm ii.: *Quare fremuerunt gentes et populi meditati sunt inania?* Then make another figure as follows:—

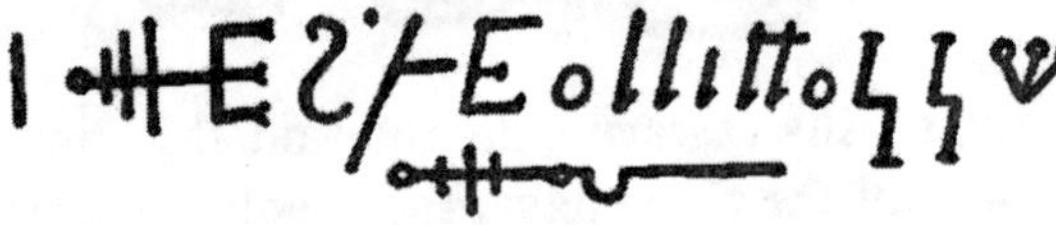

Or, alternatively:—

And recite Psalm cxv.: *Credidi propter quod locutus sum.* Finally, on the last day of the month a Mass for the Dead shall be offered; the prose shall be omitted, and also the Gospel of St. John, but at the end of the Mass the priest shall recite the Psalm *Confitemini Domino quoniam bonus,* &c.[1]

[1] At this point the process of the Grimoire becomes almost unintelligible. The recitation of the seventy-two names apparently succeeds the Psalm, and is followed by the Second Gospel, which is not omitted after all. There is then an extension of the *Deo Gratias;* this concluded the Mass, which seems immediately followed by the evocation. But the use of the Pentacles of Solomon and St. John does not appear, in the one case, till the close of the Conjurations, and not at all in the other.

In Honour of the Most Holy and August Trinity, the Father, the Son, and the Holy Ghost. Amen.

The Seventy-two Sacred Names of God.—Trinitas, Sother, Messias, Emmanuel, Sabahot, Adonay, Athanatos, Jesu, Pentagna, Agragon, Ischiros, Eleyson, Otheos, Tetragrammaton, Ely, Saday, Aquila, Magnus Homo, Visio, Flos, Origo, Salvator, Alpha and Omega, Primus, Novissimus, Principium et Finis, Primogenitus, Sapientia, Virtus, Paraclitus, Veritas, Via, Mediator, Medicus, Salus, Agnus, Ovis, Vitulus, Spes, Aries, Leo, Lux, Imago, Panis, Janua, Petra, Sponsa, Pastor, Propheta, Sacerdos, Sanctus, Immortalitas, Jesus, Christus, Pater, Filius Hominis, Sanctus, Pater, Omnipotens, Deus, Agios, Ressurrectio, Mischiros, Charitas, Æternas, Creator, Redemptor, Unitas, Summum Bonum, Infinitas. Amen.

Hereinafter follow the three small pentacles of Solomon, and that of the Gospel of St. John.

The Method of Honorius

The Beginning of the Holy Gospel according to John.
Glory be to Thee, O Lord.

In the beginning was the Word, &c., *in extenso, so far as the end of the fourteenth versicle.*

Thanks be to God. Hosanna to the Son of David! Blessed is He who cometh in the Name of the Lord. Hosanna in the Highest. We invoke Thee. We adore Thee. We praise Thee. We glorify Thee, O blessed and glorious Trinity! May the Name of the Lord be blessed, now and henceforth for ever! Amen. In the Name of the Father, of the Son, and of the Holy Ghost, Jesus of Nazareth, King of the Jews. May Christ conquer ✠, reign ✠, command ✠, and defend me from all evil. Amen.

Universal Conjuration.

I, N., do conjure thee, O Spirit N., by the living God, by the true God, by the holy and all-ruling God, who created from nothingness the heaven, the earth, the sea, and all things that are therein, in virtue of the Most Holy Sacrament of the Eucharist, in the name of Jesus Christ, and by the power of this same Almighty Son of God, who for us and for our redemption was crucified, suffered death, and was buried; who rose again on the third day, and is now seated on the right hand of the Creator of the whole world, from whence he will come to judge the living and the dead; as also by the precious love of the Holy Spirit, perfect Trinity. I conjure thee within the circle, accursed one, by thy judgment, who didst dare to tempt God: I exorcise thee, Serpent, and I command thee to appear forthwith under a beautiful and well-favoured human form of soul and body, and to fulfil my behests without any deceit whatsoever, as also without mental reservation of any kind, by the great Names of the God of gods and Lord of lords, ADONAY, TETRAGRAMMATON, JEHOVA, TETRAGRAMMATON, ADONAY, JEHOVA, OTHEOS, ATHANATOS, ISCHYROS, AGLA, PENTAGRAMMATON, SADAY, SADAY, SADAY, JEHOVA, OTHEOS, ATHANATOS, *a Liciat* TETRAGRAMMATON, ADONAY, ISCHYROS, ATHANATOS, SADY, SADY, SADY, CADOS, CADOS, CADOS, ELOY, AGLA, AGLA, AGLA, ADONAY, ADONAY. I conjure thee, Evil and Accursed Serpent, N., to appear at my will and pleasure, in this place, before this circle, without tarrying, without companions, without grievance, without noise, deformity, or murmuring. I exorcise thee by the ineffable names of God, to wit, Gog and Magog, which I am unworthy to pronounce; Come hither, Come hither, Come hither. Accomplish my will and desire, without wile or falsehood. Otherwise St. Michael, the invisible Archangel, shall presently blast thee in the utmost depths of hell. Come, then, N., to do my will.

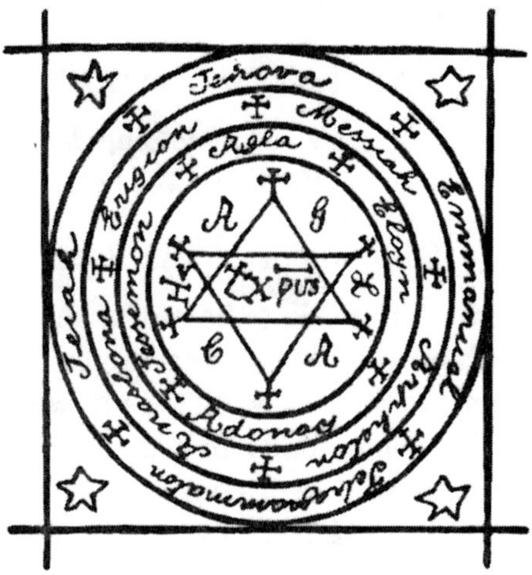

THE GRAND PENTACLE OF SOLOMON.

A. P.

Why tarriest thou, and why delayest? What doest thou? Make ready, obey your master, in the name of the Lord, BATHAT or RACHAT flowing over ABRACMENS, ALCHOR over ABERER.

L. Q. L. F. A. P.

Behold the Pentacle of Solomon which I have brought into thy presence! I command thee, by order of the great God, ADONAY, TETRAGRAMMATON, and JESUS! Hasten, fulfil my behests, without wile or falsehood, but in all truth, in the name of the Saviour and Redeemer, Jesus Christ.

DISCHARGE.

Go in peace unto your places. May there be peace between us and you, and be ye ready to come when ye are called. In the Name of the Father, and of the Son, and of the Holy Ghost. Amen.[1]

ACT OF THANKSGIVING.

Praise, honour, glory, and blessing be unto Him who sitteth upon the throne, who liveth for ever and ever. Amen.

CONJURATION OF THE BOOK.

I conjure thee, O Book, to be useful and profitable unto all who shall have recourse to thee for the success of their affairs. I conjure thee anew, by the virtue of the Blood of Jesus Christ, contained daily in the chalice, to be serviceable unto all those who shall read thee. I exorcise thee, in the name of the Most Holy Trinity, in the name of the Most Holy Trinity, in the name of the Most Holy Trinity!

[1] This is the *Liber Spirituum* of Pseudo-Agrippa, sufficiently described in Part I. The introduction of it in this Grimoire presupposes either an acquaintance in the reader or information which is omitted.

What follows must be said before the sealing of the Book.

I conjure and command you, O Spirits, all and so many as ye are, to accept this Book with good grace, so that whensoever we may read it, the same being approved and recognized as in proper form and valid, you shall be constrained to appear in comely human form when you are called, accordingly as the reader shall judge. In no circumstances shall you make any attempt upon the body, soul, or spirit of the reader, nor inflict any harm on those who may accompany him, either by mutterings, tempests, noise, scandals, nor yet by lesion or by hindrance in the execution of the commands of this Book. I conjure you to appear immediately when the conjuration is made, to execute without dallying all that is written and enumerated in its proper place in the said book. You shall obey, serve, instruct, impart, and perform all in your power for the benefit of those who command you, and the whole without illusion. If perchance some of the invoked spirits be unable to come or appear when required, they shall be bound over to send others vested with their power, who also shall swear solemnly to execute all that the reader may demand, and ye are all hereby enjoined by the Most Holy Names of the Omnipotent Living God, ELOYM, JAH, EL, ELOY, TETRAGRAMMATON, to fulfil everything as it is set forth above. If ye obey me not, I will force you to abide in torments for a thousand years, as also if any one of you receive not this Book with entire resignation to the will of the reader.

CONJURATION OF THE DEMONS.

In the Name of the Father, and of the Son, and of the Holy Ghost. Take heed! Come, all Spirits! By the virtue and power of your King, and by the seven crowns and chains of your Kings, all Spirits of the Hells are forced to appear in my presence before this pentacle or circle of Solomon, whensoever I shall call them. Come, then, all at my orders, to fulfil that which is in your power, as commanded. Come, therefore, from the East, South, West, and North! I conjure and command you, by the virtue and power of Him who is three, eternal, equal, who is God invisible, consubstantial, in a word, who has created the heavens, the sea, and all which is under heaven.

After these Conjurations you shall command them to affix the Seal.

CONCERNING THE FIGURE OF THE CIRCLE.

Circles should be described with charcoal or holy water,

THE MAGIC CIRCLE OF HONORIUS.

sprinkled with the wood of the blessed Cross. When they

have been duly made, and the words have been written about the circle, the holy water which has served to bless the same may also be used to prevent the spirits from inflicting any hurt. Standing in the middle of the circle, you shall command them in a lively manner, as one who is their master.

What must be said in Composing the Circle.

O Lord, we fly to Thy virtue! O Lord, confirm this work! What is operated in us becomes like dust driven before the wind, and the Angel of the Lord pausing (*sic*), let the darkness disappear, and the Angel of the Lord ever pursuing, ALPHA, OMEGA, ELY, ELOHE, ELOHIM, ZABAHOT, ELION, Sady. Behold the Lion who is the conqueror of the Tribe of Judah, the Root of David! I will open the Book, and the seven seals thereof. I have beheld Satan as a bolt falling from heaven. It is Thou who hast given us power to crush dragons, scorpions, and all Thine enemies beneath Thy feet. Nothing shall harm us, not even ELOY, ELOHIM, ELOHE, ZABAHOT, ELION, ESARCHIE, ADONAY, JAH, TETRAGRAMMATON, SADY. The earth is the Lord's and all those who dwell therein, because He established it upon the seas and prepared it in the midst of the waves. Who shall ascend unto the mountain of the Lord? Who shall be received in his Holy Place? The innocent of hands and clean of heart. Who hath not received his soul in vain, and hath not sworn false witness against his neighbour. The same shall be blessed of God, and shall obtain mercy of God to his salvation. He is of the generation of those who seek Him. Open your gates, ye princes, open the eternal gates, and the King of Glory shall enter! Who is this King of Glory? The Lord Almighty, the Lord mighty in battle. Open your gates, ye princes! Lift up the eternal gates. Who is this

King of Glory? The Lord Almighty. This Lord is the King of Glory. Glory be to the Father, &c.

To dismiss them, the Pentacle of Solomon must be exhibited, at the same time saying as follows:—

Behold your sentence! Behold that which forbids rebellion to our wills, and doth ordain you to return unto your

A LESSER PENTACLE OF SOLOMON.

abodes. May peace be between us and you, and be ye ready to come, each and all, as ye are called to do my will.

Conjuration of the King of the East.

I conjure and invoke thee, O powerful King of the East, Magoa, by my holy labour, by all the names of Divinity, by the name of the All-Powerful: I command thee to obey, and to come to me, or that failing, forthwith and immediately to send unto me Massayel, Ariel, Satiel, Arduel, Acorib, to respond concerning all that I would know and to fulfil all that I shall command. Else thou shalt come verily in thine own person to satisfy my will; which refusing, I shall compel thee by all the virtue and power of God.

The Grand Pentacle or Circle of Solomon will answer for the above and following Conjurations, which can be said on all days and at all hours. If it be desired to speak only with one spirit, one only need be named, at the choice of the reader.

Conjuration of the King of the South.

O Egym, great King of the South, I conjure and invoke thee by the most high and holy Names of God, do thou here manifest, clothed with all thy power; come before this circle, or at least send me forthwith Fadal, Nastrache, to make answer unto me, and to execute all my wishes. If thou failest, I shall force thee by God Himself.

Conjuration of the King of the West.

O Baymon, most potent King, who reignest in the Western quarter, I call and I invoke thee in the name of the Deity! I command thee by virtue of the Most High, to send me immediately before this circle the Spirit Passiel Rosus, with all other Spirits who are subject unto thee, that the same may answer in everything, even as I shall require them. If thou failest, I will torment thee with the sword of fire divine; I will multiply thy sufferings, and will burn thee.

The Method of Honorius

CONJURATION OF THE KING OF THE NORTH.

O thou, Amaymon, King and Emperor of the Northern parts, I call, invoke, exorcise, and conjure thee, by the virtue and power of the Creator, and by the virtue of virtues, to send me presently, and without delay, Madael, Laaval, Bamlahe, Belem, and Ramath, with all other Spirits of thine obedience, in comely and human form! In whatsoever place thou now art, come hither and render that honour which thou owest to the true living God, who is thy Creator. In the name of the Father, of the Son, and of the Holy Ghost, come therefore, and be obedient, in front of this circle, without peril to my body or soul. Appear in comely human form, with no terror encompassing thee. I conjure thee, make haste, come straightway, and at once. By all the Divine names—SECHIEL, BARACHIEL—if thou dost not obey promptly, BALANDIER, *suspensus, iracundus, Origratiumgu, Partus, Olemdemis, and Bautratis.* N. I exorcise thee, do invoke, and do impose most high commandment upon thee, by the omnipotence of the living God, and of the true God; by virtue of the holy God, and by the power of Him who spake and all things were made, even by His holy commandment the heaven and earth were made, with all that is in them! I adjure thee by the Father, by the Son, and by the Holy Ghost, even by the Holy Trinity, by that God whom thou canst not resist, under whose empire I will compel thee; I conjure thee by God the Father, by God the Son, by God the Holy Ghost, by the Mother of Jesus Christ, Holy Mother and perpetual Virgin, by her sacred heart, by her blessed milk, which the Son of the Father sucked, by her most holy body and soul, by all the parts and members of this Virgin, by all the sufferings, afflictions, labours, agonies which she endured during the whole course of her life, by all the sighs she uttered, by the holy tears which she shed whilst her dear Son wept before the time of His dolorous passion on the tree of the Cross, by all the sacred holy things which are offered and done, and also by all others, as in heaven so on earth, in honour of our Saviour Jesus Christ, and of the Blessed Mary, His Mother, by whatsoever is celestial, by the Church Militant, in honour of the Virgin and of all the Saints. In like manner, I conjure thee by the Holy Trinity, by all the other mysteries, by the sign of the Cross, by the most precious blood and water which flowed from the side of Jesus Christ, by the sweat which issued from His whole body, when He said in the Garden of Olives: My Father, if it be possible, let this chalice pass from me—I conjure thee by His death and passion, by His burial and glorious resurrection, by His ascension, by the coming of the Holy Ghost. I adjure thee, furthermore, by the crown of thorns which was set upon His head, by the blood which flowed from His feet and hands, by the nails with which He was nailed to the tree of the Cross, by the holy tears which He shed, by all which He suffered willingly through great love of us: by the lungs, the heart, the hair, the inward parts, and by all the members, of our Saviour Jesus Christ. I conjure thee by the judgment of the living and the dead, by the Gospel words of our Saviour Jesus Christ, by His preachings, by His sayings, by all His miracles, by the child in swaddling-clothes, by the crying child, borne by the mother in her most pure and virginal womb; by the glorious intercession of the Virgin Mother of our Saviour Jesus Christ; by all which is of God and of His Most Holy Mother, as in heaven so on earth. I conjure thee by the holy Angels and Archangels, and by all the blessed orders of Spirits, by the holy patriarchs and prophets, by all the holy martyrs and confessors, by all the holy virgins and innocent widows, and by all the saints of God, both men and women. I conjure thee by the head of St. John the Baptist, by the milk of St. Catherine, and by all the Saints.

CONJURATIONS FOR EACH DAY OF THE WEEK.

For Monday, to Lucifer.

This experience is commonly performed between eleven and twelve o'clock, or between three and four. Requisites: coal, and consecrated chalk to compose the circle, about which these words must be written: I forbid thee, Lucifer, in the name of the Most Holy Trinity, to enter within this circle. A mouse must be provided to give him; the master

must have a stole and holy water, and alb also and a surplice. He must recite the Conjuration in a lively manner, commanding sharply and shortly, as a lord should address his servant, with all kinds of menaces: SATAN, RANTAM, PALLANTRE, LUTAIS, CORICACOEM SCIRCIGREUR, I require thee to give me very humbly, &c.

CONJURATION.

I conjure thee, Lucifer, by the living God, by the true God, by the holy God, who spake and all was made, who commanded and all things were created and made! I conjure thee by the ineffable name of God, ON, ALPHA, and OMEGA, ELOY, ELOYM, YA, SADAY, LUX, MUGIENS, REX, SALUS, ADONAY, EMMANUEL, MESSIAS; and I adjure, conjure, and exorcise thee by the names which are declared under the letters V, C, X, as also by the names JEHOVAH, SOL, AGLA, RIFFASORIS, ORISTON, ORPHITNE, PHATON IPRETU, OGIA, SPERATON, IMAGON, AMUL, PENATON, SOTER, TETRAGRAMMATON, ELOY, PREMOTON, STITMON, PERIGARON, IRATATON, PLEGATON, ON, PERCHIRAM, TIROS, RUBIPHATON, SIMULATON, PERPI, KLARIMUM, TREMENDUM, MERAY, and by the most high ineffable names of God, GALI, ENGA, EL, HABDANUM, INGODUM, OBU ENGLABIS, do thou make haste to come, or send me N., having a comely and human form, in no wise repulsive, that he may answer in real truth whatsoever I shall ask him, being also powerless to hurt me, or any person whomsoever, either in body or soul.

For Tuesday, to Frimost.[1]

This experience is performed at night from nine to ten o'clock, and the first stone found is given to him. He is to be received with dignity and honour. Proceed as on Monday; compose the circle, and write about: Obey me, Frimost! Obey me, Frimost! Obey me, Frimost!

CONJURATION.

I conjure and command thee, Frimost, by all the names wherewith thou canst be constrained and bound! I exorcise

[1] Otherwise, Nambroth.

thee, Nambroth, by thy name, by the virtue of all spirits, by all characters, by the Jewish, Greek, and Chaldean conjurations, by thy confusion and malediction, and I will redouble thy pains and torments from day to day for ever, if thou

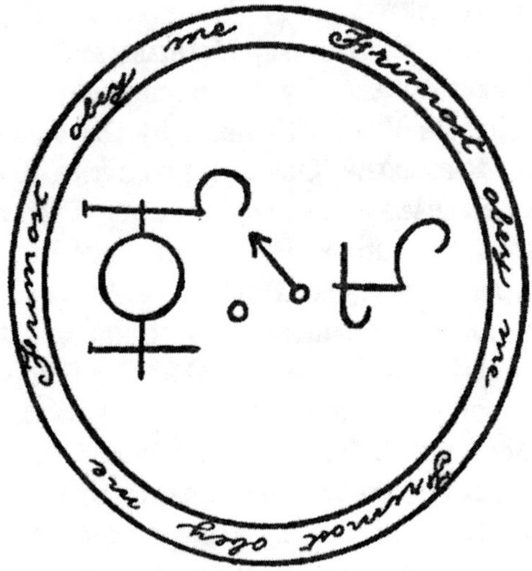

come not now to accomplish my will and submit to all that I shall command, being powerless to harm me, or those who accompany me, either in body or soul.

For Wednesday, to Astaroth.

This experience is performed at night, from ten to eleven o'clock; it is designed to obtain the good graces of the King and others. Write in the circle as follows: Come, Astaroth! Come, Astaroth! Come. Astaróth!

CONJURATION.

I conjure thee, Astaroth, wicked spirit, by the words and virtues of God, and by the powerful God, Jesus Christ of

Nazareth, unto whom all demons are submitted, who was conceived of the Virgin Mary; by the mystery of the Angel Gabriel, I conjure thee; and again in the name of the Father, and of the Son, and of the Holy Ghost; in the name of the glorious Virgin Mary, and of the Most Holy Trinity, in whose honour do all the Archangels, Thrones, Dominations, Powers, Patriarchs, Prophets, Apostles, and Evangelists sing without end; Hosannah, Hosannah, Hosannah, Lord God of Hosts, who art, who wast, who art to come, as a river of burning fire! Neglect not my commands, refuse not to come. I command thee by Him who shall appear with flames to judge the living and the dead, unto whom is all honour, praise, and glory. Come, therefore, promptly, obey my will, appear and give praise to the true God, unto the living God, yea, unto all His works; fail not to obey me, and give honour to the Holy Ghost, in whose name I command thee.

For Thursday, to Silcharde.

This experience is made at night, from three to four o'clock, at which hour he is called, and appears in the form of a King. A little bread must be given him when he is

required to depart; he renders man happy and also discovers treasures. Write about the circle as follows: Holy God! Holy God! Holy God!

Conjuration.

I conjure thee, Silcharde, by the image and likeness of Jesus Christ our Saviour, whose death and passion redeemed the entire human race, who also wills that, by His providence, thou appear forthwith in this place. I command thee by all the Kingdoms of God. Act—I adjure and constrain thee by his Holy Name, by Him who walked upon the asp, who crushed the lion and the dragon. Do thou obey me, and fulfil my commands, being powerless to do harm unto me, or any person whomsoever, either in body or soul.

For Friday, to Bechard.

This experience is performed at night from eleven to

twelve o'clock, and a nut must be given to him. Write within the circle: Come, Bechard! Come, Bechard! Come, Bechard!

CONJURATION.

I conjure thee, Bechard, and constrain thee, in like manner, by the Most Holy Names of God, ELOY, ADONAY, ELOY, AGLA, SAMALABACTAY, which are written in Hebrew, Greek and Latin; by all the sacraments, by all the names written in this book; and by him who drove thee from the height of Heaven. I conjure and command thee by the virtue of the Most Holy Eucharist, which hath redeemed men from their sins; I conjure thee to come without any delay, to do and perform all my biddings, without any prejudice to my body or soul, without harming my book, or doing injury to those that accompany me.

For Saturday, to Guland.[1]

This experience is performed at night from eleven to twelve o'clock, and so soon as he appears burnt bread must

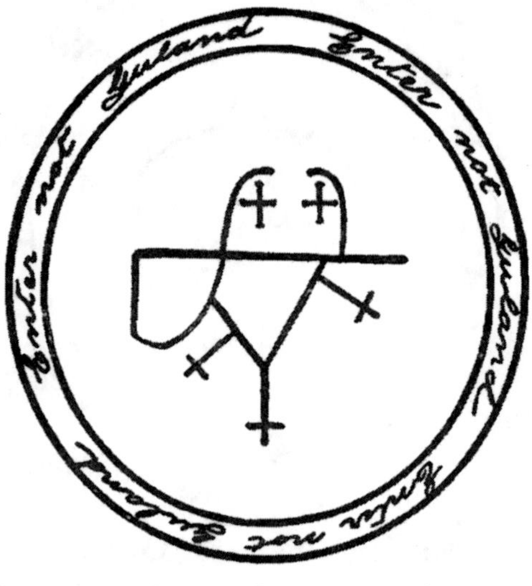

be given him. Ask him anything you will, and he will obey you on the spot. Write in his circle: Enter not, Guland! Enter not, Guland! Enter not, Guland!

CONJURATION.

I conjure thee, O Guland, in the name of Satan, in the

[1] Otherwise, Nabam.

name of Beelzebub, in the name of Astaroth, and in the name of all other Spirits, to make haste and appear before me. Come, then in the name of Satan and in the names of all other demons. Come to me, I command thee, in the name of the Most Holy Trinity. Come without inflicting any harm upon me, without injury to my body or soul, without maltreating my book, or anything which I use. I command thee to appear without delay, or, that failing, to send me forthwith another Spirit having the same power as thou hast, who shall accomplish my commands and be submitted to my will, wanting which, he whom thou shalt send me, if indeed thou comest not thyself, shall in no wise depart, nor until he hath in all things fulfilled my desire.

For Sunday, to Surgat.[1]

This experience is performed at night from eleven to one

o'clock. He will demand a hair of your head, but give him

[1] Otherwise, Aquiel.

one of a fox, and see that he takes it. His office is to discover and transport all treasures, and perform anything that you may will. Write in his circle: TETRAGRAMMATON, TETRAGRAMMATON, TETRAGRAMMATON. ISMAEL, ADONAY, IHUA. And in a second circle: Come, Surgat! Come, Surgat! Come, Surgat!

CONJURATION.

I conjure thee, O Surgat, by all the names which are written in this book, to present thyself here before me, promptly and without delay, being ready to obey me in all things, or, failing this, to despatch me a Spirit with a stone which shall make me invisible to every one whensoever I carry it! And I conjure thee to be submitted in thine own person, or in the person of him or of those whom thou shalt send me, to do and accomplish my will, and all that I shall command, without harm to me or to any one, so soon as I make known my intent.

Very Powerful Conjuration for all days and hours of the Day or Night, being for Treasures hidden by men or Spirits, that the same may be possessed and transported.

I command you, O all ye demons dwelling in these parts, or in what part of the world soever ye may be, by whatsoever power may have been given you by God and our holy Angels over this place, and by the powerful Principality of the infernal abysses, as also by all your brethren, both general and special demons, whether dwelling in the East, West, South, or North, or in any side of the earth, and, in like manner, by the power of God the Father, by the wisdom of God the Son, by the virtue of the Holy Ghost, and by the authority I derive from our Saviour Jesus Christ, the only Son of the

Almighty and the Creator, who made us and all creatures from nothing, who also ordains that you do hereby abdicate all power to guard, habit, and abide in this place; by whom further I constrain and command you, *nolens volens*, without guile or deception, to declare me your names, and to leave me in peaceable possession and rule over this place, of whatsoever legion you be and of whatsoever part of the world; by order of the Most Holy Trinity, and by the merits of the Most Holy and Blessed Virgin, as also of all the saints, I unbind you all, spirits who abide in this place, and I drive you to the deepest infernal abysses. Thus: Go, all Spirits accursed, who are condemned to the flame eternal which is prepared for you and your companions, if ye be rebellious and disobedient. I conjure you by the same authority, I exhort and call you, I constrain and command you, by all the powers of your superior demons, to come, obey, and reply positively to what I direct you in the name of Jesus Christ. Whence, if you or they do not obey promptly and without tarrying, I will shortly increase your torments for a thousand years in hell. I constrain you therefore to appear here in comely human shape, by the Most High Names of God, HAIN, LON, HILAY, SABAOTH, HELIM, RADISHA, LEDIEHA, ADONAY, JEHOVA, YAH, TETRAGRAMMATON, SADIA, MESSIAS, AGIOS, ISCHYROS, EMMANUEL, AGLA, Jesus who is ALPHA and OMEGA, the beginning and the end, that you be justly established in the fire, having no power to reside, habit, or abide in this place henceforth; and I require your doom by the virtue of the said names, to wit, that St. Michael drive you to the uttermost of the infernal abyss, in the name of the Father, and of the Son, and of the Holy Ghost. So be it.

I conjure thee, Acham, or whomsoever thou mayst be, by the Most Holy Names of God, by MALHAME, JAE, MAY, MABRON, JACOB, DASMEDIAS, ELOY, ATERESTIN, JANASTARDY,

Finis, Agios, Ischyros, Otheos, Athanatos, Agla, Jehova, Homosion, Aga, Messias, Sother, Christus vincit, Christus imperat, Increatus Spiritus Sanctus.

I conjure thee, Cassiel, or whomsoever thou mayest be, by all the said names, with power and with exorcism! I warn thee by the other sacred names of the most great Creator, which are or shall hereafter be communicated to thee; hearken forthwith and immediately to my words, and observe them inviolably, as sentences of the last dreadful day of judgment, which thou must obey inviolately, nor think to repulse me because I am a sinner, for therein shalt thou repulse the commands of the Most High God. Knowest thou not that thou art bereft of thy powers before thy Creator and ours? Think therefore what thou refusest, and pledge therefore thine obedience, swearing by the said last dreadful day of judgment, and by Him who hath created all things by His word, whom all creatures obey. P. *per sedem Baldarey et per gratiam et diligentiam tuam habuisti ab eo hanc nalatimanamilam,* as I command thee.

CHAPTER VIII.

Miscellaneous and Minor Processes

I. *Concerning Works of Hatred and Destruction.*

THE following process appears in several manuscript copies of the "Key of Solomon," but has been omitted by the English editor of that work, as others are also omitted, presumably as a Goëtic interpolation. But we have seen that a Goëtic process in a book like the "Key of Solomon" is not necessarily an interpolation, while as regards this particular instance it is very nearly evident that it is an integral portion of that dubious collection. In the second chapter of the first book we are told that the days and hours of Mars are suitable for overthrowing enemies, while the hours of Saturn and Mars, and also the days on which the Moon is in conjunction with those planets, are excellent for experiments of hatred, enmity, quarrel, and discord. In the first chapter of the second book it is said:—As for operations of destruction and desolation, we should put them into execution on the day of Saturn at the first hour, or rather at the eighth or fifteenth of the day, and from the first until the eighth hour of the night. From these statements it seems fair to infer that there must have been a section containing directions as to the performance of such works. In this case, the "Key of Solomon" is neither better nor worse than any other Grimoire of Black Magic. The apologists of the Clavicle will probably cite in defence of it a passage which occurs in Book i. c. 8, in which the author proffers his secrets on the express condition that they shall not be used to ruin and destroy one's neighbour. But when every allowance has been for this stipulation, we shall do well to remember that similar warnings are not wanting in purely Goëtic rituals. There is further another test by which the authenticity of the following process may be largely determined, and that is the manner of its wording, which corresponds closely with the prevailing manner of the Clavicle. It is a loose and general wording, covering several classes of experiment, and may be compared with Book I. c. xv., xvi., xvii., in which the same characteristics will be found.

The process itself is as follows:—Experiments upon enemies may be performed in several ways, but whether with waxen images or some other instrument, the particulars of each must be diligently and faithfully observed. Should the day and hour fail thee, proceed as already laid down, and prepare the image or instrument proper to this effect in the order and manner thereof. Fumigate with the proper perfumes, and if writing be required on the image, let it be done with the needle or stylet of the art, as aforesaid. Next recite the following words once over the said image:—VSOR, DILAPIDATORE, TENTATORE, SOIGNATORE, DEVORATORE, CONCITORE, ET SEDUCTORE. O all ye ministers and companions, I direct, conjure, constrain, and command you to fulfil this behest willingly, namely, straightway to consecrate this image, which is to be done in the name of . . . . . , that as the face of the one is contrary to the other, so the same may never more look one upon another.

Deposit the image in some place perfumed with evil odours, especially those of Mars, such as sulphur and *assafœtida.* Let it remain there for one night, having duly asperged it, observing the proper hour and time. Do likewise when the experiment is performed with characters and names, by touching the lovers with words, or by whatsoever other manner. But when the experiment is made by giving something to be eaten, the same must be performed on the day and hour proper to this work. All things being prepared, place them before you, and say: Where are ye, SOIGNATORE, USORE, DILAPIDATORE, and DENTORE; CONCISORE, DIVORATORE, SEDUCTORE, and SEMINATORE? Ye who sow discord, where are? Ye who infuse hatred and propagate enmities, I conjure you by Him who hath created you for this ministry, to fulfil this work, in order that whensoever N. [*naming the person*] shall eat of like things, or shall touch them, in whatsoever manner, never shall he go in peace.

Give then whatsoever you please to the person designated, but let it be in the hour of Saturn or that of Mars, observing all things needful for such experiments.

§ 2. *Concerning Venereal Experiments.*

We have seen that the sorcerer of the Middle Ages was usually squalid and necessitous; hence he coveted treasures: he was usually despised, and hence he longed for mastery, for the prestige of mystery, and the power of strange arts: he was usually lonely and libidinous, and hence he sought, by means of spells and philtres, to compel the desire of women. To be rich in worldly goods, to trample on one's enemies, and to gratify the desires of the flesh—such are the ends, variously qualified and variously attained, of most Ceremonial Magic, and hence the Rituals abound in Venereal Experiments.

In such as the *Grimorium Verum* there is no attempt to hide their illicit nature; in the "Key of Solomon" it is disguised, but the process for obtaining favour and love which occurs in that work is not really a more lawful experiment than that *Pour faire venir une Fille vous trouver, si sage qu'elle soit.* The "Key of Solomon" is reticent and the Grimoires are frank; the one promises the fulfilment of the operator's desire without defining it; the others are explicit and particular. It is true also that the one has recourse to Adonai and implores his assistance, while the others invoke the powers of Hell.

The Book of "True Black Magic" for once ignores the experience of the Clavicle and substitutes the following:—

§ 3. *Concerning the Experiment of Love.*

Whatsoever person be the object of this experiment, whether man or woman, it is needful in making it to observe the proper day and hour, and note further that it is performed by means of an image of wax or other suitable matter. Before composing it, say the following words over the wax: NOGA, JES, ASTROPOLIM, ASMO, COCCAV, BERMONA, TENTATOR, SOIGNATOR—I conjure you, ministers of love and uncleanness, by Him who hath condemned you to hell! Do ye consecrate this wax in a regular manner, that it may acquire the desired virtue, by the power of the Most Holy Adonay, who liveth and reigneth for ever and ever. Amen.

The image must then be composed and suitable characters inscribed thereon with the male goose-quill of the Art, after which it must be fumigated while reciting the following words:—O thou most powerful King Paymon, whose absolute rule and reign is in the western quarter! O thou, Egim, most strong King, whose empire is in the cold region! O thou, Asmodeus, who governest in the south! O thou, Aymamon, most noble King, monarch of the Eastern world, whose reign began from of old and will endure to the end of time! I invoke and beseech you by Him who spake and it was, whose sole word hath created all, whom all creatures obey; by the seat of his Majesty; by his Will and his Name; by Him who was before the ages and hath created the ages; whose Name is written with the four letters JOD, HE, VAU, HE; by the enchantments and power thereof; and by all the signal names of the Creator; I conjure you to consecrate this image, and grant that it may acquire virtue according to our desire, by the Most Holy Name Adonay, the power of which is without beginning or end.

This being done, conjure with the Conjuration of the image, and if the woman or man should not appear, place the said image beneath the pillow of your bed, and before three days you shall behold admirable things, while chains or earth shall not stay the desired person from coming to you, for the fulfilment of your purpose, nothing being excepted.

But if the experience be to find the beloved person, place the image under the door which he or she must pass. In either case a powder must be made and cast upon the person, or given them with their meat or drink. The solemnities of the hours, matters, and instruments must be faithfully observed, and the Spirits conjured by name, saying also: I conjure and constrain you, ye Devils, who have the power to disturb the hearts of men and women! By Him who hath created you from nothing and by this image, I conjure you this night into my presence, that I may have the power to compel whomsoever I will to love me, whether male or female.

When the characters and images have been prepared, say over them: I conjure you, O Anaël, Donquel, Theliel, princes of love, with all your ministers, who have power to fill with warmth the hearts of men and women, and to kindle the fire of love! I conjure you by Him who is seated upon the Cherubim and guardeth the abysses, by Him who maketh the world to tremble, whom all creatures obey!

Grant that these characters and figures may possess this virtue, that such man or woman may love me, may desire me, and burn for my love, and that it shall be impossible for him or her to love any person save me.

Place the image in a vessel for one night, operate on the day and in the hour appropriate thereto, and you shall behold a wonder.

The compiler of the *Grimorium Verum*, who seems to have selected almost invariably the most bizarre processes, instructs his pupils

How to Cause the Appearance of Three Ladies or Three Gentlemen in One's Room after Supper.

§ 1. *Preparation.*

Abstain for three days from drawing Mercury, and then will you rise up. On the fourth day, you shall cleanse and prepare your chamber as soon as it is morning, immediately after dressing, the whole fasting. But see you do it in such a way that it will not be liable to disarrangement during the remainder of the day. Note that there must be no hangings, nor anything set crosswise, no tapestries, no hanging clothes, hats, bird-cages, bed curtains, &c. Above all, put clean sheets on your couch.

§ 2. *Ceremony.*

After supper pass in secret to your chamber, made ready as above; kindle a good fire; place a white cloth on the table, round which set three chairs, and before each chair, upon the table, let there be a wheaten roll and a glass full of fresh clear water. Lastly, draw up a chair and settee to the side of the bed, and retire to rest, uttering the following

CONJURATION.

Besticitum consolatio veni ad me vertat Creon, Creon, Creon, cantor laudem omnipotentis et non commentur. Stat superior carta bient laudem omviestra principiem da montem et inimicos meos ô prostantis vobis et mihi dantes que passium fieri sincisibus.

The three persons having arrived, will rest themselves near the fire, drinking, eating, and finally thanking him or her who has entertained them; for if it be a young lady who performs this ceremony, three gentlemen will come; but if it be a man, three young ladies will appear. The said three persons will draw lots among each other to know which of them shall remain with you. If a man be the operator, she who wins will place herself in the arm-chair which you have set by the bed, and she will remain and commune with you until midnight, at which hour she will depart with her companions, without any need of dismissal. As regards the two others, they will keep themselves by the fire, while the other entertains you. So long as she remains you may question her upon any art or science, or upon what subject soever, and she will immediately give you a positive answer. You may also inquire of her whether she is aware of any hidden treasure, and she will instruct you as to its locality and the precise time suited to its removal. She will even appear there with her companions to defend you against the assaults of the Infernal Spirits who may have it in their possession. At parting, she will present you with a ring, which, worn on the finger, will render you lucky at play, while if it be placed upon the finger of any woman or girl, you shall there and then have your delight with them. Observe, however, that you must leave your window open in order that they may enter.

This ceremony may be repeated frequently at the will of the operator.

It must be acknowledged that the above experiment offers a large return for very small pains in the preparation, and hence it is very popular with the makers of Grimoires. The same observation applies to the following process, which is common to the supplementary portions of the "Grand Grimoire," the *Grimorium Verum,* the "Grimoire of Honorius," and most of the minor collections. It is described as an experience of the wonderful power of the Superior Intelligences. The nature of the superiority may, however, be inferred from the title.

To Cause a Girl to Seek you out, however Prudent she may be.

Whether in the increase or wane of the Moon, a star must be observed between eleven o'clock and midnight. But before beginning do as follows. Take a virgin parchment. Write thereon her name whose presence you desire. The parchment must be shaped as represented in the following figure. On the other side inscribe these words: Melchiael, Bareschas. Then place your parchment on the earth, with the person's name against the ground. Place your right foot above it, while your left knee is bent to the earth. In this position observe the brightest star in the firmament, holding in the right hand a taper of white wax large enough to last for an hour, and recite the following

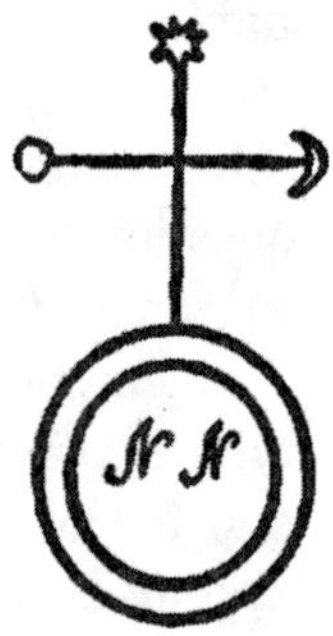

Conjuration

I salute and conjure you, O beautiful Moon, O beautiful Star, O bright light which I hold in my hand! By the air which I breathe, by the breath which is within me, by the earth which I touch, I conjure you, and by all the names of the spirits who are princes residing in you; by the ineffable Name ON, which hath created all; by thee, O Resplendent Angel Gabriel, together with the Prince Mercury, Michael, and Melchidàel! I conjure you again by all the divine Names of God, that you send down to obsess, torment, and harass the body, spirit, soul, and five senses of the nature of N., whose name is written here below, in such a way that she shall come unto me and accomplish my will, having no friendship for any one in the world, but especially for N., so long as she shall be indifferent to me. So shall she endure not, so shall she be obsessed, so suffer, so be tormented. Go then promptly; go, Melchidael, Baresches, Zazel, Firiel, Malcha, and all those who are without you (*sic*). I conjure you by the great living God to accomplish my will, and I, N., do promise to satisfy you duly.

Having thrice pronounced this conjuration, place the taper on the parchment and let it burn. Take the parchment on the morrow, put it in your left shoe, and there leave it until the person for whom you have operated shall have come to seek you out. You must specify in the Conjuration the day that you desire her to come, and she will not fail.

This process has its disadvantages, and even its difficulties. It seems absurd to suppose that there are Spirit Princes inhabiting the flame of a taper, and the treatment invoked upon the lady is of a turbulent kind, nor is there any colourable pretence on which the position of the rival lover can be justified; but it has the touch of the picturesque, and, making all allowance for the potencies which may inhere in Sator, Arepo, Tenet, Opera, Rotas, it does not suffer seriously by comparison with the method of the Clavicle.

§ 3. *Concerning the Experiment of Invisibility.*

We shall see later on that there are certain processes found in the Grimoires which do not connect with Black Magic otherwise than by their place in the Grimoires. There are also other processes which are not in themselves Goëtic, but are objectionable on account of the abuse to which they are liable. It is curious to observe how experiments of this kind will in one Ritual appear under a harmless guise, and will in another bear all the marks of diabolism. The experience of Invisibility, with which we are here concerned, illustrates all these points.

Here Ceremonial Magic pretends to place its adepts in possession of the ring of Gyges. Presuming that the "Key of Solomon" is the most ancient of all the Rituals, it is there that the formal process first occurs. It is accomplished, however, without the intervention of a ring, by means of a simple preliminary invocation and an address to Almiras, Master and Chief of Invisibility, whatsoever may be necessary for the particular occasion, such as characters and circles, being left to the discretion of the operator. There is also a complementary process by means of a waxen image which occurs in one manuscript copy, and is given by the English editor. The person who has duly made and consecrated this image is supposed to become invisible when he carries it. If we now turn to the "Book of True Black Magic," we shall find the first experiment adapted as follows:—Before making the experiment of invisibility these words must be committed to memory: Scaboles, Habrion, elæ, elimigit, gabolii, Semitrion, Mentinobol, Sabaniteut, Heremobol, cane, methé, baluti, catea, timeguel, bora, by the empire which ye exert over us, fulfil this work, so that I may become invisible.[1] The said words must be written with the blood before mentioned,[2] and the following Conjuration recited: O ye Spirits of Invisibility, I conjure and constrain you to incontinently and forthwith consecrate this experiment, so that, surely and without trickery, I may go invisible. Furthermore, I conjure you by Lucifer, your prince, by the obedience which you owe to him, and by the power of God, incontinently to aid me by consecrating this experiment, without loss of my body or my soul. So be it, so be it, so be it.

Prepare all things required for this experiment with due solemnity and diligence, as it is laid down in the chapter proper thereto: so shalt thou operate with certainty and so find the truth; but failing any of the things needful, thou shalt not attain thy desire, for not by the walls but the gate may any man enter a town.

This is merely a shorter recension of the process contained in the Clavicle, with the reference to Lucifer interpolated.

In place of these bald and somewhat unmeaning directions, the *Grimorium Verum* supplies an excessively curious process, at once monstrous and fantastic, recalling the sorceries of Thessaly, and having direct connections with folk-lore.

To become Invisible.

Begin this operation on a Wednesday before the sun rises, being furnished with seven black beans. Take next the head of a dead man, and place one of the beans in his mouth, two in his eyes, and two in his ears. Then make

[1] These names are given as follows by the English editor: Sceaboles, Arbaron, Elohi, Elimigith, Herenobulcule, Methe, Baluth, Timayal, Villaquiel, Teveni, Yevie, Ferete, Bachuhaba, Guvarin.

[2] Possibly that of a mole, used in the consecration of the instruments.

upon this head the character of the figure which here follows. (*Omitted in all the Grimoires.*) This done, inter the head with the face towards heaven, and every day before sunrise, for the space of nine days, water it with excellent brandy. On the eighth day you will find the cited spirit, who will say unto you: What doest thou? You shall reply: I am watering my plant. He will then say: Give me that bottle; I will water it myself. You will answer by refusing, and he will again ask you, but you will persist in declining, until he shall stretch forth his hand and shew you the same figure which you have traced upon the head suspended from the tips of his fingers. In this case you may be assured that it is really the spirit of the head, because another might take you unawares, which would bring you evil, and further, your operation would be unfruitful. When you have given him your phial, he will water the head and depart. On the morrow, which is the ninth day, you shall return and will find your beans ripe. Take them, place one in your mouth, and then look at yourself in a glass. If you cannot see yourself, it is good. Do the same with the rest, or they may be tested in the mouth of a child. All those which do not answer must be interred with the head.

The advantage of occasional invisibility in the pursuits of illicit affection seems to have fascinated the compiler of the "Little Albert," and he refers to the adultery of Gyges with evident relish in prefacing his process for

Invisibility by means of a Ring.

This important operation must be performed on a Wednesday in spring-time, under the auspices of Mercury, when it is known to be conjoined with other favourable planets, such as the Moon, Jupiter, Venus, or the Sun. Taking good Mercury, fixed and well purified, compose a large ring thereof, so that the same will pass easily over the middle finger of the hand. Let the collet be enriched by a small stone which is found in the pewit's nest, and about the ring let the following words be enchased: Jesus passing ✠ through the midst of them ✠ disappeared. ✠[1]

Next, having placed the ring on a palette-shaped plate of fixed Mercury, compose the perfume of Mercury, and thrice expose the ring to the odour thereof; wrap it in a small piece of taffeta corresponding to the colour of the planet, carry it to the pewit's nest from which the stone was obtained, let it remain there for nine days, and when removed, fumigate it precisely as before. Then preserve it most carefully in a small box made also of fixed Mercury, and use it when required. The method of use is to place the ring upon the finger with the stone outwards; it will so fascinate the spectators by its virtue that one may be present without being beheld. When the wearer no longer desires to be invisible, he has merely to turn the ring, so that the stone shall be inward, and close the hand over it.

But Eliphas Lévi affirms that the only authors who have written seriously concerning the ring of Gyges or its equivalents are Porphyry, Iamblichus, and Peter of Apono; that their discourse is allegorical, and that they are referring to the Great Magical Arcanum. However this may be, the Little Albert supplies an alternative process which it pretends to derive from these authorities, and also from Cornelius Agrippa, the master of Peter of Apono. The first requisite is a tuft of hair taken from the head of a hyena, and from the upper part thereof. These hairs must

[1] Compare the Magic circle of Honorius.

be plaited into a ring, which must be carried, like the other, to a pewit's nest and deposited therein for the space of nine days. The perfumes of Mercury must be used in like manner. The person who wears this ring will be invisible, and he will reappear by removing it from his finger.

Eliphas Lévi observes that the directions recall the history of the bell of Rodilard, but the criticism is scarcely commensurate, for the material is certainly obtainable, nor would it be necessary to catch one's own hyena. The point which was missed by the occultist will be evident to the ordinary reader, the head of the hyena is short-coated, and the hairs could not be braided. It is not, however, unreasonable that impossible conditions should attach to an impossible object.[1]

§ 4.—*Concerning the Hand of Glory.*

No person who is familiar with the humours of Ingoldsby will have forgotten the wondrous legend of the Hand of Glory, which includes a transcript from the Grimoires. It is less generally known that there are two processes, serving distinct uses, and there can be little doubt that they should both be in the possession of every well-equipped operator. The possession of the first alone might be a source of temptation, as it is designed primarily for the protection of burglars. The second renders housebreaking unnecessary, as it ensures a decent competence,

[1] A process was also provided against fascination and deception by means of the ring of invisibility. It consists in the composition of a ring similarly shaped, made of refined lead, and enchased with the eye of a female ferret which has had only one litter. The words *Apparuit Dominus Simoni* should be engraved about the circumference. It should be composed on a Saturday when Saturn is in opposition with Mercury, perfumed three times with the perfume of Saturday, wrapped in a piece of a winding-sheet, buried for nine days in a churchyard, perfumed, when disinterred, as before, and it then ready for use.

but is at the same time without prejudice to its companion, which will be serviceable in a number of emergencies not, at least technically, illegal.

According to the *Albertus Parvus Lucii Libellus,* the Hand of Glory is indifferently the right or left hand of a criminal who has been gibbeted. The sorcerer obtains it as he can, and in the days of Tyburn Tree such requisites might have cost nothing beyond the personal risk of the adventure; it is indispensable, however, that it should be wrapped in a piece of a winding-sheet, and this suggests that the criminal must have been previously cut down with a view to interment. Thus enclosed, the hand must be well squeezed so as to force out any blood which may possibly remain in the member, after which it must be placed in an earthen vessel, together with some zimort, saltpetre, common salt, and pepper-corns, all pounded. It should remain in this vessel for fifteen days, and when extracted should be

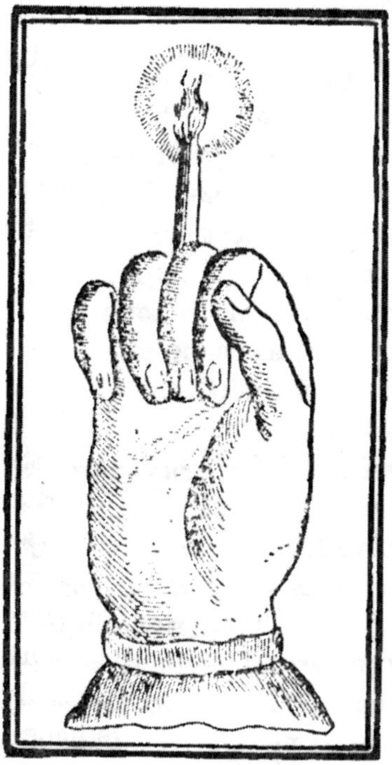

exposed to the heat of the sun during the time of the dogstar until it is extremely desiccated. If solar warmth be insufficient, it may be placed in a furnace heated with bracken and vervain. The object is to extract all the grease from the member, and therefrom, in combination with virgin wax and sesame from Lapland, to compose a species of candle. Wheresoever this frightful object is lighted, the spectators will be deprived of all motion, and the sorcerer can do what he will. It is possible to destroy its influence by anointing the threshold of the door, or other places through which entrance may be gained to a house, with an unguent composed of the gall of a black cat, grease from a white fowl, and the blood of a screech-owl. This should also be confected in the dog-days.

It is to be regretted that this signal process does not rest upon the personal testimony of its historian, but he was present at the trial of several who confessed, under torture, that they had applied it with complete success. It is to be regretted also that the alternative experiment must remain, as regards its materials, in the language of its inventor. It will be seen, however, that the Hand of Glory is not a hand, but a serpent; the process has, in fact, no connection whatever with its name, which is wholly in accordance with the genius of Black Magic.

Arrachez le poil avec sa racine d'une jument en chaleur, le plus prés de la nature, saying: Dragne, Dragne, Dragne. Tie the same in a knot, and go forthwith to purchase, without haggling, a new earthen pot, fitted with a lid. Return home at full speed; fill the said pot with spring water within two inches of the brim. Place your material therein, cover the vessel, and set it where neither you nor any one can perceive it, for the same is danger, saith the Grimoire. At the end of nine days, and at the hour of concealment, bring it forth, open it, and you will discover a small animal in the form of a serpent, which will at once spring up. Say then: I accept the pact. Touch not the creature with your hand, but transfer it into a new box, purchased expressly, without bargaining; for food give it husks of wheat only, and those daily. When you are in want of gold or silver, place as much as you need in the box, retire to rest with the box at your bedside; sleep, if you wish, for the space of three or four hours; then rise, and you will find double the amount of money which you have entrusted to the serpent. What you originally placed in the box must, however, be left therein; and it becomes therefore a sort of transcendental savings-bank which doubles its capital daily. Should the reptile be of ordinary appearance, you must not try for more than one hundred francs at a time; but if your planet give you the ascendant in things supernatural, the serpent will have a human face, and you may deposit a thousand francs. In either case, should the operator part with his possession, two conditions must be observed: the recipient must be a consenting party to the gift, and a figure, to be drawn on virgin parchment, but omitted by the Grimoire, must be placed in the box. If, however, you prefer to destroy it, let the serpent be provided, not with his usual bran, but with some of the flour used for consecration in the first Mass of a priest, after eating which he will die. On the whole, it will be simpler to retain the enchanted animal, more especially as the vague responsibilities of the pact are not apparently transferred in the one or annulled in the other case. No jest is intended, says the dry author of the *Grimorium Verum,* but the process of the Gold-Finding Hen is on the whole simpler, as it is also more cleanly.

§ 5.—*Concerning the Vision of Spirits in the Air.*

For the Masters of Black Magic, as for the author of the *Comte de Gabalis,* the air is the abode of far other beings than the bird and fly, but the process by which they are rendered visible is complicated by the exceptional nature of the required materials. It is, of course, quite possible to secure the brain of a cock, and dissection with that object may perhaps be performed by deputy; the kitchen-maid or the poulterer's assistant would be easily secured. The dust from the grave of a dead man is the second ingredient of the process; but a visit to the nearest cemetery will not be sufficient, because it is useless to collect it on the surface; that which is next to the coffin will alone serve the purpose. In addition to these substances there are only oil of almonds and virgin wax. A compost must be made of the four, and it must be wrapped in a sheet of virgin parchment inscribed previously with the words GOMERT, KAILOETH, and with the character of Khil.

The materials being thus prepared, it remains to set them alight, whereupon the operator will behold that which the Grimoire characterises as prodigious, but does not specify except by the indication of the title. This experiment, it adds, should be performed only by those who fear nothing.

It is easy to deride the process, but reflective persons will see that it is the quintessence and summary of the whole art. This is Black Magic in a nutshell, a combination in equal proportions of the disgusting and the imbecile. There are many more elaborate experiments, but few of a more representative kind. It is not necessary to add that it has been exceedingly popular, and is to be found in most of the Grimoires.

§ 6.—*Concerning Divination by the Word of Uriel.*

As there are many practices passing under the name of White Magic which are at least doubtful in character, so there are experiences described in the Grimoires, or in the treasuries of secrets which accompany them, having nothing repulsive in their nature; they belong, however, to the Grimoires; their connections in occult literature are those of

Black Magic, and they deserve a place here. Moreover, a process which in one Ritual will be merely curious or diverting, hypnotic or clairvoyant, may in another bear all the outward marks of diabolism. The mode of divination termed the Word or Speech of Uriel—signifying answers or oracles obtained from that spirit ceremonially invoked—appears in the *Grimorium Verum* as an experiment in lucidity induced by means of Hydromancy, but in the *Verus Jesuitarum Libellus* the Conjuration of Uriel appears as an infernal conjuration, and it is a process of Black Magic.

The experiment in the *Grimorium Verum* is worded as follows:—

The Invocation of Uriel.

To succeed in this operation, it is needful that whosoever makes the experiment shall do in all things as hereinafter enjoined. Let him choose a small chamber or cabinet which has not been frequented by impure women for at least nine days. Let such place be well cleansed and consecrated by aspersions and fumigations. In the middle of the said chamber let there be a table covered with a white cloth, and set as follows thereon, to wit, a new glass phial filled with spring water, drawn shortly before the operation; three small tapers of virgin wax mixed with human fat; a sheet of virgin parchment six inches square; a raven's quill cut ready for writing; a china ink-well filled with fresh ink; a small pan furnished with the materials for a fire. Let there be also a young boy of nine or ten years, cleanly and modestly dressed and of good behaviour, who must be placed near the table. One of the three tapers should be fixed upon a great new needle at a distance of six inches behind the phial, and the two others, erected after the same manner, should stand on the right and left at the same distance. While arranging these matters, recite the following words:—Gabamiah, Adonay, Agla, O Lord God of Powers, do Thou assist us!

The virgin parchment should be on the right, and the pen with the ink on the left side of the phial. The windows and door must be closed before beginning the operation. The fire should then be stirred, the tapers lighted, and the boy placed on his knees so that he can look into the phial; observe that he should be bareheaded and his hands joined. The Master of the operation shall thereupon command him to gaze fixedly into the phial, when, approaching his right ear, and in a moderate tone of voice, but as distinctly as possible, let him make the following

Conjuration.

Uriel, Seraph, Josata, Ablati, Agla, Caila, I pray and conjure thee by the Four Words which God uttered with His mouth unto His servant Moses, Josata, Ablati, Agla, Caila, and by the Nine Heavens wherein thou dwellest, as also by the virginity of this child who is before thee, that thou appearest, and without any delay, visibly in this phial, to discover, without disguising, the truth which I desire to know; which done, I will discharge thee in peace and goodwill, in the Name of the Most Holy Adonay.

After this conjuration the child must be asked whether he beholds anything in the phial; and if he should reply that he beholds an Angel or another apparition, the Master of the operation shall say in an affable tone of voice: Blessed Spirit, be thou welcome! I conjure thee once more, in the Name of the Most Holy Adonay, to give me prompt enlightenment upon, etc. [*Here name the subject upon which information is desired.*] And if for reasons unknown to us, thou art unwilling to proceed in an audible tone of voice,[1] I conjure thee in the Most Holy Name of Adonay to write upon the virgin parchment here present, between now and to-morrow morning, or at least reveal unto me that which I desire this coming night in my sleep.

If the Spirit make answer to what is said, he shall be heard respectfully; should he fail to speak after thrice making the same supplication, let the tapers be extinguished and withdraw from the chamber, closing the door until the morrow, when the operator may return in the morning, and that which was required will be found within, on the virgin parchment, unless indeed it shall have been made known in the night.

In the *Verum Jesuitarum Libellus* this experiment in the induction of clairvoyance by means of a seering cup and a fantastic ceremonial, having only one monstrous condition, is replaced by a fierce conjuration of many pages, commanding the Spirit Uriel by all the words which have ever proceeded out of the mouth of the Creator of Heaven and Earth against the Evil Angels, and on pain of compulsion and torture, to appear before the operator, an unworthy servant of God, wherever he may be, even in the abyss of Hell. He is directed to appear visibly and modestly in a human form, and to bring whatsoever is desired in all tranquility and patience, without tumult, without detriment, without blinding, without dumbness, without whispering, without thunder, without hail, without explosion, without puffing up, without trembling. It is unnecessary to quote the entire citation, as the process is not complete; but it is evident that the Conjuration of Uriel in the forged treatise on the Magic of the Jesuits is intended for the compulsion of a devil, and not for

[1] That is, in a voice audible to the clairvoyant boy, the process being obviously intended for those who are not themselves seers.

the solicitation of favours from the Blessed Spirit of the *Grimorium Verum.*

§ 7.—*Concerning the Mirror of Solomon, suitable for all Kinds of Divination.*

The following process is found in the *Grimorium Verum* and in some other compilations. It is a mode of divination akin to that given in the preceding chapter. It does not connect with Black Magic except by the use of blood, and is really an auto-hypnotic experiment fortified by conventional ceremonies.

To Compose the Mirror of Solomon.

In the Name of the Lord, Amen. Ye shall behold in this mirror all things whatsoever that ye may desire. In the Name of the Lord who is blessed, in the Name of the Lord, Amen.

In the first place, ye shall do no fleshly actions, nor sin in thought or deed, during the period hereinafter prescribed. In the second place, ye shall perform many good works of piety and mercy. In the third place, take a shining and well-polished plate of fine steel, slightly concave, and with the blood of a white pigeon inscribe thereon, to wit, at the four corners, the names Jehova, Eloym, Metatron, Adonay. Place the said steel in a clean and white cloth. Now, when ye shall behold the new moon during the first hour after sunset, draw nigh unto a window, look up to Heaven with devotion, and say: O Eternal! O King Eternal! God ineffable! Thou who hast created all things for love of me, and by a secret judgment for the health of man, do Thou deign to look upon me, N., Thy most unworthy servant, and upon this my intention. Vouchsafe to send unto me Thine Angel Anaël, even upon this mirror, who doth order, command, and ordain his companions and Thy subjects, whom Thou hast made, O Thou Almighty Lord, who hast been, who art, who shalt remain eternally, that in Thy Name they may judge and act justly, instructing me in all that I shall require of them.

Lastly, cast upon burning coals a suitable perfume, and while casting it say: In this, by this, and with this, which I pour out before Thy face, O God, my God, who art blessed, Three and One, and in the most sublime exaltation, who sittest above the Cherubim and above the Seraphim, who wilt judge the world by fire, hear Thou me!

Repeat this three times, and having done so, breathe also thrice upon the mirror, and say: Come, Anaël, come, and may it be thy good pleasure to be with me by thy will, in the Name✠ of the Father most mighty, in the Name✠ of the Son most wise, in the Name of the Holy Spirit most living! Come, Anaël, in the Name of the terrible Jehovah! Come, Anaël, by the virtue of the immortal Elohim! Come, Anaël, by the right arm of the almighty Metatron! Do thou come unto me, N. (*here repeat your name over the mirror*), and so command thy subjects that in love, joy, and peace they may make manifest unto my eyes the things which are hidden from me. So be it. Amen.

Having said and done as above, lift up your eyes to heaven and say: O Lord Almighty, who dost cause all things to move according to Thy good pleasure, hear Thou my prayer, and may my desire be agreeable unto Thee! Lord, O Lord, if Thou wilt, condescend to look upon this mirror and bless it, that so Anaël, one of Thy servants, may pause thereon with his companions, to satisfy me, N., Thy poor and humble servant, O God, blessed and exalted above all the heavenly Spirits, who livest and reignest for ever and ever. Amen.

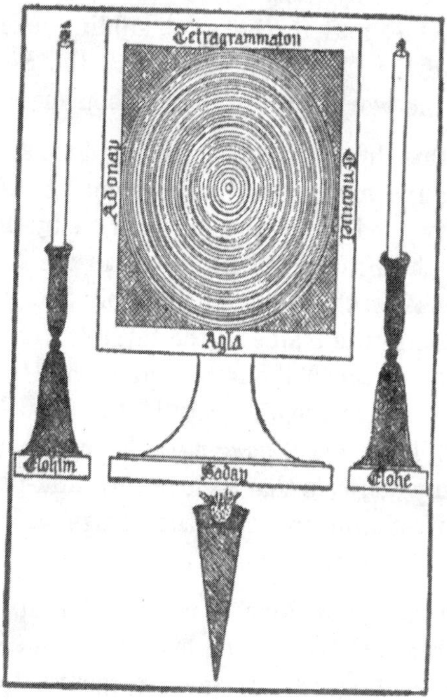
Tetragrammaton
Adonay
Emanuel
Agla
Elohim
Saday
Elohe

When you shall have accomplished these things, make the sign of the Cross upon yourself and upon the mirror on the first and following days for forty-five days in succession, at the end of which time Anaël will appear to you under the form of a beautiful child, will salute you, and will command his companions to obey you. Observe that it does not invariably require forty-five days to compose the mirror. The Angel will frequently appear on the fourteenth day according to the intention, devotion, and fervour of the operator. When he shall appear, ask of him that which you desire, and pray him to come at all times, whensoever you shall invoke him to grant your demands. On subsequent occasions when you desire to see in this mirror, it is not necessary to recite all the prayers as above provided, but having perfumed it, say only: Come Anaël, come, according to thy good pleasure, &c.

To dismiss him, say: I thank thee, Anaël, because thou hast appeared and hast satisfied my demands. Do thou therefore depart in peace, and return when I shall call thee.

The perfume of Anaël is saffron.

§ 8.—*Concerning the Three Rings of Solomon, Son of David.*

One more process, which is only incidentally connected with Black Magic, may be cited here, as the complement of those given in the preceding sections. It is scarcely a complete process, and is not intelligible as it stands in the *Grimorium Verum,* where the characters on which it depends are omitted. The experiment presupposes that the operator is in possession of a talisman inscribed with the Pentacles of Solomon,[1] when it is open to him to proceed in accordance with the following directions:—

[1] The grand pentacle, as given by the "Grimoire of Honorius," will be found on p. 242.

Compose your circle, but before entering therein, perfume it with musk, amber, aloes-wood, and incense. When invoking, the perfume should be incense only, and take care also that you have fire whensoever you make invocation, and fumigate only in the name of the Spirit whom you would call. When placing perfume on the fire, say: I burn this N. in the name and to the honour of N. When invoking, see that you hold the invocation in the left hand, having the rod of elder[1] in your right, while the ladle[2] and knife should be at your feet. These things being arranged, place yourself within the circle; if accompanied, your companions should hold each other by one hand. When within, trace the circle with the Knife of the Art, and take up the rods one after the other, saying the Fiftieth psalm, namely, *Miserere mei.* The circle being composed, perfume and sprinkle the same with holy water. Then write the characters at the four corners; let the Spirit be forbidden in formal terms to enter, after which begin the invocations, which must be repeated seven successive times. When the Spirit shall have appeared, cause him to sign the character which you hold in your hands, promising to come always at your call. Ask for whatsoever you deem suitable, and you shall be satisfied. Dismiss him with these words: Go in peace unto your places, and peace be with you until you return at my call. In the name, &c. Amen.

[1] See the method for the composition of the Magic Rod according to the *Grimorium Verum* in the second chapter of this part.
[2] Not previously mentioned under this name.

CHAPTER IX.

Concerning Infernal Necromancy

IT is only within recent times that the attempt to communicate with the dead has been elevated to the dignity of White Magic. Here it is necessary to affirm that the phenomena of Modern Spiritualism are to be distinguished clearly from those of old Necromancy. The identity of purpose is apt to connect the methods, but the latter differ generically. To compare them would be almost equivalent to saying that the art of Alchemy is similar to mercantile pursuits because the acquisition of wealth is the end in either case. To appreciate the claim of Modern Spiritualism would be to exceed the limits of this inquiry; it is mentioned only with the object of setting it quite apart. It need only be added that occult writers have sometimes sought ambitiously to represent the communication with departed souls by means of Ceremonial Magic as something much more exalted than mere Spiritualism, whereas the very opposite is nearer the truth. Ancient Necromancy was barbarous and horrible in its rites; it is only under the auspices of Eliphas Lévi and Pierre Christian that it has been purged and civilised, but in the hands of these elegant magicians it has become simply a process of auto-hallucination, having no scientific consequence whatever. The secret of true evocation belongs to the occult sanctuaries; it is not the process of Spiritualism, and still less, so far as may be gleaned, it is that of the magical Rituals, nor would the secret at best seem respected by those who possess it, because the higher soul of man transcends evocation, and that which does respond is beneath the initiate.

In any case, the Necromancy of the Rituals is, properly speaking, a department of Black Magic, and for this reason no doubt it was excluded from the theurgic scheme of the "Arbatel"; nor do even such composite works at the two Keys of Solomon and the "Magical Elements" contain any account of a process which was always held in execration. It was lawful apparently for the Magus to conjure and compel the devils, to rack the hierarchy of Infernus by the agony of Divine Names, but he must leave the dead to their rest.

Where the process is given, as in the Fourth Book of Cornelius Agrippa, it is confined to the evocation of those souls who might be reasonably supposed to be damned, and it involves revolting rites. It assumes that the evil liver carries with him into the next world the desires which have depraved him here, and it allures him by these persistent affinities with the relinquished body. In this way the use of blood came to be regarded as indispensable, because blood was held to be the medium of physical life, and so also a portion of the body itself, whether flesh or bone, was prescribed in the rite. There is not any need to say that evocations involving the use of such materials belong to Black Magic, and offer no redeeming feature to the consideration of the impartial student.

"It is also to be understood," says pseudo-Agrippa, "that those who are proposing to raise up the souls of any deceased persons must do so in places with which it is known that they were familiar, in which some special alliance between soul and body may be supposed, or some species of attracting affection, still leading the soul to such places

. . . Therefore the places most suited for the purpose are churchyards, and, better still, those which have been the scene of the execution of criminal judgments," in plain words, the immediate neighbourhood of a gibbet. A battle-field or other place of public slaughter is still more favourable, but best of all is the scene of a murder before the removal of the carcase.

The ritual of Necromantic Evocation is indicated but not given by the authority just cited; we must seek it in Ebenezer Sibley and in the supplementary portions of the "Grand Grimoire" and the "Red Dragon." The astrologer Sibley does not give account of his sources, but they were evidently not in printed books. The Sloane MS. numbered 3884 in the Library of the British Museum would appear to have been one. It is, in any case, not an invented process; it develops the principles laid down in pseudo-Agrippa, and is quite in harmony with the baleful genius of Black Magic. It is here given verbatim.

But if, instead of infernal or familiar spirits, the ghost or apparition of a departed person is to be exorcised, the Magician, with his assistant, must repair to the churchyard or tomb where the deceased was buried, exactly at midnight, as the ceremony can only be performed in the night between the hours of twelve and one. The grave is first to be opened, or an aperture made by which access may be had to the naked body. The magician having described the circle, and holding a magic wand in his right hand, while his companion or assistant beareth a consecrated torch, he turns himself to all the four winds, and, touching the dead body three times with the magical wand, repeats as follows:—By the virtue of the Holy Resurrection, and the torments of the damned, I conjure and exorcise thee, Spirit of N. deceased, to answer my liege demands, being obedient unto these sacred ceremonies, on pain of everlasting torment and distress . Berald, Beroald, Balbin, Gab, Gabor, Agaba. Arise, arise, I charge and command thee.

After these forms and ceremonies, the ghost or apparition will become visible, and will answer any questions put to it by the exorcist. But if it be desired to put interrogatories to the spirit of any corpse that has hanged, drowned, or otherwise made away with itself, the conjuration must be performed while the body lies on the spot where it is first found after the suicide hath been committed, and before it is touched or removed. The ceremony is as follows. The exorcist binds upon the top of his wand a bundle of St. John's Wort or *Millies perforatum,* with the head of an owl; and having repaired to the spot where the corpse lies, at twelve o'clock at night, he draws the circle and solemnly repeats these words:—By the mysteries of the deep, by the flames of Banal, by the power of the East and the silence of the night, by the Holy Rites of Hecate, I conjure and exorcise thee, thou distressed spirit, to present thyself here, and reveal unto me the cause of thy calamity, why thou didst offer violence to thy own liege life, where thou art now in being, and where thou wilt hereafter be.

Then gently smiting the carcase nine times with the rod, he adds:—I conjure thee, thou Spirit of this N. deceased, to answer my demands that I propound unto thee, as thou ever hopest for the rest of the holy ones and ease of all thy misery; by the Blood of Jesus which He shed for thy soul, I conjure and bind thee to utter unto me what I shall ask thee.

Then, cutting down the carcase from the tree, they shall lay its head towards the east; in the space that this following conjuration is repeating, they shall set a chafing dish of fire at its right hand, into which they shall pour a little wine, some mastic, and some gum-aromatic, and lastly [the contents of] a vial full of the sweetest oil. They shall have also a pair of bellows and some unkindled charcoal to make the fire burn bright when the carcase rises. The conjuration is this:—

I conjure thee, thou Spirit of N., that thou do immediately enter into thy ancient body again, and answer to my demands, by the virtue of the Holy Resurrection, and by the posture of the body of the Saviour of the world, I charge thee, I conjure thee, I command thee, on pain of the torments and wandering of thrice seven years, which I, by the force of sacred magic rites, have power to inflict upon thee; by thy sighs and groans I conjure thee to utter thy voice. So help thee God and the prayers of the Holy Church. Amen.

This ceremony being thrice repeated, while the fire is burning with mastic and gum-aromatic, the body will begin to rise, and at last will stand upright before the exorcist, answering with a faint and hollow voice the questions propounded unto it: why it destroyed itself, where its dwelling is, what its food and life are, how long it will be ere it enter into rest, and by what means the magician may assist it to come to rest; also of the treasures of this world, where they are hid. Moreover, it can answer very punctually concerning the places where ghosts reside, and of the manner of communicating with them, teaching the nature of Astral Spirits and hellish beings so far as its capacity alloweth. All this when the ghost hath fully answered, the magician ought, out of commiseration and reverence to the deceased, to use what means can possibly be used for procuring rest unto the spirit, to which effect he must dig a grave, and, filling the same half full of quick-lime, with a little salt and common sulphur, must put the carcase naked into it. Next to the burning of the body into ashes, this is of great force to quiet and end the disturbance of the Astral Spirit. But in this and in all cases where the ghosts or apparitions of deceased persons are raised up and consulted, great caution is to be observed by the Magician to keep close within the circle; for if, by the constellation and position of the stars at his nativity, he be in the predicament of those who follow the Black Art for iniquitous purposes, it is very dangerous to conjure any spirits without describing the form of the circle, and wearing upon the heart, or holding in the hand, the Pentacle of Solomon. For the ghosts of men deceased can easily effect sudden death to the magician born under such a constellation of the planets, even whilst in the act of being exorcised.

It must be confessed that this process is grim and depressing, and the occult student will not envy the sorcerer at the first palpitation of the corpse. Yet the rite is methodical, and even sober, when compared with the monstrous alternative of the "Grand Grimoire," which must be given on the authority of Lévi; for no available editions of the work which is in question, nor yet of the "Red Dragon," nor indeed any ritual of our acquaintance, contains it.

"There are also necromantic processes, comprising the tearing up of earth from graves with the nails, dragging out some of the bones, setting them crosswise on the breast, then assisting at midnight mass on Christmas Eve, and flying out of the church at the moment of consecration, crying 'Let the dead rise from their tombs!'—then returning to the graveyard, taking a handful of earth nearest to the coffin, running back to the door of the church, which has been alarmed by the clamour, depositing the two bones crosswise, again shouting, 'Let the dead rise from their tombs!'—then, if we escape being seized and shut up in a madhouse, retiring at a slow pace, and counting four thousand five hundred steps in a straight line, which means following a broad road or scaling walls; finally, having traversed this space, lying flat upon the earth as if in a coffin, repeating in doleful tones, 'Let the dead rise from their tombs!'—and calling thrice on the person whose apparition is desired."

The object of Necromantic evocations was much the same as the other operations of the Grimoires. If the sorcerer of old like the modern magician, had ever dispossessed the shade of Appolonius of its eternal rest, it would have been upon a question of finance. The remaining process in Necromancy will be an appropriate conclusion to our whole inquiry, as it is designed to raise up and expel a human spirit who is supposed to stand guard over a hidden treasure. It is from the *Verus Jesuitarum Libellus,* and is the *ne plus ultra* of Ceremonial Magic. The end of all things is money, says the sorcerer, and if asked to define Occult Science, he would answer that it was the method of obtaining concealed money. The testimony of the entire literature coincides with this definition.

A Conjuration for the Spirit Guardians of Hidden Treasure.

I cite, require, and command thee, Human Spirit, who frequentest this place, and in thy life has interred thy treasure herein, who also of recent time, to wit, in the day or night of . . . ., about the hour of . . . ., hast shewn thyself in the form of a fire at this spot: I conjure thee by God the Father✠, by God the Son✠, by God the Holy Spirit✠, by the most glorious and Holy Mother✠ of God✠, by the most holy wounds of our Saviour, by all miracles performed through His Divine sorrows, passion, and tears, by His material death, by His descent into Hell, by His triumphant Resurrection, by His most glorious ascension into Heaven, by His sitting on the right hand of God the Father, giving rule to His angels from thence over the whole earth✠. I conjure thee by the terrible Day of Judgment✠, by the power and virtue of St. John the Baptist✠, by all the martyrs, apostles, and prophets. Come to me. I adjure and beseech thee by the terrible, ineffable, and Divine Names inscribed on this sheet, and in reverence and confession of their power, to come before me, and to make thy sign visible, without lightning, without thunder, without noise of dread tempests, without causing fear or trembling, harm to body or soul, or annoyance of any kind. But do thou perform my will in all things, even as I shall command thee, by the virtue of the one stupendous and holy Name, which even the adverse and inferior powers of the Abyss do venerate and adore, ever confessing the Almighty, whose creatures we all are. Be this done by the virtue of God the Father✠, by His blessed Son✠, and by the union of the Holy Spirit✠, even by the Trinity in unity, which liveth and reigneth for ever and ever. Amen✠. Incessantly do I call, adjure, conjure, ordain, and require thee, Human Spirit, by the Most Holy and Undivided Trinity, by the immortality which cometh after death, by the power and victory of Hell, by the bearer of the Seven Swords, by the Most Holy and Secret Seal, by the sacred love of Jesus, by all the Ministers and Archangels of God, Ophanim ✠, Aralim ✠, Hasmalim ✠, Cherubim ✠, Seraphim ✠, and Malachim ✠, and by the terrible torments of the demons. I conjure thee also by the good angels Maluzim ✠, Penpalabim ✠, and Calizantin ✠, by all the powers of Heaven ✠, by the earth ✠, and by the torments of Hell; I adjure thee by all mysteries, by the Crucifixion, by the dolorous scourging, by the crowning with thorns, by the bitterness of the Divine death, by the Most Holy and Ineffable Name of Jesus ✠, which is sacred unto all Christians, but terror and anguish to the evil, for they have refused the salvation which has been offered them by the great living God. I conjure thee to come before me immediately, in thy proper human form, even as when thy treasure was buried. Come before this circle, answer me faithfully, without falsehood, and without enigmas. This I command thee, in the Name and by the power of the Triune God, Father, Son, and Holy Ghost. Amen.

A Conjuration Compelling Obedience.

I adjure and command thee, Human Spirit, to appear before me under the similitude of fire. By the ineffable Name of Jehovah, by the ineffable and incomprehensible Fiat, by the power which created all things and sustains all things, I conjure and adjure thee to come visibly before this circle. By the goodness of God when He created man in His own likeness, by the power of His justice, which expelled the demons, enchaining them in the Infernal Abyss, by His infinite mercy when He sent His Son to redeem us, by all Divine Names and Attributes, by the omnipotence of our Saviour Jesus Christ, destroying the works of hell, blessing the seed of the woman and empowering it to crush the serpent's head—do thou answer me and obey faithfully. By the ineffable Name Tetragrammaton, inscribed on this rod, answer me without deception or equivocation. By the power of our Saviour, who shall judge both thee and me, the quick and the dead, I conjure thee. Come.

If the Spirit be Obstinate.

I conjure thee, Human Spirit, by the ineffable name of God, written on this sheet, but not to be pronounced, by my blood, most excellently redeemed by the Lord of the

Prophets, Jesus Christ, by His most Glorious Mother, by the insignia of His humility, by the great book of the judgments of God, by the angels, archangels, and all the host of heaven. Be thou obedient unto me, a Christian baptized in the holy waters of Jordan. Answer me exactly, without enigma or pretence. Make known the power which aids thee. I command thee by the most holy Name of God, who hath condemned thee to frequent this place wherein thou hast buried thy treasure. Amen. Amen. Amen.

Citation.

COLPRIZIANA, OFFINA, ALTA, NESTERA, FUARO, MENUET.

Charge.

ALIM, JEHOH, JEHOVAH, AGLA, ON, TETRAGRAMMATON.

When the Spirit makes visible appearance, say:—

ADON, SCHADAI, ELIGON, AMANAI, ELION, PNEUMATON, ELII, ALNOAL, MESSIAS, JA, HEYNAN, TETRAGRAMMATON.

Add the following Conjuration:—

ADONAI, ZEBOTH, ADON, SCHADAI, ELION, TETRAGRAMMATON, ELOI, ELOHIM, JA, HAGIOS, HO, THEOS. Amen.

Say inwardly:—

ALLEY, FORTISSIAN, FORTISSIO, ALLINSON, ROA.

The Discharge.

OMGROMA, EPYN, SEYOK, SATANY, DEGONY, EPARYGON, GALLIGANON, ZOGOGEN, FERSTIGON.

The most barbarous and unintelligible words are said by Picus de Mirandola to be the most powerful in Black Magic. As those here cited from the *Versus Jesuitarum Libellus* seem in most cases fortuitous assemblages of letters, they are doubtless all that can be desired, but additional constraints and conjurations should the spirit of the deceased miser refuse to appear will readily occur to the reader.

Here Ends the Complete Grimoire of Black Magic